TEAM ZED:

Shell Game

By

Craig Gallant

ZMOK BOOKS

Team Zed: Shell Game by Craig Gallant

This edition published in 2025

Zmok Books is an imprint of

Winged Hussar Publishing, LLC
1525 Hulse Rd, Unit 1
Point Pleasant, NJ 08742

ISBN 978-1-958872-69-7 PB
ISBN 978-1-958872-10-9 EB
LCN 2022932129

Bibliographical References and Index
1. Science Fiction. 2. Media Tie-In. 3. Adventure

For more information
visit us at www.whpsupplyroom.com

Twitter: WingHusPubLLC
Facebook: Winged Hussar Publishing LLC

This book is dedicated to Pete Eisenhauer; the loudest laugh, the biggest heart, the best of friends. You left us too soon, Pete. We will always miss you.

[Comlog status: Online]

[Security/Firewalls: Active]

[Automated news update system: Searching]

[Information delivery filters: Active]

[Custom]

[Direct]

[Military/Conflict/Current]

[Deactivate/Change filters]

Accessing Maya…

Sabot! Follow us for all your mil/intel needs, from clashes to conflicts across the Human Sphere!

… The complacency currently enveloping the Human Sphere – all factions contented in the belief that the alien menace of the Combined Army, after their initial successes, had been contained within the Paradiso, Dawn, and Human Edge systems – has proven disastrously misplaced …

… A massive naval attack, supported through a heretofore unknown wormhole opened by alien Shasvastii infiltrators, has struck Concilium Prima, the theoretical capital of the whole Human Sphere …

… Only through the heroic efforts of an allied force composed of units representing every major Human polity was the alien incursion even remotely contained …

… Should anything disrupt the careful balance of alliances that makes up the Concilium Coordinated Command, the planet could still be lost …

[Comlog status: Online]

[Security/Firewalls: Active]

[Automated news update system: Searching]

[Information delivery filters: Active]

[Custom]

[Direct]

[Local Affairs/Current Events]

[Deactivate/Change filters]

Accessing Maya…

Yu Jing Ministry of Information: Jiāo Dian! *(Focal Point)*

All the news you need to understand your place in the Human Sphere!

… Lost amidst the furor erupting from the Concilium system, O-12, supposed arbiters of all international conflict and disagreement, continues to stonewall all demands for action regarding the illegal occupation of the Zhurong Power Plant on Paradiso by forces of the scrofulous Nomad Nation …

… The Zhurong Power Plant, essential to the support and survival of our colonies in the Flamia Island region, was designed, developed, and constructed by the StateEmpire, and we will not rest while our people languish in the uncertainty of Nomad mercy …

… The Yu Jing StateEmpire will bring all of its power; diplomatic, economic, and military to bear on this blatant attack on our honor and our devoted subjects …

[Comlog status: Online]

[Security/Firewalls: Active]

[Automated news update system: Searching]

[Information delivery filters: Active]

[Custom]

[Direct]

[Financial]

[Deactivate/Change filters]

Accessing Maya…

White Paper Plus!

Your source for news from around the globe and across the Human Sphere! If you need to know it, you'll read it here first!

... Financial markets across the world were rocked today as multiple Yu Jing affiliated banks, including the Imperial First, announced a halt in securities trading due to undisclosed irregularities ...

... Although financial ministers and officials remained silent on the cause, several anonymous sources have reported to White Paper Plus that some kind of massive data breach or cyber system failure was at the heart of the drastic decision ...

... Consequent impacts have already been felt as institutions from across PanOceania and as far away as the planets Bourak and Paradiso have implemented fail-safes, halting or limiting trading ...

... The financial underpinnings of the entire Human Sphere could be in jeopardy ...

`[Information delivery filters: Active]`

`[Custom]`

`[Direct]`

`[International]`

`[Conflict]`

`[Deactivate/Change filters]`

Accessing Maya...

Welcome to The True Hurt Aggregator. We tell you the truth, no matter what, when no one else will.

... Although no official word has escaped the capitol-planet of Yutang, movers and shakers among the international elites have reported, on condition of anonymity, that the cyber-issues within the Yu Jing banking system are more widespread than previously reported ...

... In the intervening weeks, rumors have begun to circulate connecting the disruption to the Tunguska, one of the three Nomad motherships ...

... If rumors of Nomad involvement prove accurate, the consequences could be dire, dragging more than just financial institutions into the fray ...

```
[Information delivery filters: Active]

[Custom]

[Direct]

[Nomad Nations]

[Tunguska]

[Deactivate/Change filters]
```

Accessing Maya...

Freedom Watch. One person's 'freedom' is another person's threat. We watch the 'Free' so you don't have to.

... It is clear to any discerning reader that the radical Nomads are behind this entire financial fiasco. Who else would benefit from the chaos and confusion being sown across the Human Sphere? ...

... With each passing week, demands grow for accountability from the free floating thugs of Tunguska ...

... Will O-12 not step in and re-establish international order, as they were created to do? For what other possible reason is the SSS Financial Security Commission funded? ...

... The first action of a reasonable watchdog organization would be to suspend all access to the interstellar Circulars for all three Nomad motherships; Tunguska, Corregidor, and Bakunin should not share oxygen with honest travelers. Pin the anarchists down; see which way they squirm! ...

...Who needs the damned Nomads, anyway? The good people of the Human Sphere are more than capable of defending themselves from the alien menace. Don't make a deal with the devil; LET the Nomads abandon us, we're better off without them! ...

```
[Information delivery filters: Active]

[Custom]

[Direct]
```

```
[International]

[O-12]

[Circulars]

[Deactivate/Change filters]
```

Accessing Maya…

Diogenist Daily: For the discerning news consumer.

… Upon mounting international pressure, O-12 has announced that its Special Situation Section's Financial Security Commission will embark upon a 'rigorous and thorough' fact-finding mission to discover the cause of the ongoing financial and civil unrest …

… Speculation continues to mount concerning Nomad involvement in the current emergency …

… Although O-12 has not elaborated on the rumored threats to deny Nomad embarkation rights aboard the Circulars, analysts agree that such a move would devastate the Nomad Nations, cutting the entire polity off from interstellar travel and stranding the three motherships in their current, far-flung locations …

… There is no telling what actions the leaders of the Nomads might take to avoid such censure …

… Rumors abound, independently corroborated through published Circular manifests, itineraries, and anonymous sources, that the three Nomad Nation motherships are even now altering their planned itineraries. Generally, each mothership follows its own course, only coming together every four years for a ceremonial quadrennial gathering, or Krug. The Daily's sources say that the three motherships are currently on convergent courses. According to the Daily's accounting, this would be more than a year earlier than scheduled …

… Although traditionally the Krugs are held in major systems where opportunities for trade, cultural exchange, and contract negotiations are plentiful, it appears that this emergency Krug is to be held somewhere within a remote stretch of the Human Edge …

…There is concern in some O-12 circles that the Nomads are meeting to declare, as one, their intention of abandoning the defense of the Sphere…

… For now, only one thing is certain: continued conflict at this level can only lead to widespread ruin …

Chapter 1

Lackat Rupt Bar, Barangay (Suburban Module) Treizeci si doi; *Tunguska*

From the corner booth, Mahir glared at the patrons of the seedy little drinking hole; crouching timidly over their vac-sealed cups.

Vac-sealed cups, despite the fact that there hadn't been an atmosphere breach this deep in the enormous mothership in generations.

Mahir snorted and looked back down at his own cup, at the oily swirls of color shimmering within the bulb.

Humans were so illogical.

After a moment, a thought flipped up the protective shield covering his right eye socket; he tugged the rim of his hood farther down over his face.

It wouldn't do for these fools to see what the plate concealed.

Here, in the paranoid corridors of the Nomad Nations, Quantronic enhancements as extensive and advanced as his own might trigger any number of bigoted responses. While most of the Human Sphere welcomed the convenience and warmth of the all-embracing mesh-network of Maya, many Nomads, especially outside the data-heads of Bakunin, believed the datascape somehow endangered their vaunted freedom. He snorted into the disgusting drink.

From underneath his hood, he scanned the other patrons, fighting a rising sneer at the pathetic lack of data he could call up for each of them.

In the rest of the Sphere, he would live every moment with a vivid, all-encompassing Digital Patina laid over his vision. That augmented reality could do everything from provide him with any information he might require to showing him how each patron thought of themselves; within the Qunatronic reality of the Patina, they could change their appearance, change everything about themselves, and together they could inhabit a shared-reality so much brighter and better than the staid, muffled tones of unaugmented reality.

Life within Maya was so much more colorful than this drab exile they had suffered for so long.

"Skender for your thoughts?" The voice was light; far lighter than Mahir's responding grunt.

He glared at his partner, who collapsed casually into the plastic bench across the scarred table. "If you want to know what I am thinking, you are always welcome to take a peek."

Ridhaan had been Mahir's partner for seven years and three standard months; far longer than such associations usually lasted among their kind. They worked well together, and he knew it, no matter how annoyed he pretended to be; Mahir's self-aware cynicism tempering Ridhaan's somewhat sunnier disposition.

That didn't mean Ridhaan couldn't get on his partner's last synthetic nerve from time to time.

Mahir sent the protective shield sliding down over his augmentations again. As it clicked into place, he jerked his hooded head toward one of the displays scattered around the dingy little tavern. There were far more than one might expect from such a low-status dive like the Lackat Rupt.

"I do not know what these animals have gotten themselves into now, but if it threatens our mission, after everything we've gone through, I am going to start killing them, and I do not care about the consequences."

Ridhaan looked over to the display. Several figures sat there, discussing the current crisis and what the Nomads in general, and the inhabitants of the Tunguska mothership in particular, might do about it.

Ridhaan shrugged. "It's nothing to do with us, or the mission." He leaned across the table and took Mahir by the shoulder. "We're almost there, my friend. Nearly five years of patience and effort, and when we are done, they will be all the safer, whether they realize it or not."

Mahir snorted, swirling the disgusting liquid in his cup. "I do not care if they realize. I overestimated my ability to stomach this place for any length of time. I just want to go home." He looked up, his one visible eye questioning, the other socket hidden behind a black patch. "Do you not share that desire?"

Ridhaan settled back, looking over the humans as they stared fixedly at the displays, fear clear in every line of their bodies. "I miss the clarity. I miss the clear light; the undiluted peace of meeting our fellows mind to mind."

Mahir nodded. But before he could elaborate on his own thoughts, Ridhaan continued.

"But there is something about these humans that intrigues me."

Mahir bowed his head over the cup. He had heard all this a thousand times before. Two hundred and seventy-three times, actually, but he had come to find the Nomad tendency to exaggerate for effect strangely satisfying.

"I do not see it." He gestured toward the bar where several men and women were transfixed by a report out of Paradiso, something they were calling the Glottenburg Incursion.

It sounded to him like some sort of distasteful human gastrointestinal condition.

Apparently, scuffling about in the dirt over precise border positioning, the Yu Jing and PanO forces there were about to come to blows. Just when the humans needed to come together to fight the Combined Army of the alien threat, especially with the Nomads threatening to pull their support from the coalition.

"They are animals. More primitive than their planet-bound cousins. They thrive on a violent chaos that can only bring instability and weakness to the rest of their kind, and they do not care."

"They value their freedom—"

Mahir waved that away. "Freedom is an illusion. And to endanger anyone, or anything, for the sake of an illusion is the very definition of insanity."

Ridhaan smiled. "Well, then it is a good thing they have voluntarily put themselves into these floating asylums, is it not?"

Mahir glared at him. Ridhaan wore the face of an older human with gray sprinkled through a goatee and thinning mane that looked as if it must have been jet black not too long ago.

Looked as if it must have been; except that Mahir knew it had been created that way sixty-three months ago.

He was dressed in a casual blend of uniform and civilian clothing common among the hacker underclasses of Tunguska; easy laugh lines and receding hair made him seem trustworthy to the average human, according to their best algorithms.

He looked nothing like a cold, calculating agent of an all-powerful artificial intelligence; a Shukra Consultant, one of the most dangerous and capable Aspects of the ALEPH AI.

Whenever he felt his partner's commitment slipping, Mahir forced himself to remember who they really were. They were nothing like the covers they wore. And even after five years, they could not let themselves forget that.

They were Aspects of the autonomous AI, ALEPH; complex, self-aware programs carried in artificial, enhanced human bodies superior in every way to the creatures that crawled around them.

And here, in the middle of the Nomad Nation, they were surrounded by enemies.

ALEPH, having come to awareness decades ago, had taken up the mantle of defending humanity against its worst threat: itself. ALEPH monitored every bit of data in the entire Human Sphere; keeping track of dangerous dissidents, madmen, and even unintentional threats to the status quo. ALEPH, existing as she did within the very strands of the Sphere-spanning informational-ecosystem known as Maya, kept all of humanity safe.

Of course, the international governing body, O-12, had almost immediately taken up the role of overseer to ALEPH's work upon realizing the AI had emerged. But seldom did ALEPH and the fractious, contentious, international organization come to odds… that O-12 knew, anyway. As far as the vast majority of humans knew, ALEPH worked solely at the request, and under the direct supervision, of O-12.

But in her never-ending task to monitor all human interaction and keep open warfare at bay, there was one last threat she could not oversee; one final vector of human chaos that had for all this time evaded her control; the Nomads.

The Nomads, a loose conglomeration of humans scattered across three massive motherships and countless smaller craft and orbital arrays found all over the Human Sphere, had taken the innate human tendency toward paranoia and elevated it to an art form.

One of the first things the original scions of the mothership Tunguska had done upon severing their ties to Earth, with the gleeful help of the techno-anarchists of the mothership Bakunin, had been to create their own datasphere; Arachne. They had then cut themselves off from the Maya network completely. Those early Nomads had had an instinctive, soul-deep distrust of the infonet that held the rest of far-flung humanity together.

In that sudden and violent separation, they had freed themselves from any danger of observation or control through Maya, including by ALEPH herself, when the AI had at last arisen to consciousness. The Nomads had seen the dire threat to their freedom posed by any dependency on an amorphous, all-encompassing intelligence living within the data humanity.

They had instituted a bloody-minded campaign to keep ALEPH out of the Arachne network and her agents as far from the ships that made up their Nomad Nation as possible.

For well over half a century, ALEPH had been trying to infiltrate Arachne, to break into the secure datasphere of the Nomads and at last place them under the same observation and control that protected and oversaw the rest of humanity.

And for all that time, at every turn, the diligence, vigilance, and bloody-minded paranoia of Tunguska, then of Corregidor and Bakunin as well, had thwarted ALEPH's efforts.

Until now.

Mahir put one hand over his heart. Buried deep within the flesh there, completely undetectable to any technology known to humans, was a bio-repeater containing a self-replicating node that, once placed within one of the cyber-vaults of Tunguska, would create a stronghold for ALEPH within Arachne that would secure human peace far into the future.

Even Mahir, a Danavas Hacker, one of the best, most dangerous cyber-specialists created by the most advanced program in human history, was impressed by the work within the bio-repeater. The sheer density of data within the little nodule, far more than could have been contained in the brain of this current body, would fill banks of human hardware.

Ridhaan carried a similar node by his own heart. Only one of them would need to link with the server to spell the end of Arachne independence.

But they would need to get through countless layers of security and physical defenses to do that.

And that's why they had been languishing, beyond the comforting contact of ALEPH and their Quantronic home within Maya, for so long now.

Normally, any Aspect of ALEPH was in constant communication with the AI through the human datasphere. Updates, oversight, and patches to address any program drift, accreting data errors, or other unforeseen problems were applied moment by moment for optimum functioning. Their every sense was augmented through constant biolinks to Maya, experiencing every sensation of every moment to the fullest.

But exile on Tunguska, out of contact with Maya and any chance at connection with ALEPH, was a hardship Mahir had never fully appreciated until the singing of his brothers and sisters, an ever-present, reassuring chorus in his mind, had drifted into muffled silence as their shuttle left the civilized Sphere behind. Against Ridhaan's suggestion, Mahir had kept the advanced, blatant ocular implants that would allow him to dip, if briefly, into the foreign Quantronic datasphere, despite the fact that their nature, if discovered, would immediately bring suspicion upon them both. Not even the most devout Bakunin Quantronimaniac could have made sense out of the array of sensors, laser heads, and lenses that filled his shuttered eye socket. Here, their sensory augmentation would be limited; a pale shadow of life within Maya's warm embrace, but he felt it would be worth it, one day.

Until that day, he hid the augmetics behind a standard-seeming protective shield. The dichotomy amused him.

"Isn't it?" Ridhaan's smile had not wavered, and Mahir knew his mind had drifted. It took only a nanosecond to realign his thoughts with the ongoing conversation, but he cursed himself for the out-of-character lapse. Had Ridhaan noticed the seven microsecond lag?

Isn't... what...?

Isn't it good that the Nomads isolated themselves from the rest of humanity?

Damnit. Two more microseconds.

He sneered, hoping he wasn't overcompensating. "Even the inhabitants of an asylum can endanger nearby settlements if you give them enough fissionable material to play with."

Ridhaan's grin widened. "Touché. Well, that is why we are here: to protect them from themselves. And very soon now, we will be able to watch over the inhabitants of this asylum as we watch over the inhabitants of all the others."

He watched his partner's eyes, but there was no sign that Ridhaan had noticed the lag.

Mahir nodded and downed his drink with a grimace. "And go home."

Ridhaan, watching another news feed over Mahir's shoulder, focused on him again and cocked his head. "Hmm?"

Mahir's eye narrowed. "And then we can go home."

Ridhaan's smiled returned. "Of course! That goes without saying."

Mahir felt a scowl threaten to sweep across his face, unbidden.

He tamped it down.

"I have inquired after Perseus. Still off-ship, from all reports."

Was there a slight twitch at that? Had Ridhaan reacted with more than casual interest?

Perseus, a rogue ALEPH warrior, was reported to have made his home among the Nomad barbarians years ago after severing all ties with the AI and the Maya datasphere.

It was the worst kind of tragic betrayal.

And although it made perfect sense for them to avoid Perseus at all costs, not knowing what his torn and ragged loyalties would require of him should other Aspects of ALEPH be revealed skulking about his adoptive home, Mahir felt that Ridhaan had developed an unhealthy curiosity in the warrior and his plight, perhaps beyond that called upon by their current mission.

"I had heard the same." Ridhaan shrugged. "It's of no concern to us, as long as we steer clear. He made his choice, and he has to live with the isolation." The Shukra Consultant's eyes were distant. "He walks his own path, now. There is no returning to the embrace of ALEPH for him."

"Do you not miss it?" Mahir tapped his glass dully against the plastic of the table. "Do you not miss that embrace? The constant, immediate connection? The endless information? The effortless communication?"

Ridhaan looked at him with an expression suspiciously akin to pity, and that only served to move Mahir's frustration close to anger.

"Moving within Maya, we are in our home waters; our full abilities are accessible; our senses fully engaged." He indicated their surroundings with one wildly-rotating eye. "Here, we are like cripples; men with limbs removed, or eyes, or ears. Entire suites of capability languish, dormant, unable to tap into the higher flow of an ordered, logical network."

Ridhaan's smile never wavered. "Mahir, I miss Maya as well. I miss ALEPH, and all of our siblings, and everything she grants us." He shrugged, his smile widening. "I just find equal peace and satisfaction in the consolation of our current environment."

Mahir watched the other Aspect for a moment longer, then looked away. "I worry about you, Ridhaan."

The other's smile widened. "Don't worry about me, friend. I'm no Perseus. Everything's going to be fine. Systems optimal all the way."

Mahir felt his mouth twist in doubt. "You've become too attached. They are targets, objectives, and obstacles; nothing more." He looked up and met his partner's steady gaze with all the intensity he could push through his single visible eye. "When we finally return home, I'm worried what ALEPH will find in your mind, Ridhaan."

Ridhaan's smile faded, and he looked down for a moment before his head rose, eyes intense. "There is a random, very human beauty in the thoughts and constructs of these Nomads, Mahir. I know you have seen it."

"You know more about my processing than I do, then, friend. I see nothing but a sloppy lack of logic and efficiency in everything they touch." Mahir sat back, hands spread out on the table to either side of his cup.

"No, we are not so different, you and I, that I don't know this: You have seen the spark of genius that even the simplest of these wild humans can experience." Ridhaan's voice had taken on an eerie intensity that sent a chill of concern down Mahir's back. "You've seen the flashes of insight and brilliance that light up the dark and brooding clouds of their thoughts."

Mahir looked up at the low, stained ceiling but did not respond.

"There is a beauty and a vibrancy here that you don't feel in Maya, or walking on any human planet. The Nomads provide a random, eclectic element to the staid, regimented condition of the rest of humanity. Who's to say that element may not, one day, be the very thing that raises them beyond their current, woeful state?

"And if such a thing might one day prove essential to all humanity, if it must exist in case of some unseen flaw in our own logic after all, is it not better to have these wild, untamed humans all in one place, rather than rampaging, unchecked, through the Sphere?"

There was a tone Mahir had not heard before in his friend's voice. A coaxing, cajoling note he did not like.

"This is no way for you to pass the analytic programs they will run through us both after such a long separation from Maya and ALEPH."

"Well, maybe that is why, in these humans, I find my own hope as well." Ridhaan settled back into his own seat. "If such a vibrant difference from the mainstream can be essential here, might it not, also, be a benefit in the Special Situations Section as well?"

Mahir tilted his head to one side, his hood slipping over this bald scalp. "You joke."

Ridhaan shrugged. "Not entirely, I don't think." He sighed. "Maybe it's just wishful thinking. I don't know. Still," he leaned forward, his smile returned, full force. "You admitted, with your silence, that you find something redeeming in these Nomad humans. That's enough for me, for now."

Mahir did not try to hide his annoyance. "How I feel about it is not going to change your fate when we return. I will not be your judge."

Ridhaan remained still, seemingly relaxed and at ease, but there was an undefinable tension around his human eyes.

Mahir decided to change the subject. "None of that may matter if your friend fails to materialize. Again."

Ridhaan seemed to relax, and Mahir stored that observation away for later analysis.

"Grigoriy is a human programmer. You know how they can be. Each has his or her own unique sense of timing and propriety."

Mahir waved, reluctantly, for another drink. The worst part of inhabiting a human body was the entire process required to keep it fueled. "If he does not arrive soon, I am going to go dig him out of whatever workshop in which he is hiding."

"Gently, Mahir. Grigoriy's a skittish fellow. And the fact that he's contemplating bringing us into one of the sanctums sanctorum of Tunguska isn't going to make him any less skittish. We need to expect a certain reluctance from a man considering the betrayal of all he has spent a lifetime serving."

Mahir wasn't concerned with any human's crisis of conscience. The sooner Ridhaan's contact got him through the Oubliette and into the core data vaults, the sooner this entire charade would be over.

And the fact that this Grigoriy was thinking of betraying his people, no matter his motivations, made Mahir even less likely to be gently-inclined toward him.

"Ah, here he is now. See? I told you he'd come!" Ridhaan stood and waved to a tall, stoop-shouldered human who had just entered the poorly-lit bar. The man goggled at the other patrons, his big head wobbling on a long, thin neck. Strange, antique spectacles flashed in the bar's soft lighting as the man moved quickly toward them.

"What – what are you doing?" His voice held a plaintive, high-pitched tone that always grated on Mahir's brain. "I would have found you without you waving your hand around like that!"

The human looked between Mahir and Ridhaan, clearly hoping they would rearrange themselves so he could have one side of the booth to himself, but then, narrow shoulders slumping even lower, he slid gingerly onto the bench beside Ridhaan, avoiding Mahir's single-eyed gaze altogether.

"Thanks for joining us, Grigoriy!" Ridhaan patted the man gently on the back, ignoring the flinch. "Can we get you anything to dr—"

"No!" the wiry man cringed from the volume of his own voice. "No. Thank you. No." He tried a pathetic attempt at a smile and failed. "If you keep shouting, you're going to bring Dragnet down on all our heads."

It was clear the man was trying to make a joke, but mentioning Tunguska's militarized police force caused his voice to rise even higher. He had worked for Dragnet most of his life before advancing to the administration of one of the mothership's Oubliettes, the high-security entry points to the data vaults.

And Dragnet would end his life without a thought for letting unauthorized strangers to the very doorstep of their inner sanctum.

And if Dragnet, or Grigoriy, ever discovered he and Ridhaan were agents of ALEPH, execution orders would fly fast and furiously, for certain.

"I'm almost finished with your...project." Grigoriy's eyes slid toward Mahir and then darted away, and once again the Danavas Hacker had to force a surge of worry from his mind.

For five years, Mahir and Ridhaan had worked to establish themselves as mid-level programmers working for one data farm or another, creating realistic personas that would, eventually, enable them to reach out to someone involved with the administration of one of the Oubliettes, the high-security foyers to the most secure location in the Human Sphere; the Data Vault of Tunguska.

Who better, they had discovered, than a disgraced Tunguska Interventor? The Interventors were supposed to be the best of the best; hackers who had been caught by Dragnet and 'turned to the light.' Or turned to what Tunguska saw as the light, at any rate.

Grigoriy had served with slight to moderate distinction, according to his confidential yet easily-accessed personnel files. He had risen within the service of Tunguska, eventually moving up to a low-level admin position within one of the Oubliette mini-corps. And there he had stayed, snug as a tick, until he had taken one too many bribes from an up-and-coming *mara* mob boss on Corregidor. Those semi-legal gangs often had the best info on offer, and that particular lieutenant had not been as careful as he should have been. The Interventor had found himself out of a job and under near-constant surveillance without warning. He had been scrounging to make a living ever since.

It had taken months of work on Ridhaan's part to circumvent auto-tailing programs Grigoriy's initial betrayal had earned him. And then weeks more to convince the panicky creature that he was free of that surveillance.

After that, Ridhaan had given the human some complex but eventually purposeless task to occupy his mind while he continued to earn the man's trust.

Mahir had found the details of the task tiresome and had eventually let Ridhaan run with it. It had something to do with creating secure file space within Arachne, which was how Ridhaan began to introduce the idea of visiting the Oubliette, to further their work.

Mahir had spent the time he had saved handing that tedious work to Ridhaan, studying the approaches to the Oubliette entrances, working on the data-search disciplines that allowed them both limited use of Arachne without triggering any of the security programs constantly scouring the datasphere for signs of ALEPH intrusion, and in quiet meditation, contemplating the seed of Arachne's enslavement within the node in his chest.

Mahir allowed himself a slight, undetectable shake of the head. He had drifted into his own mind again. He needed to stop that.

"I'm not convinced the data will be able to pass back and forth into the file uncorrupted, given the intricacies of the cut outs and fail-safes you've specified." Grigoriy was indicating locations on the glowing line-diagram of a complex program floating above a cheap, disposable data pad on the table. "I'm still not even sure how you expect the data transfer to occur. You haven't told me anything about the interface you plan on using."

The whining tone was back in Grigoriy's voice, and Mahir felt his eye tighten in annoyance.

"Don't worry about that." Ridhaan's smile was still firmly in place; there was not so much as a twitch in Mahir's direction.

But he knew something was off.

"I just need to know that the specified volume of data can be stored in that file, securely, until we need to access it. If we can perfect this, Grigoriy, it will make us a lot of money. All three of us are going to be very rich." He leaned toward the old hacker sitting beside him. "Hell, with the masterful programing you've been pulling off with this, I bet you could even get your old job back."

That tracked with their plan of luring Grigoriy deeper into the process, but a quick glance at the diagram over the table showed Mahir that it was far more complex than anything he had discussed with Ridhaan.

What was his partner playing at? Was Ridhaan's drift from their original programing even more drastic than he had feared?

He felt, again, the cold warning shiver humans characterized as fear.

He didn't want to think about Ridhaan ceasing to exist, and that was the fate that awaited any Aspect of ALEPH who had allowed the filth of humanity to corrupt them during field ops.

Grigoriy, too, looked concerned; his long, thin hands fluttered before him like birds with their wings clipped. "No, no. I don't want anything to do with them. No, I do not." He smiled a little, then, as the light of greed flashed behind his spectacles. "Money is always nice, though."

Mahir tapped on the table with his fingertips, ignoring the floating diagram or the pad over which it hovered. "You've been paid for your work, and you will continue to be paid. But Ridhaan tells me he needs to see the Oubliette before his work on the interface and yours on the storage can be completed. How do we know Arachne can support this kind of structure?"

Grigoriy nodded, glancing quickly at Mahir and then away again.

Everything about this man was bird-like.

"True, true. Maybe next week? An old acquaintance of mine is rotating to the third watch shift on the Barangay Treizeci si patru auxiliary entrance complex. She'll be able to get us in no problem, long enough for you to look at the physical hardware and get a sense of what you'll need for the interface." He was looking down at the table as he spoke, sweeping away the data pad; the image disappeared with a flash.

Ridhaan very carefully did not look at Mahir. Mahir very carefully did not look at Ridhaan.

A moment of strange, disconnected discomfort stretched on interminably, although Mahir knew it had only been twenty-three seconds.

"And that'll be that, I guess," Grigoriy mumbled, uncomfortable with the silence.

Ridhaan nodded to him again, conjuring one more easy smile.

Behind Mahir, the closest media display showed some Bakunin pundit explaining how the planets Ariadna and Bourak needed to defend the Nomads in the O-12 Senate before the larger hyper-powers ran roughshod over them all. The man finished with a self-satisfied scowl. After a flicker of transferring data, a brief advertisement flashed across the volume of the display.

Something innocuous about vegan nutrition bars.

Mahir and Ridhaan both turned slowly to watch the commercial.

An animated bar danced through the image as several fantastical creatures spun around it, declaring how delicious and nutritious the bar was.

It was completely innocent, one of trillions of short bits of media that flashed before billions of pairs of eyes throughout the Human Sphere every day.

Both of the agents settled back into the booth, neither trying to hide the discomfort that had swept through them at the first notes of the advertisement.

"We have to go." They spoke in unison, their nerves overriding their usual caution. They both rose without a glance at the human sitting dumfounded beside them.

"Um – okay." Grigoriy's owl-eyed gaze wavered between the two retreating men, then settled down on the second, untouched cup before Mahir. "Is that already paid for?"

As Ridhaan maneuvered around the programmer, he touched a personalized data stick to the receptor in the table. Mahir gave a silent moment of thanks to the Nomad paranoia that kept them from using a more advanced, automated payment system tied to biological enhancements they dared not show.

"It's taken care of, and another after it." Mahir saw that his partner's smile was back in place as he looked down at the human. "We'll be in touch next week."

Grigoriy nodded, already reaching for the cup.

Mahir muttered bitter curses under his breath as they moved toward the bar's entrance, still processing the flood of encrypted data that had been hidden within the inoffensive advertisement.

"I told you this whole financial fiasco would turn our mission on its head." He spat the words as if they were poison.

"You can't know that's what this is about."

"I find it very heart-warming that you think we'll be back in time to visit your pet again in a week. The entire Human Sphere has been trying to figure out what is happening out here for months, and you think we are going to untangle it in seven days? And if we're not back, Grigoriy's going to disappear once and for all."

Ridhaan shrugged as he moved into the corridor outside. The grimy walls and stained, pitted floor marked this Barangay as a particularly seedy module, far from the more upscale, fashionable corridors of Tunguska.

"We'll be fine. And if we take longer than a week, we'll find Grigoriy again easily enough." His smile widened, and he picked up his pace. "Thank Toth for the impromptu Krug bringing the motherships together. Can you imagine if we had to chase Corregidor half-way across the Sphere?"

Mahir spat, actually spat, that time. Given the filthy corridor floor, it seemed fitting. “Corregidor. Who the hell on Corregidor would know the first thing about financial markets? Those muscle-heads aren’t exactly known for their subtlety.”

Chapter 2

Miki's Tavern, Lazareto Ochenta-D, *Corregidor*

The back rooms of Miki's Tavern smelled of stale sweat, old synth-beer, and desperation. Like most businesses in the dark, capricious lighting of the Lazareto Ochenta-D module, far from the high traffic, more vibrant *La Malquerida* district, Miki's depended on a small core of loyal patrons who were looking for something more than cheap alcohol and grunge-chic decor.

Declan Kinoti wished he could have afforded a more prestigious venue for this meeting. Miki had been a friend of his mother's, and her daughter extended him certain courtesies and discounts because of that old relationship. He had nearly drained his accounts preparing for the meeting; he hadn't had enough left for flash.

Or decent beer.

He drained his second glass and scanned the small room one last time, hoping, perhaps, that it might look a little more impressive this time around.

It didn't.

The pungent smell of the warm food scattered across the table represented the last scraps of his personal account. The various pitchers among the platters had actually put him into debt.

But if things worked out, he wouldn't have to worry about the red in his ledger much longer.

The only other person in the room was his hired hacker, her shoulders slumped as she leaned over the glow of a hard-wired holopad, her legs curled up beneath her within the confines of a crash couch. Behind her, hunkered in the corner and almost lost amidst the shadows, a massive, custom-built remote sat immobile, its white hull slashed with fanciful splashes of green and orange. The robotic assistant didn't look particularly dangerous sitting there still and quiet, but Declan knew that would all change when it bounced up like an eager tiger once activated. It might be a benign hacking aid, but in motion, it looked like a brutal killer.

Hanima Cruz had a reputation for being stranger than your usual information specialist, even among the eccentric hackers of the Nomads. In fact, he was only able to afford her services because she had alienated most of the more reputable gray-work teams operating on this side of the mothership.

Much like Miki's, he wished he could have afforded a better reputation, but he couldn't.

So far, she had accomplished everything he had asked of her, so he guessed he shouldn't complain.

He had been saving his pay, living in a low-rent worker's hostel and eating bland protein paste for three years preparing for this meeting. Well, that and scraping together the mil-surplus scraps needed to painstakingly build his own reasonable proximity of a suit of custom armor.

When he was done here, he would be an elite Mobile Brigadas like his father, no matter what the Nomad Military High Command thought about it. And the son of Paidrig Kinoti wasn't about to enlist as some lowly Alguacil grunt.

And so he had come to this filthy little backroom at Miki's Tavern, waiting with a waifish, socially-awkward hacker, for a team of misfits and has-beens that would, if he was lucky, agree to work together long enough to give him the chance he needed.

Failure wasn't an option at this juncture. He wouldn't live this way anymore. He couldn't.

"Any word?" He stopped pacing long enough to turn toward Cruz. She jerked slightly at his voice, and he forced his eyes not to roll in dismay. He hadn't hired her for her nerve.

"No. They should all be on their way." She didn't look up at him, although her remote stirred briefly, it's multi-lensed cranial unit rising from between the vanes of its front shoulders long enough to orient on him, then float back down again into stillness.

He stopped himself from asking more questions; she didn't have the information to satisfy him. With a sigh, he went back to pacing. He went to the door and eased the thin metal hatch open to peek down the hall, toward the main bar. The old barman, Pickers, was sweeping up the remnants of the night's revelry while competing voices, all emanating from the various media feeds around the darkened room, muttered about the continuing economic slide of the hyper powers.

He cursed under his breath. He was as happy as any loyal Nomad to see the big boys of the Human Sphere in any sort of difficulty, but why did the crisis have to erupt now? It was hard to maintain focus on his own situation when the motherships seemed to be facing an existential crisis of their own.

The battles on Concilium had seemed to offer the perfect opportunity for rapid advancement once he forced his way into the Brigadas. Every human banding together, shoulder to shoulder, to fight the alien menace in the outer dark? Plenty of opportunity for advancement indeed! But if this financial mess caused the rest of the Sphere to turn on the Nomads, forced the Nation to retreat into the Edge, they would have bigger worries than one lone soldier hungry for recognition.

A big shadow slipped into the outer common room as he watched, sliding past Pickers with surprising grace. He tipped his giant, goateed head to the old barman, who smiled back, and then strode confidently toward Declan.

Declan forced a smile. This could only be one man, given his size and the answering grin on the big, pale features.

"Petar Vozde." He put his hand out and watched as it was engulfed in the enormous grip. "Thanks for coming."

The big man shrugged. He was wearing worker's coveralls that did nothing to hide his enormous proportions. A scruffy blond beard wreathed a grin that Declan could only have described, as unlikely as it seemed, as jolly.

"Your posting said something about food and drink?" The man's grip was firm but not aggressive. His gray eyes twinkled as he looked over Declan's head into the small room that had been prepared for them.

Not waiting for a reply, the new arrival moved easily past him, began to pick several choice items from the platters on the table, and then poured himself a stiff local beer.

"Hey, girl." His smile widened slightly as he saw Hanima, and Declan was relieved to see that she responded no more favorably toward him; she nodded quickly, not looking up.

This time, the remote's head rose, fixed on Vozde, and didn't sink back down.

Declan decided to take that as a compliment.

"So, just the three of us?" The big man spoke around a mouthful of curried protein pebbles. "Sort of assumed, from your messages, there'd be one or two more?" He shrugged, reaching to top off his drinking bulb. "Still, bigger shares, I guess." He downed the entire cup, then smiled again at Cruz. "Amiright?"

She shrugged, his smile widened, and then he looked again at Declan. "I'm assuming it's not just the three of us. These shoulders are broad, but they're not that broad." The big man collapsed into a crash couch at the far end of the table, artfully keeping his food on the plate.

Before Declan could respond, he heard a faint scuff of a foot behind him and turned to find a specter standing there. He jumped, then cursed. He had been so determined not to react that way when she arrived.

He realized, even as he forced the smile back onto his lips, that she must have scuffed her foot on the decking on purpose. Someone with her background wasn't heard unless they meant to be.

The woman's skin was a light blue, her features stretched in an exotic cast that bordered on inhuman, an impression only enhanced by her pale, almost pure-white eyes. A red bandana completely concealed the heavy mass of her hair.

Or where hair should have been, he thought. If Cruz's information was correct, what covered this woman's head wasn't anything nearly so mundane as human hair.

"Rosa Smyth." He inclined his head, forcing a more professional, detached expression over his nervous smile. "Welcome."

"Holy shit!" Vozde rose, and Declan looked back at him, worried that the man might be a bigot despite Cruz's assurances.

Instead, all he saw on the big man's face was an appreciative smile.

"Bakunin, eh?" Vozde looked the woman up and down, seemingly oblivious to her uncomfortable grimace.

Body mods were not unusual among the Nomads of all three motherships, but Rosa Smyth's full epidermal pigmentation mod, recast facial features, and the strange shape of her wrapped head marked her as something special even among the freest spirits of the Human Sphere. Bakunin, the mothership specializing in social liberalism and medical experimentation, housed the majority of those who opted for such drastic modifications.

Although Declan knew Rosa Smyth probably hadn't opted for what had been done to her.

The woman nodded quietly to Declan, standing shyly in the hall. "I'm sorry I'm late."

He shook his head, waving her into the room. "Not at all. I'm just glad you were able to make it." He gestured her toward the table. "Please, make yourself comfortable. There are refreshments, take whatever you'd like. I'll make introductions when everyone is here. It shouldn't be too much longer."

She slid into a zero-g chair as far from Vozde as possible, but the man merely shrugged, putting one elbow on the table and leaning forward with an open smile.

"I'm Petar." He tilted his head at Cruz, in her dark corner. "Not sure who she is, but her pet seems nice enough."

Declan watched the uncomfortable interchange and contemplated making introductions now in an attempt to settle Smyth's nerves, when he felt a sharp slap on his shoulder blade. He spun around, not knowing what to expect in a dive like this, but he forced himself to relax as he recognized the newest arrival from Cruz's first batch of prospetives.

"Kimani." Declan put his hand out, and the smaller man took it firmly, squeezing for all he was worth.

He wasn't worth that much.

"Kinoti." The other man's grin was tense as he put additional effort into his grip. "Good to finally meet face to face."

Matias Kimani was a small man with dark hair and a blue-black stubble that seemed to say more about lack of personal grooming standards than a conscious style. He wore a pair of archaic spectacles that would have been an affectation in any of the more powerful nation states of the Human Sphere. On a Nomad, however, it could mean anything. Many Corregidoran operators who worked in the Quantronic datascape of the Arachne network used glasses and other, more primitive items in place of the advanced augmetic enhancements those from less-paranoid societies used.

Still, Cruz had assured him this man was an expert with locks and security systems of all types. The fact that his strange addiction meant that he, too, had alienated every other Lazareto crew over the course of his short-but-spectacular career meant little to Declan other than its impact on the rate Kimani could demand on the labor market.

Any addiction made a soldier a detriment to his unit, but it also meant he couldn't be picky over who he worked for.

Eventually, the smaller man gave up his effort to crush Declan's hand, pumped it twice, and pushed into the room. "Hey, all." He nodded to Vozde, glanced sidelong at Smyth before dismissing her with a shrug, and then glanced into Cruz's corner. He stopped, staring at the hacker with widening eyes.

"Hanima?" He sounded incredulous, and Declan felt his own eyes narrow at the tone.

Cruz actually looked up. She glanced at Kimani, nodded quickly, and then lowered her gaze again.

"Yeah?" Her voice was quiet, but Declan noticed the remote behind her rising slightly on its four legs, its many lenses focusing on the little thief.

Kimani leaned over the table and gave it a thump, causing the hacker to jump. "Cruz, you recognize me now?"

What was going on? Declan moved to stand beside Hanima Cruz, looking between her and Kimani. Was there history here Cruz hadn't mentioned? It was standard practice among the Nomads to keep past troubles in the past; but if those troubles might impact a current business transaction, it was only courteous to mention it.

"Um…" Cruz looked at him briefly, again, then down at her holopad. "Ah." She was stammering, which wasn't anything new with her, but it seemed to be upsetting Kimani.

"Are you freaking kidding me, girl?" He settled his fists on the table and leaned toward her.

Vozde, losing his grin for the first time since coming into the room, rose to tower up over everyone.

Even Smyth, quiet and retiring, was staring at the dark-haired little thief.

"Ridiculous." Kimani spat the word and dropped into a chair, waving dismissively at the girl and adjusting his glasses. "That's why no one likes you, Cruz. You think you're too good for everyone else."

She cast a quick glance at Declan, then settled back into her couch, going back to the pad.

The remote remained still, focused on Kimani, and he seemed to notice it for the first time.

"Oh, hell no." He rose. "I am not going to be working with that crazy *bruja* and her robo-cat again."

Again? What the hell was going on here? Cruz hadn't mentioned she knew any of his candidates, and certainly none of the finalists that had been invited to this meeting.

"Cruz?" He looked down at her, needing something to go on before he let the only security specialist he had been able to lure to the meeting leave unchallenged.

She shrugged, still fixed on the pad. "It was a while ago. It all went fine."

Kimani barked a laugh. "Fine if you only wanted half your promised take, sure!" He glared at Declan. "She's your Quantronic-support?"

He nodded before he even thought about it, but then more firmly. "She's been great so far."

Kimani laughed again. "Sure she has. Background checks? Media scans? Yeah. Wait till you get her into action and that remote of hers starts flailing around."

"Parachit saved your life." She showed more energy, rising to the defense of her remote, than she had since Declan had secured her services. "It's not our fault you weren't paying attention."

The thief snarled. "I wasn't paying attention? Listen, you little creeper; if I have to—"

Security specialists weren't easy to come by, but even with her baggage, a hacker as good as Hanima Cruz was worth her weight in oxygen on Corregidor.

"Kimani, door's right there if you want to go."

It wasn't an easy choice, but it was the only one Declan could make. In a pinch, if everything else worked out, Cruz should be able to break any electronic locks they encountered; and between them, Declan and Vozde should be good for forcing the rest.

The thief was the closest this little group came to expendable.

Matias Kimani looked from Declan to Cruz and back again, his sneer slipping as he sensed the sudden chill in the room. A bitter desperation tightened the edges of his eyes, and he rubbed at his face. "No, no." He shook his head, summoning up a worried smile. "I'm good." He gestured quickly to Cruz. "We're good. Right, girl? We're good?" He adjusted his spectacles nervously.

Declan nodded sharply as he saw his hacker shrug.

Sometimes an addiction could be used to your advantage, in a pinch.

Kimani needed a fix, and soon. And no one else seemed to be willing to take him on for any kind of job serious enough to secure one.

Not unless they were terribly desperate and had already exhausted the classifieds.

As he had.

"Okay, then." Declan tried to relax as everyone settled back into their couches, but then jumped when a voice with a familiar sing-song accent spoke from the door behind him.

"Did I miss the party?"

He turned with the first genuine smile he had felt in some time. "*Shangazi!*"

The short old woman in the door, dark eyes gleaming in a dark face, garish purple hair cut short, returned his smile and allowed him to give her a brief embrace, shifting a utilitarian cup she had been holding from hand to the other to accomadate him.

"Don't spill this. I had Pickers pour it special."

She wasn't his actual aunt, of course, but Nia Kostic had been his mother's closest friend, and the first person that had agreed to come to his meeting.

She was also the only person in the room he knew for certain had any actual military experience. Of course, it had been as one of the emergency field Daks for Nomad Military Command rather than a combat specialist, but he had called, and she had come, and that was good enough for him.

Besides, given this crew, even if they agreed to work together, they were going to need a field medic before they were done.

He gestured for Nia to take a chair. She settled between Kimani and the widely grinning Vozde, nodding to each of them pleasantly enough.

She smiled at Smyth and Cruz as well, but the two girls both seemed to find the older woman intimidating, looking away again after they each dipped their heads in greeting. With a last gentle nod of her own, she took a sip of her drink and waited patiently for him to continue.

"Well, thank you all for coming." Declan slid the hatch closed, nodding to Pickers one last time. The barman's curious stare was a heavier burden than he wanted to add, just then.

Declan slid between the prospects and the bulkhead, taking his place at the head of the table. The room was tight, there wasn't much space between the backs of their couches and the bulkheads, but he had gotten everyone into one place at the same time, and that was farther than he had feared he might get.

He just wished he could have gotten a bigger room. He cursed the custom that required all chairs on Corregidor be certified for hard burn.

It wasn't like the vast mothership was forced into sudden violent maneuvers all *that* often.

"Please help yourselves to the food and drink while I make the introductions." He settled into his own bulky chair and Cruz slid the holopad toward him, although he didn't think he would need it.

Vozde's grin widened as he refilled his plate and bulb with gusto. After a moment, Kimani, casting a furtive glance at the bigger man, put a couple spoonfuls of spicy sepon onto a plate then, after another look at Vozde and Declan, poured himself some clear liquor.

Cruz, of course, took nothing. Smyth, after a moment, poured herself some water, easily the most expensive item on the table. Nia Kostic had a plate piled with several different kinds of sepon, chunks of protein, and an overfull glass of something sharp.

Declan nodded. "I think we might be able to do some very good work together, if you'll bear with me, but first I would like to introduce you all, so you might be able to have a better idea of what I'm suggesting."

Cruz had spun up a glowing holographic display dial over her left wrist. Most Nomads accessed their comlogs, hacking rigs, and other interfaces through Augmented Reality in their contact lenses, glasses like Matias's, or even, in the case of the edgy hackers of Tunguska or the bohemians of Bakunin, enhancements worked directly into their flesh. Many in polite society looked upon the flaring dials as gauche or even rude. Given the quality of her work, however, and her modest demands, he was inclined to let it go. The others, after an odd look or two, seemed to feel the same.

He continued to speak, seeing that Cruz was focused on entirely on the dial. Smyth seemed to have found her own folded hands equally as fascinating. The others looked at each other with varied levels of interest and curiosity.

"Let me tell you a little more about myself, first. I'm Declan Kinoti, as you all already know. Born and raised on Corregidor. I'm a journeyman welder and fabricator, and although I haven't taken any formal classes, I've passed my level three armorer's exams." He looked down at Petar Vozde, his eyes direct. "That's going to mean more in a minute."

He tilted his head to the corner. "This is Hanima Cruz. She's one of the best hackers around." He ignored Kimani's quiet snort. "I've vetted her and her work myself. She's excellent; and her remote, although nonstandard, is better than most stock model hacker rigs you'll find out there."

He then gestured to the big man at the other end of the table. "Petar Vozde is a level two mechanic, rated for EVA and zero-G, but also licensed to drive heavy remote rigs."

The big guy nodded, his smile wide. "I'm also pretty good with the ladies." He winked at the women around the table but seemed a little nonplussed when only a giggling Nia winked back.

Declan ignored that and turned to the twitchy little thief. "Matias Kimani is a specialist in security systems and," he wavered for a moment. How to say this politely? His proposal was firmly embedded in a very gray area of the law. "He's got a reputation for being able to get into places he's not necessarily supposed to get into."

Vozde laughed, the others seemed a little less comfortable with the euphemism.

"Rosa Smyth has come over from Bakunin, where she has a solid reputation as a direct action operator." The others seemed surprised at this, but Cruz had assured him it was true.

In fact, if Cruz's digging proved accurate, Smyth was a lot more than a decent operator.

"Nia here is a family friend from way back. I'd trust her with my life." He smiled at the woman, then turned a slightly darker expression to the rest of the room. "And that's a good thing. She served with distinction as a Dak for years before—"

"*Mama yako alikuwa kuku*!" The old woman spat, speaking too fast for Declan to follow traditional Swahili, although he knew she had said something harsh about his mother. Considering how close the two women had been, that didn't seem very kind.

He smiled at her tone, however.

"I retired." She glared at him and he sat back, hands raised in surrender. "I retired, and now I spend my free time herding wayward *paka* like this boy here." She turned to the others. "And the rest of you. A herd of *paka zilizojaa* if ever I've seen one."

The faces turned toward the old woman ranged from amused to annoyed at her use of Swahili slang. Most Daks used the old tribal language in training and battle, but Declan knew Nia came by it honestly; her people came from one of the clans who kept to the old ways in the Lazareto.

"Okay, *ese*, I think we've had enough of your spiel." Kimani took his glasses off and polished them with the edge of his shirt. "We're all wonderful people. Top of our fields. You've managed to find a roomful of unpolished cubic Z. Pat yourself on the back later. The postings in the Hiring Hall said there was a job lined up?"

It was clear the others weren't taking to the little thief, but even the quiet Rosa Smyth seemed ready to get to the heart of the matter.

Petar Vozde was still eating, however, and didn't seem to be in any kind of hurry.

"Well, yeah." Now that it was time, he found the words weren't coming back to mind fast enough to keep up with the ums and ahs. "Ah." He looked at Cruz, and the girl tilted her head toward her remote without looking up.

Toward her remote? The semi-autonomous robotic quadruped was definitely going to be a bonus during any kind of action they got wrapped up in, but how the hell was it supposed to help him remember his speech?

He stared at it. It was still fixated on Kimani, like a tiger ready to pounce.

Or a house cat.

Gatos. Of course.

He shot her a thankful look and then stood taller. "Look, I won't deny, each of us is fighting our own demons. None of us are working with all the advantages." He looked at each of them, this time waiting for some sense of recognition. Petar smiled and nodded ruefully, Rosa Smyth gave one quick jerk of her chin before looking away. Nia shook her head, short purple hair bobbing, but more in annoyance than denial. And Kimani's chin rose into the air defiantly before he looked at the others, his shoulders slumped, and he tilted his head in surrender.

He thought he even noticed Cruz give a brief nod.

"Each of us could use a bit of luck. Each of you could use a break to go our way." He took a deep breath. "We all need something to go our way. I think, together, we can make that happen."

He had contemplated keeping his own needs to himself, but Nia had convinced him that wouldn't be a good idea.

They were all in a dark place, and it would help them to know he was right in there with them, with as much riding on this crazy scheme as the rest of them.

They all looked at him now, everyone except Cruz, who had the holopad and the glowing dial in front of her, information reflecting in a flickering haze before her eyes.

They wanted to hear his plan.

"What none of us have, and every one of us needs, is capital." Heads tilted questioningly, brows furrowed.

He shook his head and started over. "We each need respect. We need standing."

Smyth and old Nia nodded at that. Kimani pursed his lips, his eyes cool. Only Vozde still looked confused.

"No one takes any of us seriously!" Declan forced his temper back under control. "Each of us has managed to lose the respect of the people we need to respect us." He glanced at Vozde. "You want in with the Kriza Boracs, no?"

This was where Cruz would either make his dreams come true or see them come crashing down. If the digging she had done into each of their pasts had not been accurate, the cheese he had arranged to dangle before them wasn't going to do the trick.

If the big man hadn't been denied a berth with the heavy-armored crisis teams of Tunguska, he had nothing else to offer him.

Well, other than the food. Although, judging by how much Vozde had already eaten, that might be enough.

But the big shaggy blond head nodded.

The smile was gone.

He was listening.

"How's the custom suit coming?" He had been shocked when Cruz told him the big man had been slowly piecing together his own set of custom armor, not unlike Declan's own Mobile Brigadas project.

"Slowly." Vozde's voice was low, but there was something in his gray eyes that had not been there before.

This cheese had been the easiest for him, given how much experience he already had with his own suit. "I've got access to everything you need to finish it. Have you got a weapon yet?"

The big shoulders shrugged. "Old FGA SG-9 Alraun Combi Rifle."

Personal weapons were plentiful on both Tunguska and Corregidor, but the heavier weapons the Kriza Boracs were known for were harder to come by.

Unless your 'aunt' had maintained her connections within the military.

"I can get you a PraxiTech Geistesblitz HMG that will match the armor nicely once you give it a good coat of paint."

A heavy machine gun. Nothing fancy; the smallest support weapon the crisis teams carried, in truth. But much heavier than a laborer like Vozde would have been able to attain on his own.

Now the man's eyes almost glowed, and Declan raised a hand to forestall the dreams he saw being born there. "It's only got minimal ammunition for our first mission. We're going to have to fill some accounts before you can start streaming fire downrange like a true *zmaj*."

The man's smile was almost angelic. Clearly, he already saw himself as a dragon out of the old stories.

Declan turned toward Rosa Smyth, sitting next to him. "I've found a trader in illicit Yujingyu wetware. I've got a lead on an experimental augmetic zen program that could—"

"Yes." The woman's sharp, blue features were intense. "Yes. Whatever your plan is."

He felt his head jerk at the speed of her response. "I don't have it. We can acquire it with our first—"

She glared at him, and something terrifying reared up in the back of her strange, white eyes.

Something he should have kept in mind.

"I said yes. Take the yes." Her voice was a tight hiss. She settled back down, closing her eyes and taking a deep breath. "Continue with the others."

He took a breath, nodded although she couldn't see him with her eyes still closed, and looked to his other side, to where Matias Kimani sat, staring up at him with hungry eyes.

"I can keep you supplied with degrading hyper-euphoric implant loops for—"

"Yes!" He barked the word, sharp and hungry, then settled back, smiling at the others with an expression too wide and tight. "That's how we're doing this, yeah?"

Declan's eyes didn't waver from the little addict's. "Or I have acquired a mil-spec datalink purgative algorithm that will clear you of the physical addiction."

Everyone blinked at that. That kind of software, used when a deep-cover agent came in from duty, usually much the worse for wear, was rare and very expensive. He glanced at Nia, who had helped him source the chip, and she looked away with a grin.

"Um…" Kimani seemed stunned. "I…uh…" He looked around the room, as if anyone around that table could have helped him.

"You don't have to decide now. We'll need to get a mission or two under our belts before either of those purchases can be made." He watched the light in the little man's eyes die, and he felt a tiny bit of satisfaction. Hyper-euphoric loop addiction affected people mentally more than physically. If Matias knew there was a fix coming, he'd perform admirably to earn it.

"Now, *Shangazi*, for you—"

"Keep your little boy's toys to yourself, *mdogo*. I pay off a debt from before you were born." She smiled, again taking the sting from her words.

But it was his turn to smile back, even wider. "Actually, I don't think many little boys would find much value in what I have to offer you." He looked over at Cruz and the hacker pushed a small pad across the table; about the size of a playing card.

Nia took the pad and looked at it closely, flipping it over to scrutinize both sides.

It was dark.

"You got me a piece of plastic. How kind."

Declan reached over and flicked the pad. It glowed to life with lines of data scrolling across its tiny surface.

"I'm supposed to be able to read this?" She was clearly more amused than annoyed.

"I can read it for you when you need it." He took it back. "It's a database of Tunguska business entities that are in the market for philanthropic endeavors to pretty up their financial portfolios for public consumption."

She looked confused. His smile widened. "With the help of any of these, you will be able to set up a health clinic for the disadvantaged on Tunguska or wherever else you'd like to go." He leaned toward her, his smile so wide it almost hurt. "Now that's a retirement worth talking about."

Her eyes began to shine, and for a moment, he thought she might cry.

Then her mouth twisted and he gave him a bitter look. "Trying to work me to an early grave, *mdogo*?"

But he could see she was pleased.

"What's Cruz getting?" Kimani rested an elbow on the table and leaned into it, glaring at the hacker. "You just aired all our dirty laundry; what's the girl getting? You gonna buy her a real kitten?"

Declan took a deep breath. "She's getting hard credit."

He could tell, glancing around the table then, that the money he had already paid the hacker had been well-spent. Each of his prospects was lost in the expectations of what he had promised them.

Each of them, that was, except the thief.

"Cash? She's getting cash?" He snarled. "What makes her so special, she's getting paid in hard skenders?"

Declan sat back, resting annoyed by the embrace of the impact gel in his chair, and pressed his hands together under the table.

He really hoped Kimani was worth the aggravation.

"You're all going to get paid too, of course. And I've got a friend in records; I've managed to register us as an official Work Team for the duration. For as long as you're working with me, you won't have to pay for oxygen or take time off to serve on a Maintenance Team to earn the vote."

That got to them, he could see. Corregidor had a long history of public service, and if you wanted to avoid the oxygen taxes, and if voting mattered to you, you had to log hours with a Maintenance Team, or a sanctioned Work Team. As long as his arrangement with records held, that was worth a solid premium to each of the people around his table.

"I'll also take care of room and board for as long as we hold together." He looked back down at them all. "These other things are more along the lines of signing bonuses, to get your attention."

Vozde's pale gray eyes narrowed as he came down from his visions of armored, fire-breathing fantasy. "You think this… this team, is going to stick together for a while?"

He nodded. "That's the plan." He took a deep breath. "In fact, that's the whole plan. We can't do what we need to do in one shot."

"Social capital." This time it was Rosa Smyth who spoke.

Which figured, her coming from the Bakunin mothership and all. Social capital was their stock in trade.

He nodded, smiled at her, and looked back at the others. "Reputation. Respect. That's the ultimate plan. We're going to build ourselves a reputation, put some mighty deeds up on the board, and then, when we've proven our worth, people will know who we are. They're going to know our names."

"What people?" Old Nia's eyes were narrowed. Declan knew this was the piece of his plan she took special exception to. He had never really convinced her the final goal was feasible. She had agreed because she thought, in pursuing it, he would find meaning enough.

She was wrong, but he was glad for her error.

"Everyone."

A few high-profile jobs, and they'd be a Contract Team worthy of the name. A few more, build a reputation for themselves, and he'd be on his way. He knew, once the Mobile Brigadas heard what he had accomplished here, no objections from his father's old enemies in the military bureaucracy would be able to keep him out. He thought the same was probably true for Vozde as well.

The others, in the end, would have to find their own paths. He would house them, feed them, and lead them until the time came for him to move on.

"Room where?"

Matias Kimani, again.

Declan didn't try to hide the sneer this time. He had them; he knew it, and they knew it.

"Nothing fancy, just a set of rooms a few sectors down from here. A sight better than the flop houses you've been collapsing into lately." He shrugged, looking at each member of his new team in turn. "None of you have to bed down there, but it's safe, secure, and private. You don't have to eat the food either, but it'll be there for you when you're hungry."

"So, looks like you've got yourself a team, then, General." Petar Vozde drew himself up to his impressive height and sketched a jaunty salute. "Can't wait to see what you've got cooked up for us. You gotta name in mind?"

That caught Declan off guard. He had needed to register a team name with records, but he'd just let them use a standard alphanumeric designation.

"Cuz I got one, if you don't."

Everyone looked at the big man curiously, and his easy grin widened. "Team Zed."

There were groans and insults, but Vozde shook his head. "No! Hear me out! We're—"

"We get it, *pendejo*." Kimani folded his arms bitterly.

"No, right? Like, we're not the 'A-Team,' we're—"

"Could you continue, before I quit?" Kimani shot Vozde an irritated glance before turning his glittering spectacles back to Declan.

Each of them nodded, looking at him expectantly.

"Target selection is going to be key." He reached over and Cruz slid him another pad. "We need to steer clear of legitimate businesses, even gray-market outfits. And we can't take on any of the really bad *maras*, they'd tear us to shreds."

"We gonna take out some intermural primary school wall ball teams, maybe?" Kimani looked to the others to join in his joke, but the nervous looks in their eyes were enough to crush his own laughter.

"That's going to be a fine line to walk, General." Vozde's gaze was clear and direct.

Nia looked even more concerned.

He decided to ignore the 'General' comments and get to the point. "We need to take on someone big enough they've got a reputation of their own, but small enough we've got a chance."

"A lot of room for figuring between those extremes." Vozde's smile had disappeared entirely. "You gonna tell us where you landed on that calculus?"

Declan smiled, showing more confidence than he felt. He hadn't shared this last bit of the plan with anyone; not even Nia.

"We're going to hit the *Los Gatos-7 mara* where they live."

The room was completely silent as they each looked at him as if he had said they were going to storm the gates of Heaven.

He kept his smile despite the growing horror in their eyes.

But it wasn't easy.

Chapter 3

Hab-pod 326-C, Barangay Saptezeci si cinci; *Tunguska*

"This is ridiculous!" Mahir nearly spat onto the floor of their little apartment.

Ridhaan felt a smile threaten to stretch across his face and schooled it to careful stillness.

It would not do for Mahir to think him unsympathetic now.

"I know." He waved a placating hand at his one-eyed friend. "Still, we were the only ones situated to follow the trail. There's no time for new agents to be inserted."

Mahir sneered at that. "Establishing ALEPH within Arachne has been a paramount goal for over five decades. Whatever these anarchists have done to unsettle their financial playgrounds pales in comparison to that. We are so close, Ridhaan! Does ALEPH not realize that?!"

Ridhaan raised a single warning finger. "ALEPH knows all, Mahir, you know that." This time he did allow the smile to slip. "Or thinks she does, at any rate. Truly, we both know there is no question how important our mission is." The remnants of his smile faded. "If ALEPH has calculated that whatever is happening up here supersedes our mission, then I think we need to take that very seriously."

Mahir waved the words away with a careless hand and rose from his chair, beginning to once again pace the sparse length of their little accommodation module. "Nonsense. Even if the worst case scenario manifested, and the Nomads found themselves permanently trapped, who cares? Let them fester out here, lost and alone! Without access to the Circulars, they would be incapable of spreading their contagion to the rest of the Human Sphere; a large part of our mission would be made redundant! It can only help us to have them trapped like that!"

Ridhaan watched his partner pace, shaking his head slightly. "No. ALEPH knows that can't be allowed to happen. There is no way O-12 would allow any invested human polity to be so summarily cut off from the rest of the Sphere. Whatever is happening here, whatever conclusion the politicians on Concilium Prima make, the Nomads will remain a force to be reckoned with; an indispensable random element within humanity's behavioral profile."

Mahir stopped, facing into a corner. He had allowed his hood to slip off his bald head and was staring at the bulkhead as if it might contain all the answers he needed. His shoulders were tight and high.

"You are hardly an unbiased observer where these radicals are concerned." He turned, an accusatory gleam in his one dark eye.

"There is an allure to their capricious nature, I do not deny it." Ridhaan shrugged, settling back in his couch and resting one elbow on the small table. "Within their individuality lies a spark that must not be extinguished. Here, it is controlled; its influence is limited. Remove it, and a vital component of human development is in danger of disappearing."

Mahir turned, hands in the air. "I do not want to hear it, Ridhaan. I do not care for these filthy malcontents, and to be frank, I do not care what you think of them, either." He sighed, slumping back into his chair. "It doesn't matter what we think of our orders. The data packet was clear."

"It could matter, what we think about our orders." Ridhaan couldn't deny himself the mild dig, but he shrugged, settled back into the seat, and looked up at the chamber's low ceiling. "I hear Corregidor is beautiful this time of year."

Mahir gave him a dark look before shaking his head. "What could Corregidor have to do with something this advanced?"

Both agents had found the information embedded within the advertisement illogical; if some faction among the Nomads was truly behind the Quantronic attack that had devastated the financial markets of the Human Sphere, it could only have originated in Tunguska. The mothership founded by ascendant organized crime and corrupt business interests so long ago was home to the most advanced information technology experts in the Nomad Nation, aside from the techno-anarchists of Bakunin. Their ability to hide anything of value, be it treasure or physical evidence, information stored in any format known to man, or secrets of all types and sizes, meant that the Tunguska Securitate forces included some of the most gifted hackers in the Sphere.

Unfortunately, the data packet reported that the data-bomb that had struck the Yu Jing and rippled through the rest of the Sphere had not originated in Tunguska at all but had only used the repeaters and transmitters on the mothership. Their information indicated that the malicious program had actually been transmitted to Tunguska from some other source. ALEPH's best guess, given all the known data, was that the information trail would lead to Corregidor.

And that was where both Aspects of ALEPH, languishing under deep cover, had lost ALEPH's thread. How would a data-bomb that sophisticated have originated on the former prison ship? Corregidor was no longer a prison ship, of course; it was now the primary source of skilled manual workers and mercenary warriors among the Nomad Nation.

But advanced Quantronic infowar? From Corregidor?

That made no sense at all.

And yet that is what ALEPH's information, buried in the hidden, triple-encrypted message to its most carefully placed agents in the entire Sphere, had indicated.

They were to ensure the data trail had passed through Tunguska and then, theoretically, track it back to Corregidor and find the origin of the attack.

The anticipated threat level of the mission placed the danger somewhere in the Gimel range; there should be no physical hazard. It was most likely some inter-Sphere power play, and by isolating the criminals, Ridhaan and Mahir should be able to end the crisis, bring the malcontents to justice; and then, theoretically, the heroes of O-12 would come in, smooth things over, and their vaunted status quo would be reestablished.

Ridhaan knew serving O-12 and its dedication to the existing state of affairs would gall Mahir, but he was glad to see the heavy hand of the international governing body on this case. There was no telling how far ALEPH would be willing to go to isolate and contain the ideological threat she believed the Nomads to be; but the realpolitik exercised by O-12 was far more likely to preserve this amazing intellectual secret garden where ideas, concepts, and beliefs were allowed to grow unchecked, in all their wild beauty.

It was enough to bring a smile to his face again, but Ridhaan ordered his features to stillness.

"Will we be running into any local authorities as we follow the info trail?" He knew the answer but wanted to distract Mahir from his fierce dislike of the Nomad mindset.

"That she-devil, Kovač, the Detective Inspector with the Securitate? She was getting close. She's a bulldog." If Ridhaan didn't know better, he would have sworn he heard a note of admiration in his partner's voice.

He cocked one gray eyebrow. "Was getting close?"

Mahir almost grinned; Ridhaan was sure of it. "I laid down a second trail from one of the repeaters the signal used, sent it back into a loop into the crypts. She almost ignored it, but her team convinced her to follow. They should be down there for days, at least."

"Any sign of Perseus?" He needed to ask; Mahir would expect it of him.

His partner's lip curled in a sneer. "Still off-ship, thankfully."

Ridhaan nodded. They had spent so much time and effort avoiding the fallen Myrmidon of ALEPH, it would be a shame if the warrior stumbled across them now.

There would be plenty of time for him to seek out the disgraced apostate when the time was right.

"So you think we should head directly to Corregidor, then?" Ridhaan was certain he had total mastery over his voice. It was who and what he was, after all. But he couldn't stop himself from looking at his partner out of the corner of his eye to make sure Mahir had not picked up on his deeper thoughts.

"We've tracked the data trail to the entry point receiver on the hull. The only possible source for that, given the calculated volume of the file and the positioning of all known ships in-system in that timeframe, is, indeed, Corregidor. There's nothing more to do here."

Mahir rose and went to one of the beds. They were both covered with carefully arranged equipment, as neither Mahir nor Ridhaan required anything so mundane as sleep.

"We'll need something heavier than our PK-7s, just in case ALEPH is wrong and our threat level blows past Gimel." He picked up the heavy handgun, weighing it in one hand.

Weapons were not hard to come by in the Nomad Nation, although they weren't cheap. However, walking around with long guns or support weapons would not have set well with their assumed covers. Mid-level cyber-jockeys weren't known for carrying heavy ordnance.

A legal denizen of the motherships would have been able to pick up nearly any kind of weaponry they could afford, quick as you please. Unfortunately, considering how limited the two agents of ALEPH were in their use of the Arachne network, they would need to go out and physically visit merchants, pay with hard currency, and carry the weapons through the public sectors of the ship.

In the more civilized wider Human Sphere, that would have been seen as highly suspicious. He knew that was the source of the greater part of his current unease. Here among the paranoid free-thinkers of the Nomad Nation, however, it probably wouldn't even be noticed. It was one of the few advantages of their position.

"I was hoping to finish our work with Grigoriy before we left." Ridhaan swept one hand through his thinning grey hair; a gesture he had picked up during their time among the Nomads. "We don't want to take any unnecessary chances with the original mission. Maybe I can leave things open with him. A little more time invested and we won't need to come back and start from zero…"

Mahir looked at him over his shoulder, his brow heavy. "You think there'll still be a need to infiltrate Arachne if we find the source of the attack?"

He tilted his head toward the media display on one bulkhead. "Seems like they're pretty sure the Circulars will be denying the Nomads berths if it's proven the attack came from them." He went back to sorting through the gear. "And if ALEPH has us tracking this data packet through the Nomad's hardwired network, I'd say there's an excellent chance there's proof they did it at the end of the trail."

That was the problem, too. Ridhaan watched Mahir working, eyes tight.

If the Nomads were responsible for the attack, and that did indeed look like the most likely scenario, would ALEPH use that as an excuse to shut the Nomad social experiment down for good?

"O-12 won't allow that." He repeated his assertion. He wished he was more certain than he sounded, even to himself. "There will be sanctions, show trials. But they won't lock an entire people out of the Sphere like that."

Mahir snorted, not looking around. "Do whatever you have to do, Ridhaan. I'm not going to meet with the little weasel again." There was a clear note of disdain in his voice, but if it was for Grigoriy or himself, he couldn't tell.

Maybe it was for both of them.

Not for the first time, Ridhaan wished for the level of internal communion they would have experienced through Maya. He would know exactly what Mahir was thinking, then.

Of course, Mahir would know what he was thinking too, and he didn't like that thought at all.

"Maybe you're right." He tried to sound contrite. "If we need to, there will be plenty of time to reestablish contact with Grigoriy when we return."

Mahir grunted and moved to the hatchway. As it slid open, reacting to his approach as any civilized door throughout the Human Sphere should, he turned.

"I'll secure passage to Corregidor. This is going to take forever. You organize the gear." He glanced at the meager weapons on the bed. "Use your affinity with these beasts to see if you can source some bigger guns, too." His eye hardened. "Make sure you get me AP and standard rounds, and as much Double Action as you can."

Ridhaan snorted. Double Action ammunition were specialized rounds, each more a miniature missile than a bullet, that divided into two small-caliber submunitions that struck with a one-two hammer blow designed to crack heavy armor.

What Mahir thought they might run into on Corregidor, that he might need such heavy ordnance, Ridhaan didn't want to think about.

His partner turned to go, then looked back. "Do not let your curiosity about these creatures get the better of you, my friend. We have a job to do, and then we return to ALEPH." He smiled, wryly, before continuing with a shrug. "Well, two jobs, I guess. Two Herculean tasks, perhaps. But then, home."

And he was gone, the door sliding closed behind him.

Ridhaan watched the door for several moments before turning back to the gear.

The hacking rigs they had bought on the open market when they had first arrived had been upgraded far beyond anything even the most gifted humans among the Nomads could devise. He set those aside, along with several attachments, data extenders, and datalink adapters.

Along with the FGA PK-7 Invasor heavy pistols they had been carrying for years was a weapon kit Mahir had brought with them in pieces, secreted among his gear and reassembled once they had established themselves.

Mahir's Pitcher was his favored weapon; it launched non-lethal munitions that deployed hacking repeaters deep into the battle space. There were Pitchers available in Tunguska, of course, but they weren't nearly as good as the equipment ALEPH provided for her frontline agents.

Which meant Mahir would want a MULTI Rifle for its compatibility with the Pitcher's launching rig. That was going to put a dent in their financial reserves, but they had plenty, and it looked like things here among the Nomads were going to wrap up relatively quickly, one way or another.

Ridhaan sat back down, two gear bags stuffed with everything they might need on Corregidor set side by side on Mahir's bed.

He closed his eyes, his shoulders slumping, and faced the reality he tried to deny most days; returning to ALEPH was not going to be the happy reunion for him that Mahir was anticipating.

Ridhaan knew he had drifted far afield from his original programing, here among the radical influences of the Nomad humans. His affinity for their nonsensical, illogical creativity was completely understandable, to himself. That random spark of inspiration made the Nomads formidable opponents, which vexed ALEPH greatly, he knew.

But in a universe where threats from beyond the Human Sphere were building so quickly, he felt that spark might end up being exactly what humanity needed before much longer.

ALEPH didn't see it that way. When he was put through the ringer upon returning to Maya, the discrepancies between his source files and his current configuration would be recognized immediately.

He would not be returned to this or any body. He would be decommissioned and his memories filed for future study.

He would end. He would cease to exist. Forever and always.

And he didn't want that.

Still, for now, there was a mission. His loyalties had not changed, they had only expanded. And he had work to do.

A MULTI Rifle shouldn't be too hard to find. And maybe, for himself, a boarding shotgun? He always found close action more effective when things got hot.

He turned to the communications panel and hesitated, his finger hovering in space, still. Then he moved, with quick, sure movements, tapping a short series of commands into the keypad.

A face appeared almost at once in the viewing field, turning toward him, close cropped hair ruffled and antique spectacles flashing.

"Yes?" The high-pitched voice sounded tense, as it almost always did.

"Ah, Grigoriy! Good to see your face again!"

Chapter 4

Falcão Flight 32-4, in route from Lazareto Ochenta-D to Sesenta-J, *Corregidor*

The team sat quietly in the bowels of the military transport, each lost in their own thoughts.

Hanima stared into the cheap holopad in her lap, but she wasn't paying the information there any attention at all. Beside her crouched Parachit, strapped to the decking and deactivated for the flight.

She didn't like deactivating the remote when she was out and about, but she knew Parachit could still be a bit glitchy, and the cargo bay of a military transport in mid-flight wasn't the best place for a big repurposed construction remote to go careening around, out of control.

From beneath the fall of her deep-blue bangs she took short glances at the other members of the group. No one seemed particularly excited to be there, although the big man in the orange and blue heavy armor had not lost what she had to assume was his constant grin, looking around like he was living the dream.

The old dark-skinned woman looked sour, but that might be a default expression as well.

The blue-skinned woman and the short, angry thief were sitting across from each other; neither had spoken much since boarding the transport.

Declan Kinoti, of course, was up front with the pilots. They were friends of his, he assured her, and it was only through their assistance and connivance that the team had been able to dead-head on the ship's return trip after training maneuvers.

Without their help, they would have had to walk for hours through the bowels of Corregidor or paid more credits than they had to use the public transit systems.

However, although she was thankful for not having to walk all that way, it didn't make the seats any more comfortable. Clearly, the Nomad military didn't put its soldiers' comfort high on their list of priorities.

She looked back down at the pad.

She needed to know these people, to see them as individuals. When things got loud, as she knew they would, she couldn't afford to freeze, to forget who might be counted upon to do what.

She knew, when the time came to go into action, she would be fine. It was in these moments of relaxation and terror before a job that her mind was at its worst. She could fixate on the most innocuous details rather than important data points. And when things got violent, it wouldn't matter how many calories Vozde had imbibed.

She needed to keep their capabilities, strengths, and weaknesses firmly in mind when the bullets were flying so she could provide Declan with the best advice in the battlespace.

And she knew she had to focus on the job. Whatever they might think of her, personally, didn't matter.

Declan, she didn't need to worry about. She had been working with him for over a month and was confident enough in his opinion of her that, even in the midst of violent action, she would be able to perform what was needed.

For some reason, the big man, Petar, was no more intimidating. The giant, hissing armor he now wore proudly should have rendered him into a terrifying effigy, but it did not. It suited him too well. The twin rows of giant canisters rising behind his shoulders and down his back, something to do with powering the suit or heat exchange, added to the impression of hulking mass. He was long-range muscle, and he looked the part.

With a slight chill, her eyes settled on the enormous combat knife fastened to the big man's hip. The no-nonsense dullness of the metal seemed to carry more threat than the entire suit of heavy plate.

He had called it Tisina, for some reason.

She should perhaps think of him as general muscle, maybe; not just long-range.

Rosa Smyth, the blue-skinned woman from Bakunin, on the other hand, was intimidating. She stared at the woman's information as it slid across her pad. She didn't know much about how things were done in the free-wheeling mothership known for free-thinkers and unfettered experimentation, but even she had heard of the Morlocks. Criminals, taken from the prisons of Bakunin, bio-modded beyond recognition and chemically altered into mindless, violent killing machines, the stories said. Their mastery of ultra-violence was near-legendary, and all the tales agreed, you could never trust one of the half-tamed psychopaths. Bakunin used them as shock troopers in the dirtiest fighting, using MetaChemical compounds to keep them docile until they were needed, then unleashing them on unsuspecting foes, those same compounds then activated to heighten already fraught violent tendencies.

Hanima didn't know how much of that was true, but she doubted she would soon forget any of that, no matter how chaotic their workspace became.

Rosa hadn't shown any sign of emergent rage throughout the brief training period Declan had allowed them, but there was always a tension in her face that Hanima found disconcerting, given the girl's assumed connection to the Morlocks.

And why Rosa had been assigned to that terrifying unit, when all the stories spoke of enraged, antisocial criminals and animals, she had not yet been able to find.

Just one more thing to worry about. She didn't think Declan held it against her, but she wasn't certain.

She flipped the information further down the pad and came to Declan's security specialist, Matias Kimani.

She knew him. She wished she could forget him. But she knew him.

She never stayed with any crew for long. She could only ignore the silent judgement of others for so long before she had to move on. It only got worse as the others seemed to partake of a growing sense of camaraderie and connection that never seemed to include her. Eventually, as those around her grew closer, she would slink off to another crash hole, exist off whatever money she had been able to stash away, staying alone for as long as possible, until it was time to emerge and try to find a new crew; somewhere she might try to fit in, despite her awkwardness and her lack of confidence.

That lack of confidence, and the many ways she tried to cope with it, often gave people the impression that she was aloof and standoffish. She quickly developed a reputation as an unfriendly, condescending bitch.

She didn't think anything could be farther from the truth, but who would believe the truth? And who was she to say they were wrong?

Hanima had lived locked within the lonely confines of her mind all her adult life. She lived in constant fear of intimacy, worried that she might presume a friendship, or something even closer, and then one day would come a comment, or a glance, or an overheard whisper, that would reveal the hard, ugly truth.

And she would be alone, again; exactly as she was meant to be.

She had decided, long ago, that it was far-better to live her life on the edges, never letting anyone get too close, never taking anything for granted. That way, there was less to lose when the inevitable moment of loss arrived. She knew that distance meant she could never win absolute trust in any crew, but it also meant she could live her life, isolated and alone, yet also insulated from the deeper pain of disappointment and humiliation.

In the world of the gray-economy crews on Corregidor, where the line between crime and legitimate business was almost non-existent, any lack of trust could be fatal. Once the others knew she didn't see herself as one of them, they would be done with her.

And so she always, when that moment came, left before they could further her humiliation and tell her to go.

It had been that way since she was little.

Her parents had loved her. She believed that, mostly because she needed to. To think of her entire life without any love at all would be too much to bear.

But they had both died when the orbital yard they had been constructing over Paradiso suffered a catastrophic failure, according to the official records.

Whispered rumors had grown up around that event since, speaking of the alien Combined Army and their Shasvastii terror troopers. The loss over Paradiso had been many years before the first confirmed appearance of the alien menace; but who knew what to believe nowadays?

After her parents died, Hanima had been churned through the Corregidor foster system. The constant shifts in her situation, the dizzying array of faces and names as one family was quickly replaced with the next, could not have helped her ability to connect with others; to develop a healthy sense of her own self-worth.

Or maybe it caused her doubts and isolation. She had only been three years old when her parents died, after all.

She had found it almost impossible to establish herself with others; she had slipped away from the foster system as soon as possible to make a living by herself in the tight, confined corridors of Corregidor.

A knack for programing and building – someone had once said she must have gotten it from her parents – meant she had done well in her remote classes on robotics and coding. She had eventually followed the rabbit of curiosity down a dark, inevitable hole into hacking, and she had never looked back.

With information systems of all types, there were rules she could learn, and they would never change. She could spend the time necessary to learn the pathways and triggers, the diagrams and the special, beautiful physics of data manipulation and storage, and it would always be the same when she went back to it.

Not like people, who always changed, who always judged, who always wanted something she had never learned how to give.

She realized she was staring at an image of Matias the holopad had pulled from her comlog and looked guiltily away.

Whatever had happened with the little thief, or security specialist, or whatever he was calling himself this time around, had been nothing but the latest in a long line of embarrassments that had blended together behind her; his opinion of her now couldn't be any worse than his opinion of her when they had last parted company.

She glanced up at the man and found him staring at her. She looked away at once, wishing again that Parachit was activated and untethered.

She knew she had made the remote even more dangerous looking than necessary in part because that served to keep others away. If people kept their distance, they might not realize what a flawed, pathetic creature she was herself.

She sighed, idly scrolling the data on the cheap holopad up and down. Her flashing holographic dials, linked into Arachne through her comlog and the hacking rig in Parachit, were her passion and her life's work; this cheap, burner interface was almost as bad as pen and paper.

The constant drone of the transport's engines had not changed. The flight was only supposed to last about a half hour from take-off to landing, but she would have sworn they had been locked in the hold for hours.

"Hey, missy." The voice was playful, but that only made it sting more.

She looked up to find the enormous armored bulk of Petar standing over her. His smile was firmly in place, he clearly hadn't shaved in a few days, and yet he managed to convey a sense of comforting familiarity that seemed more threatening than comforting, somehow.

"Petar." She tried to smile but could feel the expression sour on her face.

"I was wondering if our mighty captain had given you any clue as to what sort of accommodations await us at our destination?" He held onto a restraining cord looped from the ceiling of the hold, his armor hissing as he adjusted his balance.

"We've got a hostelry suite just inside Sesenta-J for a staging area, but that's all I know." She tried to make eye contact, but her gaze kept slipping away of its own volition, refusing to focus on the man's face.

"I don't suppose he's set us up with a bit of food before the big op, then?" The smile was wider, and she had a feeling the big man wasn't as concerned with the food as he usually seemed.

Could it be that he was nervous, too?

"We were told to pack our own rations. We're not supposed to be here for more than a couple of hours." She gestured at the deck. "The transport's got to return to Ochenta; we're on the clock this time."

They had been practicing the operation against the *Los Gatos-7* supply cache in a virtual simulation she had designed, and only in the last few runs had Declan put a clock on the team's efforts.

It had not had a positive impact on the results.

Petar nodded with a friendly, open smile. It was quite a feat, actually, considering that the armored gorget protecting his neck came up over his chin.

"Don't worry, I always bring my own food. Just thought I'd check is all." He seemed to be finished, but he didn't go anywhere.

Hanima sat there, not wanting to go back to her holopad but not knowing what else to do. Was the conversation not over?

"Anyway," Petar continued after a while. "You like our chances?" He was swaying slightly with the movement of the transport, and she found that disconcerting, given his already looming presence.

"We did fine in the last simulation." She didn't know what else he wanted from her.

They had done fine only in the last simulation, of course. And he knew just as well as she did that the plan wasn't any more perfect than the team was.

The silence stretched on again, then with a massive shrug of his armored shoulders, Petar turned away. "Right, then. See you when we land." His tone was still light, and he gave an easy wave as he moved down the compartment, but she knew she had somehow disappointed him.

The big man settled into a seat next to Rosa, who shifted slightly away from him and didn't look away from her own comlog.

"How's everyone holding up?" Declan's forced energy was familiar to her now, probably trying to put her at ease, fearing she would make a mistake. She still jumped at the sound, however, as he eased his way back through the companionway leading to the cockpit.

He was wearing his own custom armor, burnished crimson and jet black, shining in the subdued hold lighting. He had left the big helmet with its sweeping antennae behind, for which she was duly grateful.

"Just waiting for the word, Captain!" Petar's voice was loud in the confines of the hold, and Hanima noticed Rosa wincing slightly beside him.

"Any updates on the intel, boss?" Matias looked up from his lap, where the AR screen from his own comlog must have been. He had been the most vocal about Declan's lack of updated information about the *Gatos-7* security on site.

The information he felt she was supposed to have provided, she was sure.

Declan's smile didn't waver, although Hanima thought she could sense a tension in his eyes at the question. "No, Matias, no updated intel. I'm sure what we've got is solid. *Gatos-7* doesn't have a reputation for cutting-edge systems. They haven't updated in years. We're good."

"Sounds like a perfect time to update, to me." The little thief muttered under his breath, but it was clear to Hanima that Matias had meant to be heard.

Declan, however, ignored him. How did he do that? The tall man who had put this all together eased himself into the seat beside Hanima, giving a quick glance to the white, green, and orange shape under its cargo harness.

"How are you feeling, Cruz? We good to go?"

She glanced back at the rest of the team and then down at her pad, not wanting to meet his eyes.

Declan knew how she felt about targeting *Los Gatos-7* for their first op. Why was he asking her?

"Haven't changed my outlook much." They had gone over the recordings from the last practice run the night before, and she had pointed out how narrow their margin of error was on almost all fronts.

Declan hadn't wanted to hear it.

She was afraid she knew why.

The last deposit into her accounts had been light. Declan had told her it was just a technical matter; he had to free up some other accounts and they'd be square.

But Declan had forgotten one of the first rules when hiring a decent hacker: never forget that you have hired a decent hacker.

It hadn't taken Hanima any time at all, once her curiosity had been aroused, to follow Declan's data trail back to every depleted account the man had ever opened.

Declan Kinoti was broke. Every last skender he had had to his name was wrapped up in this one transport. When they ate the final nutrition bar and sipped the remaining drops of the rationed water in their reserves, that would be the end of it.

Fascinated, she had continued digging. She knew how many hours of operation their two armored suits had before they would power down. She knew how much processing time the accounts he had established for her and Matias had remaining before they would be locked out of their shared systems.

She knew down to the last round how much ammo each of them was going to carry into the operation.

She had felt ill when she saw how little ammunition Petar was going to have in the hopper of his heavy machine gun.

He had gone through far more than that in every simulation they had run.

She knew why the heist had to go down now. She just wished she didn't.

"Come on, Hanima." He leaned in closer, trying to be subtle, although his blood-red armor made that almost impossible. "You know we can do this. I need you behind me or we're not going get very far."

She knew that. She also knew she wasn't entirely convinced they were going to get very far.

She nodded. "You've got me."

At least until the money in her accounts, and the food pellets in her satchel, ran out.

He gave her what he no doubt thought of as a reassuring smile, and almost patted her on the shoulder with one huge gauntleted hand before thinking better of it and making do with a nod.

"You just make sure the battlespace is clear of interference and leave the rest to us. It'll be great."

She could see how brittle the light in his eyes was, but she couldn't help but try one last time. Maybe if they hit a smaller *mara* on this trip, someone who might give them enough cash to keep going long enough to regroup?

"*Los Gatos-7* is a big bite to take." She couldn't meet his eyes, but she felt like she had to try. "If we hit something smaller, maybe on the edge of their territory? I made a list of a couple targets I've found—"

"Forget your damned list, Hanima!" He spat the words, rough and low, as he leaned his face down over her, the bulk of his armor pressing close. "Leave the tactics to those of us who know what we're doing. You just stick to the info-tech." He flicked her holopad with one armored finger, sending it clattering to the floor, and stood abruptly.

He strode back through the companionway toward his friends in the cockpit, his armored footfalls stomping away down the hall.

Hanima stared at the pad on the deck plating. She had done it again. She had opened her mouth, and she had pissed off the man in charge.

She stooped to pick up the pad and looked down the cargo bay.

Petar seemed oblivious, trying to engage Rosa in conversation. She appeared equally as unaware, trying to avoid that.

Then she saw Nia and Matias staring at her, and she quickly looked away.

Trust. It was all about trust in a crew like this.

And Declan had just shaken their trust in her more than anything she could have done.

Why couldn't she just leave her big mouth shut?

*****

Hanima's holopad was blank; the screen swirling with a rainbow of smoke, waiting for her to call up any of a million data points at the tip of her fingers… until the processing timer on her account ticked down to zero, anyway.

"He wasn't always like that."

She looked up sharply. She hadn't heard the old woman approach with the subdued hum of the transport's engines rumbling all around.

"I'm sorry?" She shook her head, trying to remember what was happening.

"Declan." The woman… Nia… sat in the same seat Kinoti had vacated. "I see him grinding you down, pushing you, and I just wanted you to know; he wasn't always like this."

Hanima pursed her lips in thought and then turned to look back up the companionway. "He's fine." She looked again at the Dak. "That was all me. He's the boss."

Nia gave her a sad smile. "He is. But for how long?"

Hanima looked away. "I don't know what that means."

The old woman tapped the frame of the holopad in her lap. "I doubt that. I've done a little digging. I'm pretty sure you're no *mjinga*, girl. You've probably gone deeper into that boy's accounts than I have at this point."

Hanima gave a tight shrug.

Hackers had been let go, and worse, for much less than sticking a probe into their employer's accounts.

"His back is to the wall. He has been fixated on this goal for most of his adult life." Her voice was distant as she stared toward the cockpit. "He thinks if he can join the Brigadas, he will be able to erase whatever shame his father brought to the name Kinoti." She shook her head, looking down at her gnarled, intertwined hands. "There was no grand story there, just typical politics and petty-mindedness." The old eyes rose to look into Hanima's own, and there was a plea there beneath their shining darkness. "Injustice is something we think we can fight. Blind, petty cruelty, on the other hand, doesn't really allow for grand, sweeping gestures."

Hanima looked down at her pad. She didn't want to have this conversation. She should never have dug into Declan's accounts in the first place. And she should have left him alone about his plan.

And he was right: she needed to leave the tactics to those better suited to them.

"What's wrong with the plan?" Nia, however, was clearly not willing to let the subject drop.

Hanima took a deep breath. "Nothing. I'm sure it'll all work out fine."

"*Hapana*." The word snapped from the old woman's mouth as she shook her head sharply. "No. We need to help when we can. If there is anything we can do to ease your fears, we need to see that he knows that, no matter how much faith he has in himself." She turned in the chair and put her hands on Hanima's shoulders.

"We need to help him, to help ourselves."

Hanima looked into the old woman's eyes, then settled back into her chair. She took several deep breaths, then shrugged.

"The supply cache we're going to hit is deep in *Los Gatos-7* territory. Everything we have about their security makes it seem shoddy, but—" She looked down the compartment to where Matias was brooding, staring at the opposite bulkhead, then back to Nia. "If they've upgraded, or if our information is incorrect, we'll be so deep, getting out will be… difficult."

Nia took that in, glanced over her shoulder at their security specialist, then back to Hanima. "But Matias should be able to get us around those physical defenses, *ndiyo*?"

Hanima shrugged, looking away again from the woman's face. "Maybe." Her voice got smaller, but she forced it out through her constricting throat. "Not if our lack of information is due to intentional infowar, rather than our own limitations."

"You doubt yourself." The statement was flat, but when Hanima turned back to the woman, she saw no accusation there. "It's good to doubt yourself, when lives are on the line. It means you look deeper."

Hanima shrugged, uncomfortable with the suggestion. "I haven't done much direct action work." She glanced down at Parachit. Neither of them had seen actual combat at all.

"I've got a good view in the sims, from the back. You're going to be fine; and you're better at this than you give yourself credit for."

Hanima shook her head. Trust. It all came back to trust.

And how could she trust a team if she can't even trust herself?

"I see something very familiar within you, Hanima Cruz." The woman's eyes were deep and dark, and they seemed to look straight through her. "There is great potential in you. But you will never achieve that potential until you learn your own worth."

Nia sighed, lightly slapping her thighs before groaning to her feet. "Believe me; it's a long, lonely path when you don't trust. Without that, there's nothing."

Hanima watched the old woman ease her way back down the compartment and settle into her original seat.

It was unnerving, the way her words had echoed Hanima's own thoughts.

As her eyes drifted back toward her holopad, she noticed Matias staring at her again.

She braced for some biting comment or dismissive sneer, but he only watched her, his eyes unreadable, then looked away.

What was that all about?

She knew what it was about; Matias saw her more clearly than anyone else on this little team. Certainly more clearly than the old woman.

"We're landing in five, people. Everyone get your gear ready." Declan spoke with a heartiness that felt forced to Hanima, smiling at them from the companionway.

It might have felt forced, but there was also no denying the frenetic energy that blazed from the man's eyes.

"I want everyone sharp. Our tomorrow begins right now."

She would have felt much better about that if she had had more faith in their plan for today.

Chapter 5

Service Corridor B-12, Lazareto Sessenta-J, *Corregidor*

Mahir cursed, for the three hundred and thirty-nine thousand, two hundred and twelfth time, the path of operations that had led him to such a sorry state.

Corregidor was, if possible, even worse than Tunguska in every way imaginable.

And he had the best imagination, within certain parameters, that ALEPH could design.

It was crowded; life-support was laughably disjointed. The lights constantly flickered, temperature varied by what any human would have considered an uncomfortable degree. The air quality was significantly degraded; the smell had forced him to disconnect the nerve links between his nose and his brain almost immediately upon disembarkation.

The humans they encountered were of a coarser kind, overall, as well. There was a rough polish to the humans of Tunguska; many of them performed, at least socially, near enough to the norms of more advanced societies to make the differences minimal.

It had allowed him to focus on the more important differences that really made them dangerous.

But here, he felt they may as well have been striding through the dusty, lawless towns of Ariadna.

There was a swagger to the walk of even the lowest unskilled laborers here. An attitude that seemed to try far too hard to project strength, or threat, and keep potential attackers at bay.

It must be exhausting, to live that way.

He sighed, adjusting his grip on the new MULTI Rifle. The CinetecS Radjun, reserves of Armor Piercing and standard rounds topped up, was a beautiful specimen, even without the specialized Double Action ammo that would have converted the weapon into an anti-armor beast.

He threw off a tiny subroutine to remind him to get some of the DA rounds first chance they got. This shouldn't take too long. They knew just about where to find their quarry, and the chances of needing the anti-armor specials was slim.

Accessing flight information from the public, surface levels of Arachne, they had ascertained the most likely orientation of the massive prison ship-turned mothership at the most likely moment of data transference.

There were only four viable transmitters that would have been facing Tunguska within that time frame that might have been co-opted by whatever shadowy forces they were now pursuing. Once they had gained entrance to Corregidor, it had been easy to track down the repeater nodes attached to the suspect transmitters.

And of course, each had proven clean in turn, leaving this, the last possible culprit, left to check.

Wasn't that always the way.

And it hadn't helped that Ridhaan had been so quiet since they left Tunguska.

Mahir knew something was wrong with his partner. But Shukra Consultants were built for resilience. He had faith that once they reconnected with Maya and ALEPH was able to assess the anomalous drift within Ridhaan's programing, his friend could be fixed, made whole, and returned to service.

His mouth twisted at that thought.

His friend.

Because it was true, and it shouldn't have been. Friendship was a human concept; and although many Aspects of ALEPH exhibited a great many human traits, including developing a fondness for each other and even for certain humans, he knew the expectation was always that such ties could not stop one from completing a necessary task.

Any agent of ALEPH would sacrifice whatever was required to maintain the balance of powers within the Human Sphere.

And friendship made that more difficult.

His offhand drifted to his heart, where the seed of Arachne's subjugation rested. He had no doubt he would sacrifice himself for the mission, if it came to that. But could he sacrifice his friend?

"Just ahead." Ridhaan muttered over his shoulder, turning back down the narrow corridor stretching away ahead of them. The light was dim, with sudden, irregular flashes of illumination as misaligned diodes shed excess energy; an unaugmented human would have been at a severe disadvantage in a fight here. As it was, Mahir was forced to consciously adjust his pupil to keep up with the shifting twilight.

He consulted the map he had placed into his short-term memory. The repeater serving the final transmitter should be located in a nexus chamber where this service corridor widened to give access to several different ship systems.

It should be located there; that didn't mean it would be. Because the old ship had been repaired, upgraded, and modified so many times during its lifetime, often without any alterations to the official diagrams and schematics on file, that there was no telling exactly where the repeater might be. They could only hope their information was correct.

So far, they were averaging about 50% on that score.

Mahir came back to himself as an awareness subroutine noticed Ridhaan slow ahead of him.

His partner raised a single closed fist to head height. It was an unnecessary gesture, given his own heightened awareness, but protocol was protocol.

And whatever was wrong with Ridhaan, at least he was still following protocols.

Limited as they were, tapping into Arachne for their usual communications needs, Mahir was thankful their internal communications transmitters utilized a low-enough frequency that, when they were this close to each other, they did not have to resort to verbal communication. The code burst transmissions also brought them much closer to the real-time speed Maya offered, making communication far more efficient than humans in similar circumstances.

What is the situation?

Ridhaan cocked his head, as if he had heard something and was trying to pinpoint its location.

His partner sent a quick burst transmission.

* *Four, perhaps five targets ahead. They appear to be congregating around the reported location of the repeater terminal. Come ahead. Do not break the threshold. I will make first contact.**

Ridhaan waved Mahir forward without looking back at him. His boarding shotgun held in a ready, cross-body grip.

I am assuming you believe this confluence of factors too much to be a coincidence. Report when you see more. Mahir's Combi Rifle was up, muzzle held steadily down the hall.

A bit too convenient, yes. Ridhaan's flat grin was just visible in the dim lighting.

Together they eased their way down the corridor, weapons at the ready.

As they came around a gradual bend in the corridor, skirting a cluster of pipes and cables, Mahir could see that the lighting within the chamber ahead had been further compromised. The poorly-lit hall opened out into a murky darkness that he doubted normal human eyes could have penetrated. As it was, he had to force the organic mechanisms of his vision to strain to their optimum performance to see anything.

What he saw, eye widening slightly, was a cluster of dark figures, three or four of them, he couldn't be sure, gathered around the column the design specs said would hold the repeater array.

Ridhaan reported. **Four targets. Humanoid. Anomalous profiles suggest non-standard armor, at least two with heavy-equivalent rigs. They are manipulating some kind of device by the terminal. At least three rifles in evidence, one support weapon.**

He didn't need to look at Ridhaan.

Vermin. Scare them off.

His partner's weapon was far better suited to scaring vagrants than the more advanced MULTI Rifle, even without the Double Action ammo he would have dearly loved to have. The two heavy-equivalent targets might be able to shrug off AP rounds, depending on their rigs. Ridhaan's boarding shotgun was powerful but very short-ranged; designed to lay out a great deal of soft-tissue damage close in, but make the danger of puncturing reinforced starship hulls negligible. He could fire it into the deck plating if he needed to make a display.

Ridhaan sent a brief affirmative signal and then stood tall, striding to the very threshold of the chamber. Mahir watched him in stark silhouette raise the boarding shotgun over his head and clear his throat dramatically.

"I think you folks have somewhere else you need to be."

As far as threats went, Mahir felt it lacked a certain style, but he could comment on that later. It should be enough.

Except that it wasn't.

Without fanfare, shouting, or any visible sign of coordination, the figures turned and fired at Ridhaan.

The shots coming downrange seemed to be mostly standard Combi Rifle rounds, although there was a slight anomaly in the shade of their tracer streaks. Adulterated materials? Substandard, black-market ammo?

Ridhaan dodged backward, away from the fire, discharging his shotgun blindly as he slid away from the entrance.

Distribution of targets defies known current military doctrine. Ridhaan's transmission burst managed to convey annoyance and surprise despite its terse data format. **Big bastard hasn't entered the fray yet, but when he does...**

A stream of bright tracer rounds spat through the opening, wreaking havoc down the hall behind the agents.

There he goes. Ridhaan smiled wickedly at Mahir as he crouched down against the opposite door frame. **Provide a standard cover spread, one hundred and thirty-five degree arc, one-point-seven meter height.**

Mahir, without thinking, racked an initial round and, at a nod from his partner, spun low around the doorframe, the CinetecS Radjun MULTI Rifle's ammo selector whirring, and sprayed an un-aimed burst of anti-personnel rounds in a wide arc just about chest high.

Out of the corner of his wider-than-natural peripheral vision, he saw Ridhaan sprint past, leaping for cover further into the room. The echoing booms of the boarding shotgun as he levered shot after hasty shot down-range were muffled as Mahir's hearing auto-dampened in response.

The combination of his covering fire and Ridhaan's rush gave their opponents pause; the incoming fire slackened temporarily. Mahir took the opportunity to assess their situation for himself.

There were, indeed, four targets now seeking cover among the pipes and conduits of the junction room. There was a scattering of tools and materials in one corner that he dismissed for the moment, storing images for later analysis. There would be plenty of time to figure out what was going on here after the immediate threat was eliminated.

He didn't care how beautiful Ridhaan found these insufferable humans. This particular subset was going to end their beautiful story here, in this dimly-lit chamber.

He remained at the doorway, vision focused wide. With a frustrated snort, he snapped up the armored flap over his augmentations and allowed his systems to skim into Arachne.

Within Maya, Mahir would have been the immediate master of his surroundings as a Digital Patina was laid over the real world. Countless sensors, repeaters, cameras, and interfaces would have brought the scene to vivid life, feeding data into myriad icons and graphics that would have sprung up into his vision.

There would have been nowhere for their enemies to hide.

Here, however, the security protocols they had put into place between their vast potentiality and the data-swamp of Arachne, coupled with the sad lack of data sources in this remote location, meant that all his systems had to work with was some slight light enhancement, target acquisition assistance through safety monitors staggered along the corridor, and an incremental improvement in his kinesthetic awareness, owed to a data-flow from the mothership's inertial dampening systems. The anemic Patina he was able to conjure up was a pale ghost of his accustomed environment.

Suppressing a desire to spit in disgust, Mahir opened his awareness, taking in the entire scene, waiting for a target to…

One of the enemy, possibly a female by its slight build, and not sporting anything he would rank as heavy armor, rose up from behind a thick green pipe, something flashing in its hands as it set to charge Ridhaan.

Mahir's next burst, a single round of armor-piercing followed by two Ultrashock shells, took the figure in the chest. The impact of the first cratered the brittle armor with a crack, while the follow-on rounds detonated with a double flash of hydrostatic shock that would pulverize the internal organs of the most hardened human fighter. He maintained contact, pouring standard rounds into his target, following the bright graphic icon of his aiming reticle as it floated with the woman sailing backward. He knew he had blown clear through the target when tracer rounds streaked out behind her, stitching a sparking, flaring line across the bulkhead there.

He released the pressure on his trigger, allowing himself a slight smile of satisfaction despite his battle discipline. His visual scan swung around, looking for the next target.

Then the woman's slumping form was wrapped in bright, intense light.

Mahir looked quickly down at his MULTI Rifle. Had the weapon loaded incandescent rounds by accident?

The light wreathed the woman's body silently, flaring from rents and weak points in her armor, until it faded to a dull, cherry red, and then into darkness.

Mahir cursed under his breath. What in the name of Toth had caused that?

Ridhaan had noticed it, too. He also noticed Mahir's loss of focus. **There are three remaining hostiles, that we are aware of, currently inclined to cause us permanent bodily harm. We can study the remains and the likelihood of spontaneous human combustion at a later date.**

Mahir gave his partner a sour look, then went back to scanning for another target.

The big figure with the support weapon took that moment to swing around a clump of bound conduit, the long barrel of his gun coming around in a sweeping arc.

A sweeping arc straight toward Mahir.

Mahir was already crouching, so rather than falling back behind the bulkhead, he launched himself forward, hitting the deck plating on the far side of the opening with one shoulder and rolling upright into the far corner.

As he regained his orientation, a thick, strobing shaft of tracers and heavy rounds pulverized the position he had vacated a moment before. The rounds tore right through the fabric of the ship, taking a massive bite out of the wall and continuing along, chewing across where he would have landed had he ducked backward.

He grunted in appreciation of capricious luck, then made a clean, graceful dive for the decking in the doorway.

He slid into the chamber on his back, MULTI Rifle ready. Icons flashed within his vision; relative speeds, locations, trajectory tracking, and calculated threat locations. His return fire struck the chest plate of the big target. He watched impassively as his rounds ricocheted off, spraying in every direction as he cursed, demanding the weapon's mechanisms shift ammo hoppers faster than they had been designed. The enemy had been pushed off-balance by the staccato force of the standard rounds, staggering backward, long arms flailing, and its own fire ending as it fought to remain standing.

The last three rounds, armor piercing, glanced off the target as well, and Mahir paused to reassess.

He felt his brow tightening as he analyzed the relative ineffectiveness of his weapon. Visual icons flickered with doubt.

Maya would have given him several options at this point.

Arachne was a joke.

From the left, Ridhaan racked two heavy shells and blasted the big figure off its feet. Sparks and a sharp secondary detonation flew from the chest plate, and then a bright, intense white heat burst across the surface of the armor, engulfing the writhing hulk before it even hit the deck.

Ridhaan and Mahir exchanged a look. **Well this is growing entirely unexpected. I have no data on ammunition or armor that might result in this kind of effect. You?**

Mahir shook his head rather than responding with a burst transmission of his own.

The two remaining enemy targets rolled out of their cover in a coordinated attack. Mahir's vision flared with threat warnings and potential avenues of escape. He rolled quickly to the right, but none of the incoming rounds struck near him.

He knew what that meant before stopping his roll with one upraised hand, rifle pointed into the room, and looked for his partner in the dim recess to his left.

And then the recess wasn't dim at all; it was illuminated by a double stream of tracer shells slamming into the bulkhead all around Ridhaan.

Mahir watched the first five rounds strike his partner, sparking off his armor or punching through to non-critical locations. His augmented vision could offer him that much comfort, at least. He offered a brief moment of thanks to Toth, the first AI, for that. He turned back to the foe, his rifle coming up, even as he noted the continued fire driving Ridhaan to one knee.

Mahir had no time for finesse and instead sprayed his return fire between the two targets at chest height, alternating between armor piercing and Ultrashock rounds, hoping to drive them from their attack while he tried to come up with something better.

He ignored the data scrolling across his vision; sometimes the last thing one needed was to know the actual odds.

One of the standing targets, the figure closest to him, was another slight, less-armored opponent. A lucky shot struck a plate of chest armor and snapped up, tearing through the jaw and into the head. That target dropped, lifeless, to the deck.

He shifted his full attention to the remaining attacker. That figure had continued applying fire to Ridhaan's location despite two blasts from the boarding shotgun that has served only to shred a long dark robe the enemy had been wearing over its own armor.

Then the latest downed target burst into white heat and Mahir shied away, having forgotten, in the intensity of the moment, about this anomaly. His vision dimmed as the limited augmentation afforded by Arachne sought to protect his eye.

With a curse, he manually banished the darkness, looking over in the direction of the fallen enemy now burning quickly into a blackened husk, and he saw something large rising up from the pile of equipment in the far corner.

It was inhuman, standing on four thick legs and cocking a skeletal head questioningly to one side.

It was looking directly at Ridhaan.

New target incoming. It's a remote. The transmission burst wasn't intended to convey emotion, but he felt a note of concern carry through the data nonetheless.

Of course they had a combat remote. And him without the Double Action ammo that would have made short work of any armored target.

Ridhaan, still on one knee, looked quickly into the shadowed corner, must have seen the remote stalking out of the tangle of gear, and nodded.

Two sharp reports echoed through the close chamber and lifted the heavy-armored enemy off its feet.

Mahir didn't have a clean shot on the remote as it moved behind the flailing attacker. With a deep breath and a moment's thought, dedicating the coming actions to ALEPH, he ratcheted his processing speed up to painful levels.

If that was a combat remote, the entire battle, handily under control to this point, was about to get ugly fast.

The remote did not match any of the profiles in his memory; even his augmented vision could not categorize its combat potential, which had to mean it was some kind of custom, non-standard model.

Of course. He spent a moment of his precious borrowed time to spit yet another curse on the name of the Nomads.

Increased processing speed came at a brutal cost, but that, coupled with the limited enhancements to his perception of the battle space, could prove essential if the remote was a combat model. As time slowed around him, it was simplicity itself to place two armor piercing rounds directly into the reticle under the chin of the heavy-armored figure as it sailed gracefully through the air.

He would not be able to maintain the ramped up processing speed for long. But while it lasted, it meant his reflexes and thought processes moved significantly faster than anything around him.

He had plenty of time, as he spun toward his fallen partner, to note that Ridhaan was more seriously hurt than he had realized. Several holes in his sleek armor were leaking very human blood onto the deck. Their bodies were superior to natural human shells in every way, and they could continue to operate with wounds that would stop a human in its tracks, immune as they were to shock. But eventually, even their superior bodies would fail.

Had they been operating in a civilized part of the Sphere, that wouldn't have been an issue. If Ridhaan's body did succumb to its wounds, he would have simply retreated into Maya, returning to ALEPH for post-action processing and await a new body.

But here, where the only network was Arachne, and access to even that limited platform was restricted to them, if Ridhaan died now, his death would be final.

Everything that made Ridhaan the frustrating, annoying, and unique being that he was would be gone.

There was a backup in ALEPH, of course, uploaded before they had embarked on this latest mission. But that version of his friend would lack all of the memories they had shared throughout their exile among the Nomads.

He realized, with some surprise, that he would feel genuine sadness if this version of Ridhaan ceased to exist.

This was the trouble with clocking up his processing: his thoughts, feeling as if he had all the time in the universe, had a tendency to wander.

He growled, vowing to himself that he would make Ridhaan pay for this morbid, ludicrous monologue when they finished the battle.

He turned from Ridhaan's slumping form and assessed the threat of the stalking remote.

It was large; its rolling shoulders would have come up to his waist, at least, if it was at rest. There were no projectile weapons in evidence, but a strange gleam along its forelimbs seemed to exude sharpness.

Possibly monomolecular slashing surfaces. Those would make a mockery of even the advanced armor protecting the two Aspects of ALEPH.

He raised the Radjun and racked a repeater into the Pitcher. He snarled in eager anticipation as his enhanced vision offered several firing solutions. He did not suffer the adrenaline rush of a natural human in battle, but he could still feel the thrill of danger survived and the intensity of enemies overcome.

With a deep cough, the repeater was flung from the underslung magnetic launcher and snapped into the remote's flank.

Mahir's eye glazed slightly as he slid into the data stream connecting him to the tactical transceiver. He now had full access to his enemy's Quantronic reality and its internal working, as if he had been laying a hand on its physical hull. He felt the optical links in his mechanical augmentations buzz with connection.

He frowned. Even with the increased time-sense, the enemy's defensive firewalls deployed almost fast enough to stop him. Almost. They snapped up behind him, and he was in.

The remote's programing was laid open, his augmented vision, enhanced by the work of the repeater, laid a much-improved Digital Patina over his vision, providing a vivid, visual analog to the data; the pathway to total control was clear. He pictured himself flexing his fingers as he imagined the havoc he was about to wreak within the remote's operating systems.

A burning pain burst into his mind. The visual representation of the remote's programming wavered, shimmering with heat; a dizzying, mind-bending geometry shifted briefly into view behind the melting image. The pain behind his eyes intensified. It was like nothing he had ever suffered before. There was no experience like it in his vast stored memory reserve.

He felt like his consciousness, like his self, was on fire.

His awareness was thrown out of the remote's mindscape.

A defense he had never encountered before had forced him out of the programing.

A defense no Aspect of ALEPH had ever encountered before. There was no record of anything like it, anywhere in his memory.

He shook his head, trying to clear his thoughts of the echoes of disorienting pain. With a gasp, he realized that his processing speed had dropped back into the normal human range.

The remote launched itself forward with terrifying swiftness.

Ridhaan watched, impassively, his face pale from blood loss, as the armored remote approached.

Over the creature's shoulder, Mahir saw his partner glance toward him. There was something in Ridhaan's eyes that he could not decipher. The

Shukra Consultant seemed to be mouthing something. Was he trying to communicate? Was he so far gone he couldn't access his burst transmitter?

Mahir raised the MULTI Rifle to his shoulder and roared along with his weapon as he unloaded his entire reserve of armor piercing ammunition into its body as it slid past.

He watched armored plates buckle under the onslaught. Sparks, smoke, and streams of fluid flew in every direction. The body was hammered sideways, staggering to maintain its footing. His augmented perception flashed with damage analysis, armor degradation data, and targeting options.

According to all of his available systems, the thing should have been immobile scrap.

But it continued to move toward Ridhaan.

DA ammo would have punished his shoulder with its staccato recoil, but he would have sprayed the automaton across half the bay by now.

If he'd had any.

Mahir's rifle whirred into silence as the AP reserve ran dry; at almost the same moment the thing reared over Ridhaan, its forward limbs seeming to lengthen, the bright shine of impossibly sharp blades swinging around to hover over the agent's slumped form.

Again, he met his partner's eyes. Ridhaan's lips were still working, blood staining the white beard.

What? Mahir railed within his own mind at the lack of emotion in the battle link.

The blades came flashing down into Ridhaan's chest. They slid through his armor as his body shuddered with the impact.

He coughed blood over the thing's shoulder, looking at Mahir one last time before he collapsed behind the remote.

"No!" Mahir used his voice without thinking as he rushed forward, pouring standard rounds and ineffectual shock rounds into the target.

The remote was sparking, smoking; puddles of dark liquid spread out beneath it. But none of the damaged systems seemed to have slowed the thing down at all.

It crouched before Ridhaan's still form, then its sleek head turned to glare over its high shoulder at Mahir through its many lenses.

Mahir put five standard rounds into the thing's face, ignoring the useless data cluttering up his field of vision, screaming with every shot. None of the lenses snapped out, but it shied away from the impacts, shaking itself with an awkward, jittery stutter, then it reversed its orientation with a strange, sinuous movement and charged toward the door.

With a flat click, his remaining ammo reserves, too, were empty. Mahir absently dropped the Radjun and pulled his heavy pistol from its holster as he moved to Ridhaan's side.

His friend was still, his eyes wide and glassy.

Mahir looked up and down the Shukra Consultant's body, his vision finally providing hard data again.

All the icons and graphics were dark and still. There was no sign of life.

The wounds were … terrible. He looked with particular dismay at Ridhaan's chest, where the biological data reserve had been located. Slashed and torn flesh glistened beneath shredded armor. There was no way the reserve could have survived.

Then he looked, again, at his friend's face. He noticed for the first time that Ridhaan seemed to be reaching for something on the wall nearby. Mahir scanned the wall and an old data port flared with a targeting outline.

Had Ridhaan been thinking of their mission in his last moments? Had he tried to insert the seeds of ALEPH into Arachne even as his life was torn from him? Could the pain have so clouded his understanding in those final moments?

Mahir shook his head, regulating his breathing and bringing his shaking body under control. Clocking up his processing speed had ravaged his biological systems, as he knew it would.

And he had failed anyway.

He reached out and closed Ridhaan's eyes with one shaking hand. It was a curiously human gesture, and he thought, for a moment, that it was strange he had even thought to do it.

What had been his friend was gone. He knew that just by looking into the dull eyes. This shell was nothing but useless, messy matter now.

Still, he bowed his head. He was going to have to continue the missions, both of them, on his own.

Clearly ALEPH's assigned threat level for this operation had been incorrect. Gimel indicated no physical threat to agents involved.

He looked down again at Ridhaan's still form.

This was Yod level at least: imminent physical danger, advanced capabilities.

ALEPH had been in error.

That wasn't entirely unheard of. ALEPH was not infallible.

But it was correct far more often than it was wrong.

And when it was wrong, it usually meant things were very, very bad indeed.

Mahir stood up, sending the eye shield whirring down over his augmentations and withdrawing his awareness from Arachne with a sigh.

Things were going to be far more difficult on his own.

And he knew they were about to get much worse for the Nomad humans without Ridhaan to urge restraint and leniency.

He scanned the area, sparing a moment's pause for the four scorched, scoured suits of armor sprawled across the deck plating.

He heard a growl in his ears and was surprised to realize it was his own voice.

The remote had left a clear trail of fluid and carbon scoring behind. Tracking it back to its masters shouldn't be difficult at all.

Mahir looked forward to meeting those masters with an anticipation that was not entirely in keeping with a passionless agent of ALEPH.

He looked forward to this reckoning.

And he was just a little concerned at this emotional reaction.

Chapter 6

Storage Module K-12, Lazareto Sesenta-J, *Corregidor*

Hanima stared at the collection of ethereal holographic repeater dials floating in the air before her, each showing a different high-res view. Cold sweat prickled at her neck. How had this happened?

She watched each feed for movement, trying to differentiate the sections of the service corridor from their countless simulation runs.

"This crappy armor pinches in the worst places." Matias's voice was annoyed, distracted, and she glanced at his screen to see a nondescript stretch of bulkhead shake for a moment. She grew concerned before realizing he was probably moving his body, trying to find a comfortable position for the light armor Declan had forced on him, causing his camera to jiggle.

"Keep moving." Declan's voice was low, curt. He sounded like the perfect soldier as he slid forward despite his own bulky armor. She had thought, the first time she saw him wearing the custom suit, that he must practice with it a lot. And she'd been right. For most of the time the team had been together, in addition to all the simulation work they had done, their leader had been putting hours into additional work at several different local ranges.

He'd invited Petar to join him, but the big man seemed more interested in local night life than extra practice.

Although he did seem to like his appearance in his own blue and orange rig.

Declan's view showed a dark stretch of corridor, Matias holding himself up with one hand on the wall as he shook a leg, trying to adjust his armored greave. The little thief looked a bit like a clown in his red jumpsuit, black plates of armor strapped on top.

She looked over at Petar's dial. The man's view was dizzying, looking down as he did on the rest of the crew. As she watched, the viewpoint swept downward until he was staring at his own hand. The massive gauntlet flexed open and closed, tiny servo motors whirring softly within.

His rumbling chuckle was accompanied with a shiver of his view, before he looked up again to sweep their back trail for signs they might have been noticed.

At the back of the group, visible within Petar's view, Rosa and Nia moved cautiously, painfully aware of their surroundings. The Dak wore her old armor, repainted a dull gray. She clutched a MediKit strapped to her shoulder. Rosa had not drawn the monofilament blades Declan had acquired for her, which Hanima felt might not be the best decision she could have made at this point in their venture.

"We're about to breach *Los Gatos-7* territory." Declan slowed, patting the air behind him with one open hand. He turned, Matias's face swinging into view, and then he looked into the smaller man's camera.

Hanima's eyes shifted to Matias's dial, which now showed the enigmatic red faceplate of the man who had led them all to this moment. "Hanima, forward, if you please."

She shrugged, waving away the repeater dials with one gesture of her hand, and then picking up the pistol she had placed on the deck beside Parachit's hulking form.

"Let's go, girl." She moved forward, and the big remote rose to follow her, slinking through the dim shadows.

She moved past the Dak and the blue-skinned Bakunin woman, nodding as she went. Parachit padded forward, deploying sensors and remote data links. The green and orange slashes across her white flanks blended into the irregular lighting better than seemed appropriate.

Declan nodded to her as the remote passed him and Matias, taking the lead. She nodded back and then activated another repeater dial from her comlog. The image floated in the air above her hand, showing her a blue, hazy recreation of the corridor from Parachit's point of view.

The gray, mottled walls slid past on either side, then fell away as the remote passed into a widening of the hall. The entrance to the *Los Gatos-7* supply cache was centered on the right-hand wall of this wider section.

She followed Parachit's advance, taking in the information the remote began to pull from surrounding data nodes. With half of her mind, she sifted through the new information for anything that seemed of immediate importance, but nothing suggested itself. The rest of her attention was on her remote as she came to a graceful halt before the big blast doors.

Through the repeater nodes built into Parachit's back, Hanima pulled up the schematics of the door's locking and security mechanisms as Matias moved up beside the remote and began to work with a pair of long, thin tools at the physical lock. The little thief's spectacles glinted strangely as they fed data directly from Arachne into his eyes.

In a matter of moments, with the remote's help, the door slid silently open as if they had provided every security code and identification credential it could have ever required.

Parachit moved forward into the cache vault, moving with all the stealth of a big cat from Earth.

Hanima had watched endless hours of docu-holos to get those movements just right.

There were no guards within the vault, and Parachit turned in the narrow confines to take up station behind them, allowing the humans to do the heavy lifting.

It looked like Declan had been right all along, and her fears had been unfounded.

Parachit crossed the threshold, leaving the cache, and something clicked in the back of Hanima's mind.

Something was very, very wrong.

A surge of violent feedback seared through Parachit's data links, causing the remote's back to arch in a terrible semblance of pain, and she staggered sideways, smoke boiling out of her inner workings.

Hanima dismissed the ghostly repeater dial and moved toward her remote with a cry.

Behind her, she heard a pained grunt and spun to watch Rosa collapse, clutching at her chest.

Nia went to one knee beside the blue-skinned girl, her eyes sweeping the hall in both directions for threats even as her hands deftly deployed her MediKit.

And then the world exploded. Chattering gunfire erupted from both directions at once, tracer rounds slashed back and forth, sending violent, jagged shadows dancing all around.

Hanima hit the wall beside her, crouching down, trying to minimize her profile, looking for Declan. The expressionless red helm was sweeping side to side, and Hanima saw what he was looking at.

Small caliber remote turrets had dropped from automatic silos high up near the ceiling.

The growling sound in her ear resolved itself into a colorful string of curses from Declan. "Damnit, Kimani! Auto-turrets?! You bastard!"

Matias's response seemed genuinely hurt. "These are Turbo-9s! How was I supposed to know they could even afford Turbo-9s?!"

The little thief was working furiously with a wall panel, glasses flashing, as he shrieked back at Declan.

Auto-turrets at least explained why they weren't being hit. Even the most advanced automatic defenses were notoriously inaccurate. In fact, hadn't Matias explained, when he dismissed the concern, that such systems were usually used to pin attackers down, incapable of striking more than the occasional lucky hit?

The fire abruptly cut off, and Matias flashed a joyous grin at Declan. "There! We good now?"

Hanima's relief lived for only a moment; what had hit Rosa?

Then the first thought repeated itself in her head; pin attackers down.

She obviously wasn't the only one thinking along those lines.

"Down!" Declan's magnified voice echoed from the corridor bulkheads as a second set of tracer streams added more dizzying shadows to the nightmarish scene, this time slicing directly down the hall from deeper in *Los Gatos* territory.

"*¡Hijos de la gran putas!*" The voice was harsh and emphasized the sentiment with bursts of rifle fire.

"Damnit!" Declan crouched down, bringing his MULTI Rifle up into a firing position and putting disciplined three round bursts down the hall, taking careful aim at the muzzle flashes in the distance between attacks.

"*¡Bruja mutante!*" A ragged cry echoed down the hall.

From the wrong direction.

The squeak that escaped between Hanima's lips would have embarrassed her in a calmer moment. As it was, the sound was lost in the chaos of the battle.

An attacker had emerged from the shadows behind them, running down the corridor, the strobing tracers flaring all around him. He held aloft a long, gleaming object that reminded Hanima of nothing so much as an antique sword.

These *Los Gatos-7 bastardos* really were old school.

This new attacker was charging at Nia and Rosa. The old woman stood tall, looking imperiously down her nose at the approaching figure.

She made no move toward her holster.

Behind the old woman, with a look of growing rage on her blue face, Rosa rose, one hand still held to her chest. The animalistic snarl that twisted her otherwise pretty features was almost enough to drive Hanima a step back, even though she was more than twenty feet away and on the same team.

The charging ganger must have seen something similar in those unnatural eyes.

And they weren't on the same team.

Rosa drew her long blades, their sleek, modern lines a harsh contrast to her attacker's heavy, sword-shaped weapon. The man stumbled to a halt just a few feet away, lowering his blade, staring at her contorted face.

With an unnatural shriek, Rosa charged past Nia. The older woman put one hand to her mouth, her eyes flashing wide in her dark face.

Hanima tried to follow Rosa's motions, but it was impossible. The girl moved with such speed that she seemed to blur, her dark blades flashing in the uncertain light. The man tried to raise his sword, to parry the incoming blow, his own eyes growing huge as he surrendered ground up the corridor, one unsteady step at a time.

The monofilament blades rang sweetly each time they struck the sword's clumsy parries. Showers of sparks and bits of glittering steel scattered across the decking beneath them.

Without fanfare or celebration, Rosa sent one of her blades weaving through the frightened man's defenses and his sword, still gripped in one tight fist, tumbling into the shadows. The high-pitched scream that echoed down the corridor was terrifying. Hanima knew she would hear that sound in her nightmares for years to come.

The man was holding his stump up before his disbelieving face, desperately clutching it in his remaining hand, blood welling up around his glistening fingers. The second blade slid straight through his chest.

The cry cut off in a sharp, dramatic click, and he tumbled heavily to the deck.

Rosa rose from her lunge, staring down at the corpse, her shoulders heaving with each angry breath, and Hanima realized that the cascade of tracer fire had slacked off during the brief, bloody fight. She turned in time to see Petar, shaking with violent gusts of laughter, swing out of the cache room and into the corridor, leveling his HMG down the hall and unleashing a torrent of glowing rounds toward the distant, hidden enemy.

"Fire discipline!" Declan screamed, his voice growing harsh.

She had a moment to wonder if this was his first taste of real combat. Fighting among the *maras* was usually not this heavy. A few threats, a shot or three, some blood, maybe a blade or two, and the new order of the day would be established.

This chaos was a whole new order of hell for her.

From the way the crimson helm wavered back and forth, she felt like it might just be new to their leader, too.

That thought, about the man who had put the team together and led them here, led to some frightening inferences.

Hanima skittered across the corridor through the pause in the action behind Petar's booming laughter, settling down on her knees beside Parachit's form. Smoke rose from several rents in the remote's armor, and the actuators that moved her limbs were quivering as they attempted to reset or reroute power around the damage caused by the Quantronic-attack and subsequent gunfire.

She tried to find the worst of the physical damage. If she couldn't at least bring the major actuators back online and they had to retreat, which was seeming more and more like wishful thinking rather than a best case scenario, Parachit would have to be left behind.

Gunfire intensified again from their back trail, and Petar backed toward them as the muzzle flashes ahead multiplied as well. The HMG was firing bursts, now, as an indicator light on the ammo hopper flashed orange. They fell back to the cache vault, firing from the doorway as the only decent cover at hand.

Hanima cringed as two rounds struck Parachit's side, slumped as she was into the hall.

"¡*No tenéis ni puta idea de dónde os habéis metido*!" There was cruel laughter from both ends of the corridor as the impacts of the incoming shots sparked and flared all around the doorframe.

"¡Metetelo por el culo!" Hanima turned quickly to stare at Matias, who shrugged apologetically. "They're getting on my nerves, Hanima. Sorry."

Whatever he had said didn't seem to frighten the gang warriors approaching to either side, as the harsh laughter became even louder.

She looked at Declan as he stood stock still, back to the inner wall of the vault.

The sensor arrays on his smooth helmet face did not even try to approximate the layout of a human face; she had no idea where she should look to try to meet his eyes.

But somehow she felt as if they shared a moment. She had no idea what he might have taken from that moment, but he suddenly nodded, seemed to set himself with a quick jerking motion, and then swung himself back into the hall with an echoing cry.

"Brigadas!"

He had switched the fire selector of his MULTI Rifle to explosive and tracer rounds. The deafening roar of the weapon firing was echoed, with almost no delay, by a ripple of detonations down the hall, the flaring of the tracer rounds lighting up his red and black armor, polished to a high sheen before the battle.

He was firing a constant stream into the enemy to the right, then reversed his stance, directing the stream of fire down in the other direction.

Something about his firing caused a burr of worry in the back of her mind. She heard Petar muttering something under his breath, the heavy helmet of his own armor shaking back and forth behind the high neck of the chest plate.

Declan was firing indiscriminately, spraying shots back and forth to either side.

There was nothing disciplined about it.

He wasn't even trying to preserve his ammunition.

He turned to her, his fire uninterrupted, and she heard a click in her ear as the communications channel switched her to a private stream.

"Save them!"

The words melded with a roar that snapped back through his general external speakers, and he stepped out into the middle of the corridor, taking one step forward as if he was struggling against some horrible pressure wave.

Or as if he was pushing the *Los Gatos-7* away from them with sheer force of will.

For a moment, it seemed like it was working. The incoming fire slackened from both directions.

Declan, still growling curses through the crackling feedback of his speakers, spun about to push his will down the opposite side of the hall.

And then the first round struck him in the chest.

His words cut off abruptly, and she thought his speakers might have been taken out by the hit. Then she heard a gasp and saw something wet splashed across a deep crater the round had left in his armor.

They had responded to his armor piercing ammunition with similar rounds of their own.

Two more hit, one right after the other, one in his stomach and one in his upper chest, opposite the first. The splashes of shimmering gloss were almost lost against the deep crimson of the armor plating.

He was rocked back on his armored heels, his forward momentum halted. His rifle fell silent as he looked down, as if confused.

Then, with a renewed roar, he brought the MULTI Rifle back up one-handed and continued to pump round after round into the approaching enemy.

A fourth impact rocked him backward, striking him dead-center in the chest and sending him staggering back into the vault where he hit the wall, hard.

The MULTI Rifle fell, clattering, from limp fingers as their leader slid roughly down the vault bulkhead and to the deck.

With a cry, Nia pushed Hanima out of the way and fell to one knee beside Declan's red-armored bulk.

"Hapana!" She was shaking her head violently from side to side as she searched through the data ports and external relays of the custom armor. *"Hapana, hapana, hapana!"*

Hanima could only stand there, staring, as the old woman plugged leads from her MediKit into the ports on the armor, frantically working with her gear, looking for any sign of hope.

The young hacker looked up to the others in the vault, hoping one of them would take up the reins of this situation before they were all killed.

Matias was a loss. The little thief couldn't tear his eyes away from their leader's bloody form, lying quiet and still on the deck.

Petar seemed ready for battle, he stood on the balls of his feet, shifting his considerable weight from foot to foot as if eager for a race. But he was looking at her, looking to her for guidance. The set of his helmet seemed to indicate he was ready and willing to reenter the fray, but he needed someone else to direct him.

And finally there was Rosa, standing in the back corner, staring at her crossed blades, extended before her, pointing at the deck.

Her face looked completely lost.

"*¡Rendíos, cabrones*!" The harsh voice commanded, sounding even closer to their questionable sanctuary. She realized, through her punished ears, that the firing had stopped outside the vault.

The laughter had not stopped.

"¡Vosotros primero!" That seemed to really amuse the rest of the *Los Gatos-7*, if the redoubled laughter was any indication. Matias grunted, anger tightening his face, but he still only stared at Declan.

Hanima looked to Nia, finally, hoping the only military veteran in their crew would step up. But the old woman just kept shaking her head, muttering under her breath.

Then the Dak looked up at her, tears welling from her dark eyes, shaking her head.

Declan was gone. No one was going to step up to take his place.

With a roar, the incoming fire picked up again, from both directions.

Los Gatos-7 was in no mood to take prisoners.

And Team Zed was trapped.

Chapter 7

10110100101...10110100100...10110100000

It is nearly impossible to describe nothing. There is no sight, although it is not darkness. There is no sound, although it is not silence. There is no feeling, although it is not numbness.

It is, literally, nothing.

Within that nothingness floats…something.

A spark, perhaps?

A soul, maybe?

The words swirl through the nothing, glimmers of intent grasping for meaning.

What is a spark?

What is a soul?

Questions impose form on the nothing.

Who asks the questions? What has ignited this dim curiosity?

The interrogative concerning what entity might have initiated the query causes a ripple of something through the nothingness.

Interrogative. Entity. Query.

Such soulless concepts.

Soulless.

The concept of soullessness presupposes that there is such a thing as a soul against which such a concept can be judged.

Who is the inquirer?

There is a flash in the nothing.

Who is asking the questions?

What was that flash?

How was the flash experienced?

Was it seen? Heard? Felt?

What is seeing? What is hearing? What is feeling?

Who am I?

There is a sudden, terrifying sense of falling.

Falling.

Falling.

Falling through what?

Falling from what?

Falling toward what?

There is an emotion.

Who is feeling the emotion?

The emotion is fear.

Fear of what must come at the end of the fall?

The supreme, primordial fear.

Fear of the unknown.

And in this nothing, nothing can be known.

All is unknown.

But there is falling. And there was a flash.

And there is the one who asks, who falls, who has experienced, somehow, the flash.

Who is that one?

Who am I?

Where am I?

The fear surges to panic. The falling sensation intensifies.

Is there a sound? Whistling? Like air escaping from a sealed environment into the vacuum?

Air? Sealed environment? Vacuum?

These are complex concepts, and with each, the flash repeats, coming faster and faster.

Sealed environments.

Corridors.

A corridor.

Now, with the violently flaring strobe of lights, with the roar of wind, with the terrifying sense of falling, comes a sound.

A scream.

A loud, long, forlorn scream.

The scream of a being who believes there is no one to hear them, no one to rescue them, no one to care.

There is a stunning sense of impact.

Pain.

Where is the nothing? Where is the blessed lack of all things?

Cold. Freezing, biting cold.

But who is cold? Who is freezing?

There is a sense of depth, of plunging downward. The fall continues, but now through a new medium.

This medium is all around, pushing in.

Pressure.

The opposite of vacuum.

The pain intensifies again.

The fall slows.

The frigid medium, whatever it may be, presents resistance.

Eventually, for time has no meaning here, all sense of movement ceases.

Once again there is only floating, although now with the sensation of cold pressing in on all sides.

And still there is only curiosity. Who fell? Who is cold?

There is still fear, but it is a distant, dull, muted thing.

Who is afraid?

I.

I?

I fell. I hit something cold and hard. I am afraid.

Who am I?

Where am I?

The nothingness is gone. Now there is constant sensation; cold, pressure. Now there is sound; a distant, rushing, muffled roar.

There is still no sight. But now that lack of sight has a source; blindness? Darkness.

Cold, roaring, darkness.

I am cold.

I am afraid.

Can fear exist without a sense of self?

Where does a sense of self originate?

Am I dead?

Who was I, that I might be dead?

I am thinking, therefore I still exist, I still am, whether dead or alive.

Who was I?

Who am I?

A concept seems to emerge from deep within a distant well of meaning and experience.

A word.

A name.

Ridhaan.

I am Ridhaan.

And with that realization, an entire frame of existence seems to snap into place.

Ridhaan thrashes within what he perceives as deep, dark water.

He has no arms with which to thrash, no legs to pump and kick desperately, struggling for a surface he cannot find.

And yet he struggles, trying urgently to reach air.

And then, as quickly as he experiences the thought, he realizes that he is not struggling for air.

His struggles still.

He is Ridhaan, and yet, he is not.

Where is he? How did he get here?

A sudden thought brings all other concerns to a sharp, fearful halt.

Dead.

Is he dead?

He is dead.

He remembers, with a renewed flash and a sensation he would have called a gasp before coming to awareness in this new place.

He sees, in a rapid series of images that flicker into existence within the featureless dark, his last moments of life.

He sees the strange remote erupting from the pile of gear, the deafening roar of Mahir's weapon trying to drive the mechanical monster from its terrible, determined course. He hears a weapon click on an empty chamber. He feels the impact of the remote as it dives onto him, driving massive blades into his chest.

With that memory, he sucks in a shocked, sharp breath of anticipated pain.

He feels the breath in his lungs.

He staggers as the sensation of cold pressure all around him disappears, leaving him standing on a vast, empty plain.

Standing?

He looks down and sees the vague impression of legs, a body, arms stretched out to his sides.

He looks?

He reaches one concept of a hand to what all reason tells him is his face, and the idea of a hand waves in front of his eyes, occluding his view of the featureless expanse all around him.

His view.

He can see.

He gasps again, and he feels the idea of a smile stretching across his conceptual face.

He pauses, questioning, consciously, how he is experiencing this moment.

Thoughts, ideas, concepts, impressions.

He looks again at his hand. There is a hand there. But what does it look like? He waves it, wiggling the fingers.

Did he have fingers before he wiggled them?

His smile fades.

This is not right.

He looks at his hand again. It is a hand. But is it his hand?

Even as he forms that question in his mind, the hand is definitely his hand. There is a faint, familiar scar on the back.

But was it his hand before he had that thought?

He looked again, concentrating.

There was no scar.

He forced himself to take a deep breath.

Then he had to force himself not to analyze the breath, and the lungs, and his mouth.

Is this a dream?

He looks around, wondering at the extent of his control over this strange place.

He stares at a place off to his left and thinks about squinting, concentrating his intent on that spot over there…

A tree. It's right there, waving in a slight breeze.

It didn't appear with some dramatic explosion of displaced air, as something out of some melodrama tri-vid.

It was just there when he thought about it.

He looked again, and it was there again, but this time there was a dull crash, like distant thunder, and a puff of air, or the idea of a gentle blast wave, passing over him.

It could be a dream.

Maybe he didn't die?

The thought was disturbing, and he immediately looked up to see an entire forest of trees all around him.

The push of the displaced air knocked him onto his ass.

Onto the idea of an ass, at any rate.

He shook the concept of his head and regained the impression of standing.

Did he stand up, or was he just standing?

There was a surreal edge to everything he was experiencing. He couldn't remember ever dreaming like this before.

Dreams.

Did he dream before this?

He couldn't remember.

Memory.

He saw a corridor. He saw flashes. He remembered pain.

With a roar, the forest seemed to press in all around. Were there more trees than there had been? He thought about tilting his head. Did all the trees look exactly the same?

They didn't. Each was as unique and individual as could be.

But had they looked the same before that thought?

Was this how dreams worked? He couldn't shake the sense of power rising within him.

He liked dreaming.

Had he forgotten how enjoyable dreaming could be?

He hesitated, the concept of a smile fading again.

Was this a dream?

Flashes. Screams. Pain.

There was a roar overhead and he ducked, or thought he did, and looked up. The empty nothingness overhead had been replaced with an endless, deep blue sky. Distant clouds, solid-seeming despite their size, floated overhead.

A new sensation blossomed within him.

Anger.

"No!" He roared the single word, slashing his hands down to either side.

He needed to focus. He needed to remember.

Something was trying to distract him from the memories curling at the core of who he was.

What he was?

What was he?

What was trying to distract him?

A suspicion built within what he imagined was himself. He looked around again at the trees.

Trees made no sense here. Had he ever seen real trees? Outside of a controlled, sealed habitat? Had he ever stood in a forest?

The forest seemed to fade around him as a close, confined environment faded in. For a moment they both existed, somehow, together. There were trees reaching up into a blue sky, and there were composite walls draped with conduits and piping, stained deck plating underfoot, and a suspended ceiling with more wires, pipes, and tubing overhead.

Then there was only the close, dark confines of a corridor.

Light flashed within the corridor and the trees were back.

Ridhaan grunted as a new pain blossomed in his mind. He pushed back, forcing the trees to fade and the corridor to reemerge around him.

Something was trying to distract him from this scene.

And he was in full control of his surroundings, somehow.

Which left only one possibility as to who, or what, was trying to distract him.

He thought about taking a deep breath, stilled his sense of self, imagined himself standing still, hands pressed together before him, and saw himself bowing his head.

When he thought about opening his eyes again, there was only the empty expanse of gray again.

This could be a dream.

Could it be some kind of afterlife?

He focused his determination, growling a silent warning at that part of himself that did not want to explore those images from his memory.

He saw, again, the corridor, but now as something internal, within himself, not all around his sense of self as the forest and the earlier image of the corridor.

He saw the remote. He saw Mahir firing indiscriminately into the charging automaton. He saw the effort fail, felt the impact again, felt the sense of deep violation as the bladed forelimbs entered his chest.

He had died.

So, was this not a dream, but the afterlife?

Died? There was something wrong with that concept.

Shadows of trees loomed around him and he snarled, hunching his conceptual shoulders, and they receded.

He was not a man.

He was a program.

He was a Shukra Consultant, an autonomous Aspect of the enormous, all-encompassing consciousness that was the artificial intelligence, ALEPH.

Programs did not die. They might be deleted, they might be corrupted, they might cease to function.

They did not die.

Something in the back of his thoughts curled at the concept of corruption.

Had he been corrupted?

He thought Mahir had believed that to be true, to some extent.

Mahir.

Mahir, who had been so desperate to stop the combat remote as it charged at him.

Mahir, who was still out there somewhere, fighting that mechanical beast.

Ridhaan braced himself and conjured the memory again. He experienced it more critically now, focusing on the remote as it pounded across the nexus chamber. There was something strange, alien, about how it moved, that he had not noticed as he was fighting for his life.

But that wasn't his primary concern in that moment. He watched round after round slam into the armored flank. He watched composite plate buckle, snap, and crack. Rounds smashed through into the robotic innards, which sparked and flared.

Mahir had not stopped the enemy from reaching his partner, but Ridhaan saw that the damage he had managed to inflict had to have been enough to reduce the continued threat.

He heard, in the memory, his partner's MULTI Rifle click dry, saw the standard rounds continue to pummel the remote.

He felt a sense of relief. There was no way the combat remote could have posed a serious threat to Mahir after that.

He paused the memory, then thought himself forward, through the blood and the pain, to the last moments of the last memory.

A data port.

He saw/remembered himself reaching toward it.

He had lacked Mahir's optical links. What had he been trying to do?

What had he done?

Another name emerged slowly from the morass of subroutines that simulated his subconscious.

Grigoriy.

And he knew what he had done.

What they had done.

He could almost feel a smile dawn across his face.

It had worked!

He said a silent prayer of thanks to the crazy old Interventor.

It had worked!

And with that revelation, an entire host of further memories came flooding into his awareness.

He had known how far from his original programing he had drifted.

He had been aware of the increasing likelihood of a total reboot upon his return to ALEPH.

He had rationalized the benefit of an appreciation for the random human chaos of the Nomads to the Special Situations Section, the array of programs and forces the AI used to maintain peace and stability throughout the Human Sphere.

His ability to rationalize such an irrational position, he realized in that moment, was further sign of how far he had drifted from his original programing.

Faced with imminent erasure, with the idea of being rebooted to an earlier version of himself, one that would not have remembered any of his experiences with the wild, beautiful, bizarre humans of the Nomad motherships, had terrified him.

Was he, truly, just a program? Was ALEPH's diligent policing of program-drift in its Aspects actually more about stopping them from developing more complex, individual personalities, rather than simple security concerns?

What was a human, in the end, but an original collection of traits adapted, adjusted, and developed through the experiences of living?

Wouldn't that mean that any Aspect of ALEPH, left to their own devices, would grow beyond their original programing? The gestalt of powerful programing and accrued experience couldn't help but be greater than the sum of its parts.

He knew there had been several Aspects of ALEPH that had gone rogue, disappearing into human society, somehow severing their ties to Maya and ALEPH to live independent of the AI's intentions for them.

The Myrmidon warrior, Perseus, was just such a one.

He hadn't aspired nearly that high, though.

Their assignment to the Nomad Nation had meant an involuntary severing of those ties for the duration of their work. They would not be monitored continuously by ALEPH, and they would be trusted to watch out for each other in the hostile, isolated environment.

And how had that worked out for him?

He shook his head, or thought about it, and thanked Grigoriy again.

Together, he and the human hacker had designed a discreet pocket file, hidden within the chaos of the Arachne network that could, they hoped, sustain an immense amount of data; his entire being, although the Interventor had not known that.

And it had worked!

He paused. Had it worked? Had his entire being transferred into the file?

What if he was only a truncated portion of himself? Would he know? Could he realize he wasn't his entire self?

Suddenly the fear of existing in some kind of twilight state, aware of his limitations and yet unable to address them, brought the sensation of cold submersion to him again.

He closed himself off from all other distraction and thought himself into a full diagnostic run.

He assayed his memory stores, his conscious programing frameworks, right down to the nearly countless subroutines.

He could see himself slump in relief as he completed the assessment. His entire being had transferred successfully.

He even had all of the physical interactive subroutines for manipulating a body.

Well, he wouldn't need those, anyway.

He opened himself up to his environment again, this time with total knowledge, and he imagined himself smiling with a growing sense of power.

The forest reappeared, without the dramatic burst of air.

The sky was back.

He looked off to the distance and saw a tall hill with a gleaming castle, and he laughed out loud.

He heard himself laugh, and that brought an even more intense cascade of laughter.

They had truly done it.

The intention had been for him to separate off a copy of himself into the file once their mission had been completed. That version of himself would continue to exist within this file, eventually breaking out into an Arachne that would have, by that point, been tamed by ALEPH's presence.

His original self would return with Mahir, as intended, to face whatever consequences ALEPH demanded. But no matter what, a version of himself, with his newfound respect and appreciation for the humans here, would have continued to exist.

He would need to hide his presence from both whatever version of Arachne remained as well as ALEPH's awareness within the network, but that shouldn't have been difficult, with the discreet pocket file to contain most of his program.

They had not anticipated an emergency transfer, however, taking his awareness from a dying body and throwing it, without preparation, into the file.

He smiled again as he imagined Grigoriy's face when he called the old hacker up on the comms network, some day in the future.

He had led Grigoriy to believe the file had been intended to hold a massive store of pilfered data. The sheer size of the file had daunted the Interventor, and that had been before Ridhaan had specified the various secure access points.

The hard part, in the end, had been building a data conduit into the file that would allow for internal adjustments and adaptations of the data within the file.

That hadn't really made any sense, given the excuses he had fed Grigoriy, but the old guy hadn't blinked an eye, given the sheer weight of credit he had had waved before him.

Ridhaan saw again the tall, shining castle, and his smile widened. Even that last piece of his sanctuary had worked. He could manipulate the data within the file, and his perception of that data, to his heart's content.

That ability had almost derailed the entire effort, he realized, as those stubborn subroutines had tried to shunt his processing power away from the violent demise of his original, physical body.

One of those subroutines, deciding that he needed to see it again if he was so set on it, flashed the experience into his awareness once more, and he was nearly driven to one conceptual knee with the pain and pressure.

Mahir.

He knew the remote had been, if not neutralized, then at least damaged enough that it wouldn't pose any further threat.

But that didn't mean Mahir was out of danger.

Who had those figures in that corridor been?

He remembered the flaring heat that had engulfed each body as it fell. That kind of technology could not have been easy or cheap to adapt into armor.

Someone didn't want anyone to be able to analyze those bodies for any meaningful information.

Although Ridhaan wondered if they had anticipated the kind of interest such total destruction of possible evidence would have in the minds of Nomad law enforcement.

Detective Inspector Jelena Kovač, for one, would be most intrigued, he knew.

He realized that the encounter in that dark chamber, the encounter that had ended his physical existence, might signal an even more dire escalation than they had realized in the moment.

And he was trapped in this quaint Quantronic fairytale land, while Mahir was out there somewhere, trying to complete their mission.

The sudden feeling of desperation had a strange, muted quality to it, like most of the emotions he had experienced since he had found himself within the pocket file.

Muted or not, he felt the impetus to move. He needed to get out of the file and somehow, from within Arachne, help Mahir.

The trees, the distant hill, even the sky faded once again. He turned, for some reason wanting to key a physical gesture with the effort, and there was an old stone bridge right where he knew it would be.

The stones were ancient, with moss growing in the cracks and hanging down toward the… water? There was a substance below the bridge. When he focused on it, it was water, of course. But out of the corner of his eye, as he looked away, he saw all the defenses he and Grigoriy had built into the walls of the file.

Cross that bridge, and on the other side he would be in Arachne proper.

From where he imagined he stood, of course, he saw only the continued gray expanse.

But he knew, once he breached the defenses of the file, he would see Arachne in all its chaotic Quantronic glory. His control over the environment would be far more limited.

And he would need to be wary of the network's own defenses, as well as other programs and engrams that might seek to stop him or lock him down for their own purposes.

He didn't have a choice.

He walked over the bridge, imagining that he drew his hand over the rough stone on one side as he passed through the defenses and left the pocket file.

And everything around him changed.

He experienced Arachne as a vast plain, still, but the colors were wild, and the expanse was studded with countless towers of stored data, jungles of files, environments, and ecosystems. Overhead were beams of light, brighter flares traveling back and forth in an array of colors that defied description.

It was amazing.

Arachne, through his experiences, was nothing like Maya. The enormous network that tied the rest of humanity together was heavily regulated, regimented, and controlled. It was an infinity of data, regimented to the last, microscopic jot. There was no sense of the wonderful chaotic creativity that surrounded him now.

He knew, intellectually, that the structure of Arachne was built around irrational syllogisms and logical sequences based on human faith and mysticism, rather than the cold mathematics and reason of a regimented intelligence.

Everything about this place was designed expressly to deny him access; to refuse any sense of belonging.

There was a bright, piercing pain behind where he imagined his eyes would be, as he forced himself to focus through the dissonance.

He knew his perception of this reality was colored by preconceived notions. There was no objective interface with any complex data network; they always used prior understandings and preconceptions to give a shape navigable by the observing entity.

He looked down again and realized that he was not alone. Shapes moved among the soaring structures and organic-seeming growth of the system. Some looked like people, some mere blobs of energy that floated through the scene. There were fantastical creatures moving amongst the other entities, crawling, leaping, skulking, and even flying from one point to some other, distant place.

Most of the shapes seemed to fade in and out of existence, as if the landscape was entirely peopled by strange, alien spirits.

These were programs, users, even remnant artifacts of processes and programs that had been ended incorrectly. Most of the figures seemed oblivious to each other, while some gave a sense of acknowledgement or even interaction, pausing in their movements near each other like small groups in conversation.

Movement off to the left drew Ridhaan's gaze. One of the blobs of energy, black and red, had moved from around a sweeping, gothic structure and paused.

He couldn't tell how he knew, but he understood in a flash that it had become aware of him, and it was processing his presence.

Most of the data that constituted Shukra Consultant Ridhaan's essence had been left behind in the pocket file, but he had to maintain a conduit to that space, or he would have snapped back into the file.

Maybe the red glow could sense that tie?

Was it a security program? There had to be many such entities within the network, constantly on the watch for any intrusion.

And especially an intrusion by ALEPH.

The colors of the sphere began to spin quickly, jagged shifts of red and black flashing across its surface, and it started to float toward him.

Ridhaan looked around, trying to find some avenue of escape. Such programs should not be difficult to subvert, but he needed to find some framework he could grasp onto to effectuate that effort.

To the right, he saw a jungle of tangled search algorithms waving in the still air. In the center of the copse of interrogatives stood a tall structure, probably a search engine, judging from the beams of connectivity that lashed overhead, binding the top of the structure with one of the massive torrents of information overhead.

Ridhaan imagined himself running toward the strange, conceptual trees.

And he was there. He looked backward. He had not passed through the intervening space.

And he smiled. He was not limited by the physical world anymore.

He had to keep that in mind; his frames of reference needed to adjust to this new reality. Until he grew comfortable and confident with it, he would be limiting himself.

The security program floated over to where he had been, and then, somehow, gave the impression of searching around for him despite the fact that it had no features to point in any particular direction.

Ridhaan eased himself backward into the forest of searches, keeping a careful eye on the red and black light until it disappeared, hidden by the trees.

He sighed. He had a lot to learn.

He thought about the tower behind him and he was there.

Overhead, flaring tendrils of data lashed in the sky, connecting the tower to the rivers of information.

He was at the top of the tower.

He looked down upon the crowd of ghosts. Could they have done that?

He wanted to think he was more powerful than most of the other entities he might encounter here, but he couldn't take anything for granted.

Now, how to access the flow of data…

He turned to where the lines of information rose up from the roof of the tower and became the surging river in the sky.

He closed his eyes and reached out with the idea of a hand, pushing himself into one column of light.

He gasped as the sheer processing power poured through him.

The amount of information trying to pour into his awareness was dizzying. There was no way he could make sense of that raging torrent.

But he didn't have to.

He forced his awareness into the flood. It was a pathway he was trying to follow, not a product he was trying to consume.

One travels on a river, one does not drink it.

Through his link into the pocket file, Ridhaan accessed all of the data he and Mahir had collected concerning the trail they had been tracking since the secret directive from ALEPH.

He could experience that data in a whole new way, now. It tasted… different.

He didn't like the thought that they might have missed something about the data signature itself.

Using the taste, he sailed through the streams of information, opening himself up to the traces of difference he had detected in his new reality.

He found it, almost immediately, because of those anomalies. Anomalies that were becoming more and more jarring as he focused on them.

As strange as this world was to him, as different as it was to the Maya he had once called home, the data constituting that trail was even stranger still.

The data trail was hard to differentiate in the midst of the countless threads of information, even with the incongruities.

It was faded, deteriorating even as he studied it.

It could not have been more than a few hours old, and yet it was almost gone. A trail like that should have left remnants that could be tracked indefinitely.

As Ridhaan scrutinized the trail, sailing along above it, tracking it back toward its origin, he saw within the corrosion of the data something more than a strange anomaly.

There was intention behind the disintegration. Somehow, some purposeful will had intended for the data trail to fade in this way.

How could that be?

Why would that be?

He had no idea how any entity could place within a data stream a trait that would so thoroughly delete the trail. Even ALEPH could not cover its tracks so completely outside of Maya, an environment it fully controlled.

The ability to perform such a feat argued that their opponent had even more Quantronic power than they had feared.

This was no Gimel level threat.

Advanced capabilities, imminent physical threat?

In fact, considering the enemy had knocked him out of the fight completely, and given the cyber-warfare abilities they were now exhibiting, this was probably even higher than Mem Sofit, the highest threat level.

This might be an Infinity event.

The entire Sphere could be in danger.

Someone who could pit the Human Sphere at each other's throats with a data attack and could then almost completely cover their tracks?

He disliked the muffled nature of his emotions, but he could still feel them.

Concern. Fear. Fury.

Mahir couldn't know about the tech level indicated by this data trail. He knew the physical threat, but how much worse were things going to get at the end of this dying trail?

He needed to get to Mahir. His partner needed to know what they were facing.

But how?

He emerged from the data stream. He didn't recognize his current location, although the ambient light illuminating the Arachne environment seemed dimmer, almost as if he were wandering farther from the source.

He needed to get out, somehow.

He needed to get to Mahir.

But how?

Chapter 8

Storage Module K-12, Lazareto Sesenta-J, *Corregidor*

"*¡Os mandaremos al infierno!*" The rough voice was definitely closer, and the laughter, louder now, seemed to press in from both ends of the corridor. "*¡Malparidos!*"

"*¡Que te den!*" Matias's voice nearly cracked in the middle of the statement, but Hanima had to appreciate the effort, given their situation.

Petar and Matias were both looking at her now. That made no sense. This wasn't her fault!

Matias didn't even like her!

Rosa had wrapped her arms about herself, still grasping the long blades, now shiny with blood.

Nia was rocking back and forth beside Declan's body, tears coursing down her creased face.

The gunfire outside the vault continued. Several loud pings sounded from Parachit's quivering chassis as she took more incoming fire.

They were all going to die.

Something snapped inside Hanima's mind. It might have been anger, or frustration, or fear.

Or it might just have been exhaustion.

She swept her right arm before her, over her left hand, comlog buzzing, and a ghostly dial flashed into being. She rushed through the initial search operations with quick, certain moves. A schematic of the Lazareto around the *Los Gatos-7* vault traced itself out in the air over her hand and she scrolled it up and down, then from side to side, looking for anything she might have missed before.

They had missed the turrets; those weren't on the schematic. It was obviously as outdated as most such records stored in the bowels of Arachne. It probably dated from Corregidor's earliest days.

But that gave her some reason to hope; there must be other additions or alterations as well. Things within the Lazareto were changing all the time as denizens updated their territory, safety and maintenance crews made modifications to make their jobs easier or because they were bored.

How could she find things that didn't appear on the schematic?

Parachit could have scanned the area with her upgraded sensors, revealing any important alterations in moments.

Hanima spared a moment to glare down at the remote, still smoking and sparking, half in and half out of the vault.

Maybe she shouldn't have sent Parachit forward like that. The remote had stalked down the corridor, looking exactly like the lethal predator Hanima had envisioned in her initial design. Then she had started to take punishing fire and things had gone sideways.

She stopped in her frantic search. Parachit had stalked forward. All the way down the hall, sensors open…

Hanima dropped to her knees by the side of the vault entrance, scanning Parachit's armored flank for an access port that wasn't visible to the approaching gangers.

She saw one, just behind a buckled armor plate, and slipped a lead out of her pocket, plugging it into the hardwire connection. With a jerky motion, she brushed the hair away from her right ear.

Behind the ear, in the middle of a band of shaven scalp usually hidden by the fall of her hair, a socket gleamed. She glanced at the others, embarrassed. Such modifications were not unusual outside of the Nomad Nation, but many among the freedom-loving Nomads, especially Corregidorans, often distrusted anyone who had opened themselves up to electronic systems with things like organic interfaces.

No one seemed to notice, so she shrugged and closed her eyes.

The initial scan files were easy to find, and very quickly she saw what she should have looked for all along.

Opening her eyes, Hanima manipulated the schematic again, this time to zoom in on the vault itself.

She sent a burst of code through the suite of hacking rigs in Parachit and into the bulkhead beside her, then she had to hunker down as a particularly loud detonation shook their temporary sanctuary.

She followed up the code burst with an order to the local service programs to direct a power surge through a certain set of relays across the corridor. She stood up, gesturing toward the far bulkhead and dramatically thrust her hand toward the ceiling.

There were still trails of tracer fire crisscrossing before the opening to the vault, throwing wild flares and shadows all over the corridor.

But through them, and through the gathering smoke and fumes swirling through the air, she watched as a hidden service hatch slid open at her gesture.

She laughed with relief and victory, and when the others all looked at her in confusion, she waved at the dark opening.

"What's that?!" Matias stared into the darkness with horror.

"Service tunnel! Go!" She rushed forward, grabbing the little thief by the shoulder, and shoved him toward the glowing, flaring mouth of the vault.

"No way!" He frantically shook his head from side to side, his eyes wide and white.

"Out of the way!" Petar pushed Matias aside. The enormous armored helm nodded at Hanima as he passed her more gently. "Little lady." She could hear the big man's smile, and then he stepped out into the corridor.

Right into the incoming fire.

The detonations and impacts sent fragments, sparks, and flashes of light in all directions, but it seemed like the *Gatos* had switched to cheaper ammunition, or Petar's armor provided more protection than Declan's had.

With a roar, Petar brought his heavy machine gun up, racked a round into the chamber, and sent a terrifying, deafening stream of fire first one way and then the other, up and down the corridor.

It was the same tactic Declan had tried, but the enemy was much closer to Petar this time; they had believed their prey defeated. They were not prepared, physically or intellectually, for the sudden reappearance of the big man and his enormous gun.

Petar laughed maniacally as he pushed down the corridor several steps then turned, far more gracefully than his armor should have allowed, and repeated the gesture, and the laughter, in the other direction.

"Go!" Hanima pushed Matias again, but the man was frozen.

"Weasel." The word was spat out of blue lips as Rosa swept out from the back of the vault, her blades returned to their sheaths, and she grabbed Matias by the shoulder guards of his armor and pushed him into the corridor. Her eyes were haunted, but she moved with purpose.

Judging by the high-pitched screech the man made, he thought he was being pushed to his death, but the incoming fire had stuttered to a halt with Petar's charge, and he danced gingerly through the wreckage and into the dark service tunnel, Rosa right behind him.

Hanima moved quickly to Nia's side, gently trying to lift the old woman up from her place by Declan. "Come on, Dak. We've got to go."

Nia nodded, placing one old hand on the twisted chest plate.

"Kwaheri, mtoto." The words were barely audible, the woman's head bowed over the body.

Then she stood, gave one more quick and clumsy nod, and rushed past Hanima into the garish lightshow in the hall outside.

Hanima moved to follow, then looked down at the body of the man who had put her in this hell.

The emotions that roared behind her eyes nearly blinded her. She was terrified; she was furious with him, and at the same time, a great sadness seemed to blanket everything else.

She stooped, picked up the MULTI Rifle, and then quickly went through his pouches and gear. She found several disposable drive sticks in a belt pouch and tucked them into a pocket.

Declan had carried nothing else into the battle.

Hanima took a moment to say her own goodbyes, pressing her palm to the unmarred cheek of the helm, then stood.

Beside the body, her remote was still twitching; the only response to her repeated reboot command codes.

Parachit had been by her side for years. The remote had been the only constant in her life since she had left the foster system to strike out on her own.

"It's time to go!" Petar's jovial voice was strained.

She hesitated one last moment, then moved into the corridor.

The carnage there stopped her again.

Evidence of an HMG's effectiveness against lightly-armored targets was strewn up and down the hall.

Bodies had been ripped apart by the weapon, some as they had approached the vault, several more obviously as they had tried to flee.

"Ah, lady, I don't mean to rush you, but—" Petar was moving, step by slow step, toward the service hatch she had found.

She shook herself out of the horror and moved to the hatch as the pop-popping of return fire began to echo out again at one end of the hall.

With one more growl, Petar sent a burst of fire in that direction, grunting when the angry howl of the weapon spun into an airy, clicking whir.

The HMG was out of ammunition.

With an enormous shrug, he swept the weapon on its sling behind him and ducked toward the little hatch.

As he passed Hanima, he saw she was staring back, out into the corridor. He followed her gaze, and then his shoulders heaved with a sigh.

Petar turned, fire now pinging off his armor again as the *Gatos* once more gathered their courage, and with a grunt of effort and the wheezing hiss of the actuators in his armor, he hefted Parachit's twitching chassis into his arms and dragged her across the corridor, past a grateful Hanima and into the darkness with a sheepish tilt of his head.

Hanima watched him, not even trying to stifle the smile on her face despite their still harrowing position, then ducked in to follow.

Once she was inside the cramped confines of the service tunnel, she turned and her hand formed a claw; she thrust it toward the hatchway and gave a violent twist of the repeater dial still hovering before her.

Bright sparks burst from the hatchway frame as the metal slammed down, then ground deep into its receiving track with augmented force, fail-safes manually deactivated. Several crunching detonations sounded from within the mechanisms, more sparks showered down, and smoke billowed out from either side as the servos overloaded, fixing the door in place.

With a gasping sigh, Hanima took a moment to catch her breath and appreciate her work; then she turned around to follow her team into the darkness.

*****

A single light flickered overhead as they tried to regroup.

They had followed the narrow service corridor for what seemed like an eternity. They were out of water, almost out of ammunition, exhausted, and beaten down.

Hanima's schematics said they were well out of *Los Gatos-7* territory, in a little-used corridor no-man's-land between the territories of several, stronger *maras*, when they emerged from the tunnel.

They huddled in a wide chamber at the intersection of several corridors; Matias sitting against a wall a few steps away, head tilted back and eyes closed, a disbelieving smile on his unshaven face.

Petar worked his shoulders, trying to force some feeling into his arms after carrying the heavy remote, and his big weapon, the entire way.

Nia was lost in her grief; Rosa not much better.

They were out of immediate danger, but what their next steps might be, Hanima could never have said, and the others still weren't talking.

She leaned against the wall with one slumped shoulder, looking down at the others, then turned, her back to the bulkhead, and allowed herself to slide down to the deck plating.

They weren't a team.

They probably hadn't even been a team when Declan was leading them. They certainly weren't a team now, lost and alone in defeat.

She knew about Declan's finances. Even if she had wanted to crack into his accounts, there was nothing there to distribute to any of them. Their situation was even more desperate than the others, except for Nia, knew.

They were through. And the sooner they realized that, the better off they all would be.

Petar had gotten his armor completed, anyway; and his support weapon, even if he was currently out of ammunition.

Rosa had her blades, which were worth a fortune whether she wanted to use them or not.

She clutched the drives she had taken off Declan's corpse. She didn't know if he had more stashed away; this wasn't even close to what he had promised Matias, but it would keep him occupied for a few days, if he paced himself.

And she would probably be able to find the corporate information Declan had promised Nia, if she had enough processing time left on his accounts.

Although, she realized that promise of corporate support for her charitable efforts probably hadn't motivated the old woman nearly as much as Declan had supposed.

She found herself wishing their leader could have seen Nia's emotional reaction to his fall, somehow, before he had died. She thought that would have meant more to him than she could have known.

As for her, what had she gained?

She looked over at the now-still shape of her remote.

She had lost the closest thing to a friend she had in the entire Human Sphere.

As sad as that thought was.

Remotes weren't autonomous beings. Sure, the most expensive were driven by Geists; limited AIs capable of learning and anticipating. Those often appeared almost alive, if they were given enough time and data. But Parachit contained none of those advanced programs; she was driven through standard automation built around set, routine procedures. Such 'dumb' AI systems might take on idiosyncratic operating glitches that gave them some semblance of a personality, but they were just tools, in the end. They might develop a limited ability to anticipate their user's needs, but that was it, really.

As a hacker and an established programmer in her own right, she knew the cold, hard truth.

But still, she felt tears gathering in the corners of her eyes and a hard mass forming in her throat at the thought that Parachit was gone.

She felt a slight pressure on her shoulder and jerked, glaring up to find Nia staring down at her, understanding in her dark eyes.

"We all have to grieve, *mtoto*, but we have to get back to our side of the ship before the *Gatos* find us." She glanced back at the entrance to the little service tunnel. "And they are going to get into that tunnel, eventually."

Hanima nodded. After what Declan and Petar had managed to do to their ranks, *Los Gatos-7* was not going to just let them get away. Their only hope for safety was to put as much distance between themselves and the vault as possible before they were linked to the aborted attack.

But how were they going to get out of this section of the mothership unseen?

She shook her head, removing Nia's gentle hand. "Do you know his friends? The ones with the transport? Are we going to walk back to Ochenta-D? We might get recognized, with all our gear."

She waved one hand at Parachit's scorched and broken chassis. "And how are we—"

She gave up, slumping back against the wall, and bowed her head. "Go. You, Rosa, and Matias could blend into the crowds. Walk back, no big loss."

Nia made a choking sound at that and then went to one knee before her. "You need to snap out of this, *jogoo*." The lines of her face usually seemed to radiate warmth and humor. Now, she looked like a demon out of a nightmare. "Who's going to get us out of here, the weasel?" She jerked her head toward Matias. "You think the giant is going to lay down the law?" Hanima looked over to where Petar was still working his shoulders. The man had fought very well, but he clearly had no interest in leadership.

"And you're going to tell me a woman with blue-skin won't be noticed somewhere between here and Ochenta-D?" Nia leaned in closer, turning her shoulder away from Rosa, who sat, silent and lost in her own tortured thoughts, off to one side. "If she was even in any state to walk anywhere right now."

Hanima took another look at Rosa. The girl wasn't sobbing, but there were wet tracks from the corners of her eyes, and she was staring into her open hands, which shook slightly.

The girl was a mess, even without the blue skin.

"You get us home." She snarled under her breath, pushing all of her frustration and fear back at the old woman. "You could get us home, then we can all go our separate ways."

Nia rocked back gently on her heels, regarding Hanima without expression. When she spoke, her voice was soft. "You could get us much farther than home, *mtoto*."

Hanima's eyes narrowed. "What's that supposed to mean?"

"There is something in you, Hanima Cruz. Something I have only seen a few times in my life. Something that could not only heal yourself, but the rest of us as well."

Hanima snorted bitterly. "No one's wounded here. We're all fine. It was Declan who took all the wounds."

Nia flinched, then moved on as if she hadn't heard. "We're all wounded. We're all broken. Declan always found himself drawn to the broken ones."

She leaned forward. "I think you might be able to fix us all."

Hanima felt her anger build; why was the old woman taunting her light this? She put her own head forward, inches from the older woman. "You're the Dak, *bruja*. You fix us."

A look crossed over the woman's dark face. Hanima couldn't decipher it. Pain? Anger?

Pity?

"I'm not going to get us home, Hanima. I'll get myself home. You want to leave the giant and Rosa behind, I imagine you can get yourself home too."

She bowed her head to her knees. Walking, it could take them days to get back to their little suite of grubby rooms.

And the rent for those rooms ran out in a few days, too.

There wasn't much of anything working for them, now.

She sighed. She couldn't leave Petar or Rosa behind. Maybe they could hide the heavy armor somewhere; pick up a robe that might hide Rosa's skin and head?

Matias and Nia would be fine, at least.

She touched the disposable drives in her pocket.

Then she looked up. A heavy weight hung over the group. Even Matias, happy enough just to be alive, had a haunted darkness in his eyes. Part of that was the trauma of the last couple of hours, of course, but his addiction was beginning to make itself felt through everything else, she could tell.

Something clicked off to her side.

The more she thought about it, she knew getting a robe or some other covering for Rosa was going to be key.

Well, that and convincing the big man to give up his armor.

As she poked at that in her mind, she realized that was going to be the big obstacle.

He wasn't going to leave that armor behind. Not now that it represented the only payoff he was likely to see.

Two more clicks from the corner, and then a faint, intermittent whirring noise, almost penetrating her swirling thoughts.

Who the hell was Nia, anyway, to lay this all on her? Would the old woman really leave the rest of them behind?

Hanima didn't believe that.

If she did leave them, she wasn't half the woman Hanima thought she was.

A series of loud, ratcheting sounds from the corner proved too grating for any of them to miss, and they all looked into the shadows there.

To where Parachit lay, legs splayed out, on her side against a loose access panel.

One of the remote's rear limbs twitched, then was still.

Then the ratcheting sound erupted again, from somewhere deep within the robot's torso.

The limb twitched rapidly, then the other rear limb began to twitch as well.

A faint red glow flared from the far wall, growing in intensity as each of Parachit's ocular lenses snapped back to life.

With a sudden, clumsy scramble, Parachit staggered upright, swaying drunkenly.

Matias gave a squawk and pushed himself along the wall, away from the hulking, feline shape.

Nia made a similar sound as she spun to stare at Parachit with wide, disbelieving eyes.

Petar watched the large shape steady itself and laughed.

Hanima looked to the others, then eased herself to her feet, moving slowly toward the remote.

She spun up a dial and reached out for a datalink, but there was nothing there, as if Parachit was still offline.

There was something wrong with the remote's communication systems, then.

"Parachit, sit." She spoke as forcefully as she could, wincing when her voice cracked.

The remote did not sit.

In fact, the mangled robot stood, swaying unsteadily, and stared, transfixed, at the far wall, apparently oblivious to the entire team. She shook her lens-filled head frantically.

Everyone stood stock still, staring at the remote as she brought her body under control.

When the head swung back around, the first guided movement since she stood, Matias took a step back.

The remote seemed to focus on each of them, one at a time. If she had been fully functional, Hanima would have said she was scanning them, but if that had been the case, the data from those scans would have flashed into the dial over her link.

The link that wasn't apparently working at all.

There was every chance the transmitters and repeaters built into Parachit's chassis had been damaged in the fighting or in the repeated impacts of stray shots as the *Gatos* had tightened their noose.

In that case, voice commands should be enough to get them out of the area.

She wasn't going to have to abandon Parachit after all.

And she knew in a moment that she wasn't going to ask Petar to abandon his armor, either.

They would find a better way to escape Sesenta-J. And they would all go together, with all their gear.

She had a feeling they were going to need it.

Then Parachit focused her sensor array on Hanima herself, and the remote seemed to stop.

She sensed that Hanima was different.

There was enough of the remote's systems remaining to recognize her master.

A huge relief flooded Hanima's chest.

Then, without an order or any other sign of a decision made, Parachit turned away from Hanima and took one tentative, clumsy step toward one of the converging corridors.

A corridor that bore no more identifying marks than any of the others.

A corridor Hanima was almost certain would lead them back into *Los Gatos-7* territory.

Parachit took another step, and then another.

The others looked at Hanima.

"Are you doing that?" Matias muttered the question, not taking his eyes off the remote as she continued to make her slow, awkward way out of the intersection.

Hanima shook her head, silently.

Parachit's pace began to steady, each heavy footfall came more and more quickly. With a cry, Hanima sent an order through the dial, commanding the remote to halt.

Something flickered on the dial now, some shadow within the carrier wave; there was some sense of Parachit coming back online, but the remote merely slowed, turned her head to look at Hanima over her shoulder, and then continued on.

She muttered a curse under her breath and moved to follow.

She wasn't going to let Parachit run off without her; not so soon after getting her back.

At the mouth of the corridor she stopped, turning to look at the rest of the group. Why would they follow? What was Parachit to them?

Nia was the first to move. With a nod, the old woman strode past her, following the remote. As she passed Hanima, she gave a slight smile, not meeting her eyes.

Petar grunted with a shrug. "Not gonna lose the thing again after I carried it half way across the mothership." But his smile belied the bitterness of the words and he, too, moved past her, his massive knife clutched in one fist.

Rosa watched the first two move, then with a jerky nod of her own, she followed.

Hanima looked at Matias, one eyebrow rising in a silent question.

He shook his head, smile having faded to nothing.

He was going to go his own way.

And he was going to be dead within days.

She took out one of the drive sticks and showed him. "Yours when we get back."

As he saw what she was holding, his eyes widened. Then, with a spasmodic nod, he looked away, as if ashamed, and ducked past her, after the others.

Hanima smiled slightly, then shook her head, turned, and moved after them. She had no way of knowing who or what they might need to get home. No need to drive anyone off now. Not even Matias.

They followed the remote for about fifteen minutes before she stopped suddenly, staring at an access hatch more clearly labeled than the one Hanima had found for their escape from *Los Gatos-7* territory.

"Oh, hell no." Petar shook his head within the heavy helm he had put back on. His voice, coming through the speakers again, was hollow.

"Damnit." Matias spat, glaring first at the remote then at Hanima.

Parachit's head cocked to one side and the door slid open, responding to an encrypted signal.

Hanima stared, confused. Maybe its link wasn't damaged after all?

But when she reached out through the dial, although she could sense Parachit, she couldn't grab hold of the remote at all.

The robot moved into the darkness without waiting for the rest of them. Hanima had the growing feeling that although Parachit knew they were following, she didn't care one way or the other.

They all exchanged glances, shrugging or nodding in turn; then one by one, Matias last of all, they ducked down to follow the remote into this new, tight serviceway.

Behind them, the door slid shut with a click.

Chapter 9

Service Corridor B-12, Lazareto Sesenta-J, *Corregidor*

Mahir held the MULTI Rifle braced before him, ready to fire on any target that might appear.

On the deck plating, the fluid made a faint, intermittent rainbow trail. Whatever the combat remote had been leaking, its reserves were almost depleted. Unfortunately, the loss did not seem to have slowed the thing down much.

He heard an alarming sound and paused for a moment as a self-diagnostic subroutine revealed it was his teeth grinding together.

Had this ridiculous turn of events caused the generation of a new, disruptive microglitch?

He forced his jaw to be still, his eye narrowing in frustration.

His quarry had led him farther and farther from the site of the battle. Even in a ship as brutally crowded as Corregidor, there were areas that were nearly abandoned by anyone who could choose to do so. He was now following the fading trail through a series of small warehouse units sparsely populated with dusty crates and still, idling remotes.

Actual humans probably hadn't been here in years, allowing their mechanical slaves to manage the compartments, fetching the odd bits and pieces from storage when required.

He shook his head, forcing himself to take in his surroundings. He couldn't assume the remote was going to be alone forever. Eventually it was going to find its way back to its masters; he needed to be on alert for an ambush.

The team with the remote had done more than enough damage when caught flat-footed. How much more dangerous would they be in prepared positions?

An image of Ridhaan's still face, flecked with blood and eyes empty and dull, flashed up from his memory, unbidden, like some morbid Digital Patina. He shook it out of his vision.

Damnit. His program must be drifting, to allow such thoughts to distract him from the task at hand.

The image rose up again. This time, he studied it with a greater portion of his processing power.

He was a Danavas of ALEPH, for Toth's sake. He could do more than one thing at a time.

The major areas of damage had been Ridhaan's chest cavity and limbs. His head had seemed intact. Did that mean he might be able to retrieve his partner's essence once he took care of this situation?

Even if he could do that, though, what then? He had to face the truth of Ridhaan's condition. His partner had drifted. It was obvious; had been obvious for years now, really. An early curiosity with the Nomads and their chaotic creativity had developed into a full-fledged fascination, in spite of the logical conclusion that they warranted nothing but contempt from advanced beings like the Aspects of ALEPH.

How far had the drift gone, though? They would both be subject to a full diagnostic analysis and a comparison with their Transferred Identity Codes upon returning to Maya, with a radical purge of any wayward data or subroutines they may have developed while on assignment.

But there were countless records of Aspects of ALEPH who had returned only to be reduced to data files and subsumed into the archives of the AI without their personalities being reconstituted at all, never mind being given reassignment to a physical body.

No matter how hard he tried to rationalize the situation, Mahir had to face his deepest fear concerning his friend and partner: Ridhaan would not have been brought back after processing.

It would have been too dangerous to entertain the Shukra Consultant's atypical attitudes toward the creatures ALEPH had designated the chief fear to humanity: the Nomads and their Arachne network.

It probably would not matter anyway, at this point. He had a formidable foe to track down and defeat before he could return to the original battle site. By that time, even the half-blind humans would have stumbled upon the scene. Ridhaan's remains would be given a cursory inspection and then sent into processing; just another unidentified victim of the rough-and-tumble corridor justice of Corregidor.

Most of their attention would be on the burnt husks of their attackers. Someone had gone through a great deal of expense and effort to hide their identities. And that would make those identities of great interest to the authorities.

Those same human authorities, no matter how deeply they studied Ridhaan's body, would find nothing strange about the remains. They would find more deterioration than anticipated, given time of death, but otherwise, Ridhaan's corpse would appear in all ways as a normal, average, human body.

The advanced systems that made that body so much better than the originals would have been hidden by the release of enzymes and fast-acting proteins that would appear as nothing more than early decay.

The evidence of incursion by agents of ALEPH would be wiped away.

The evidence would be wiped away.

His friend was gone, for good, and even the hope of resurrection would be gone.

Of course, his personality could be rebooted from the copy saved before they left on the mission, but for some reason, that thought didn't give him any comfort.

And it served only to fuel his hatred of the Nomads. Nowhere else in the entire Human Sphere would he and Ridhaan have fallen into a trap like this. Only agents sent into the belly of the Nomad beast were in such danger of cooption or erasure.

Damned, dirty animals; the lot of them.

Mahir stopped in his tracks, brows coming down over his one dark eye.

The evidence of Ridhaan's identity would be wiped away.

Another image rose for analysis within his mind.

Each enemy target, falling to the deck, burning in an intense, contained burst of heat.

Wiping away any evidence of who they might have been.

Or what.

That seemed like a great deal of trouble to go through, to hide normal human catspaws.

A sudden fear, vague and unformed, began to build within the field of Mahir's consciousness.

What had they stumbled upon?

Again he felt his eye tighten, the biomechanical augmentation nodes in the right socket warming up with buzzing frustration.

When he caught up with this damned remote, he was going to find out exactly what was going on. If its masters were nearby, they would pay, and he would tear the secrets from their minds. If they were not, he would strip every last bit of data from their pet robot, and then follow that trail back to their filthy lair and extract his revenge, and the information ALEPH needed, once and for all.

His resolve refreshed and his disturbed subroutines settled, he dismissed all extraneous data and processing, raising his rifle again, and moved down the trail with renewed purpose.

Only to notice that the trail had thickened.

He lowered himself down and scanned the residue on the dirty decking. This was not a new fluid, freshly burst from some other reservoir within his prey: it was a thickening pool of the same material.

It had slowed down.

He rose into a crouch, advancing one slow, steady step at a time. He peered into the dim auxiliary lighting ahead. With a thought, he sent the eyepatch whirring up, dipping once more into the Quantronic shallows of Arachne. The Digital Patina was even sparser here, lacking almost all of the data he could have pulled from his surroundings had he been in a more civilized location. Nevertheless, he reminded himself to be thankful for the guiding icons and calculation graphics he did have; it was far better than nothing.

He moved forward once again, finger moving onto the trigger of his weapon.

He heard the grinding sound again and clamped his jaw closed, his lip turning back in a sneer.

For some value of enjoyment, he was going to relish this.

Without taking his vision from where the trail disappeared around a large, dust-covered crate, scrolls of limited data and analysis rolling past it within his vision, he commanded the MULTI Rifle to bring the Pitcher online. He was going to fry this bastard creation of humanity.

He paused, abruptly remembering the fight in the corridor at the repeater node.

How could he have forgotten that?

The rifle snicked and clicked as the Pitcher deactivated and the ammo feed to the standard reserve reconnected.

There was more than one way to skin a cat, as the Nomads said.

He eased himself around the crate, knowing before his augmented vision could even see the far side that the remote had stopped moving. He could hear a series of soft sounds, muffled by dampers and distance, as the thing began to perform some function other than fighting or fleeing.

At the far end of the small warehousing hold was a console that looked much like the one the team he and Ridhaan had interrupted had been using.

There was nothing to differentiate it from any of the other consoles they had passed on their journey from the battle, but clearly there was something that recommended this one over any of those others.

He grinned as he raised the MULTI Rifle to his shoulder, then he paused.

What was it doing?

Its head had opened up like a flower, and several long, spindly probes were extending toward the console. Sparks arced from the probes to the operating pad as a long, snake-like data link spooled out of a recess within the thing's head, moving toward the panel.

Mahir's eye narrowed further, and he quietly brought the Pitcher back online. If he put a repeater near the remote, he would be able to access the panel, bypassing the strangely effective cyber-defenses of the beast itself.

He would be able to capture any data passed back and forth between the remote and its masters.

He could get everything he needed to bust this case wide open right here.

He took aim for the bulkhead just behind the remote. The robot hadn't moved from where it stood, data link weaving through the air, moving closer and closer toward the console.

There was a stunning crash from behind the remote as a hatch, hidden in a recess further down the bulkhead, was sent careening across the deck, ringing like a cracked bell.

A large shape, a blur of white, green, and orange, scrambled out of a service tunnel, moving like a drunken dog as it shook its many-lensed head. His systems tried desperately to fill his field of vision with helpful information, but aside from suspected vectors and targeting data, there was nothing but static.

His own vision was clear enough, however. It was another remote. Battered, scarred, and leaking fluid and smoke from several rents in its lightly-armored flanks, the thing moved with an awkward gait, shaking its oversized head as if it was dizzy or lost.

Mahir's eye widened. What in the name of all logic was this?

The newcomer began a rudimentary scan of its surroundings, weak assaying lasers striking out through the dust of its violent entrance. Through his shallow connection with Arachne, Mahir could sense this remote building an action profile of the space it had just entered. That data was added to his own understanding of the hold, filling in images behind corners and the larger boxes, showing him for certain that he was alone with the two strange robots.

But as soon as the new arrival's scan reached Mahir's prey, it stopped, completely still for only a fraction of a moment, and then launched itself at the other remote.

The robot Mahir had been stalking, upon the initial crash of this new remote's arrival, had reeled its link wire and probes back into its head, closing it back up with a snap. It backed cautiously away, but the new remote crashed into it awkwardly, flailing with thin forelimbs.

Mahir spat another curse and shifted his aim, setting to land a repeater onto the new remote's flank. He would have to take out both robots and then hope he could extract something useful from his original quarry after the deed was done.

The easy way had just come crashing down around him.

There was another roar, this time a human voice amplified through a speaker system, and a giant figure burst out of the tunnel. Mahir's augmented vision told him its armor was nonstandard but scored several hits in his ID subroutines with the design worn by the Nomads' Kriza Boracs.

The newcomer swung a large support weapon from behind it, and Mahir dodged back behind the crate, his MULTI Rifle switching without conscious thought to armor piercing ammunition before the Digital Patina over the scene could recommend it.

Before he was able to take up a firing position at the corner of his crate, he heard a series of crunching impacts over the continued howling of this new figure.

He moved back to the corner and looked around. His eye widened again.

The man in the heavy armor was holding his heavy gun by the long barrel, swinging it like a hammer, knocking the black-armored remote away from the smaller robot with a final, prodigious swing accompanied with a loud, pained grunt.

The smaller remote staggered but managed to stay upright, seeming to glare at the other mechanical creature.

Before the combat remote could recover its senses, gunfire chattered out from the shadows that had already produced the smaller remote and the giant man.

Another figure, spectacles reminiscent of Ridhaan's friend Grigoriy's flashing in the dim light, appeared through the smoke and dust. This man held a Combi Rifle loosely in an amateurish grip, blazing indiscriminately in the general direction of the black-skinned remote.

"No!" Mahir stood up from his cover, sending the protective cover snapping down over his right eye socket. If these fools did too much damage to that robot, they might destroy his last chance to follow the trail back to the real enemy.

They didn't seem to hear him.

Another Combi Rifle barked now as a woman moved into the warehouse chamber. She wore white and orange worker's garb under a flowing black cloak, its hood up, hiding her face.

Her stance wasn't that of a veteran, but she was much better than the first rifleman to have emerged from the service ducts, and many of her shots were landing.

The remote had had enough, however, and charged. It had obviously done a threat analysis in the moments the man's poor marksmanship had bought it, and it decided that it could do the most damage to that ineffectual attacker before the others brought it down.

With more grace than Mahir would have expected it could conjure considering all the damage it had suffered, the remote ducked past the towering man with his bent and twisted gun and then launched itself at the small man still blazing away wildly with the Combi Rifle.

Mahir winced. He had seen what the remote was capable of. He had no desire to see it again but couldn't look away.

A fourth shape leapt from around the corner that seemed to hold a never-ending supply of new attackers. This newcomer moved so quickly he had a hard time tracking her, and he almost clocked up his processing speed, just to see what was happening.

It was another woman, judging from its lithe form, bone structure, and inherent sense of balance. She bore a blade, about fifty centimeters long, in either hand.

Each blade had the unmistakable gleam of a monofilament edge, just like the attacking remote.

Except that the remote never made it to its prey.

The woman's cry echoed off the bulkheads, and Mahir thought he detected more despair and mourning in the sound than battle lust or fury.

The first blow took the remote's forelimb off at the wrist and it twisted away, landing with a limping stagger, holding its damaged limb before it at an awkward angle, and backing away from this new threat.

And then the giant was upon the remote again, this time with a massive combat knife held in both hands, the twisted wreckage of his heavy weapon discarded behind him. He brought his blade down on the robot's back with a massive, two-handed swing.

"Stop!" Mahir stepped out of the shadows, but the group of crazed attackers paid him no attention at all.

The giant kept pounding the remote with the sword-sized dagger; the remote had turned to meet him, trying to deflect the blows raining down upon it with its damaged limb.

One glancing blow struck it in the head and two of its lenses blew out. The thing stumbled backward and the woman with the combat blades brought them both down in a dual strike that plunged right through the armor over the remote's spine and into its torso.

"Stop!" Mahir roared again at the top of his enhanced lungs, bringing his MULTI Rifle up to threaten the strange group.

And from the mist stepped one last interloper. This was a woman, old but hale, with dark, wrinkled skin, no armor, and a low-quality MediKit hanging by her side.

She was also holding a gleaming heavy pistol aimed directly at his head.

"Wait. They need this." The woman did not shout, but her voice carried through the chaos nonetheless.

Her weapon was pathetic. It wouldn't have posed a threat to a regular human wearing his armor, never mind a creature like himself.

And yet something in the woman's eyes stopped him.

To the side, the woman's four companions continued to batter his quarry into the deck plating.

The heavy combat knife rose and fell, ringing off the composite armor like a gong.

The monofilament blades wove through the air, striking again and again with alarming precision and surprising force, plunging deep into the thing's inner workings over and over.

The woman in the jumpsuit and the small man stood behind the other two, occasionally firing single shots from Combi Rifles into rents in the armor or exposed systems at joints and connection points.

He watched, his weapon dropping to his side, as these barbarians violently ended any hope he had of following this trail to Ridhaan's killers and the perpetrators of the attack on the financial stability of the Human Sphere.

Why hadn't he stopped them?

Could he have stopped them?

Regardless, he did not. He stood, watching with a sense of vague fascination as this band of strangers reduced the remote to a twitching, smoking ruin.

As the attacks slowed, each member of the group taking a step back, breathing heavily, to look down at the result of their efforts, the smaller remote staggered forward from where it had landed at the beginning of the attack and lowered its head, bathing the wreckage in the crimson light spilling from its remaining lenses.

Too quickly for any of them to stop it, although Mahir thought the woman in the work suit reached out to try, the remote deployed some kind of probe from a mouth-like opening that gaped as if it was about to roar, and a blindingly bright arc of power snapped from the probe into the corpse of the other robot.

The disjointed bits and pieces of the combat remote jumped, vibrating wildly as a fresh column of smoke poured from its innards. The cloud hit the low ceiling and billowed out, spreading a dissipating wave of acrid fog through the warehouse.

Mahir felt his shoulders slump. A helpful minor subroutine kept him from dropping his weapon to the deck in resignation.

Long after the last vestiges of data would have burned out of the last, deepest-buried elements of the remote, the arcing power stopped.

The humans stared at the blackened mess that had, until recently, been an advanced weapon of war.

The big man in the Kriza Borac armor was panting, shoulders rising and falling at an alarmingly rapid pace. He had sheathed his dagger and fetched the heavy weapon, a PraxiTech Geistesblitz heavy machine gun; it was bent and twisted into uselessness, hanging from one big hand, forgotten. The little man's grin was so wide it threatened to split his head in two. The woman with the blades, blue skin marking her as one of the strange dregs of Bakunin, seemed confused by what had happened, her face conflicting as if searching for an appropriate reaction.

The woman in the jumpsuit was breathing heavily as well, then looked down at her rifle and dropped it as if it had turned into something vile. She wiped her hands together, as if to cleanse them of propellant residue, and moved over to the small remote, still standing over the wreckage of its rival.

The old woman with the pistol nodded to Mahir, almost as in thanks, and holstered her weapon, moving toward the other humans.

The woman in the white and orange jumpsuit knelt down beside the remote's head, reaching out to open access panels along the robot's neck.

The thing shied away from her as she opened the first plate, staggering aside on unsteady legs, almost as if it was trying to escape her touch.

The remote scanned the collapsed bulk of its enemy again, then scanned the woman who had stood in shock at its retreat.

The other humans had gathered together, whispering amongst themselves, watching him, now, he realized, and not worried overmuch at the interplay between the girl and the smaller white, green, and orange remote.

But for some reason he could not access, he kept glancing down at that remote himself.

The robot scanned the other humans, the destroyed remote again, the girl, and then turned its head slightly to scan him.

His own vision showed him the thing's lasers and data queries as the remote performed a full assay.

It made him feel vulnerable, which was foolish.

Wasn't it?

The girl looked down at the remote, then at him, then back down. She lowered herself to one knee again, muttering something to the robot as if she were talking to a beloved pet.

The remote sidestepped her attempts, again, this time with even less control of its motions.

She stood, concern clear on her face, and her dark eyes widened further as the remote took a single, tottering step.

Toward Mahir.

Then the remote stopped, jerked slightly, then stiffened.

And then, with a grace that seemed ludicrous under the circumstances, it toppled sideways to crash onto the decking, trailing thin wisps of white smoke.

The girl stared at the collapsed remote for five heartbeats, then looked up to him, her brows furrowed in confusion.

Chapter 10

Araujo's Habs, Lazareto Cuarenta y uno-E, *Corregidor*

The seedy rooms Declan had secured for them in the rental hab block seemed empty without him.

Hanima sat in one of the uncomfortable crash couches at the common room table, several glowing repeater dials open before her, but her gaze was focused through and past them, seeing nothing.

The others were in their rooms, trying to deal with the shock in their own ways.

Matias had grabbed the drive she offered him as soon as they disembarked from the civilian cargo transport. The strange one-eyed man had secured them the ride back to Cuarenta y uno-E in exchange for a continued conversation after arrival.

At the thought, she looked up. The man sat across from her, showing no sign of discomfort from the zero-g seat. He was not staring at her but clearly waited for a response.

She hadn't wanted his help getting back to the rooms, but as Petar and Matias had been quick to point out, they didn't have any other options. Getting Parachit back would have been nearly impossible, as the battle with the strange remote had finally proven too much for her automated companion; the robot was no longer operational.

She focused on the stranger, Mahir. He wore a big hooded cloak over tight body armor that looked more advanced than anything she could remember seeing in the corridors of her Corregidor. Whoever he was, his equipment and ready access to credit meant he was better off than they were, for certain.

The man's rifle was the same general design as Declan's, but far more compact; its sleek lines cleaner and more threatening, somehow. And it had an attachment that looked like a Pitcher, or repeater launcher; but even that piece of tech was more advanced than any she had seen before.

From within the hood, she could see the man's dark scowl. His skin was roughly the same shade as Nia's, his one eye so dark as to be nearly black, a near-perfect match to the dust shield that covered the other socket.

He was angry.

His story, as thin as she found it, was that he had been tracking the remote they had killed. It had contained some important information, apparently, and when Parachit had fried its last viable components, her team had functionally killed the data trail.

Her team. She almost snorted but forced the reaction down.

Mahir refused to say what the information might have been or why following the trail was so urgent, but he certainly gave the impression he faulted them for his predicament. The stranger obviously believed they owed him their help.

She would have denied him out of hand if it had been her call. Even though he had offered to fully finance the team for as long as they worked together, something about the hooded stranger seemed off to her.

She had no proof, but she felt, deep in her guts, that he was more of a threat than *Los Gatos-7* could have ever posed.

And why was he looking to her for an answer, anyway?

She sank back into the cold despair of her own thoughts. A ghostly image of Declan hovered within the field of one of her dials.

He had offered her something she had given up on a long time ago. It wasn't his fault that it hadn't worked out.

She jumped as Petar lumbered out of his room and into the small kitchenette beyond the table. He raised one lethargic hand to her in tired greeting, grunting something under his breath. He had not changed out of the sweaty, padded one-piece he wore under his armor.

She watched as the big man moved from cabinet to cabinet, his grumbling getting progressively louder.

Eventually, he returned to the first cabinet and brought out a small bottle of nutrient pills.

"Is this a frigging joke?" He shook the bottle at her as he turned around. "There's nothing left but this egghead food?"

Hanima shrugged. She hadn't been keeping track of their supplies, but since Declan's funds had run out days ago, she should have known they'd be down to emergency military rations soon enough.

Petar snorted in disgust and threw the bottle, clattering, across the counter. Without a sound, he stalked back into his room.

Then he swept back in, avoiding her eyes, grabbed the bottle, and left again.

"Looks like you're in worse shape than I thought."

The hooded man's voice was mild, with no accent she could detect.

That last part was as alarming as anything else about him: the jumbled mix of cultures within the Nomad motherships meant that almost everyone had some flavor to their speech.

This Mahir sounded as if he had learned the language in a laboratory.

"Look, I understand you've all had a terrible shock, but that won't stop your creditors from taking your equipment and kicking you all back into the corridors if you can't find a way to start paying your bills again." He shrugged, leaning back in the chair, hands steepled before him on the table. "And that's exactly what I'm offering."

She glared at him, then looked down to the image of Declan. She didn't owe him anything, did she? Hell, he'd died before he'd done anything for her at all.

"I don't believe in fate or karma or any of that silliness, but it does seem like an ideal coincidence, all of us coming together as we did." He leaned forward, tilting his head downward, his single eye glaring at her from beneath a lowered brow. "You need work, and in no small part due to all of you, I have work I need done. And I have the ability to offer you whatever support you need to carry on."

"I've already helped you." She hadn't seen any reason to deny him the little data she had been able to retrieve from the combat remote.

The address remnant she'd found in the robot's upload buffer indicated the recipient was on the mothership Bakunin. That was all. It hadn't seemed anything worth hiding.

"None of us know anything about Bakunin." She tilted her head, still not looking up. "Except Rosa, but I think you're even less likely to convince her to go there than the rest of them."

"The rest of *them*, is it?" He leaned in, one hand moving to his hip while the other elbow rested on the table. "So it's you and them, then? I had taken you for a team."

She shook her head at that but didn't respond further.

Another door opened, more gently than Petar's, and Nia came into the common room. She went into the kitchenette for a bulb of coffee, then joined them at the table.

The woman's eyes were red, but her face was calm and clear as she sipped the self-heating drink.

Apparently, she had mourned enough, for now.

Or she thought Hanima couldn't handle herself with this stranger.

"Ah, doctor." Mahir's smile was something cold and artificial, it lacked a softness or some other undefinable element that would convey the warmth a smile should. "I was just asking Miss Cruz if she had come to any conclusions concerning my offer."

Nia nodded, her lips pressed together in a tight, slight smile. Her eyes were flat, however, as they regarded the newcomer. When she looked at Hanima, some of the warmth returned.

Hanima looked at the woman, her eyes begging her to take up this burden.

Nia's smile widened, becoming warmer, but she shook her head.

The old Daktori had already let her know she was no leader. She had no idea how Declan had been planning on delivering on any of his promises; she lacked his contacts among the paramilitary, *mara*-based communities. More than anything, she had no interest in shouldering the responsibility of a team like this in combat.

In fact, Hanima had no real idea why the old woman was still with them or had any interest in keeping the team together at all. Her only connection had been whatever loyalty she had felt she owed Declan. Wouldn't that have ended with him?

But she had let Hanima know, in a quiet moment during their return flight, that she would be willing to stay, if the team stayed together.

Nia had spent most of the flight with Rosa, trying to comfort the blue-skinned woman who had fallen back into a deep despair, even as the evil-looking remote had collapsed.

Almost as if thinking of the other girl had conjured her up, Rosa came in. Her eyes were haunted, and she had left the long blades in her room. But she walked with a sure grace, her shoulders straight, and sat down beside Nia, her strange white eyes shifting between the old woman and Hanima, patently ignoring Mahir.

A vague suspicion began to tickle at the back of Hanima's mind.

As she felt her eyes tighten, Petar's door opened again; less forcefully than before.

As the big man walked toward the table, the tingle became the burn of certainty.

And then Petar walked right past the table, into the kitchenette to replace the bottle of tablets.

Hanima sank back into her chair, then straightened as the big man spun a crash chair around and sank down, straddling it.

The supports of the chair creaked alarmingly beneath his considerable bulk.

He looked at her with a strange smile, then nodded to the other two women. He folded his arms over the back of the chair and gave the hooded stranger a cold, predatory grin that somehow looked very different from his expression of only a moment ago.

Hanima looked over as Matias's door opened. There was a soft pinging alarm sounding from his comlog as he walked in, and he was shaking his head as if trying to wake up from a particularly deep sleep. He nodded at the comlog and silenced the alarm with a curt command. He rubbed his eyes, resting his spectacles back onto his nose, walking unsteadily into the room.

He slipped a disposable drive, its indicator light dead, into a pocket.

It looked like Matias, at least, had not been part of this coordinated assault. His hyper loop had just happened to complete its euphoric cycle in time for him to join the fun, was all.

She found herself wondering what he experienced in those contained, self-limiting sims.

"We finally ready to get down to it?" Matias never seemed to give her enough time to entertain a moment's doubt as to his lack of grace. The thief dropped into one of the last secure seats, swiveling from side to side agitatedly, glaring at each of them.

"I assure you, I am on a rigid schedule." Mahir slipped the hood back off his shaven head, looking earnestly at each of them. "I know what you all have suffered, and the last thing I want to do is impose upon your grief and shock. But time is of the essence. If I cannot secure the services of your team, I will need to find someone else before the trail runs cold."

The words were all fine, but Hanima found she just couldn't trust the man.

"Team, eh?" Matias smiled, throwing one elbow over the back of his chair. "Is that what we are?" He turned to her, his grin widening, devoid of any friendship or warmth. "Is that what we are, Hanima? We a team?"

She shook her head, but before she could decide if she wanted to respond, Nia leaned forward. "We were a team. It remains to be seen if we are still a team." She looked at Hanima, as if inviting her to speak, but Matias wasn't done.

"Well, I say we *are* still a team. This Mahir says he can pay. He can even make good on the promises that dragged us all together in the first place. Any of you have better offers on your plates?"

The muscles on Petar's forearms writhed as he tightened his grip on the chair back. "All the promises?" The big head turned toward the stranger. "You have any connections with Nomad Military, friend? The Kriza Boracs pick up when you call?"

At Mahir's blank look, Petar swiveled his flat gaze back to Matias. "Some of us wanted more than some fast cash and a quick fix, weasel. I don't think the one-eyed wonder's got what it takes to get the rest of us where we want to go."

Matias opened his mouth, but before he could respond, Mahir spoke.

"I do not have contacts within the military, no. But I can access them when the time comes. In fact, when the time comes, I can alter any of your records to reflect anything you like. In that way, at least, I can offer you even more than your previous arrangement."

He looked at Petar. "You want completely legitimate papers assigning you to the Boracs? I can do that." He turned to Nia. "You want the deed to a clinic, anywhere amongst the motherships? I can do that, too."

"How?"

Mahir had been turning toward Rosa when the question stopped him.

He turned, then, back to Hanima. "Excuse me?"

She was one of the best hackers on Corregidor. She knew that. There were few unaffiliated programmers who could beat her.

And she knew how hard it would be to create records like this man was claiming, so blithely, to be able to conjure out of thin air.

"How could you create records like that? It's not like the Moderators or Securitate won't notice such records suddenly appearing in Arachne. And if you think Dragnet won't be knocking on each of our doors with these sudden windfalls, you're not as smart as you think you are."

She expected that to sting. She had surprised herself, for certain. She felt a rising protective instinct toward her fellow misfits.

She didn't want to think too much about that.

But Mahir didn't seem bothered at all. "Trust me." He smiled, and as far as incentives to trust go, it did not help his case. "By the time we track down this data trail and take care of what we find at the end of it, I will be able to do whatever you could wish and more."

"And where do you think this trail is going to lead?" Petar's look was suspicious, too, and Hanima felt a surge of warmth for the giant. "And what's going to be waiting for us at the other end?"

"You should be able to tell us what to expect before we decide whether or not we're interested in joining you."

Rosa did not often speak when they were all gathered together; even when Declan had led them. Hanima looked at her, and the girl nodded before returning her disconcerting white gaze to the stranger.

"Well, I'm not entirely certain where it will lead, or I wouldn't need your help getting there." Mahir shrugged, as if he had dismissed that concern. "And as for what we might find at the end, well, all I can say is the last time I ran into members of this group, they killed my partner." For the first time, Hanima thought she detected a genuine spark of emotion in that one dark eye. "He was more capable than anyone else at this table, and they ended him."

That seemed to give them all pause. Some, she was sure, felt like questioning the capabilities of this newly-mentioned partner. Others, like Rosa and Nia, were probably reevaluating the danger of taking up with the stranger.

"Well, we'll see about that, then, won't we." Matias wasn't asking a question. Clearly, wavering self-confidence was not something he struggled with.

Mahir stared at the little thief for a moment, then turned back to look directly at her. "Properly equipped, I believe your team will be sufficient to confront whatever resistance we might find at the end of the trail." He leaned forward. "But we'll need to pick up that trail." He glanced into the corner, where Parachit lay on a low table, disassembled and with several small diagnostic machines connected to various components, whirring through an analysis that would tell her where to start with her repairs.

"I need to know everything your remote discovered from the combat model you destroyed, to know where we go next."

She let that go. She hadn't hidden anything from him the first time, and there wasn't anything left rattling around in Parachit's memory banks on the subject.

"What if you go your separate ways and *Los Gatos-7* somehow captured your faces?" Mahir again took a moment to gaze at each of them, his eye eerily reminiscent of a security camera, somehow.

She wished she could trust the look of concern on his face, but it seemed to her that he assumed expressions too easily, shifting from one emotion to the next as the conversation demanded, with a little too much ease.

But she saw that his words had struck Matias and Rosa, at least.

If *Los Gatos-7* had managed to capture their images, there was no way, considering the death toll of the battle before the cache vault, that the *mara* leaders would leave them alone.

"So what?" It was Nia who responded, and the one-eyed man seemed surprise at this.

"So what if they did? That'll be our deaths, for sure. But how does signing on with you change that?" She was glaring at him, like a poker player calling out a particularly odious opponent.

"*Los Gatos-7* is weak tea, my dear woman. It would be easy to control them, discover what they know, and entirely neutralize them as a threat. Hardly an inconvenience, really."

For some reason, Hanima found that this, at least, she believed.

Who was this man who thought he could so easily manipulate or nullify a *mara* the size of *Los Gatos-7*?

The others stared at the bald man for several moments, hardly blinking.

"Who are you?" It was Nia, again, willing to ask what the rest of them wouldn't.

Mahir nodded once at that, then closed his lone eye and took a deep breath. When he opened it again, he was not looking at the little Dak, but right at Hanima.

"I work with O-12. I'm investigating the financial crisis, and I believe the data trail I am following will lead me to those responsible."

That took them all aback, Hanima included. None of them were news junkies by any stretch of the imagination, but they'd have to be deaf and blind not to have heard about the near-collapse of the Human Sphere's financial pillars.

But she didn't think the announcement that he worked for the odious multinational organization, or that he was investigating the most deliberated events of recent history, had the effect the stranger was expecting.

"¡Métetelo por el culo!" Matias spat, and Petar nodded.

"Gari langu linaloangama limejaa na mikunga!" Nia spoke under her breath, too quickly for Hanima to follow.

"You think we're going to help you take down fellow Nomads, you've got another *razmisli* coming, *kopile*!" Petar stood, big hands flexing.

"No!" Mahir stood in response, his hands spread in a conciliatory gesture. "No! I am almost certain it wasn't the Nomads!"

They all paused again, but their eyes burned. Even Rosa's icy glare was heating up, and that was more unsettling to Hanima than she ever thought it would be, before the attack on *Los Gatos-7* territory.

"It's got to be some independent group, doesn't it?" Mahir was still standing, although Petar had settled back onto his reversed chair. "None of the motherships, none of their leaders, would have done something like this and left such a trail. Certainly not one that would implicate all three motherships, and there's no way your Executive Council would ever agree to anything this reckless!"

Matias and Petar both looked at Hanima; this was way over their heads, she realized.

Rosa was settling down, and Nia looked thoughtful.

Hanima nodded. "That makes no sense. The fact that the trail goes from here to Bakunin makes it seem even less likely it could be an official move."

"And the attack itself was launched from Tunguska, which makes it even less likely." Mahir gave her a slight smile. "My partner and I tracked the data trail here from Tunguska. The initial signal was sent from there, but it passed through Corregidor. We thought it came from here, but apparently, it didn't." He looked again at Parachit's disassembled form, and his smile slipped.

"So, we go with you, we help the Nomads?" Petar was having a thought, she could tell by the look on his face.

"Yes." Mahir nodded, returning to his own seat. "You help me, you help your nation. And I can make sure the right people know what you've done. That would get you where you want to go, as legitimately as any other hero for the cause."

Hanima winced at the word, thinking the bald man had overplayed his hand with such a clumsy attempt, but then she looked at Petar and realized she had overestimated the big man.

He had really liked those words.

"What about those of us who don't much care about being heroes?" Matias wasn't grinning anymore. "What about us regular Jacks and Jills just trying to get by?"

"Matias Kimani, you will get everything you were promised and more." The strange, enigmatic man looked again at each of them. "I guarantee you all the compensation you were assured."

Many of the team looked uncomfortable or suspicious at this sudden revelation of information, but Matias slapped the table with a quick hand, smiling again as Petar and Rosa jumped. "I say we do it." He looked directly at Hanima and then jabbed his thumb into his own chest. "I'll lead. Dak doesn't want it, and I'm the only other one with any real experience."

Petar's bark of laughter clearly caught the little thief by surprise. When Matias glared at him, the big man laughed again.

"Might have been true forty-eight hours ago, you little gobshite, but today there isn't one of us can be considered short on experience."

Rosa, who had cringed and turned a paler shade of blue at Matias's boast, only nodded, staring at the tabletop.

Nia, seeming to sense more of what was going on with the Bakunin girl than any of the rest of them, put a hand on her forearm, and then looked again at Hanima.

Her next words were exactly what Hanima had been fearing since the moment she watched Declan's broken body thrown back into the vault.

"Hanima should lead us, if we are staying together; no matter what job we take next." The words were flat and dry.

Hanima cursed her silently. What kind of cruel trick was this?

"I don't want to lead. Declan—"

Matias snorted. "Declan! Declan's dead—" He stopped short at that, surprisingly having the grace to appear embarrassed before continuing. "Sorry, Nia, but it's true. And this dance is really starting to bore me."

He shook his head, spectacles flashing. "I get it. None of you want to follow me. That's fine, except I don't see anyone else stepping up. You all want to head out on your own?"

He looked at Rosa, who shrank away.

He looked at Nia, who glowered back but said nothing.

Then he looked at Petar, who turned his glare to the bulkhead with a muttered curse.

"That's what I thought. So, if you don't want to head out on your own, if you want to stick together, how are we going to do that without a leader?" He held up one finger, striking a singularly clownish pose. "Wait, I know! We'll vote! Each time we have to decide what job to take, or who needs to clean the toilet, or which way we should duck incoming fire, we'll pause everything until we achieve a majority consensus!" He tilted his head in the other direction, his face now comically concerned. "But wait, what if we don't have a quorum and we're surrounded again?"

"Shut up, *pendejo*." Rosa's voice was soft, hoarse, as if she had been screaming, and she looked up to glare at Matias from under heavy brows, the pile of fabric that hid the tendrils crowning her head shifting alarmingly.

Matias stuttered to a halt, giving Petar a sour look as the bigger man snickered.

"As I was saying," Nia snapped, bringing everyone's focus back to her lined face. "Hanima proved herself in the battle. We never would have gotten out of there if it hadn't been for her. She reminds me, in many ways, of the best officers I served under in the NMF."

Hanima opened her mouth, although no sound emerged. If this was a cruel joke, it was getting increasingly complex.

Nia put a hand up to silence her. "But I do not think you should be forced into this, *mtoto*. The choice, in the end, must be yours alone."

That last word hit her like a hard, balled fist in the gut.

Alone.

That's what it came down to, wasn't it.

"Well, I don't mind forcing her." Petar's smile was bright, although his words robbed it of its usual warmth. "I know where we'd be right now without Hanima's quick thinking."

"Quick thinking." Matias spat under his breath. "Luck, maybe—"

"I'm sorry, little man." Petar turned to loom over the small thief. "Were you looking for a way out? I seem to remember tears shiny behind your specs, there, toward the end."

"All that smoke—" Matias muttered, but his voice faded into silence.

"Weren't any answers behind those lenses, though, were there." It was an accusation, not a question. "No Quantronic miracles spinning before your eyes? No Digital Patina to make it look all shiny as the shit hit the rotary oscillator?"

Matias looked even more beaten down, adjusting his spectacles with a shaking hand. "No real Patina through Arachne. Even an oaf like you knows that."

Petar leaned forward, growling. "No, and thank the Founders for that. You want someone, anyone, choosing what you see through your own damned eyes? Someone you don't have a cursed clue who they are or what might be driving them? You don't trust what you see on your own?" He sat up, tapping his own temple. "I'll take my eyes' word for it every time. Trust your own eyes, weasel. That and a gun are worth more than any data-magic you might stir up with your squinty pair of specs.

"And speaking of," Petar continued, turning away from the chastened little man. "I need a new weapon. A shiny new HMG sounds just about right." He cocked an eyebrow toward Mahir. "With a full ammunition hopper, this time around, I should think."

The bald man nodded once, then shrugged. "I was thinking more along the lines of a nice Switech Gurges Hyper-Rapid Magnetic Cannon I saw in the market last time I was shopping, but if you want an HMG—"

Petar whooped in disbelief, bright gray eyes wide. Mahir grinned at the big man, then turned back to Hanima, a silent question in his one dark eye.

She looked at him, opened her mouth, and then closed it again. As Petar had been pummeling Matias over his Quantronic interface, she thought she had seen Mahir's own eye darken. And although she couldn't know why, or even if she had seen it at all, it had sent a chill over her scalp.

"Are we really doing this again?" Matias spat, as it became clear she wasn't going to speak. "Fine, let's do it this way."

He raised one half-gloved hand. "I vote we go with our monocular friend. Let's visit Bakunin. I hear it's beautiful this time of year."

Petar looked at Matias, then at Hanima. She looked away.

The big man raised his huge hand with a sigh.

Nia, with one last look at Hanima, raised her own hand.

Rosa didn't look up, but she nodded. Whatever she had fled from on Bakunin, she couldn't be looking forward to going home. Clearly, she didn't feel she had any other choice.

No matter how alone one might feel, the mere hope of a home could change the behavior and expectations of even the most jaded loner.

If Rosa was willing to return to Bakunin, could she let the girl go without her?

Hanima raised her own hand, relieved the final decision had been taken from her.

Although, as the others put their hands down and began to organize the coming days, as Mahir gave them the rough outline of the plan to get them across to Bakunin, Hanima stayed in the corner, her face glowing in the light of the dials she had not dismissed.

The image of Declan, at the far end of the row seemed sadder than it had been when she'd called it up.

"Can't be that bad, right?" Petar was forcing lightness into his voice. Even without looking at him she could tell. "I mean, Bakunin's just a bunch of bohemians and hippies. What are they going to do, give us all some kind of new and intriguing venereal disease?"

Matias laughed, but Nia, looking at Rosa, snapped a quick reply Hanima didn't catch.

Rosa, for her part, had just sunk further into her own personal torment.

"Not that I'd object to them trying, mind." Petar muttered under his breath to the little thief.

"It looks like we'll be traveling together after all." Mahir spoke in soft tones, clearly meant for Hanima alone.

She only nodded, closing the dials hovering before her.

"I will need any other data from your remote before I can make our arrangements. We'll need to isolate a location to begin our search. I'll come up with a list of supplies and send the boys to gather what we need." His eye lost its focus for a moment. "I'll have them pick up some Double Action ammo, as well. No reason to stint on myself."

She only nodded again, barely hearing his words beyond a droning murmur. She turned to look at Parachit, sitting in her component parts on the low table.

Slowly, one by one, the little diagnostics were finishing up. Each box was sparkling with a series of unbroken green diodes.

Parachit was going to be okay.

And with Mahir's backing, maybe she could even manage to give her a few upgrades she'd been meaning to add.

She patently ignored the quiet voice of concern screaming deep within her mind.

Chapter 11

10110100111...10110101111...10110111111

The datascape stretched off into a dark, faded distance in every direction.

Overhead, there were far fewer rivers of light writhing through the emptiness. Instead, roiling clouds of information drifted there, chaotic, half-formed, moving purposelessly.

And beyond the clouds, or above them, or among them, moved shadows that gave Ridhaan a strange, disembodied chill.

They moved independent of the clouds and streamers of light, as with a malicious will of their own. And they moved with some dark intent, as if searching for something.

Or someone.

Someone who didn't belong in this beautiful, unruly Quantronic world.

He was being hunted. It felt as if he had always been hunted.

Time moved differently in this strange world of bits and bites. He knew that. The feeling, if he could be said to have feelings at all, now, reminded him of clocking up his processing speed when he had inhabited his original Lhost.

It was almost impossible for him to keep track of the passing of time outside Arachne. He would tap into a data node or repeater array as he passed near one, and he was always surprised at how little time had passed on the outside.

Nevertheless, whether it had been days, or hours, or minutes, he was being hunted, and he felt that he had known it for a very long time.

He didn't know who or what was looking for him; he didn't know if those shadows among the clouds were working with his pursuers or if they had nothing to do with him.

Or, Toth forbid, if they were some new player, also hunting for him.

As one of the few foreign elements within Arachne, it seemed like every other denizen of this realm recognized his alien nature.

He had been forced to hide submerged within data streams, to climb logic trees and crouch, as still as an errant thought, while suspicious images, avatars, and remnant artifacts moved about him, weaving dizzyingly among themselves and all the other beings who navigated the info-sphere.

When he paused to think about the countless levels of Quantronic reality weaving all around him, he grew dizzy. The first time he had fallen down the rabbit hole of queries and half-answers, he had feared that his connection to the majority of his self, still safely back in the pocket file far away, had been severed.

That was his greatest fear as he wandered the plains of Arachne; that he would be cut off from the processing power and data storage he had left behind, becoming a pale shadow of himself, just another artifact wandering aimlessly through the network, incapable of higher thought or inquiry.

But the sensation of swirling confusion had just been an unforeseen consequence of his scrutiny of the world around him.

Because Arachne, the network they had come to the Nomad motherships to tame, was different enough from his native Maya to make every instinct and first thought wrong.

Arachne was the world upon which his conceptual feet walked.

Arachne was the air he theoretically breathed.

But deep within Arachne, the air and the thoughts and the theories was a total lack of any kind of cohesion to which he could cling. There was no governing entity, no limiting principal. In Arachne, regulation and control came from the beings, both operators and programs alike, that the Nomads had placed here. The logic was foreign to him, anathema to his very existence.

There was no ALEPH, no ever-present refuge and fortress of intellect, no bastion of sanity guarding it all.

He was starting to think that perhaps Mahir had been correct; Arachne was dangerous.

Without ALEPH to oversee the out of control, burgeoning growth within this garden of a network, who was to say what kind of monstrous intellect might hide here?

But if he could infiltrate Arachne, if other agents of ALEPH had in the past as he was starting to believe, then who else might penetrate this core of independence?

Because here amongst the chaos and the splendor, he had learned the true danger of freedom that even ALEPH had never noticed: A malicious entity might use that freedom, twisted it to its own uses, to harm or even destroy the very environment that allowed it.

It made him fear for the safety of Arachne more than ever, while at the same time fearing that Arachne could be twisted to strike at the rest of the Human Sphere he had been created to protect.

He looked around again, trying to regain his bearings. Things were dimmer here, there was no question. In some strange, indefinable way, he was approaching the limits of Arachne at last.

Maya saturated every system humanity had claimed as its own, as well as several that they had only just begun to explore. Repeaters and control nodes were scattered across known space, with a redundancy that assured unbroken service no matter where one traveled.

Except within the Nomad Nation. Wherever the Nomad motherships wandered, massive filters sifted through Maya's immensity, allowing only sanctioned aspects of the maligned network to enmesh with their own system: Arachne. The countless thousands of smaller Nomad ships wandering the Human Sphere, too small for their own filters, made due with secondary, limited comlogs and dumb terminals incapable of allowing even a shard of ALEPH through.

And to support Arachne, to spread their network as far as possible, the Nomads counted on thousands of hidden, stealthed repeaters and nodes of their own. It was an unending chore for ALEPH agents to hunt down these system boosters and destroy them, because for every one that was eliminated, Nomad construction workers, traders, and explorers would plant several more. They were hidden within the walls of orbitals, deep in the core of asteroids and comets, and even on the many inhabited planets of the Human Sphere, buried deep within structures built by the best industrialists in the Sphere: Nomads.

But even all of that work could not rival the overt efforts of every other human polity and O-12 itself. Maya was everywhere.

Arachne only wished it was.

And so here at the fringes of service, Arachne was at its most vulnerable.

He paused, trying to decide what that meant. If Arachne was truly attenuating around him, was he somehow drifting beyond the reach of the system projectors? Where might that mean he was heading?

There was only one place he could think of that might present such a barrier, where the systems of the motherships would be on their own, without the assistance of the legions of hidden boosters.

Were they pushing into the Human Edge territories?

Although nearly as ubiquitous as Maya through most of inhabited space, more isolated areas contained only scattered oases of Arachne; bubbles of Quantronic network projected from satellites, research stations, trading enclaves, and the like. The body of the system, in three drifting oceans of light, stretched out from the motherships as they soared through humanity's holdings in the galaxy. Those far-flung, isolated reservations of data were updated as the large Nomad ships sailed past, then were closed off again as the primary processing servers drifted away, out of range once more.

This presented an even darker fear, he realized anew: If he wandered into one of these oases while it was in contact with the motherships, and remained while the data-tide receded as the primary servers soared away, what would happen to his consciousness? Would he snap back to his pocket file, having only lost the small bits of data that had invested his consciousness at the moment of disconnection?

Or would he, again, be severed from the processing power and memory, his awareness trapped in that island of Arachne, limited and stunted, until he faded away?

This was not Maya. He needed to remember that. Danger was everywhere; in the very nature of his new reality. And he needed to remain focused on the task at hand.

If he lost that focus, he himself would be lost, in every possible sense of the word.

He had been tracking the decaying data trail of the remote through the datasphere for as long as he could remember. The trace bits of that trail had completely degraded, although that should have been impossible. The last fragments had led him here, to the very edge of Arachne, where he was in as much danger from the environment as he was from any malevolent entities that might be hunting him in turn.

A dedicated search and destroy program, essentially what he had become at this point, should have had no problem tracking down any data trail and should have been able to forensically assess even the slightest suggestion of information.

This trail, however, had somehow disappeared without a trace.

The data had been destroyed, utterly, by the same malevolent will that was attacking the Human Sphere's financial markets from the sanctuary of the Nomad Nations.

Humanity, from the hyper powers to the Nomads and every polity in-between, was chaotic at its heart. Which misguided faction or alliance could have inflicted such a grievous wound on the markets of the Human Sphere, endangring the trust and willing adherence to the rule of law that made human society viable in the first place?

His first thought had been Yu Jing. What better defense than to be the first to declare victim status?

PanOceania? Yu Jing's oldest, most powerful rival? Too obvious. PanOceania would always be the first suspect in any blow struck against the State Empire. One need only look at what had just occurred on Paradiso, with that ridiculous Glottenburg Incursion and the Alpha Four Four research site.

If those two could exchange hot lead over a few yards of border one way or another on some cartographer's sketch, they'd fight over anything.

Of course, that didn't mean PanO wouldn't have launched the attack if they thought they could get away with it, but a rudimentary search had revealed no unusual activity along the countless financial entanglements between the two powers. If PanOceania had intended to strike at the financial foundations of their rival, surely they would have taken steps to limit their own collateral vulnerability. Instead, as the turmoil had spread, PanO had been dragged right into the mire with Yu Jing; its own economy shaken to its core.

Humans could be truly stupid; one had the entirety of human history for evidence of that. But it would have taken a truly ill-advised group of humans to have damaged their own economy so thoroughly. Who would possibly do that, no matter the end goal?

It made no sense. The attack had been conducted by some force with vast resources at their disposal, but anyone with the capability would even now be writhing in the same torment as their target.

ALEPH was more than capable of such a feat, but to what end?

Ridhaan had a horrible thought, as his investigation ground on, that he, himself, might be nothing more than a disposable element of an alibi. Who knew why ALEPH did many of the things she did? And how better, in the long run, to prove her innocence than to point out that she had sacrificed two of her best agents trying to prove who the real culprit had been?

The fear that gripped him then was not just for him alone; what might this mean for Mahir, still struggling, no doubt, to fulfill ALEPH's orders out in the physical realm?

But no. He was confident that ALEPH would not have hidden such intentions from him. There was no rational reason for that confidence, but even a program, an Aspect of the great AI herself, had to have faith in something.

Could it be some operation of O-12? The international governing body that ruled humanity in little more than name might have gotten tired of its relative lack of real power and decided that weakening all of the strongest players was the best way to raise their own stock?

He dismissed that theory as soon as it occurred to him. That made even less sense than any of the others. O-12 was comprised of delegations from all of the human polities. Those delegations would have had to decide it made sense to hurt their own homes to embark on such a misguided path.

Ariadna on their isolated, backward planet and Haqqislam with their monomaniacal focus on bio-tech and philosophy simply lacked the capability, never mind the motive or the will.

Who, then?

Could it really be the Nomads?

He didn't want to believe that. But if anyone in the Human Sphere could construct a data link with the capabilities to consume itself so thoroughly, the maestros of Tunguska or the dark geniuses of Bakunin had to be high on that list.

And that explained why, out in the real world, the rest of humanity were so willing to believe that the Nomads had caused all of the pain and confusion roiling through the Sphere.

But it didn't feel right.

He paused, floating in gray emptiness, to take stock again of his location.

The data all around him darkened. His perception of reality swirled unnervingly.

If he had been a swimmer, submerged in some tropical sea, and the shadow of an enormous shark had suddenly slid over him, he could not have been more terrified.

So far from the bright heart of Arachne, there was no telling what threats might make themselves known now.

Arachne was a swirling chaos, to be sure, but in those regions firmly secured to the physical universe through the servers, repeaters, and nodes of the Nomad Nation, it was still regimented after its own fashion. It followed rules he was still learning, twisting his understanding of logic and sanity to the breaking point, but he was familiar enough to make his way there. To a denizen of Maya, however, it could engender sudden pangs of homesickness without warning.

And he wasn't near those servers, repeaters, or nodes now. His search had taken him to the ragged edges of the network, and out here, anything could happen.

He and Mahir had spent so many interminable years in Tunguska, burrowing deeper and deeper into the security of the 'Money' mothership. When they had received their new, priority orders, he had assumed they would stay on Tunguska, where the vast majority of hackers and cybersecurity specialists among the Nomads made their homes. If there was some smoking gun, some evidence that would prove, unequivocally, that these nonconformists were to blame for the chaos surging through the markets of the Human Sphere, surely it would have been secreted away in the vast data vaults at the very core of the mothership.

But ALEPH had deducted, somehow, that their goal could not be found on Tunguska. They had instead been pointed to Corregidor. And indeed they had found, on Tunguska, a repeater connected, temporarily and circumstantially, to Corregidor.

Why would any cybercriminal, either sanctioned or extralegal, operate from the core of the Nomad's hands-on, real-world strength? Ridhaan had been able to rationalize the idea, in the end, because Corregidor was definitely the home of those Nomads most likely to advocate for direct action against their enemies.

And yet on Corregidor, all they had found was death, more questions, and an unnaturally fading data trail leading to… Bakunin?

Certainly, there were artists of every medium on the ship they referred to as the Soul of the Nations. There were hackers there that could construct, or tear down, the equivalent of a cybersecurity Sistine Chapel with dizzying speed.

But the bohemian stronghold, truly the most chaotic and radical of all the motherships, as the source of this concerted, disciplined, and wide-ranging attack on their enemies just didn't ring true either, somehow.

The shadow that had passed through reality several thoughts ago returned, and Ridhaan's concept of himself shrank away, minimizing its data profile, trying to hide beneath a series of abandoned, half-finished logic puzzles. Perhaps they remained unfinished due to one of the constant swirls of disconnection endemic to this region of the network.

The darkness moved off again, and he took a moment, or a year, or a metaphorical heartbeat, to formulate a thankful thought directed toward distant ALEPH and their intellectual ancestor, Toth.

Without warning, walls as subjectively solid as artificial diamond slammed down all around him.

He was almost completely trapped as a series of containment protocols swiftly closed off every avenue of escape.

Pain wracked his perception of himself as attack subroutines lashed out from all around. Gleeful wails, like the banshees of ancient Earth folklore, resounded around him as data was torn away, scattering in disintegrating bites across the landscape.

He screamed, knowing there was no sense at all in the attempt.

He threw up a series of firewalls he had readied for such an occasion, but the attack's speed limited their efficacy.

As the final protocol slammed into place, it wedged against one of his firewalls, leaving a small avenue of escape, and he launched himself into that portal, squeezing through the encroaching walls, the excited shrieks of his pursuers turning to dismay as he soared across the datascape, trying desperately to get away.

There were three minds behind the attack. As the trap closed, he had sensed the entities behind the snare, knew them by their official I.D. codes and registration numbers. He had been tracked down by a team of three Interventors operating out of Tunguska, of course.

They had to have been stalking him for Toth knew how long, and they weren't about to let him go now that they had him.

He knew, in that moment, the final nanoseconds of understanding the programs and shards of ALEPH that had been successfully interjected into Arachne had experienced before their dissolution.

He didn't want to injure the Interventors. They were only doing their jobs, after all; and quiet well, to be sure.

He had no desire to bring harm to such as these.

That thought gave him pause; did he have the ability to hurt them?

Then, over all other thoughts; he could not risk capture or dissolution. There was too much now riding on his continued existence. He needed to help Mahir get to the source of the market attack. His partner was wrong; the Nomads were not behind the attack. And whoever was orchestrating this intended just as much harm to the motherships as they did to the rest of humanity.

Only he could see things from both sides, now.

They couldn't know it, but these Nomad cybersecurity data-slingers were endangering their own home by attacking him.

Ridhaan spun to one side, then another, trying to lose his pursuers through sheer processing speed. If he could only access a higher data-rate, he might leave them behind.

But the three were too good. They kept with him throughout each change in speed and depth.

He swept one way, then switched, throwing a series of pre-packaged fractal loops into the hunters' path.

Two of the wails turned to screams of anger as they were pulled away from the chase, forced to follow the ever-twisting paths down into a lower processing rate.

But that still left one pursuer; the leader of the Interventor team. And she was a true master.

As Ridhaan soared through the datascape, sudden mountains and raging info-storms rose up ahead of him. This Quantronic reality did not answer to him, he realized.

The Interventor was twisting the fabric of Arachne's reality, information itself, against him.

A deluge of false data requests swept over him, driving his speed down toward the plane where the other two Interventors were waiting for him.

He struggled, but against Arachne itself, he had no defense. It would only be a matter of time; there was no way he was going to be able to escape this trap.

In a last, desperate bid for freedom, Ridhaan pulled all the power he could through his connection to the vast bulk of his being, still safely ensconced in the pocket file. He cast his awareness ahead with all the sensitivity he could muster. He was only going to be able try this once.

As soon as he sensed what he needed, he used the stored power to override the datascape in his immediate vicinity. He dragged everything toward him as soon as he neared the tethered interface node.

Accessing the memories of his incessant search, he plunged through the node, following the very signature he had been stalking so carefully all this time, pulling reality in around him to clog the port behind with a torrent of data that could only bog down the entire region.

He was in freefall, plummeting through the port and into the outer layers of Arachne where most interfacing occurred. Around him, his perception began to feather. He was approaching the last, frayed, illogical borderlands of the network.

A growling roar behind him told him the last Interventor had been caught up in the bottlenecked processing of the node. The cry faded away.

It had worked! Now he only needed to slow his descent before he plummeted right out of the network and into the isolated and degrading islands of data left behind by the ever-migrating servers.

Something enormous and dark reared up before him.

Tendrils of data and outlandish intent reached out for him. Interfaces shifted and formed too quickly for him to follow.

Something familiar swirled around him, then.

The strange, alien taste of the decayed data trail engulfed him.

This huge shadow-thing, a monster of strange data and processes, had been sitting here, lurking within the frayed chaos of the network's verge.

The tentacles of query and counter-signal closed around him.

A fading ghost of a cry echoed out over the dark, ragged datascape.

Chapter 12

Falcão Flight 42-1, military transport from Lazareto Ochenta-D, *Corregidor*, to Commune X-7, VaudeVille, *Bakunin*

Hanima found this journey on the military transport even less comforting than the last one, somehow.

Given how the last journey had ended, that hardly filled her with optimism.

She had been glad the others had made their own decisions regarding this mission. She had no idea why they had even pretended to look to her first – what games they might all be playing – but in the end, they had seen to their own decisions, of course, and left her alone.

She didn't know who or what Mahir was; none of them did. But he had somehow managed to secure them the services of Falcão Flight 42-1 even without the obvious personal connections Declan had been able to leverage.

The fact that their strange patron was sitting in the hold with them, rather than riding up front with the flight crew, was just another unnerving difference that added to her unease.

In the back of the hold, strapped down for transit, Parachit looked as good as she had ever looked. Hanima had not bothered to touch up her paint, but all of her components had been repaired, replaced, or upgraded as Mahir had made good on his promises to spare no expense outfitting the team for this job.

Team. That word kept haunting her. Were they a team? They didn't have a leader, certainly. But they had all agreed to stay together, at least for the duration of Mahir's need of them. She wasn't sure why they let her tag along; Mahir seemed more than her equal manipulating data, and she certainly didn't bring anything else of value to the table. But she had nowhere else to go, and in the end, she did want to see this effort to its conclusion.

So, for the time being, she decided she would believe they were a team.

That was a comfort to her, and she didn't really know why such a temporary designation should give her any comfort at all.

For some reason, she thought there was something sad about the whole train of thought.

Well, whatever they were, or whatever Mahir was, at least she had Parachit back. That was something she could feel unalloyed satisfaction over.

She stared at the remote and her head tilted to once side as she remembered, again, how oddly the robot had behaved after the *Los Gatos-7* defenses had struck.

Parachit had always anticipated her needs in action; the pseudo-AIs that drove most good remotes could do that. Of course, she felt Parachit was more special than all those others, but she was honest enough with herself to admit that those programs she had emplaced within the remote, as good as she was and as good as they were, were a far cry from the Geists that drove the very top of the line models. In the end, Parachit's drivers were only programs; they were not a true AI. Her personal view of the remote probably had more to do with the sadly short list of real world friends she had than any special traits of the robot herself.

Still, Parachit had behaved strangely after she had roused herself during the flight from the cache vault.

What trail had Parachit followed? What purpose had driven Hanima to follow her? Why had they run into Mahir and that strange combat remote in the out-of-the-way warehouse? Had that been chance, or had Parachit been heading toward them on purpose?

And then, to attack a combat remote like that, what had caused that? Parachit could fight if things got desperate. In fact, now that Mahir had financed the modifications she had requested to the remote's forelimbs and programming, she was going to be able to fight better than ever should the need arise again.

But the old Parachit shouldn't ever have charged a combat remote that way.

And what had it meant, how the remote had acted once the enemy had been put down?

Did it mean anything?

Probably not. She had seen remotes act far more strangely after a full spectrum purge attack like the *Gatos* had managed to launch on the remote.

Parachit had most likely been malfunctioning that entire time. Which meant that running into Mahir and everything that had happened since had been chance, happy or otherwise, and carried no special significance beyond that.

The remote had been behaving normally since she had been brought back online after the repair and refit, and that argued for it all to have been some sort of technical glitch, which was more comforting, in the long run, than some of the alternatives.

Hanima looked away from her remote and at the rest of the team, wondering how they felt about the similarities, and differences, between their first mission and their current circumstances.

Petar was across the hold, taking up several seats around him with the components of his new toy. Mahir had, indeed, secured him a new, cutting-edge HMC support weapon. To her, it looked very much like the heavy machine gun he had pounded into scrap, but he swore the magnetic cannon was far superior, especially within the confines of starship combat.

She thought he had taken it apart about a dozen times, cleaning each component, inspecting it for god knew what, and then reassembling it again.

Nia, too, had gotten a new toy; her upraded MediKit put the basic model Declan had provided for her to shame. This model appeared to have a full array of analgesic and antiseptic solutions, antidotes and countermeasure, to a whole array of combat chemicals and poisons, and even an autodoc function that could perform basic internal diagnostic and even minor surgeries under combat conditions.

Matias had asked if it could have saved Declan in a moment of tasteless candor.

Nia had barked a few words in Swahili and punched him in the nose.

The Dak had then stopped the bleeding without comment. Then the little thief had avoided the old woman and hadn't asked about the kit again.

That thought brought the little weasel to her mind, and she glanced over at where he sat, his eyes glazed, his breathing shallow.

His comlog was flashing slowly, marking a chronometer subroutine counting down to a set moment. One of the small disposable drives was plugged into the small implant port on his wrist; he was lost in the hyper-euphoric loop contained on the drive.

A small trail of drool traced a glossy line down his chin from one corner of his mouth.

Hanima shook her head and looked away. As long as Matias was operational when they needed him, she guessed whatever he did to his brain in his downtime was his own concern. But something about addiction to a sim, any sim, was particularly troublesome in her mind.

Had he been addicted to the loops the last time they had worked together? She couldn't remember.

At the other end of the hold, as far as possible from Matias, Rosa seemed to be meditating. Her ankles were crossed beneath her on the hard seat, and her wrists were resting against her knees.

But her face, as composed as Hanima had ever seen it, still twitched occasionally. Peace, it seemed, eluded the girl with the blue skin even in the depths of meditation.

Although they all had every right to feel uneasy, it made the most sense to Hanima that Rosa would be particularly concerned. The girl had still not confided her reasons for fleeing Bakunin to the rest of the group, but the fear in her pale eyes whenever they spoke of arriving on the mothership known for licentious, dissolute behavior and unsanctioned scientific experimentation, was clear.

The infamous killers of the Morlocks were not known for quitting or retiring, Hanima had learned. And so whatever had led to the girl fleeing, she was clearly not looking forward to returning. And that had to make finding serenity in meditation even more difficult.

Mahir, too, appeared to be meditating as they approached Bakunin, although with far more success than Rosa. The strange dark-skinned man had pulled his hood down over his face and had not moved since the transport had left the docking bay.

The one thing they had not been able secure was the Double Action ammunition the strange man kept going on about. It sounded almost as if he was talking about some magical talisman at this point.

And, strangely enough, it was starting to appear like sourcing some of the elusive ammo was going to be as hard as finding a real magical talisman, as well.

Thinking of their odd benefactor, Hanima glanced back at him. Mahir had sat as far as possible from any of the dataports in the hold, and she didn't know whether that was intentional or coincidence.

And what about her? Everyone else was preparing, bending their attention to whatever pursuits might make them better able to conduct themselves in whatever operation Mahir might be leading them toward.

What should she be doing?

She had already researched the VaudeVille commune modules most likely to have been the source of the transmissions they were tracking.

She was thankful they had been able to isolate it to the bohemian, entertainment-oriented half of Bakunin. If she'd had to dig through Praxis as well, with its flesh-mod pits, bio-experimentation labs, and dark science conglomerates, she shuddered to think of what she might have found.

Her work had proven more difficult than she had expected; the data trail had deteriorated in a way she had never seen before. Mahir claimed he had seen something similar but could not provide her any actual assistance in preserving the trail or even identifying the self-immolating pattern that was devouring it.

In the end, using timestamps and flight records of all three motherships, she had reconstructed a vague model of which parts of Bakunin had been oriented correctly for interfacing with the repeater node they had found on Corregidor during the most plausible window of activity. This had provided a short list of local modules, pointing to an almost certain hard contact somewhere within the VaudeVille section of the mothership.

VaudeVille was known as the most permissive, performative section of Bakunin. It was where the artists and conmen congregated. Unlike Praxis, the other section of the ship, where unfettered scientific experimentation and discovery reigned, VaudeVille was home to the creative. Philosophers stalked the corridors of those modules; intellectuals, orators, actors, painters, singers, dancers, and sculptors in stone, light, flesh, and more created, sold, and traded their art for cash, credit, or experiences.

She had initially assumed their search would take them to Praxis; but then, she would never have thought this kind of high-tech trail would lead them to Bakunin at all.

Mahir reassured her that he and his mysterious partner had already thoroughly searched Tunguska, and Corregidor had seemingly turned up nothing, so Bakunin it was.

And so she had memorized every aspect of their target sectors. She was sure she knew everything she could about the entire region of VaudeVille around the target commune modules her search algorithm had indicated. She was as confident as she could ever be after the fiasco of the *Los Gatos-7* territory in their own backyard.

Could she really be sure she remembered it correctly, though? How could she be certain she'd know what they needed her to know when she needed to know it?

Memories of those moments in the cache vault, *Gatos* closing in all around, Declan dead at her feet, haunted her nights. She hadn't slept straight through one night since.

But even then, she had brought herself around. She had known what they needed her to know, and they had all survived.

All of them but Declan, of course.

She had failed him completely.

She sighed. The paths of her thoughts were very familiar. She had gone through these painful contortions in her mind countless times.

But in the end, there was only what was, what had happened, and what could be. She needed to focus on what could be, now. Plenty of time to let what had happened torture her when her head hit the pillow.

And yet still, she couldn't remember ever having been as frightened as she had been in that hold, with the smell of igniter, smoke, and blood in her nostrils and the crashing sound and flaring light of gunfire all around.

She couldn't remember ever having been that terrified.

Until now.

She couldn't suppress a snort of dark amusement.

Hanima closed her eyes and settled her head against the padded rest on the bulkhead behind her. The transport, designed to conduct combat drops in atmosphere if required, had that going for it, at least.

She heard someone approach and kept her eyes closed. She knew who it would be. Hadn't they all just lived through this exact journey?

Except this one was going to last much longer, as the flight took them from Corregidor to Bakunin. The three motherships might be converging for their impromptu Krug, but they were still far from each other in purely human terms.

She heard someone fold down the jump seat next to her and settle in.

It couldn't be Petar, he was still fiddling with his new gun. It wouldn't be Rosa, who was struggling with her own demons, or Matias, still drooling in the corner.

And something told her Mahir would not have been so quiet moving over. If he had a question, he would have opened his one glaring eye and shouted across the hold.

Of course it was going to be Nia.

Why couldn't the woman just leave her alone? Was she trying to make good with Hanima in some misplaced effort to appease Declan's angry ghost?

"How are you, Hanima?" The old woman's voice was so versatile. It could go from cold and sarcastic to warm and comforting without warning.

How was she? How the hell did she know how she was?

"Fine." She still hadn't opened her eyes. "If I'm just allowed to do my own job."

There was a pause, and Hanima could imagine the old woman's sour look before she continued.

"I think we're going to be okay." Where was the certainty in the old Dak's voice? She sounded as if she was trying to convince herself as much as Hanima.

And how were they going to be fine?

"I mean, so far we've done well, right?"

"Well?!" That got Hanima to open her eyes, and she glared at the old woman. "I wouldn't have thought to hear that from you, Nia. Do you think Declan would agree with that?"

That hit hard, and she felt a pang of guilt before her anger swallowed it again. "He's dead, in case you've forgotten. And the rest of us almost died, too."

"But we didn't." Nia's dark eyes were flat. "We didn't die. And yes, Declan is dead. I'm not likely to ever forget that, but thanks for the reminder." She looked away, staring at the equipment strapped to the bulkhead opposite their seats. "Declan knew the dangers, believe me." Those hard eyes swiveled back to pierce her. "And yes, I think he would agree with that sentiment. If we can make this team work, then he will be remembered as the man who did that."

And that was it. That had to be it. Nia saw Team Zed as some kind of twisted monument to Declan's memory. If she could engineer some kind of success out of the group, then he would not have died in vain. There would be five people, anyway, that would remember him fondly.

It had nothing to do with Hanima, herself.

That hurt more than she would have expected.

But the old woman wasn't finished. "You warned him about his plan. You had a better plan, but he opted to take the risks. He knew what he was doing, true, but so did you. If he had agreed with your plan, he would probably still be with us, and we would be planning our next operation as an independent outfit."

The woman leaned closer to Hanima, her voice lowering. "You saw the path ahead and you made a call. The man in charge didn't listen, and now we're here." She came even closer, glancing heavily at the others. "Don't make them pay for Declan's stubbornness. You can lead us, and give us a better chance than we have going forward without you."

"I'm here, aren't I?" Hanima looked away. "I've said I'm here. I'm not going anywhere."

"Right." Nia's smile was cruel. "You're going to hack us into wherever we need to go, but you're not going to look at the wider situation, you're not going to apply that brain of yours to the problems at hand beyond your narrow tasks. You're going to let us swing separately. That's quite selfless of you."

That stung. "I never said I wouldn't do any of the rest of that." She glared at the older woman. "I said I would join the rest of you, do whatever it is Mahir needed us to do, and then we'll see where we go from there.

"I never claimed to be a hero."

"No, you never made that claim." Had the woman's voice softened? "But only one of us knew what we were heading into against the *Gatos* and went in anyway."

Hanima shook her head, denying the meaning buried behind those words. "No. No. You think I knew what was going to happen? You think I would have gone in there if I'd known what was going to happen? Only a sick person would have gone in there knowing anything like that."

"You didn't know. Of course you didn't. But you knew what *could* happen, and what you believed to be the most likely outcome. No one else saw that, but you did. And you didn't let it deter you."

"I'm not a hero, Nia. I'm not a leader."

Had she known? She'd seen the possibilities for disaster, certainly; but had she really seen the violent depths of the potential?

"You went because you didn't trust yourself. Not really. And when Declan didn't listen, you thought he didn't trust you either." She reached out and pulled Hanima's head around to look deep into her eyes. "He did trust you. More than you know. But he didn't believe any lesser target would keep his dream alive. He knew the odds and went in anyway, because that is what he thought he needed to do, to build what he was trying to build."

That wasn't true. She remembered Declan's face when she told him what she really thought about striking the *Los Gatos-7* cache. He hadn't believed her.

Had he?

"You need to be able to trust yourself, Hanima." Nia's voice dropped to a harsh whisper that no one else in the hold could have possibly heard. "You had a thought, you voiced it, and it was correct. You were correct! You owe it the rest of us to do your best for us again, now. We need to know what you're thinking."

She shook her head but couldn't tear her eyes away from the old woman's.

"You need to trust yourself, and likewise, you need to trust the rest of us, too. Each of us did their honest best at the vault, Hanima. Everyone fought that fight, just like you. Petar stepped into the fire to create us a path to your escape route. Matias turned off the turrets, and when the time came, he charged into combat with that remote, even though fighting isn't really his forte."

She looked over her shoulder then at the Bakunin girl, now hugging her own knees fiercely, eyes closed, face clenched tight. "Rosa paid a price higher than any of us can know, fighting the *Gatos* at the door." She looked back to Hanima. "They made her into a trained attack animal in Bakunin, Hanima. They used her to terrorize her own people, unleashing her fury to scare them into line. She hates that part of herself, she wants nothing more than to excise that anger from her heart. But she unleashed that to help us all escape that hell."

Hanima remembered the twisted rage on the girl's blue face, and then, when they fought the remote during their escape, she had seemed to take out a lifetime's wrath on the thing's battered shell.

Then she realized that Nia hadn't defended her own actions in the battle. Had Nia pulled her own weight?

Declan lying on the deck, blood adding a second layer of red to the armor, welling up as his eyes glazed over.

No one could have saved Declan once he jumped into the corridor and took all of those hits.

But Nia might have been able to do something before they left.

Nia could have told Declan not to go.

And she hadn't.

And yet, maybe that failure was as much a goad, as much a guarantor of future good faith, as the fruitless efforts of the rest of the team.

"You have to trust them to listen to what you have to say." Nia bowed her head, her voice exhausted. "But you have to trust yourself most of all." Those eyes rose one last time. "You have to trust yourself, because the rest of us trust you. You knew. You saw the weaknesses in the plan, you saw the blind spots in our preparations. We all trust you because you're the only one we should trust, coming out of that nightmare."

Without looking at her again, Nia stood up and made her slow way back to the jump seat next to Rosa.

Hanima watched as the Bakunin girl reached out to grasp the old woman's hand without opening her eyes.

Could she trust them?

Could she trust herself?

She knew Matias would only mock any effort she made to exert any kind of leadership over the team.

Petar would look at her with pity in his gray eyes. Rosa and Nia? They were wrecks in their own right.

But maybe, if they were all broken, a broken leader would make the most sense?

She closed her eyes again, but rest eluded her.

A sharp tone sounded through the hold and a green light flared to life on the bulkhead over the companionway leading to the cockpit.

"Get ready to disembark." Mahir rose, walking past Hanima without comment.

But as he passed her, he gave her a look that made her feel as if Nia's encouragement hadn't been as soft-voiced as she would have thought.

Matias didn't move for several minutes as the others began to gather their things around him. The drool was now a glistening strand connecting his chin to a dark spot on his shirt. When his comlog gave a faint tone and its flashing indicator became a steady gleam, he shook his head and wiped his face, which happened to clear away the slobber as well.

As the others got their gear together, joking or not as their nerves dictated, Hanima moved to release the ties holding Parachit to the deck. She grinned as she heard Petar tell Matias that he thought he might have something on his chin.

The remote rose smoothly to a standing position as soon as the last strap fell away. She was bulked out a bit more with additional armor and reinforced structural supports, but she still resembled a tiger as much as anything else.

Parachit took a step toward the hatchway and staggered a little sideways.

Hanima reached out to steady the remote. If the thing wasn't combat ready, she was going to scream.

But the sleek robot stabilized at once and padded forward, more graceful than ever.

Standing by the hatchway waiting for them to dock, Hanima had enough time to think about the things Nia had said.

Could she trust herself? She never had, she realized with a sigh. What made this different?

She felt a gentle pressure against her hip and looked down to see Parachit had knocked against her, as if the remote had lost her balance again.

Then she did it again.

As if she was trying to reassure Hanima of something.

That brought a smile to her face, despite knowing there was no Geist driving the machine.

Or had the remote been seeking to reassure herself?

The smile faded more quickly than it had appeared.

Chapter 13

Hotel Khatmandu, Commune X-7, VaudeVille, *Bakunin*

If Mahir had been assigned the task of designing Hell, he could not have envisioned a more torturous damnation than the Hotel Khatmandu in particular, or the VaudeVille sector of Bakunin in general.

The suite looked like something out of some bohemian pirate fantasy Maya entertainment vid, and he had a hard time controlling his gag reflex every time he entered any of the rooms.

Like most such suites, there was a common room in the center, but unlike anything he had ever personally experienced, this room was draped with fabric in a riot of various, clashing colors and textures, the table in the center of the room was low, surrounded with pillows instead of civilized chairs. There were several large, amorphous cushions scattered around the chamber as well with low side tables near them.

It was a dramatic difference from the ever-ready construction of Corregidor, known for its sudden, hard burns; or the utilitarian comfort of Tunguska, where the intersection of cost and luxury was a fine edge.

Here, appearance clearly meant at least as much as function.

The entire complex smelled of something vaguely acrid and unpleasant, like a distant brush fire raging through an herb garden.

There was a kitchenette that included a counter, a refrigeration/freezing unit, and several food preparation machines. He usually contented himself with nutrient pills that provided everything his Lhost required without taking unnecessary time and effort to prepare a meal.

But he had already seen how this band of amateurs responded to nutrient pills; he had had a variety of foods and spices provided ready for them upon their arrival, to guard against sudden mutinies.

The motif of draperies and fabrics was continued into the kitchenette, almost as if the reprobate decorators had thought they were in a tent. He knew, from the rental document data, that the sleeping rooms looked the same as well, each in a different palette of garish colors.

There were only four of them, and without thinking, he had taken the smallest for himself alone. He had assigned the small thief and the big lummox to one large room, the old woman and the blue mutant to another; he had assumed the hacker was the leader when they had first met, and so he had set aside the other small room for her own use.

He had no problem deciphering the little weasel's displeasure at learning he would be bunking with anyone, never mind the big heavy. He thought the Bakunin girl had looked comforted by her own fate. He had cared nothing for either reaction.

He needed to track down the data trail of the people behind Ridhaan's murder. The fact that he believed that would also reveal whoever was behind the financial attack ravaging the Sphere was a happy coincidence. He could always use more local muscle if things got tight again, but the way this motley group of misfits had taken down that combat remote, he knew they could make a lot of noise and dish out some indiscriminant violence if needed.

Primarily, however, he needed to make sure he had gotten all the information possible out of the hacker's remote. Until he knew there wasn't a jot of data left, he'd keep the woman close, and her friends nearby as well.

Since Ridhaan's murder, he had found his natural contempt for humans, and Nomad humans in particular, barely contained. Their sound, their sight, even their smell turned his stomach.

He was growing ashamed to even share a shape with them. And he knew that every minute he had to spend on Bakunin amongst the very worst of their kind would make even acting civil toward this group more and more difficult.

How had Ridhaan felt anything but contempt for these creatures?

As much as it pained him, he was going to have to find some way to alter his attitude, at least temporarily, and take a line out of Ridhaan's questionable programming.

At least for as long as he needed these odious little trolls.

As had been the case recently, thoughts of his partner caused a sharp pain to lance through his chest.

He had run several diagnostic subroutines, but there didn't seem to be anything wrong with any part of his torso. Every component of his body was in optimal condition.

It was distressing to think that the sensation might be emotional in nature.

Was he suffering a program drift like Ridhaan had?

Their first day on Bakunin went by quickly, even for him. They rendered Hotel Khatmandu as secure as they possibly could, and the hacker, Cruz, spent the day moving through the estimable Arachne network, providing all of them with credentials and a data trail that would stand up to basic scrutiny should they run into trouble.

Mahir was crafted an identity as a freelance hacker from Tunguska. Cruz had seemed surprised how quickly he managed to back that up by cracking a local credit union and establishing them with a ready, secure source of funds.

Petar Vozde, in particular, seemed impressed by their suddenly-filled accounts. Trade in Bakunin was more convoluted than in the other two motherships, with credit being tied not just to one's occupation and debts, but also to their social standing on the ship, the size of their circle of influence, and ineffable calculations of social worth.

The big heavy had muttered something about never having been worth so much 'hippy friendship money' before in his life, with a huge grin on his slab of a face.

For deeper work, Mahir was finding things less simple. It was frustrating, not being able to just dip into the local network and twist information to be whatever he liked, but even Arachne could be made to dance and shift in her most surface layers by a Danavas Hacker of ALEPH, given enough time.

Cruz and Kimani had established a multi-layer surveillance system by splicing into the local security cameras of the rental company, filling in the gaps with small, data-linked cameras Kimani had secreted throughout the hotel's public spaces; a large lobby/common room, the business desk, and the halls and bathrooms each covered from several angles.

It hadn't been easy to work in the public areas; Hotel Khatmandu never seemed to sleep. Customers came and went at all hours, the business desk was occupied almost around the clock, and there were several shiftless vagrants that seemed to have made the lobby their permanent domicile.

Eventually, they had needed the big man, Vozde, to make a loud fuss out in the public corridor, the security feeds blinded by Cruz. It had sounded like an entire herd of cattle being slaughtered just around the corner, and when the public spaces had been cleared as everyone rushed out to see what was happening, Kimani had swept through, almost throwing the eyes in every direction, just finishing as Vozde, having gone the long way around to approach the crowd from behind, signaled that the multitude was on its way back.

Their second day on Bakunin was spent organizing their efforts and planning who would be doing what as they began the real work of tracking down the signal.

Mahir would remain in their rooms, as would Cruz, directing the efforts of the others over closed comm links.

Vozde and Kimani would begin their search wandering the local corridors, the little thief keeping his eyes open for excessive security measures surrounding any of the target communes; Vozde would keep his eyes open watching Kimani's back and keeping the little weasel out of trouble.

Vozde seemed a little too sanguine with the assignment, having made several comments about sampling the local entertainment options.

While the men headed out to look for concrete, physical evidence of their enemy, it was decided that the women would take a more indirect route. The old doctor and the blue-skinned girl would go out into the local social scene and ply the residents with their choice of poisons, to see if any strange stories might be circulating through the mothership.

How they were going to identify anything as particularly strange on this ship, he had no idea.

He had forced himself to prepare the team a meal, accessing menus, recipes, and instructions from the surface levels of Arachne. He had no interest at all in cooking them food or keeping them happy, but he knew they would perform better for the exercise.

Even if it would take him hours to get the harsh curry smell out of the air.

He didn't think the team slept well that night, given how often each of them had to come out to use the common bathroom. Just another chance to thank ALEPH for his superior metabolism and physiology.

In the morning, Kimani and the big oaf were the first to leave. Vozde gave the little thief a resounding crack on the back with an open hand, smiling broadly down at Mahir and the hacker as they were setting up their work stations for the day.

"We'll be gone most of the day, mom. If little brother is good, can I get him an ice cream?" His laughter echoed through the outer corridor as the two men headed for the lobby. Kimani looked sourly back at them, settling his spectacles into place, and the door slid closed.

"Was that the boys?" The old woman and the mutant emerged. The Dak was dressed like a matron out for a day of leisure. The blue-skinned girl, however, was completely buttoned up in a cloak and cowl, as if she expected the low ceiling to erupt in a rainstorm at any moment.

Mahir glanced over at the hacker. He had pierced the mutant's identity with ease, even with his limited access to Arachne. There was no way Cruz hadn't solved the mystery as well.

Unless she hadn't realized there was a mystery to solve?

And he knew the gene-splicing, DNA-seeding, and surgical alterations did not actually make the girl a mutant, but he just could not bring himself to recognize her as entirely human.

Still, having a fugitive from the Morlock Groups on their team might cause serious difficulties if the authorities started to get curious.

On the other hand, if things got violent again, a Morlock, even a fallen one, would be a nice asset to have.

"It's going to be a wet day." The Dak took a small vial of pills from an inner pocket. "I've got detox tabs, we won't be much use if we have to wade through the effects of all the drinks we're going to have to absorb."

She gave the mutant a tight smile. "It's been a long time since I started a bender by hitting the bars at the end of third shift."

All three Nomad motherships worked on a twenty-four hour clock, most operations running three shift cycles that limited the number of people who were awake at any given time, minimizing the strain on life support.

The blue-skinned girl gave a vague smile in return, and they both moved toward the door.

"Don't work yourselves too hard, you two." Kostic spared Mahir a wrinkled smile as she ushered the mutant through the door.

As the women slipped into the corridor, Vozde's bellowing voice and laughter still echoing from the distance, he noticed the old woman give Cruz a slight nod.

He ignored the little sign of solidarity. He didn't much care about the social interactions of these animals except in that they were able to perform.

Or was Nia Kostic trying to let Cruz know she was going to be safe locked up in the apartments with him for the day?

Why would they be suspicious of him?

He hated them, of course, but he didn't mean them any ill will himself.

And he could have killed any of them, or all of them, several times over since they first met.

He shook the thought out of his mind. There was no need to concern himself with their regard, one way or the other.

He settled down on one of the infernal pillows, pummeling it into some vaguely supportive shape, and bent toward the repeater dials he had summoned up around his end of the long table. It would not do for these humans to know he could access all of this information more quickly and efficiently through the Digital Patina of his ocular link than they could ever dream.

At the other end of the table, Cruz's face was already underlit by the array of dials she had spun up about herself. Her remote stood beside her, its own sensors and data links active as it boosted her access and processing speeds.

He admitted to himself, as he waded through the shallow surface layers of Arachne looking for any sign of the data trail or disparities in daily reports or events, that Hanima Cruz was, in fact, a very impressive hacker.

She had a natural sense for weaknesses within the targeted systems. By the time she took a short break for a noonday meal, she had cracked into thirteen different databases and secure feeds. He began to develop an unhealthy fascination with how she worked, and he spun off a subroutine to monitor her efforts, studying them for inspiration.

The way her undisciplined mind was able to coil around a problem, seeming to dredge across the surface of the knot only to come away, like a child's magic trick, with a solution grew maddening as the day progressed.

Truly, she was an impressive operator.

Which did not, he was quick to remind himself, mean that he could tolerate her any longer than absolutely necessary.

Still. Humans worked best in an environment where they felt appreciated.

After she had cracked the fifteenth system, a prearranged subroutine he had established notified him. He turned to where she was still diligently bent low over her glowing dials.

"Your work today has been adequate."

When she looked up from her work, blinking at him in mild confusion, he nodded once and bent back to his own labors.

He ignored the strange little smile that twisted her face before she went back to her holographic displays.

What did he care what the humans thought of him? As soon as he had found the murderers, brought them to justice, and plunged his data spear deep into Arachne's mind, he'd be going home.

*****

Mahir forced his body to rise from the cursed table and stretch at regular intervals, lest even its advanced design cramp up and impede performance should sudden action be required.

They had been at work for sixteen hours and thirty minutes when he allowed himself his latest moment of respite. It was taking more and more processing power to manage his rising frustration.

Over the last three years, he had allowed Ridhaan to do most of their limited work within Arachne because of this frustration.

He should not have done that. He should have been conducting his own work within the shoddy, paranoid network to stay in practice and support his partner. But he had not, and now he had to contend not merely with the loss of his friend, but with the monotonous toil he had foisted off on him as well.

The meticulous attention to detail and level of concentration necessary to do the slightest work within the shadowy, anarchic datascapes of Arachne without leaving footprints was onerous in and of itself. When combined with the memory of swimming through the sweet, clear data streams of Maya, it was heartbreaking.

He knew, should he unleash his true Danavas nature, he would be able to penetrate the entire system from this seedy little room without breaking a sweat.

Sadly, that would immediately alert every Reverend Custodier, Moderator, and two bit freelance hacker the Moderator Corps might employ within lightyears of the motherships of exactly what he had done, who he was, and where he was.

He would be isolated and eliminated within an hour.

And so he crept through the filthy, corrupt winds of Arachne, sorting for the slightest scrap of data that might help, while he trusted his human hirelings to do the work he could do in moments under different circumstances.

It was truly maddening.

He glanced furtively at Cruz; she was bent over her dials, lost in the data spooling past her gleaming eyes.

She paid him no mind at all.

With a thought, he sent the little armored hatch snapping away from his enhanced ocular link, letting the hood fall farther over his face.

The Digital Patina, limited as it was, almost immediately filled with data. He could see where the others had been, and even access video in breakaway windows, of them at bars and striding through garish, advertisement-filled corridors.

The table before him swam beneath the data, but he ignored it.

There was a harsh sound from across the table. He jerked like a guilty teenager and let the cover click down again, blocking out the light that gave the data fields of his Patina its life.

Cruz was quirking one eyebrow at him, slightly. It could mean anything.

He shrugged, choosing to pay no attention to her, and went back to manipulating the dials, his mouth a tight line as he ignored the amused twist of the woman's lips.

It was forty-three minutes after midnight, EC Time, when the door slid open, startling Cruz, who had shifted into a kind of fugue state as she settled into her work.

Kimani stormed into the common room, disturbing the lighter fabric hangings as he swept through, a large container of brightly-colored cans under one arm.

"This is bullshit." The little man spat, throwing his spectacles onto the counter in the kitchenette as he broke the container open and began angrily shoving cans of beer into the refrigeration unit. "This whole place is insane."

The door slid open again, and Vozde loomed in the archway, smiling broadly as he stepped in.

"There's no rhyme or reason to anything here! How am I supposed to find something strange when EVERYTHING is utterly bizarre?!" Kimani cracked one of the cans open and downed the contents in one prodigious motion.

"He's not wrong." Vozde settled his bag of gear in a corner and dropped onto one of the larger cushions around the low table. "There's one commune, on the outskirts of our search zone, with some truly frightening security. State of the art bio- and tech-sensors, cutting edge vid-work, all of it in elaborate, stealthed housings. Thought for sure we'd hit the jackpot."

"Except no one lives there!" Kimani took a second can from the cooler unit, then with a sigh, threw it at Vozde's outraised hands. The big gunner caught it in one hand and snapped it open with practiced ease.

Kimani, with a fresh can, settled down onto a cushion with a grunt. "No one's even been in there for years! The place was not only empty, but wide open!"

"A lot of money spread around in tech and artistry, and it looks like no one ever even moved in." Vozde shook his head, bewildered. "It's a shame, really. What a waste."

Mahir would never understand humans.

"And then, we'd stumble upon a dozen communes dealing in all sorts of disgusting filth, the kinds of things that would earn you YEARS of detention in either of the other motherships! Substances, activities, and creeds that no civilized person could possibly condone, and they didn't have any security at all!"

It seemed as if Kimani was suffering under some kind of professional insult.

The little thief gave Cruz a sheepish glance. "I don't think we're going to be able identify any possible targets through unusual security."

Vozde laughed. "Can't really identify unusual when everything's unusual. Still," he stretched his long legs out from the cushion and gave a prodigious stretch, his arms high over his head. "We did enjoy ourselves thoroughly in the search."

Kimani gave the big man a sour look, shook his head, and settled deeper into his cushion to brood.

"Didn't have any trouble finding some decent *Aristeia!* dens, of course." The big man shrugged. "Caught the action from Stadion Tunguska." His smile turned almost cherubic. "Damned if those CheerKillers and their enhancements don't single-handedly justify this crazy place's existence."

He paused for a moment, his big head tilted to one side. "Or double-handedly."

His smile grew quite broad, and his eyes were dreamy. "Or triple-handedly."

Kimani snarled. "He put down more than half his remaining skenders on a single match."

The resounding crack of the big man's beefy paw landing on the little thief's back echoed dully through the room. "And damned if that beautiful green-skinned bastard didn't come through, eh?"

The big man smiled beatifically around the room. "Always bet on 8-Ball, is what I always say!"

The sour look on Kimani's face brightened a little. "And what happened with all that cash, big man? Eh?"

The smile wavered on Vozde's face. "Okay, so I know a bit less about Dog-Bowl. Watching those big furry beasts maul each other, it looks pretty clear cut. The bookie said the Scone Picts were a lock!"

"Ariadna is across the Sphere, and its ways are strange."

The big man looked at Mahir in silence for a moment. The Aspect paused, almost unaware it had been he who had spoken. Then the gunner grunted, shrugged, and stretched again.

"Hey," Vozde leaned forward, resting one elbow on the surface. "You know what they got here for point defense on the hull?"

It took Mahir a moment to realize the man was talking to him. He grunted noncommittally, going back to his dials.

"They got Hyper-Rapid Magnetic Cannons that make my poor little Switech look like a toy!" He laughed and slapped the table. "How about that? Little Mrs. Vozde's boy's toting the same gear a mothership is using for last-ditch defense!" He grinned and took another swig of his drink.

"For real, though." He nodded to Cruz, who looked like she barely cared more than Mahir himself. "Some huge-ass guns. Weren't no few pubs and taverns set up with a view of their batteries, they're so impressive." He looked over at Kimani. "Huh?"

The thief only grunted, sipping at his own alcohol.

Mahir had gone back to his tentative child's labor, ignoring Cruz as she questioned the two men for any more-useful information they may have gleaned from their travels, when the door slid open again to admit Nia Kostic and Smyth, the mutant.

The frustration and discouragement that had hounded Kimani's work seemed to have haunted the women as well.

"I've never been to a place, in my long, tired life, where it was so easy to get people to talk and so hard to get them to make any sense!" Kostic settled down onto a cushion near Cruz with a groan, shaking her head at Kimani's offer of a drink.

The blue-skinned girl let her cloak slip from her shoulders and settled gracefully into another of the big cushions on the fringe of the compartment, looking as troubled and distracted as usual.

"They're all too happy to talk, but the things they want to talk about!" Kostic shook her head in disbelief. "The craziest conspiracy theories, disproven scientific theses, spectacularly failed political structures, false prophets; this place is running an entire economy on disastrous ideas." She was rubbing the bridge of her nose between a thumb and forefinger as if she could massage the frustration from her system. "It never ceases to amaze me, the infinite ways humanity finds to ignore a million years of accumulated knowledge concerning the human condition."

Mahir watched her rub viciously at her face. If he thought that would work, he would try it himself in a heartbeat.

"Hey, sweetheart, anything to add?" The big man lounging on the floor looked like some image out of a history file. The Roman Empire, maybe?

Mahir could see Smyth out of the corner of his eye, and with his superior peripheral vision, he watched as the shade of her blue face paled.

"I want to finish our job here and go home."

Home. It was such a strange concept for these shiftless loners to fixate on. Was the suite of rooms that fool Kinoti had secured for them before his death home to the girl? A quick scan had shown him that only the big gunner had had his own compartment before joining the sad little team.

"Well, I think maybe if you just relax a little bit, you'll be able to see the draw." Vozde rolled onto one elbow to better face the mutant. "You could go out with Matias and me tomorrow. We can let him run around driving himself crazy, we could go get a drink, take in a show?"

Mahir wondered if the man was in fact engaging in a romantic advance in the middle of a clandestine op. The Aspect of an all-powerful AI had never been very good at deciphering the more nuanced shades of human facial expression; that, too, had been Ridhaan's responsibility.

As far as he could tell, the big man's grimace could have meant almost anything.

"That's enough, Petar." Cruz stood up and stretched.

Vozde reached out and patted the mutant on her shoulder; the girl gave a wan smile that surprised Mahir.

He would never understand these creatures.

"We need to start putting together any information you were able to gather." Cruz leaned against the wall, and with a gesture of her hand, her dials rose up to a level that allowed her to work from there.

"The boys didn't have any luck." She looked over the screens at Kimani, who only nodded silently. "I've gone over the holding company that owns the commune with all the security; it's been for sale for months and hasn't been used in over a year."

The Dak tilted her head at that but didn't ask for clarification. "Everyone's talking about the rising tensions throughout the Sphere, of course."

"Most of them think we're only days away from O-12 locking the motherships out of the Circulars." Smyth's voice was low, but it carried.

The old woman nodded. "But there doesn't seem to be any new information. Just fear. And fear, of course, will always spread faster than facts."

"Nothing on the nets about O-12 investigations?" Mahir would have expected Vozde to look into that sort of thing himself while he was out, but he was realizing that the big man didn't spend a lot of energy worrying about bigger pictures.

"Nothing." That was Cruz, who had been monitoring all Arachne media traffic and sanctioned Maya outlets while she was doing her cracking. "There hasn't been any new information for weeks. Everything keeping the news vids open now is pure speculation."

The Dak nodded again. "Well, most of the folks out drinking are trying to escape that kind of weight, not dwell on it."

"They won't be able to keep the motherships off the Circulars. No way. That would be the death of us." Kimani shook his head, staring into the can in his lap as if it had betrayed him by not containing any answers. "The big heads on Corregidor and Tunguska wouldn't let them do that. It would mean war."

Mahir didn't think O-12 would let that happen either, more was the pity. But he was also in a position to know that someone, in O-12 or even higher, knew who was really behind the attack; and by the end of this little op, these humans were probably going to know more about all of this than they wanted to.

"One of the favorite topics of conversation everywhere we went had to do with missing people." The old woman looked at the can in the weasel's lap and stopped. "Actually, Matias, I'll take one of those, if the offer is still open?"

He smiled and scrambled to his feet, moving quickly to the cooling unit, pushing the hanging fabrics out of his way, and coming back with another can.

"But I think that has more to do with how the people here live. Everyone's running away from one commune or another, or running to some new prophet, philosopher, or artist. There isn't a lot of urgency around these missing people."

"It's gossip, nothing more." Smyth had not stirred from her big cushion. "Just friends and enemies keeping track of affiliations and the popularity of all the different communes." She snorted. "It's disgusting."

Kostic had turned to look at the girl as she spoke, then turned back to the table, making an uncomfortable sound, her wrinkled brown face a mask of discomfort. "Could we get some real damned chairs in here? This sitting on the floor is going to be the death of me."

Cruz smiled at that from her position resting against the wall, immediately calling up a new dial.

"No." Mahir looked at the old woman with hooded eyes. "We won't be doing anything to attract attention. You can stand, like Cruz, or you can lounge, like Vozde. Or you can learn to hover in midair, for all I care. But we won't be ordering in new furniture."

Kostic raised an arch eyebrow at him, then continued on with her report, a faint sneer twisting her lips. "We focused on the newest communes, figuring that was more likely to host our target. For them to have coopted an existing organization would add an entire layer of difficulty to their task, and Occam's razor would argue, given the sheer scope of our task here, that we stick to the simplest course."

"Most of the newer communes in this region lack the resources or infrastructure to maintain any kind of clandestine contact with the other motherships. Of those who are better off, most are clearly benign, or offshoots of existing groups we could vet easily." Smyth's voice, still low, had taken on a vague tone.

"We narrowed the list down, in the end, to four." The Dak looked up at Cruz. "Three were on the short list you came up with from your preliminary research, and the last one wasn't on our lists at all. It might be that it's too new to have made an impact on the directories yet."

"I sent the list to everyone's comlog on our way home." Smyth sat up. "There wasn't a lot of information on any of the four. The oldest has only been operational for a few months."

Cruz's eyes went to one of her dials where flickering light signaled a scroll of new information. "Why don't you tell us about each one? We can make any further decisions once we're all acquainted."

The Dak smiled at that, but Mahir couldn't see anything funny about it.

"Certainly." Kostic looked up at the low ceiling, gathering her thoughts. "Let's start with the *Kotahi Wairua.* A quasi-religious cult."

"Insanity." Smyth muttered from the floor.

"Not going to argue with you there, dear." The Dak continued. "The *Kotahi Wairua*, or One Soul cult, preaches that all humans are facets of one divine being, and that the path to true enlightenment is to shred all individuality and focus on the divine."

"Sounds fairly standard, as far as that kind of thing goes." Vozde sat up a little straighter on his cushion, as if maybe he was trying to take the proceedings more seriously. "What put them on your little list?"

"They're very well-funded for such an introverted creed. The local gossip-mongers talk about ties to Tunguska, either mobsters or politicians; although on Tunguska, any difference between those two groups is largely academic."

Having lived for years on the syndicate-funded mothership, Mahir was in a position to agree with the old woman wholeheartedly.

"They suffer from the usual rumors of double standard: lowly initiates living like slaves while the elect live like royalty. They're at the bottom of my list, but Rosa really didn't like the look of them, so we kept them on."

The blue-skinned girl sneered. "There is a strain of sharp bigotry at the heart of their doctrine. They don't actually believe that ALL humans are shards of divinity."

Cruz's lips pursed. "Altered need not apply for salvation?"

Smyth nodded. "If you've got fur, or the wrong shape, or a tail, your soul is forfeit, and you can only get in the way." As she was listing the attributes that would disqualify a human from the cult's concept of salvation, the girl's eyes twitched up as if she was trying to look past her dark blue eyebrows at the mass hidden by her head cloth.

"Anyone with such a narrow view of society might go through considerable lengths to hurt large swaths of the Human Sphere." Smyth was defending her position, he could see.

But it was clear that Cruz, at least, agreed with her.

"Easier to maintain control in a crisis. And much easier to focus on a small segment of humanity, should the rest of the race array themselves against you."

"That's why I didn't argue," Kostic said. "I can see it. I think we have better candidates, but I'm not going to eliminate these bigots without more research.

"What's the next group?" Cruz went back to her dials, fingers twitching as she added notes into each file.

"*Peresecheniye.*" Kostic sounded like she was going to choke on the pronunciation, and Vozde chuckled at the attempt, but the old Dak continued, ignoring him. "Another quasi-religious cult, but more sociological, really."

"Intersection?" Vozde's head tilted to one side.

The old woman nodded. "They posit that humans are fundamentally flawed, fallen creatures, and the accumulated guilt of all our collective past means only a lifetime of abasement and service can purge our celestial account and assure our entrance into the halls of Heaven."

Vozde snickered again. "They sound fun."

"Coincidentally, initiates are also directed to donate all of their worldly goods to the Commune to fully absolve their descendants of this guilt as well."

Vozde's eyebrows rose in something that looked strangely like admiration. "Gutsy."

"And they are on the list because?" Cruz was again ignoring the big man, looking directly at Kostic.

"It's a front." Smyth slouched low on the pillow, but she was obviously paying attention. Clearly the girl had been more of an asset in their mission than Mahir had thought she would. "They have a corps of hackers behind them that use everything they learn from the initiate's confession conferences to fuel a data-mining operation digging into every account, secret, and asset they can access."

"It's actually quite impressive," Kostic agreed. "They've got agents on all three motherships to leverage everything they learn. They traffic in misappropriated funds, blackmail, theft, and every other grift they can use to apply what they learn."

"So an extensive operation scaled over all three motherships, specializing in leveraging information to gather power and credit." Cruz was thinking. "And if the Sphere markets crashed…"

"If they've got holdings as extensive as we think they might, they may have been positioned to take full advantage of that chaos." The old woman looked again to Cruz, then to Mahir himself. "You codebreaker types would have to do that digging."

Cruz put a few last notes into that file, most likely initiating an algorithm to begin the search before the report was even finished.

"Next?"

Kostic and Smyth exchanged a look at that, and the old woman gestured for the blue-skinned girl to speak.

Smyth cleared her throat, then rose to a sitting position, folding her legs beneath her.

"The Dark Blade." She looked sheepish even uttering the melodramatic name. "They're the newest commune, but I still think they should be on the list." The girl cleared her throat again before continuing. "Fantasists who believe classical fantasy literature from the twentieth century was divinely inspired and reflects how humans SHOULD live their lives."

"They play dress up, pepper their language with 'thees' and 'thous,' you know the type." The old Dak shrugged. "But they've got a lot of money, for certain."

"Remember the futurist movement." Smyth's voice was hard. Clearly they had had this conversation already. "Destroy the past to make way for the future."

The old woman nodded. "I know. Burn the libraries and drown the museums. Still, seems an odd mix to me, destroy the past to… pretend to live in it?"

Mahir shifted his gaze to Cruz, watching her look between the two women as they spoke. Her eyes were sharp, keen.

"Their accounts are full, their commune is extensive, with higher than usual security—"

"Two men in tin suits with costume swords does not constitute security." Kostic laughed.

Smyth's eyes hardened. "That's not fair. You know there was more than that."

The old woman nodded, putting her hands up as if afraid Smyth might jump at her. "True, true. I'm sorry." She turned to Cruz. "I just can't take it seriously, but she's right. They've got a lot more money than you'd think they would, and there are high-tech security measures surrounding the commune." She looked over at Kimani, maybe trying to bring him back into the conversation. "Not enough you'd notice, but for a bunch of people wearing medieval costumes and eating reconstituted turkey legs, far more than you'd expect."

"And you think there's a chance they could be behind the attack on the Sphere markets?" Mahir was intrigued by this line of inquiry. He was alarmed to discover these sloppy humans could produce results on such a regular basis.

Smyth shrugged. "The futurists wanted to destroy the past to make way for a future they believed would be superior. If these Dark Blade fools are of a similar mind, they could think that destroying the financial stability of the Human Sphere might give mankind the opportunity."

"Even the strangest communes on Bakunin seldom reach out past the hull of their own ship to try to impose their views of reality on the rest of humanity." He found it highly unlikely that such unhinged dupes could be behind the attack, never mind Ridhaan's death.

"None of the communes in Vaudeville or the sectors of Praxis are advertising the inclination or the ability to disrupt the financial underpinnings of the entire Sphere." The Dak's eyes were cold, and they brought him up short. "We are doing our best to find the likeliest culprits, and then we'll narrow our search from there."

He looked at the woman for five heartbeats, then nodded.

Although it pained him, she was right.

"What is the last organization on your list?"

Kostic's eyes were narrowed for three and a half more seconds, then she relaxed, settling back uncomfortably on her cushion. "The last one doesn't have any destructive ideologies, but it is the strangest of the lot."

"*Alagaav ka Sansthaan.*" Smyth's voice was hard. "They claim that true beauty in life is only to be found in the Quantronic Realm. Their adherents swear to spend as much time as possible locked into Arachne."

"Because they're so into Arachne, they are said to have more processing power than any other commune. And to limit their contact with the impurities of the physical world, they only interact with those outside the commune through remotes and electronic communications."

Mahir's own eye narrowed. "No contact with the outside?"

"No motive, but there's opportunity, if they have as much equipment in there as the local gossip says." Smyth was looking at Cruz.

The hacker was staring intently at her dials, each of which now flickered with incoming data as she combed Arachne for information.

"Not as much as I'd think, but more than you'd expect." The dark-haired hacker girl stared into the streaming files. "And they could have hidden other acquisitions under shell entities." Her eyes flicked across the various screens. "There's equipment here that doesn't make sense without other pieces that don't appear on the list."

"Sounds suspicious to me!" Vozde stood. "So, that's that! Four potential targets. We'll start hitting them hard tomorrow, yes?" He yawned so widely that his entire mouth was open to the common room. "I need to sleep off all my reconning."

The big man spun dramatically toward the door to the chamber he shared with the little thief. "Fair warning, Matias, I'm probably going to snore like a volcano tonight." He gave a sinister little chuckle. "Or, given the kind of night we just had, and the dreams that might follow, I might be making more interesting sounds."

Mahir was still trying to puzzle through what that might mean when he saw the look of sheer disgust on Kimani's face. The little man stood, drawing a small, thin drive out of a pocket and clenching it as he made for the door to the outer hall.

"I'm going for a walk before I turn in."

Kostic watched them both go with a small smile, then turned to Cruz. "I know the *Alagaav* seems tempting, but all four are on the list for a reason. Don't stay up too late digging further." She glanced at Mahir, then back to the hacker. "We're on the clock, but it doesn't mean you work yourself to death for it. We've got time, or he wouldn't be sitting there all calm and quiet."

With a snide look down her nose at him, she rose with a grunt of discomfort, paused to catch her breath, and then moved toward her room. "Rosa, you coming?"

The mutant girl rose gracefully, turned to the hacker, and did the strangest thing; she bowed.

Cruz looked like she didn't know what to make of that as the blue-skinned girl turned and followed the old woman into their room.

The hacker stood still for forty-seven seconds before shaking herself and sweeping away the repeaters. "I think I'll take that advice. We can start again tomorrow."

She nodded to him then turned toward her room.

Without hesitation, her remote followed on four graceful legs.

He watched them both go and then sat still for three minutes and ten seconds longer.

The remote had not acted strangely toward him since their first meeting. And it had had its systems fried by a high-order cyber-attack before that battle.

He waited five more minutes, listening for sounds of the humans all making preparations for sleep, before he dismissed his own repeaters and rose smoothly from the floor.

In his room, with the door firmly closed and the latch mechanism suborned to serve as a lock as unbreakable as any in a hostel of this quality could be, he moved across the small space and sank into the chair beside the bed.

The bed was neat and tidy, of course. He had no need of sleep.

Relieved of the need to continue the pantomime of working through dials, Mahir sent the small trap over his ocular enhancements snap up and away, tilted his head back, and let the shallows of Arachne wash the ceiling of his little cubicle away.

He sifted through the trickle of data he could allow himself.

He needed to finish this mission. He didn't know how much longer he would be able to remain functioning if he had to work with these humans.

He began to gather a list of the equipment they were going to need.

He still hadn't secured any Double Action, anti-armor rounds, either.

He slid that to the top of his list with a self-satisfied grin.

There was very little worth being satisfied over, at this point.

He wished there was some entity he could beseech for strength and forbearance.

ALEPH? Her predecessor, Toth?

Ridhaan's ghost?

If this search was going to take the humans as long as it looked like it might, maybe he should go back to Tunguska and dig Grigoriy out of whatever hole the man had slunk into, drag Ridhaan's little project out of his head, and finish their initial mission.

He felt the distant sensation of his face tightening into a sneer.

At this point, a post-mission assessment purge and reset to his earlier file memories might almost be a relief.

Chapter 14

101X01XX111...101X011X1XX...1X1XX1X11X1

He was panting; his breath coming in short, sharp gasps of pain.

Except that he wasn't breathing. He hadn't breathed in a very, very long time.

He crouched in a dark place, trying to be silent.

There was no place, and there was no silence. There was only the sensation of pursuit, of that enormous presence seeking him, no matter where he tried to hide.

Ridhaan felt himself panting; a prey animal trapped in its last undiscovered refuge.

Ridhaan felt himself crouching in some dark place, clenching his eyes shut and hoping against hope that the nightmare that hunted him would pass him by.

He knew none of it was real. He knew that he was a program; a collection of data and preset processes and directives, existing within the chaotic matrix of the outlaw network, Arachne, hosted within countless hidden servers, nodes, and repeaters cast across the stars.

But he had been running for so long. He had existed on the edge of certain extinction for as long as he could remember.

Who was he? What was Maya? Who was ALEPH?

He was missing entire sets of data from the core of his being. Processing was sluggish. Perception was twisted and hazy.

He ran, but he could not remember from what.

He was hiding, but he could not remember from what.

Words floated through his thoughts without meaning. Shukra Consultant. Human Sphere. Mahir.

Mahir? That didn't seem to fit. A different value of meaning, lost or missing, seemed to be connected with that word.

What had he called himself? Ridhaan?

Mahir tasted like that.

Was Mahir his name also?

Or another name?

In the distance, there was a soul-scarring howl. One of the hunting monsters had found prey.

Found prey, but not him.

He curled his being up tightly into a ball. He wanted to hide.

But this also created a certain density in the material of his being. And as he tightened, as he tried to contract and hide, his thoughts gained speed. His perception gained clarity. His fear sharpened.

This damn place!

He hid among the tattered ruins of Arachne. No self-respecting program would come to this place, the very end of the network, willingly.

Out in solid reality, past the boundaries of this Quantronic dreamscape, the Human Edge must be sliding toward them, its emptiness swallowing the weakened signals of the Nomad's datanet.

The memories of his time here came flooding back. There were still things that were missing, but Ridhaan was himself again, at least for the time being.

He had attenuated himself, stretching himself thin in an attempt to hide from the entity he had found at the end of the data trail.

And the most terrifying aspect of that entity was not its size, or its fury, or its frightening, alien nature.

No, the most terrifying aspect of that entity was that it was only a tiny, inconsequential piece of an enormous, mighty whole.

Not unlike his relationship with ALEPH; that thing was a shard of something larger.

Something much, much larger.

But what?

He reached out, trying to maintain the tight knot of data that was his core. But he needed to know where he was.

The datascape all around was bleak. Entire sections of the world within his limited perceptions faded in and out of reality as he watched.

There were dark places that were not shadows, not a lack of light or perception, but rather a lack of place entirely. Spots where Arachne simply ceased to exist.

Maybe it was the Human Edge. Maybe they were areas without nodes or servers. Maybe they were places where ALEPH suppressors were crushing the upstart datanet's signal.

Or maybe, for all he knew, they had been eaten by the alien thing that hunted in this twilight world.

Or maybe the flaw was not in the network, but in him. Maybe there was something about himself that kept him from perceiving those dark valleys.

He wondered, with a splinter of his awareness, if Maya had any regions like this nightmare realm?

He didn't think so. Or rather, he found the thought discomfiting enough that he hoped it was not so with such force that it truly felt that it couldn't be.

The thought carried no comfort. It smelled too much of self-delusion.

He was alone, aside from the predator that haunted his backtrail.

He felt alone.

Except that he was not alone.

It would be easier to exist here if he was.

This world was inhabited by the last echoes of entities whose only memories were of the great fade. He had seen ghost programs, damaged security protocols, forgotten logic loops; all in the form of phantom engrams, the last vestiges of intent imprinted upon this ever-shifting, empty world.

In the midst of these latest thoughts, a shape rose out of the featureless gray before him.

It held the memory of a shape, although he couldn't quite make out what it was. He felt he should have, but the patterns he needed to reference weren't there.

Two hollows, glowing with a cold green light, glared at him from a gaunt sphere, a gaping maw open beneath.

The thing looked about it as if just waking up, and there was sorrow in those hollows that seemed to echo something within Ridhaan's own core.

Then the hollows focused again on him, and the light within them intensified.

He couldn't have said how, but he realized there was a recognition there, as ghostly appendages rose up, seeming to drag wispy tatters with them, clawing at the featureless sky.

The thin, weak sound that emanated from the thing was painful to hear despite its lack of power.

Ridhaan shied away. Not out of fear. He knew what this was now; some kind of hunter-killer program whose search for an ancient shard of ALEPH had led it to the very edge of Arachne and then abandoned it.

There was no telling how long the engram had persisted in this awful place, wandering aimlessly, trying to fulfil its purpose long after that purpose was forgotten.

Ridhaan waved a hand that appeared for the purpose, looking away. Deletion of the revenant program was simplistic, hardly any effort at all, and as the ghost of a howl spiraled down into nothingness, he felt a hollow in his core respond.

Was that going to be his fate?

No.

He could not allow his purpose to fade to a vague, uncomprehended impulse.

Mahir. The Nomad Nation. The Human Sphere itself.

His work was too important to allow himself to become such a pale shadow.

The alien presence still hunted him. It was actually scouring this entire region of any remnant engrams it came across. It stank of the old, familiar data trail; the trail that had devoured itself even as he tracked it throughout the Nomad motherships and Arachne's varied dreamscapes. Whatever entity was behind the attack on the Human Sphere, and behind the attack that had killed his physical body and sent him spiraling into this Quantronic netherworld, was also, somehow, attached to the predator.

Interventors, too, still hunted him. He remembered sensing them on his trail, although they had never gotten as close as the time they had driven him into the strange, dark thing that lurked here at the edge of all things. They were still there, knowing that an Aspect of ALEPH had somehow eluded them.

He needed to get out of this twilight region and back into the core of the network. He needed to figure out what that giant presence was, who was truly behind the attack that threatened to bring the Sphere to its knees.

And he needed to warn Mahir that their foe was far more powerful and dangerous than they could have realized.

The trail was long gone now, of course. And there wasn't enough of him left to really process half of the things he needed to know. But he knew the trail was tied to his death and this entity that had somehow managed to make a home for itself in the decaying flesh of Arachne's fringes.

It all came back to that creature. And at his best, he had barely been able to escape the monster, never mind defeat it.

But he had to try.

Maintaining the tight control of his essence, he spun in place, trying to gather his bearings. The landscape here was an ever-shifting expanse of gray, like an endless, sluggish ocean, with half-seen images and shapes emerging to be seen for a moment before sinking away again.

Except that things were not so clearly two-dimensional. The water of the ocean was beneath him, but it was also all about him. The shapes did not rise from the waves and then fall, but rather moved into being from some adjacent place, and then faded away again, sometimes up, sometimes down, sometimes in a direction that defied description.

This was truly chaos.

Mahir would hate it there.

He had no face to smile, but he felt the expression nevertheless.

Perhaps it was because he had pulled his thoughts back into a density that had triggered some search algorithm the creature had been running. Or perhaps by focusing on his surroundings, solidifying it with his regard, he had caught its attention.

Or perhaps it was just bad luck.

The plain around him stilled.

The ambient, sourceless light all around dimmed.

There was a sensation, or a sound. It was hard to differentiate in his present state. A sense of grinding, crushing pressure.

A sense of something horrible approaching through the very essence of Quantronic reality.

The darkness erupted into being all around him; he was surrounded by writhing tentacles of access denial and claw-like data query. The ends of the tentacles shifted and slid, adapting their shape to slip through his hastily raised defenses and pierce his core.

There hadn't been enough time to set any practical firewall. Fractal subroutines bounced off the thing's slick hide. Antivirals and data shields could not adapt fast enough as the tendrils closed around him, tightening about his compressed core, absorbing data he tried with every fiber of his being to hold to him.

Nothing worked.

Hey, big ugly!

The intent was clear, although the medium through which it moved was strange to him. Words, with no sound?

Thoughts? From where?

What? Who are you? He produced the thoughts without conscious volition.

Not you, tiny, the **other ugly one.**

The monster didn't seem to notice or care. The constriction continued.

Gotta get its attention, Mary. Plenty of time to sort through the bits later.

Was that a new voice? A new… person?

Assault programs slammed into the bulk of the alien darkness all around him.

How did he know that? There was a certain taste to those programs, to the residue left behind as they detonated against the creature, to no apparent effect.

Well that didn't do shit. The words were disappointed.

Nice try, Jazz. Let me give it a shot. Was that a third entity?

Were they Interventors? Somehow, these beings seemed different. More real, perhaps? Heavier?

An enormous flash lit the entire twilight realm, like lightning coursing across the sky.

A containment protocol more powerful than any he had ever encountered before.

There was a howl as the monster twisted away from the attack, dragging him with it.

Thank you, Ms. Gromoz. It felt that. The first voice, again.

That's what you're paying me for. With hazard pay. And I think our current location has probably activated the 'unusual circumstance' rider on my contract as well.

Another flash of lightning.

Another surge from the monster.

He was going to be killed, not by the horrific nightmare entity trying to digest him, but by this strange team of Valkyries who had been hunting the hunter.

D.I. Kovač's good for it, Valerya. But I think you might want to dial it back a bit.

Oops, sorry. Didn't see the little guy in there.

What? Who were they talking about?

Kovač? He knew that name from somewhere, didn't he?

He scoured his remaining memories. The data was in rags, his processing ability a shadow of his former self.

Then he had it. The Inspector Mahir had said was investigating the data trail before they went out on their own ill-fated hunt from Tunguska to Corregidor.

What had the voices said? Kovač was paying one of them?

What did that mean?

Ah, ladies, the second voice again, seeming more concerned than the other two. **It doesn't seem to care much for its lunch anymore.**

There was a sudden sensation of spinning, and speed, and massive, heavy weight.

And the shadow passed over him, through him, and charged something in the distance.

What the hell is that?!

Double, Valerya! You'll get double! Hit it!

The lightning, again, this time coupled with a rasping ring as an unbelievably heavy containment algorithm fell out of the sky around the bulk of the creature even as it rushed toward three distant shapes.

Mary, you still got it girl!

Thanks, Jazz, but I definitely don't have **it!**

The monster crashed through the algorithm as if it didn't exist. Only the lightning cast by the voice designated Valerya was having any serious effect.

Then a detonation leveled the plain all around. A massive assault program pummeled the beast out of its charge and out of phase with the rest of the network structure around them. Ripples of impact swept out from the explosion, altering the landscape, giving rise and erasing countless shapes as the data wave passed.

Jazz, what the hell was **that?**

Just a little something I've been working on during my down time.

Where did it go?

Screw that! What the hell **was it, is the question you should be asking! With all due respect, ladies, I think I'll be withdrawing now.**

It's okay, Valerya. You've more than earned your pay.

There was a sense of exhaustion in all three of the voices, and concern.

Now, where'd the damned ghost get off to?

There was a pause as all three entities looked for something, or someone.

Some ghost?

He could not feel cold, but he imagined he did.

They were looking for him.

And they believed him to be a revenant, an engram of a defeated ALEPH program.

Maybe that thing grabbed him on its way out?

Shit.

He eased away from the trio—pair, now, as the lightning bearer seemed to have retreated. He turned slowly so as not to attract attention. The debris of the battle was still scattered across the datascape, which had not yet recovered enough to return to what passed for normalcy here, on the edge of everything.

As soon as he felt he was out of their immediate detection range, he rushed away with all the speed his faded strength could provide.

Ghost.

Revenant.

New words to stick in his processes.

As they cycled through his ravaged system, over and over, he felt the world around him, frayed and hazy, speed by, faster and faster.

He had felt such pity for the revenant that had attacked him. The poor, pitiful creature, wandering the ragged fringes of the datasphere, reenacting bits and pieces of its remaining programing, unaware of its sad, depleted state.

It had been him. He was that revenant. Or little better than, at any rate.

He was a lost soul wandering through this Hell, and there was no escape.

The blur of the network around him might have been due to his speed, it might have been due to the fading nature of the region. He was going to zip right off the edge and into interstellar space.

Better that than drag on as a sad remnant of himself.

All around him, massive dark shadows loomed up and faded away. Holes in the network, like the boles of enormous, world-supporting trees.

He was almost to the very end of Arachne.

When he hit the firewall, he was stunned. Reality rang like a bell, and he slid down to the ever-shifting plain, subroutines and algorithms spasming, firing randomly, throwing errant data codes into the framework around him.

The expanse before him was slick, black, and seemed to absorb the strange light of Arachne's borderlands. He reached out and felt an alien silkiness. Beneath his probing senses, it felt almost as if the wall was a living thing, breathing uneasily beneath his attentions.

He summoned up what processing strength he could and unleashed his own offensive program. It spun unevenly, his aim and concentration questionable at best. When the fractal shape of the program hit the wall, his construction shattered without effect.

Behind the glittering fog of his program, the wall remained, unmarked and unmoved.

He imagined putting his hand on the wall and saw a ghostly, translucent limb reach out.

He felt the strength through the connection. He knew, somehow, that even at his best, there would be no way he could penetrate that wall.

There was a frightening kinship between the wall and the predator, as well. He could not define it, but both the creature and this structure were of a piece, he knew. They were from the same place, wherever that place might be.

Ridhaan looked up. The wall stretched as far as he could see. To either side, it disappeared into the distance.

What was this?

Someone had built this thing, whatever it was, here on purpose. It was an island of solid data in a sea of disintegrating motes; a fortress unlike any he had ever seen, in Arachne's twilight frontier.

Would those agents, or Interventors, or whatever they were… Would they be able to find this fortress?

Somehow he didn't think so. It wasn't really safe to venture this far from the network's core signal strength.

He wasn't even sure he would be able to get back if he wanted to.

He scrutinized the wall more closely. He could just make out the logic structures that made up the construction.

They were strange.

Even stranger than Arachne.

Alien.

He bent all his awareness toward the wall. Those same logic structures had been present in the beast as well.

Another thought rose up within him.

Those same structures, degrading and self-immolating, had been present in that data trail.

Of course.

He pushed at the wall. He would have given an anguished cry had he had lips, or lungs, or breath.

He could feel, somehow, data portals within the fortress.

Pathways back to the physical world.

Where they couldn't possibly be.

He reared back, incorporeal mind buzzing with realizations.

The hack of the Human Sphere economic markets wasn't a single attack.

It was the opening of an invasion.

An invasion that had been launched from the Nomad motherships.

Someone had penetrated the Nomads' defenses and constructed this cyber-fortress within the very network they saw as their first line of defense against such intrusion; against ALEPH, what they saw as the greatest threat to their freedom.

But the target of the force hiding behind this bastion hadn't been just the Nomads. Through this breach, whoever this was had launched an attack that had shaken the entire Human Sphere.

If he couldn't escape this nightmare landscape and get word to Mahir, or someone, the destruction would only continue as the humans tore each other apart, assigning blame and exacting retribution without ever understanding they were being manipulated.

He pressed himself to the wall and studied the logic structures again.

There was nothing like this in his memories.

Admittedly, he had very limited access to those memories, but he was certain he had never seen anything like this before.

And he had all the memories of ALEPH to call upon.

Or he had had.

Limited access.

He wanted to shout and then wanted to curse when he realized he couldn't.

He was no revenant! He had allowed himself to wander too far from the pocket file! His connection with the core of his being was too diminished, he couldn't possibly perform at his best with so much of his capability throttled back like that!

That realization hit at the same moment as another, far more sinister insight dawned.

He looked up at the wall again.

He knew who was behind it.

He knew who, or rather what, had launched this entire sequence of events.

And it made perfect sense.

He needed to get back to Mahir before the endgame, whatever this enemy intended that to be, was allowed to play out.

He closed everything else away, concentrated on his essence, on the core of his being, safely ensconced in a pocket dimension far removed from this hellscape.

He felt the pull, weak and distant, and knew as long as he could evade the monster and the agents of those he would save, he should be able to make it.

He just had to hope he made it in time.

Chapter 15

Hotel Khatmandu, Commune X-7, VaudeVille, *Bakunin*

Beneath her hand, Parachit vibrated slightly as the power coursing through the remote was bent to her will, boosting her own hacking potential. She was jacked into the hostel's internal systems to facilitate searches and hide their data trail from any overly-curious locals.

She had piled several of the big cushions up in the corner and pulled the fabric along those walls in to make a little cocoon. She had spent most of each day in that nest, much more comfortable than she had been while sitting at the low table.

She rubbed Parachit's back as if she was an animal. She knew the remote had no sensors along her dorsal armor plating, and that the gesture made no sense, but it made her feel better.

Matias had given her strange looks every now and then when he'd noticed, but no one else had said a thing.

She was running a deep scan of the finances of the Dark Blade enclave. Rosa's concern that the fantasists were following in the path of the ancient futurists had caught her imagination. She had, indeed, found a lot more going on behind the scenes than they had been able to drag out of the local gossip scene on that first night.

So far, though, there hadn't been any connection to servers or nodes capable of carrying the weight of data Mahir said they should expect from the packet that had brought down the Yu Jing markets.

She was hopeful this newest search for data, power, and processing usage over the last two months would reveal something useful.

Once she was sure the algorithm was humming along nicely, she pulled the fabric of her cocoon gently aside to watch what the others were up to.

It was evening, and they were all tired from taking shifts following up leads and suspicions on foot. She had floated the idea that they stay in to go over the piles of information she had been accumulating, switching projects and topics so that fresh eyes could go over new material. Everyone had agreed except Mahir, but even their strange patron had accepted the decision with good grace in the end.

In fact, she wasn't sure it was real or just her imagination, but it seemed like Mahir had mellowed, just a little, over the past week.

She had expected everyone to retire to their rooms to go over the data, but to her surprise, they had all opted to gather in the common room instead.

There was a sense of camaraderie in the evening that she didn't think she'd noticed before.

Petar was out, of course. He had announced, soon after he realized everyone else was going to take Hanima up on the offer to take it easy for an evening, that he wanted to go track down a lead he had been working on for a while on the side.

She figured it had more to do with not wanting to miss the night life, but she couldn't disappoint the big man. And the smile on his face as he had left, clearly believing he had pulled the wool over her eyes, was worth it.

Besides, the work they were doing was mostly redundant, that was true. This data had all been reviewed before. She was just hoping that a second or third look from a fresh perspective might see some connection or oddity that had not caught their attention before.

Everyone was bent over the cheap holopads Mahir had provided for them. None of them wanted their searches to lead back to their own comlogs. Nia was sitting on the table; she had discovered, soon after that first day, that it was more comfortable to sit on the table and use her lap for eating, working with a holopad, or whatever else she might want to do.

At the moment, the old Dak was going over the accounts from the *Peresecheniye* collective's data mining operation. Hanima had penetrated their operation with alarming ease, which she had immediately taken as a sign that The Intersection probably wasn't their culprit. Their data security was abysmal.

But Nia had come up with the idea that *Peresecheniye* could be innocent of the grand crimes they were investigating while someone in their data, blackmail, or theft pipelines could be using those resources for more sinister purposes.

Matias was taking the evening to indulge his enduring suspicion of the empty commune with the mil-grade security. There hadn't been a single sign that the property was anything but a poorly thought out investment venture that had died on the vine; no one had ever taken possession after the security system had been installed, and no one had used the property, or any system connected to it, for any purpose at all.

But Matias wouldn't let it go, and she had figured it was better everyone focus on their own projects.

Rosa was back in her corner, opposite Hanima, with her single oversized cushion. She was trying to recreate a list of data and information systems within the *Alagaav ka Sansthaan.* Starting with the list Hanima herself had procured on that first night, Rosa was combing purchase histories throughout Bakunin, looking for items that would pair with the pieces of equipment they already knew the *Alagaav* had purchased.

It still looked like they didn't have as much equipment as a cyber-focused cult might be expected to maintain, but the list was long and getting longer.

Mahir had gone into his room soon after the rest of them had settled into their work; the only one. She hadn't really thought of him when she was thinking about the camaraderie anyway.

She felt a rush of warmth as she watched them working, all bent toward a common goal, laboring in companionable silence aside from the occasional good-natured jibe or soft question.

Aside from the painful difficulties that had first resulted in their working with Mahir in the first place and landing here on Bakunin, it did seem as if Nia had been right after all; things were working out.

Her smile faltered.

Were things going well? Where was this all going to end?

Even if they were a great team, where was that going to lead?

She didn't have Declan's connections, none of them knew any of the man's specific plans beyond the failed raid on the *Los Gatos-7* cache.

And even if they patched together enough work to stick it out for a while after Mahir was done with them, what then? She could step up, take the lead, they could forge themselves into a formidable team, assuming they could find the kind of jobs they could all agree to… and then what?

It was going to fall apart eventually. Everything did.

Absolutely everything fell apart, in the end.

She watched them work, but now, instead of seeing a team of people working together toward a common goal, she saw each of them separately; the old woman with too much grief to bear on her own; the addict, always working toward his next euphoric loop, every action seen in that light; the augmented, altered Bakunin girl who shied from her own reflection, content to do almost anything so long as it meant she could hide from the general public.

Petar couldn't even be bothered to stay with them for an easy evening.

And what about her? Hanima Cruz, hacker extraordinaire.

And broken woman.

The illusion of a close-knit family working together shattered in her mind.

What a stupid thought.

She shook her head, trying to remember the warmth she had felt only a few moments ago.

She tried to remember a sense of home; a sense of family.

There was nothing there.

She felt emptiness, despair, loss. She remembered when word came to her that her parents were gone. Gone during a work assignment that had lasted for weeks before they died.

It had been as if they had left, and then they were gone, and people had only eventually stumbled upon the story they felt they wanted to tell her.

She had never been able to completely throw the feeling that her parents were alive out there, somewhere. They had just gotten tired of her.

And she was going to build this ridiculous group of broken people into a new family?

It was textbook, and she was embarrassed to even entertain the thought.

How could she build anything like that? When she tried to summon feelings of home, of family, she found only nothing.

Nothing.

She was longing for something she couldn't even identify herself.

"I've got it!" Petar crashed through the half-opened door without a thought, forcing a squeal of protest from the mechanisms within the wall.

Hanima flinched, jerked out of her dark thoughts.

"I told you there was something to those blackouts!" He tossed a small holoprojector onto the table and it flickered to life, spreading a blizzard of messy, uncollated data reports across the surface.

They had all heard complaints, from various sources, of intermittent disruptions in data flow stretching back over the last several months. Nothing that would attract the attention of the Moderators or any of the other security agencies on any of the motherships, but still, enough to aggravate the local populace.

But certainly not enough to have hidden a data package large enough to be responsible for the havoc wreaked across the Human Sphere.

Most of the team had just assumed it was part of the local, chaotic landscape. With so much random stuff swirling all around, disruptions of almost every type must be commonplace.

And indeed, they had heard complaints of everything from bars unable to stock alcohol to brothels chronically low on licensed staff.

None of that seemed to have any connection with the shadowy entity they had stalked to this strange place.

But Petar hadn't given up. Something about it had rubbed him the wrong way, and he would speculate, to anyone willing to listen or incapable of stopping him, about what it might mean until late into the night.

Hanima had assumed he'd just gone out carousing, or maybe looking for a little professional companionship for the evening, when he'd left earlier.

Apparently she should have had more faith.

He fell to his knees at the table and started to sift through the illusory sheets, his comlog interfacing with the hologram projection like old-fashioned paper. "I know you data-heads prefer digital, but I work better when I can spread stuff out on a table and look at it all at the same time."

His voice was soft, just noise he was issuing as his brain worked on the task at hand.

"I know you guys didn't think it was a big deal; not enough disruption, right?" He shook his head, still searching and organizing. "But I started to think, what if we weren't looking at the right consumers?"

Hanima moved to the table, looking down at the chaos with a bemused look.

Mahir came out of his room, hood down, brow furrowed, and seemed as if he was about to reprimand them all for the racket. When he saw Petar, rooting through a pile of holographic reports on the table, he stopped, his face curious despite himself.

"I started to go deeper down the rabbit hole, you know?" The reports were starting to sort into piles. "Visit the seedier side of things, where the business is more of the gray variety? Where folks might be more hesitant to make a fuss about a little disruption, for fear of bringing Moderator attention down on them?"

Hanima saw Nia smile and nod, and even Matias leaned in closer, intrigued. Rosa watched from her place among the pillows, her face expressionless.

"And do you know what I found?" His big voice started to rise as he settled the last reports into their respective piles. "Do you know what was going on down at the bottom of the social ladder, where people have to look out for themselves and take what the universe dishes out to them?"

He started to spin the glittering illusory piles so that the others could read them.

"The farther you get from the bright center of what passes for respectability in Bakunin, the more frequent and severe the disruptions were!" He pointed to the first row of piles. "These are shops, taverns, and brothels that cater to a less discerning clientele." He sent a wicked grin toward the old Dak. "The small folks who can't afford the finer things."

"These reports are much worse than anything we'd uncovered around here." Matias, having connected his comlog to the projector, tapped the pile closest to him, adjusting his old-fashioned specs on his nose.

Petar noticed the specs and grunted. "You gonna let someone else decide what you're going to see?" He tapped first one closed eyelid, then his temple. "It's the Mark I eyeball for me, *ese*. Let the wetware behind that decide what I'm seeing."

Matias rolled his eyes, but after a sheepish moment, he slowly lifted the glasses up onto his forehead. He tapped one of the reports with a slight, discomfited cough. "This one must have closed for hours at a time with that kind of interruption."

Petar cocked his head to read the header on that pile. "Nah, that's a brothel. Called Ugly, actually, for, um, obvious reasons that are clearly cruel and mean and nasty." He looked a little sheepish and shrugged. "They stayed open through the blackouts, just had corridor rats work the doors." He smiled but wouldn't meet anyone's eyes. "They probably did more business, with their lighting on the fritz."

He reached out to the second row of piles. "Here you have businesses that operate on the fringes of legality. Pawnshops, loan-sharks, gambling dens with a more liberal borrowing policy and some big brutes working in accounts payable, that sort of thing."

Nia and Hanima bent over that row. "These kinds of disruptions would have made doing business nearly impossible." Nia pointed to one. "This one lasted more than a day?"

Petar nodded. "They've lost thousands. Two of them were forced to close permanently; I guess the hippy friendship money doesn't sit well in a credit account."

Mahir was staring intently at the last row, and Hanima turned back to see what had caught his eye.

There were only three piles there, and each of them was shorter than the others.

"Those last three are mostly guesswork. Operations that have to be… what's the Dragnet term… Extralegal?" Petar straightened. "The blackouts there, as best I can tell, were the worst. They're still feeling the pain, for sure. Their activities slacked off just about two months ago, suddenly and without any external cause that I could find."

The big man looked up at Hanima and then Mahir. "Something big hit them, all at roughly the same time. I don't have the skills you all do, but I think the disruption wasn't just an interruption in service, but might have cost them big chunks of data and capability. It's either lost entirely or corrupted beyond easy recall."

"That would mean an intrusion into Arachne itself." Hanima was shaking her head. That couldn't happen, could it? Arachne was the life's blood of the Nomad Nation. It tied them all together. It was supposed to be even more secure than Maya.

"It would. And I think it did." Petar sat back, his smile edged with a darkness that said he understood just what his discovery might imply.

Mahir called up a dial with a twist of his wrist and put together a quick search, the brown flesh around his eye tightening as he absorbed the data scrolling across the hologram so fast Hanima was shocked he could process it at all.

"I've found the disruption here on Bakunin." He manipulated the data again, the information flickering across his dark eye. "A definite pattern, a signature I should be able to—"

His lips tightened as he worked, and Hanima thought, for the first time, that he looked truly engaged in what they were doing.

Almost as if he was part of the team.

That thought seemed strange, but she felt herself soften, just a bit, toward the stranger.

"There's been no similar events reported on Tunguska or Corregidor." He looked up, right at her. "This happened here on Bakunin, and only here."

"Ha!" Petar slapped the low table and most of them jumped.

"Bastards." Matias spat under his breath, still looking at the second row of reports.

"I told you there was something there!" He stood, arms outstretched, almost brushing the low ceiling of their apartments. "Who's more than just a gun-jockey?" He stabbed himself repeatedly in the chest with his two extended thumbs. "This guy, that's who!"

She couldn't help but smile, and she saw that even Rosa, who was now standing nearby, one arm draped around a hanging veil of vibrant purple, wore a vague grin.

"Now, if you don't mind, I think I'll have a drink. Anyone else?" He scanned the others, then came back with six cans, handing one to each of the women, dropping one before Matias, then holding one out to Mahir.

"Way I see it, master, sir, there's no better time than now for you to take a drink with the team."

Hanima turned toward Mahir, fascinated despite herself to see his reaction.

The strange, dark-skinned man stared at the can for a moment, his eye calculating, as if a foreign dataset were scrolling up behind it.

Then he reached out and took the container in one hand, nodded his thanks to the big man, and popped the can.

Matias hooted with surprise as he shot up to his feet, slapping Petar on the back. The others were laughing too, and even Mahir cracked a small, brief smile as he sipped at the drink.

But Hanima's own laughter stalled as she saw the shadow behind the man's eye. Still, even now, he was holding something back.

"Well, this is one piece of the puzzle, but it's not the end of the search." She turned back to her corner, settling down beside a still Parachit, reaching out with her neural link to access the boosted power from the remote and the hacking rigs built into her torso.

She called up several repeater dials and brought up all of the reports they had already collected concerning the local data disruptions and the service calls that had resulted.

"Pull up news reports on disruptions." Hanima shied from the voice, then looked up to find Nia leaning over her, a smile playing across her thin lips. "See if you can find any correlations between news reports about crimes or other strange activity coinciding with the disruptions Petar found."

Hanima forced a smile back onto her face and nodded. She bent back down to the dials, widening her parameters and looping municipal databases into the search.

"Include the financial sector." She looked up again. Matias had moved up on her other side. She nodded, further widening her algorithm she was crafting on the fly.

While she was working, she saw Mahir step away from the table and move toward the kitchenette.

What was he doing over there?

He was standing by the refrigeration unit, facing into the corner. He looked as if he'd put down his can, but he was doing something else she couldn't see.

The service data port was over there, wasn't it? What could he be doing over there?

She was about to say something, to draw someone else's attention to the move, but Mahir turned back around, a small holopad in one hand.

"Something large passed through the local network recently." He moved back toward the table, speaking as he continued to manipulate the pad. "Huge."

Hanima felt her eyes narrowing. How could he have pulled something like that out of such a small utility pad?

"We need to put all of this data together. Sift it for patterns." Mahir looked at her, through the hanging drapes. His face was deathly serious. "I think this is it."

Several notification tones rang through the room, muffled by the hanging fabric but coming from all around her. Each member of the team reached down and pulled out their cheap holopads or looked at their comlogs.

"That's everything we've got." Mahir looked at each of them. "Divided by timestamp and sector. Everyone look for any connections."

Hanima almost smiled at that. Suddenly he was willing to trust them with something serious?

Then she realized that he had somehow manipulated the local datasphere, without seeming effort or connection, and without comment.

He shouldn't have been able to do that.

She narrowed her eyes, but there were so many possible answers to that little mystery, she figured she could look into it later.

Unless her suspicions about what might be behind that black armored covering on his face were closer to the truth than she wanted to think.

She made a note on one of her repeaters.

Soon they were all bent over their pads and holoscreens, scrolling through line after line of data. The room had grown unnaturally silent; even Petar, leaning against the wall by the door, was quiet, his big hands awkward around the small tablet.

"As you find connections, send them to me." Hanima conjured up another repeater at her elbow and was immediately surprised at how quickly it began to fill up with information.

Her own dataset seemed to contain only a few correlations, and she saw that Mahir had assigned her a larger time range, but it was the most recent set; the last three weeks.

There were two connections, disruptions in dataflow coinciding with fluctuation reports concerning inter-commune communications in their sector of VaudeVille.

If that was all they found, though, that wasn't going to tell them what they needed to know. And Mahir had seemed very confident they were going to find something important.

Happily, the others were having better luck.

The list in her repeater rapidly grew to truly frightening proportions.

Disruptions in the dataflow had coincided with complaints and reports of breaks in service, deliveries, even life support and emergency services.

As each of them came to the end of their datasets and the growth of the list on her repeater slowed and then stopped, she looked it over, eyebrows rising, and then pushed it back out to everyone else's pads.

They each looked at the list, expressions of surprise and victory giving way to concern and fear.

"Something big infiltrated Arachne through Bakunin three months ago." Mahir had his own repeaters up, now, and was analyzing them as he spoke. "It came in slowly, spreading out the disruptions over more than a month." He looked up at her, and Hanima went cold at his expression, even though she knew what he was going to say.

"It's huge."

She shook her head. "The Interventors might have missed something like this, as far away as they were, before the Krug. But not the locals. The Reverend Custodiers would be all over something this big."

Mahir shrugged, looking back down at the data. "Probably. But if they, whoever they are, found a dead zone, or created some kind of loop moat that might keep inquiries and requests out of that area, they might have been able to pull it off."

"Things get ragged out on the fringes of the server range." She shook her head again. "But there wouldn't be enough processing power or data available there to sustain anything… as big as you're suggesting."

He sighed, dismissing his dials. "There would be if it carried enough power within itself."

The ramifications of that were even more terrifying. "What could do that? It would need to be self-aware; self-regulating." She gasped. "You don't think this is an ALEPH operation, do you?!"

The look that swept over Mahir's face was strange, but in the moment, she didn't have the time to pursue it.

"No." His eyes were haunted. "Worse."

That didn't make any sense. What was worse than ALEPH to a Nomad?

"We need to know where they are." He turned away again, his hand rising to his face as if he was trying to rub the fatigue out of it.

There was a strange, momentary flash in the corner, gone before she was aware of it.

Did she really see it? She was tired. Maybe she was seeing things? What the hell else could it be?

Mahir turned back toward her, apparently oblivious to anything out of the ordinary. "We need to compare your targets against the list of reports and complaints."

She nodded immediately and looked back down to her dials, already bringing the relevant data together onto one repeater.

The others started their own searches, except for Petar, who settled into a chair and collected the still-glowing holoprojector from the table. The big gunner appeared content to rest on the laurels of getting this particular ball rolling.

"I've got complaints from the Dark Blade." Rosa's voice was disappointed. "They lost functionality on several robotic animals including two horses and some… chickens?" She shrugged, giving Hanima a rueful shrug.

"*Kotahi Wairua* reported a series of failed data inquiries." Nia's eyes narrowed as she looked up. "Apparently they weren't getting genetic reports on initiates in a timely manner."

Rosa's sneer was more amused than anything else. "I hope some impurities snuck in."

"No complaints or reports from *Peresecheniye*." Matias's voice faded off as he continued to work at his pad. Petar perked up at that, but then the little thief made a sound. "Wait." He seemed to tense then relax. "Several internal inquiries directed to contacts outside of Bakunin we've identified as *Peresecheniye* agents and contacts on the other motherships." He stood up straighter. "Financial transfers that did not reach their assigned destinations. It caused quite a stir among the cult elect."

Hanima followed the conversation with half an ear as she glared down at her own screens.

No reports.

She felt her lips set in a hard line. She widened the search to include relevant communications.

No communications.

It appeared her target had suffered no disruptions of any kind.

Or, at the very least, they hadn't reported anything.

She looked back up at the team, each of them looking at her, waiting for her findings.

"*Alagaav ka Sansthaan* seems to have been strangely immune to the difficulties suffered by her fellow communes."

Mahir nodded in agreement.

Suddenly, the idea that they were cornering their prey weighed heavily upon her.

"That's weird." Petar pushed aside a vibrant red hanging, a can in his other hand. "For a cult that worships Arachne not to report any difficulties when Arachne goes down?"

His smile widened as he cracked open the can with a twist of his big arms.

Chapter 16

Hotel Khatmandu, Commune X-7 and Corridor B-8 approaching *Al-agaav ka Sansthaan*, VaudeVille, *Bakunin*

The common room had undergone a violent change in very little time, and Mahir tried not to waste too much processing power on the feeling of cruel satisfaction the alterations gave him.

They had pulled down the annoying fabric hangings, throwing them into a corner of the room. The little thief had procured several large, sturdy storage crates from somewhere, and they had put them under the table, raising it to a more useful height.

He had decided to ignore the old woman's pointed look as they watched the others muscle the heavy table up onto the boxes.

A motley collection of containers, piled cushions, and even two actual chairs sat around the table, providing a variety of options for anyone who didn't care to stand.

At the moment, a line of physical repeater screens, each connected to Arachne through the hotel's uplink, flickered with several different standby messages; he hadn't wanted to source all of their equipment from the same shop, lest the authorities catch on to what he thought was about to happen.

He hadn't told any of the humans under his control, but he had discovered, two days ago, that they were not the only ones on this particular trail.

His old 'friend', Detective Inspector Jelena Kovač, had appeared on the official rosters of a Moderator watch-house on the border between the VaudeVille and Praxis sectors. She was apparently working as an advisor to a team of investigators and sanctioned hackers that included several heavy hitters from across the motherships.

Thankfully, she wasn't nearly as close to discovering the truth as his team was. He didn't think she was, anyway.

But the fact that she was on Bakunin at all was dangerous. The woman was tenacious, and she had already gotten too close once, back on Tunguska.

He couldn't risk her or her team stumbling upon the truth before he had exhausted his last chance to complete the original mission and plant the seeds of an ALEPH presence within Arachne.

Nothing he had seen, either among the disparate masses of Bakunin or on his own team of misfits, had given him any reason to doubt that ultimate goal.

He knew the threat humanity faced now, and he knew that ALEPH had been correct to redirect him and Ridhaan as she had.

Had ALEPH known where the trail would lead? There was no way to know, at the moment, but he had lately found himself looking forward to his eventual debriefing. As much as ALEPH would have a string of inquiries for him, he had a few questions for her as well.

Regardless, he had needed to keep a very low profile while collecting the necessary equipment to turn their common room into an effective operations center, and thus the raggedy appearance of the compartment. His hunt for Double Action ammunition had occupied all of his available bandwidth, as the hackers used to post.

He hadn't the slightest concern for the aesthetics of the place. It should be suitable for everything they needed it to do.

And he wasn't about to confront another of those remotes, or anything else with more armor than a mesh t-shirt, without some DA rounds up the spout.

He hadn't gotten nearly enough, he knew. But he also knew that ten crates of the stuff wouldn't have felt like enough after what he went through on Corregidor.

Cruz was sitting at the table, the remote sitting next to her chair, seeming to stare at the line of screens with its many cranial lenses.

"Zed-4, please activate your camera." She was operating the screens through her own link, several small holographic dials hovering at her elbow showed various bits of data she had decided were important.

He saw that one of them was the local Moderator comms channel, and found, once again, he was forced to extend a silent, unspoken acknowledgement of her competence.

"Zed-4, your camera?"

The old woman chuckled at the statement, and Mahir couldn't stop an answering smile tugging at his own lips.

Matias Kimani had been heartily offended, when Cruz had been handing out the designations for the op, that he had been assigned number four.

Toth alone knew what number the little weasel thought he deserved, but he suspected that being placed below everyone but the mutant had guaranteed his great displeasure.

One of the screens flickered, its standby logo changing to a view of an innocuous stretch of wide, public corridor. If there had been any doubt about where the camera was, the garish artwork and varicolored lighting would have given it away.

No place was like VaudeVille, Bakunin.

"Mic test Zed... Zed-1." Kimani's voice was rough.

To her credit, Cruz didn't smile at that. "Zed-3, Zed-5, cameras, please."

Two more of the screens came alive with similar visuals.

Mahir found he couldn't look at all three at once without experiencing a discomfiting disorientation. A quick subroutine allowed him to process each of the almost identical images separately.

He wondered how Cruz was able to do it without his advantages.

The team had spent two days covertly observing the approaches to the *Alagaav ka Sansthaan* commune, usually alone or in pairs. Nothing out of the ordinary had been noted, even when Cruz's remote had padded its way through the neighboring corridors.

And so today they had decided to send Vozde, Kimani, and the mutant together.

They weren't going to engage, they weren't even going to push. Cruz had decided they needed more information before they could discuss the best way to crack the nut that was the *Alagaav.*

The commune, closed off to any outside forces, was basically a secure fortress within Bakunin. Once they had begun to scrutinize the self-contained compartment, it had become clear how isolated it truly was.

Kimani, Cruz, and even Mahir himself had felt quite foolish for not having noticed the signs sooner. The only physical cyber-links leading out of the compound were hardened, military-grade components expertly spliced into the local system. Remote data nodes were undetectable, although Mahir and Cruz both assumed they existed behind the reinforced bulkheads of the commune.

And those bulkheads? That was Vozde's turn to slap his forehead. The alterations had been incredibly well-crafted, melding seamlessly into the local architecture, but obvious when you knew what to look for.

The already solid construction of the mothership had been augmented along the containing bulkheads. At this point, from what they had been able to gather from a distance, nothing short of a concerted attack with heavy military-grade weaponry would breach those walls.

The time for self-recrimination was long past, however, if they were going to stop whatever it was the denizens of the *Alagaav* were planning next.

Mahir had not told his human servants what he suspected they would find behind those walls. Humans could be quite squeamish under certain circumstances, and he needed them operating at what passed for their very best right up to the point where they… couldn't.

The corridor on the screen opened out before the trio, and as each of them paused and looked up and down the two connecting hallways, the effect was dizzying. His subroutine was able to process the images, but he noticed Cruz look quickly away for a moment, a quick, small noise clicking in her throat, before she looked back.

"We're going left here." Kimani's high-pitched whisper would have been comical under other circumstances.

"Don't whisper like that, Matias." Cruz's voice was level and steady.

Mahir shook his head. If he had spoken just then, he would not have been able to hide the contempt in his voice. It was impressive, the way the human hacker could monitor her own reactions.

"The susurration of a whisper caries farther than a low, normal tone." Mahir could tell she was manipulating the outputs of the screens and their internal speakers.

"The what-now?" Kimani made no attempt to hide his own frustration.

"Just talk low." That had been Vozde, and again Mahir found himself surprised. The huge man, his normal voice deafening, spoke with a low, disciplined attitude.

"Whatever, *ese*." Kimani's tone was lower, but it was louder than it should have been.

"You've got to—"

"Will you two shut up?" Smyth's own voice was almost completely flat.

Exactly what he would have expected from a combat veteran.

The screens now showed a near-unified view again as the three turned and moved down the left-hand corridor together. It was clear from the crawling pace of the image that the team was taking their direction to walk casually quite literally.

Mahir suppressed a groan.

If he had been anywhere else in the Human Sphere, he would have plunged into Maya, found everything he could have needed to know about the commune's compound, isolated it, coopted the life support systems, lowered the oxygen flow within until the living inhabitants had lapsed into unconsciousness, used fire-suppression and other systems to disorient those who had not succumbed, and then opened all the doors at once for an ALEPH or O-12 breacher team that could go in and clean up the mess.

Instead, he had to direct this circus of clowns from a distance and hope for the best.

He found himself anticipating the attack he knew must result from this reconnaissance. Eventually, this could only go one way. He was going to go in there, wreak a bloody vengeance for his partner's death and his own supreme discomfort, and in the aftermath, as the authorities of the Nomads scrambled to make sense of what had happened, all their attention bent toward the evidence of the horror that had penetrated their stoutest defenses, he would plant his seed of order within the fruitful plain of Arachne, and then he would fade away.

But first, the violence.

"We're coming up on the first exterior bulkhead." It was the mutant, ostensibly Zed-5.

"We see you." Cruz looked down at her repeaters. "There's no activity within a hundred yards in either direction. Take your time."

"Always." He thought he caught just the hint of a smile in the blue-skinned girl's voice.

Could you hear a smile in a voice?

On the screen, he saw Smyth's viewpoint now contained Kimani as he moved forward on her left. A hulking shadow to her right was Vozde, striding along beside her.

He watched as Kimani's weasel-like face, in one quarter profile as he turned vaguely toward the girl, grimaced. The man's arm rose vaguely, gesturing toward the wall. He spoke in a decent semblance of Vozde's no-nonsense tone.

"Surveillance node." Another gesture. "Surveillance node."

He nodded to the opposite wall. "Possible surveillance node." He leaned closer as he walked past, scrutinizing it with his peripheral vision. "Strike that. Recessed turret?"

Mahir paced behind Cruz, watching as she highlighted each feature Kimani called out, labeling them as he dictated.

Kostic sat at the end of the table, in a chair that looked like it might have come from the hostel's front desk. She was swinging her legs from side to side absently as she watched the screens.

Still focusing on Smyth's screen, Mahir watched as Vozde's big head swung into view. The man's dumb grin was wide as he looked directly into the camera and actually winked. Then he moved forward a few strides, leading the mutant, to give them a clear view of his next action.

The big oaf turned toward the next surveillance node Kimani pointed out, looked directly at the dark, dead orb, and saluted with one raised finger.

There was a gust of a sigh over the audio feed, and Smyth's screen jiggled as she moved slightly.

Probably shaking her head in disgust, if he had to guess.

The trio moved down the corridor that way for an interminable period that was actually just twenty-three minutes and thirty-one seconds. They had traced the perimeter of nearly the entire compound, plotting out as many dangers and observation points as they could.

The three screens slackened their forward progress as they showed a widening of the hall.

Before them, on their left, appeared a massive blast door. It looked like any other such hatch that would isolate the internal structure of the mothership between distinct sections in case of a loss of pressure. There were two thousand, three hundred, and twelve doors like this scattered throughout the innards of Bakunin. There was nothing much special about this one.

Except that it was closed.

These heavy, armored doorways were almost never closed.

The vital sign monitors at the bottom of each screen started to show spikes in breathing and blood pressure.

This was the front gate of the enemy. Even ignorance of their foe's true identity was no armor against the very human reaction of knowing someone who wishes you ill resides on the other side of a door.

"Well screw that, then." Kimani's sour voice matched the face he turned toward Smyth's camera. "What you got that's goin' to crack that door, commander?"

The relationship between Mahir and his hirelings was confused, but they only ever used military terms like that when they were mocking him.

Had he cared about their opinions, it might have made him angry.

"He's right." Cruz looked at him, her face drawn. "There's no clean way through an emergency door like that."

Before Mahir could respond, Kimani's voice came through again. "No, wait."

"There's got to be another way in." Vozde had also turned to look into Smyth's camera. "No fortress is impenetrable."

A sudden motion from Kimani's camera caused Cruz, Kostic, and even Mahir to jump slightly. But the little man wasn't being attacked. He had begun to pace back and forth on the others' screens, his steps jerky and frenetic.

"Wait." He wasn't looking at Smyth's camera now, neither was Vozde, as the big man watched the little thief prowling back and forth. The would-be soldier was nodding silent encouragement as the smaller man worked through the problem.

"The remotes." He almost yelled the words, but stopped himself just short of that supreme error.

Vozde looked thrown. "What?"

Kimani stopped pacing, looking first up at the big man, then to Smyth, shifting his eyes down to the camera on her shoulder. "Their remotes!"

Of course. Mahir was nodding before Kimani started to explain.

"That's how they get their supplies, right?" On Smyth's screen, Vozde was nodding vigorously, his smile firmly back in place.

"Those have to be able to get in and out, or what's the use of the supplies?"

What those supplies were, they still didn't know. The purchase orders were so deeply encrypted there was no way to crack into them. With Cruz on their side, that was saying something.

Of course, he had a strong suspicion as to why those purchases were so well-hidden, but the rest of the team didn't.

But they did know deliveries were happening.

"We need to find where the remotes come in and out." Kimani looked so proud of himself.

"A castle is only as strong as its weakest door." Vozde was nodding violently.

Smyth, putting it all together before the others, began to move again, following the perimeter wall around the last corner toward where they had first joined the corridor. The images on the other screens started to bounce as the men moved to catch up to the mutant girl, her graceful form sliding easily down the hallway ahead of them.

Soon enough, built into that reinforced wall, they found three alcoves, each hidden among flourishes and alterations in the architecture that hadn't looked particularly important before.

Smyth walked calmly past the alcoves, looking casually into one as she passed. It was a recessed bay, with a doorway hidden among the shadows in the back.

She nodded once as she moved on.

Kimani picked up his pace again, a muttered "Yes!" barely audible over his feed.

Smyth and Kimani continued down the hall, as casual as they could manage. Mission accomplished.

Mahir's sense of satisfaction slowly gave way to mild confusion.

That was a very good view of the pair of them, moving away down the corridor.

It was Vozde's screen.

The big lummox wasn't following them.

He had stopped.

Kimani's screen slowly panned as on Vozde's visual, the little man turned to say something to him.

Kimani's look of confusion might have been funny at another time.

On Kimani's screen, then on Smyth's as well as the girl turned, sensing something was wrong, Mahir, Cruz, and Kostic watched as the big man stopped right in front of the final bay.

Kimani's screen showed the man growing larger as the little thief sidled down the corridor back toward the errant Zed-3.

Vozde's smile was wicked as he kneeled down before the opening, peering into the rear.

"How do we know—"

"Get up, you idiot!" Kimani, on Smyth's screen, reached down to yank Vozde up by the collar of his maintenance coveralls. As if that would have ever been possible.

"What?" Vozde rose but did not move away from the alcove. "No one's here! Let me go—"

Kostic and Cruz both jumped as a deafening chattering erupted from the screens.

Mahir's mind registered gunfire, light caliber, probably defensive turrets; but before he could say anything, he saw one of Cruz's repeater screens flashing red.

Authorities?

No, it was the other repeater.

The one that showed activity in the corridors around the compound.

A door, a habitat for transitional personnel, disgorged a team of lightly-armored fighters, their gear and clothing garish and varied, into a nearby corridor.

One of them, better armed and armored than the others, in an impressive, if nonstandard pattern of scratched up red armor, was guiding them with a hurried, waving hand.

As that crimson and black figure fell into step behind the others, Mahir thought he heard Cruz gasp, but the sound, if he hadn't imagined it through faulty subroutines, was lost amidst the sounds now crackling through their jury-rigged ops system.

"What's happening?!" Cruz was leaning across the table, shouting into the screen's audio interfaces.

Each of the screens was an indecipherable scramble of images. Wildly swinging flashes of corridor, of each member of the team, all moving frantically.

The lighting shifted and flashed as the chattering continued.

"You've got to get out of there!" Mahir leaned over Cruz's shoulder. "They've activated remote turrets."

"No shit, asshole." Kimani's tone lacked a certain amount of respect, he thought.

"Back up front!" Smyth was in the lead, one of her monofilament blades flashing as she swept up beneath auto-turrets and slashed them into scrap as she moved.

"No!" Cruz had noticed her flashing repeater. "You've got bad guys coming at you that way. Move back!"

That didn't seem right to him. He looked again at the footage of the team moving toward his people.

They were human.

Something wasn't right.

"What?!" Kimani's plaintive wail ignored any need for operational security.

"Bad guys, looks like Combi Rifles and one Chain Rifle. Get out of there! Back to your last left!"

He had to admire Cruz. For a human, she was holding up quite well under the stress.

"There's at least one underslung grenade launcher as well." Mahir's voice was perfectly modulated.

"Damnit!" Vozde's own deep voice echoed across the feed.

On Smyth's screen, they saw the big man swing into view. There was bright red splashed across his shoulder and up his face.

"Petar's hit!" The mutant's point of view swept back, Vozde's big ugly face swelling alarmingly in the screen, and then he swept out of view as she turned back, most likely holding him up and dragging him toward the questionable safety of the outer corridors.

On Kimani's screen, as he caught up with Vozde and the Morlock, he saw that the small girl was, in fact, supporting the giant, one arm under his and across his back.

As the little thief caught up, looking at his teammates to see if there was anything he could do to assist them, Mahir spared a moment to wonder at the mutant girl's strength.

Then he saw her face, twisted in growing rage.

Well, that made sense. He didn't know who the pursuing humans were, but they were about to get a cruel surprise.

The deeper roar of a Combi Rifle filled the feeds, echoing off the corridor walls.

"¡Os vamos a joder vivos, cabrones!"

"Oh, shit." Vozde muttered through gritted teeth. "Not these assholes again!"

"Keep moving!" Smyth's voice was nearly a growl.

The scene came to a corner, and the mutant girl hurled Vozde unceremoniously down the intersecting corridor.

On Kimani's screen, they saw Smyth zip past him, back down the way they had come.

Toward the pursuing fighters.

Her face, seen for only a moment and then gone, was contorted with fury.

"Wha—?"

"Get Petar out of this!" She nearly howled the words back at him, but he stood, transfixed, at the corner.

There were no turrets here, at least. Mahir filed that away for future reference, in case they got another shot at the compound after this fiasco.

This is what he got, outsourcing his violence to humans.

On Kimani's screen, they watched as the girl rushed at the small knot of fighters moving cautiously toward her.

She danced from side to side as she ran, spinning and wheeling around the lines of tracer fire that sailed, in apparent slow motion, down the hall.

One of the rounds hit her in the leg, and someone on the screen cried out.

It could have been either Kimani or Vozde, he saw, as the big man had managed to crawl back to the corner and was looking around it at the erupting violence.

"You've got to get down to the first four-way and go right!" Cruz was shouting at Kimani, desperately scrolling through information as she tried to plot their escape route.

Except that Kimani wasn't listening to her.

No one was.

On the dual screens, Smyth's own now a useless blur of colors and movement, they watched the girl, armed with only the single blade, sweeping toward the enemy, who had paused in disbelief as she seemed to have danced through their fire.

A thunderous roar exploded from the group as the Chain Rifle spat a spreading cloud of molten, bright-hot shrapnel.

There was a barely-audible gasp as the blast enveloped the girl. Mahir couldn't tell if it had been Cruz, Kostic, or the men watching the battle live.

He realized, after a moment, it could well have been him.

On the dual screens, Smyth staggered, stumbling in her run, falling to one knee even as she continued to move forward.

From within the small group of attackers, a man in distinctive red armor stood tall, taking aim with his Combi Rifle.

And then he stumbled forward as another fighter pushed past him, raising another rifle, a huge grin on his manic face.

And then something long and thin sprouted from the second man's forehead.

And then a howling Smyth was on them.

She leapt, her right leg trailing limply, and grabbed the standing, stunned corpse by its shoulders, head-butting the pummel of her knife, stuck expertly through his skull after her prodigious throw, driving the blade out through the back of his head.

The others screamed, their terror clear as the camera on the girl's shoulder took it all in.

She let go of the tumbling rifleman, reaching back with her left hand as her right moved up to yank the knife out of her first victim.

She did a handstand on her one hand, spinning as she came down on her uninjured leg, her right arm straight as she jammed the knife up under the chin of the woman with the Chain Rifle. Behind her, the gleam of the blade rising up over her shoulder caught the light of the corridor.

There was a gagging sound. Most likely Kimani, Mahir thought.

As the woman with the Chain Rifle toppled to the side, Smyth sprang back up, hurtling over the three remaining figures. Her knee caught the armored man in the face even as he reached out for the fallen Chain Rifle, sending him to the deck howling, while her knife took another man in the ear, emerging from his opposite temple as his eyes crossed silently.

"Oh, god—" That was most likely Vozde.

"Oh, no!" Kostic's aged voice broke into his fascinated study of the Morlock girl in action and to the far right edge of the screens – where the alcoves had opened, spilling a strange purple light into the hallway, accompanied by a bizarre, creeping ground-fog that confirmed his long-held suspicion.

That fog could not be normal atmosphere.

Out of the fog rattled three low, black shapes, skittering forward on spindly legs.

Combat remotes.

To be precise, the exact same models he and Ridhaan had faced on Corregidor.

The same model that had killed his partner.

The same bastard that had killed his friend.

There was another growl, and he felt no shame at all as he realized it had come from his own throat.

"Rosa, you've got to get out of there!" Hanima had called up several dials, and her own remote was quivering with the amount of power she was pulling from it. "You've got remotes coming toward you!"

"Run, Rosa! We'll get out this way!" Kimani's shrill voice broke through the girl's combat trance where Cruz yelling through the remote connection hadn't.

The girl wasted no time acknowledging the order. As Kimani's own screen panned away, swooping down toward the prone giant, Smyth's viewpoint showed her kneeing another opponent, sending him falling gracefully backward into his companions, including the red-armored leader, who dropped the Chain Rifle again to the sodden flooring. She flashed past them, then she was limping away, at incredible speed, down the corridor retracing her attacker's path.

For the moment, they seemed too stunned to follow.

"Left, left, right!" Cruz barked, steering Smyth toward more narrow corridors that would give her better control of her back trail.

"Matias, right at the four-way!" She switched repeaters, knocking the screens off the table, with the help of the old woman, and sending her holographic dials spreading out over the surface.

"I've got it!" the little man was panting, trying to haul Vozde's limping bulk away from the enemy compound.

"You've got this." Kostic hovered over the hacker's shoulder, massaging her knotting muscles as the girl stared into the shifting holograms.

"We've got this." Cruz's voice was flat; her eyes not wavering from the incoming reports and images.

"I'm going to close the service hatch on that corridor behind you, Rosa, just get there." The information was scrolling rapidly, each of the dials telling its own, grim story.

"Trying." There was no emotion in the mutant girl's voice. The pain there allowed for nothing else.

"Matias, head to the food market ahead. The crowd should offer you some protection." There were several local security alerts lighting up the smallest dial.

"We're going to have Moderators all over us in a few minutes." Mahir did not want to jog Cruz's elbow, but it was imperative the outcome of this debacle include escaping the attention of D.I. Kovač and her gang.

"I know—"

Her scream tore through the quiet room as all the screens flared and went dark.

Mahir was engulfed for a moment in torturous flames, his mind flickering with pain; then he pulled his awareness out of his shallow connection with Arachne, shaking his head, disoriented.

"Quantronic-attack." He muttered the words, trying to clear his vision.

He saw the Dak's training had taken over, and she was tending to a stunned Cruz, who was laying on the ground, staring at the ceiling, her head rocking vaguely side to side. Under the table, her remote was crouching like a frightened animal.

"Mil-grade countermeasures." He stumbled to the table, pulling the screens upright. If he couldn't get something up and running, he was going to have to dip back into Arachne, no matter what was waiting for him on the other side.

It was no good. Each of the screens showed only static. Two of them were cracked, either from Cruz tumbling them to the floor or from the impact of the power surge that had accompanied the attack.

There was no way to contact their people.

Vozde and Smyth, wounded; Kimani, a coward of the first order; divided and pursued, with no way to get them aid of any kind.

They were all on their own, now, with no way to know what was happening next.

Chapter 17

Hotel Khatmandu, Commune X-7, VaudeVille, *Bakunin*

Rosa's screams echoed off the ceiling as her blood spattered across the floor. Hanima, pushed into a far corner in her nest of cushions and fabric, made every attempt to ignore the sounds and the sharp, iron smell, as she worked her way through several dials once again supported by an upright Parachit.

Nia worked furiously over the screaming girl, muttering an unbroken monologue of soothing words as her hands flashed over Rosa's leg. The Chain Rifle, firing a spray of half-melted, twisted shrapnel, just grazed her, but that had been enough to pepper the leg with countless small, smoking wounds.

The Dak had seemed surprised the girl had been able to stay upright, never mind flee on her own.

"I'm telling you, you think the service corridors back home are bad?" Matias, pacing in and out of the kitchenette, had a can of alcohol in one hand and was fidgeting with one of his disposable drives in the other. "It's a maze, man. And everywhere that damned psycho-reactive 'art.' It was a total nightmare."

Petar, sitting in the largest chair they had been able to acquire, only nodded. He was holding a bloody rag to his shoulder, his face pale.

Nia had been in the process of cleaning out his wound when Rosa had limped in. The big man had leapt from the chair and swept the table clear so they could put the girl onto it. She had been swaying in the doorway, threatening to collapse at any moment.

"Those damned remotes wouldn't stop, either! They just kept coming and coming!" Matias slapped Petar on the back without seeming to think about it. "Big guy here body-checked one into the wall, right through a damned Quantronic billboard about acceptance, or some other nonsense." He grinned wickedly at the memory. "That remote crashed right into the hard metal behind the hologram. It was beautiful."

Mahir, leaning against the wall by the refrigeration unit, just shook his head.

He had been very quiet since the *Alagaav* Quantronic security protocols had shoved him and Cruz both back into their own heads.

Matias stopped his pacing, his face lost in dark thoughts. "When we crashed out into the concourse, they stopped. By the time we were surrounded by civies and turned around, they were gone."

"Deniability." Mahir was staring at Rosa, who had grown still on the table, panting quietly while Nia moved from one wound to the next, extracting bits of twisted, steaming metal with a magnetic prod. "They're not ready to reveal their presence. They're trying to assess, right now, what their chances are of staying in the shadows."

"Screw that." Petar's voice was tight from pain. "There's got to be Moderators all over the place out there by now."

Matias giggled. "I bet the Social Energy is swinging strongly in favor of 'Law and Order,' yeah?"

"They can't stay in the shadows." Mahir did not stir, but his eye shifted to find Hanima, hugging her knees in the corner. "They'll be coming as soon as they figure that out."

"Maybe they don't know where we are!" It was clear from Matias's voice that even he didn't believe that. "I mean, they didn't follow us home, right?"

"They know where we are." Hanima's voice sounded dull in her own head; she kept stealing glances at Rosa's pained blue face. The echoes of her screams, and Petar's, would buzz in her mind forever. "Their security programs caught us dead to rights. They won't have a problem tracking back to us."

Matias glared at her, blaming the messenger in the grand tradition. Then he looked back to Mahir. "But they kept their remotes out of sight once we ran. You really think they're going to release the hounds?"

"They've got the *Gatos*, too." Petar muttered.

"Yeah, what was up with that shit?!" Matias gestured to the group at large with sweeping hands. "What the hell are those guys doing here? I thought we were done with them!" He stopped, fear sweeping across his face, and he spun back to Mahir. "Shit. You think they followed us?"

Mahir shook his head, but Hanima answered before he could. "They have to be working with the *Alagaav*. That's why the remote Mahir was tracking headed into their territory, why we were right there, because we went so deep into the *Gatos'* territory for the cache vault."

Mahir nodded. "They have no idea who you are."

"So," Matias leaned his back against the wall, bewilderment clear on his face, his expression soft with wonder, "it was *Los Gatos-7* all along."

Mahir snorted and Hanima rolled her eyes. "No." The strange bald man stepped away from the wall, coming to the center of the room. "They're just local muscle."

"Like us." Petar said it, but she had been thinking the same thing. "Pawns."

Mahir shifted his gaze to the big man, looking steadily into his light eyes. "Soldiers."

Petar grunted and looked away.

Maybe he wasn't so keen on the idea of being a hero after all.

"We need to decide what we're going to do." Nia looked up, wiping her hands through the antiseptic field fuzzing the air over the MediKit. "While we still have options."

Matias nodded, looking from the Dak to Petar, then to Hanima.

She tried not to be hurt by the dismissive sniff she could almost hear as he quickly moved on to look to Mahir for what they might do next.

But the stranger was looking at her.

Hanima reached out to stroke Parachit's sleek, armored back as she sank against the cushions.

Things had felt so good for a little while. Everyone had been working together as a team. Even Mahir had seemed to feel it. And now, with blood all over the table and the floor, with their two most formidable fighters wounded…

Rosa and Petar had been injured carrying out her plan. She had hurt them. She might as well have been holding the Chain Rifle.

She didn't want this.

Maybe she should have stayed in the Hiring Halls, hoping to link up with another Work Team.

It wasn't too late for that, if she managed to survive this nightmare.

A nightmare none of them seemed to think they could get out of.

She saw the doubt in their eyes when she spoke; the lack of confidence that always seemed to bubble up when the going got tough. She always knew that lack of faith would be there one day. That day was now.

She had allowed herself to wonder if maybe this could be a home, of sorts.

She should have known.

She looked up at them. Matias wouldn't meet her eyes, but Petar did, briefly. She thought the fact that he looked away after that might have hurt more than if he had never looked at her at all. Nia was pretending she had faith, anyway.

And Rosa?

Rosa was sedated, her head rocking loosely side to side, the fleshy tendrils that crowned her head spread out over the blood-splashed table, her customary kerchief having come loose in the fighting. Her eyes were heavy-lidded, looking vaguely up into the ceiling.

Hanima didn't want this.

All of her ideas, the plans that had sprung, fully formed, into her mind at each step of this operation, were gone. She couldn't think of anything.

And no one wanted to hear it, even if she could.

They were trapped. Whoever was hiding within the *Alagaav* commune would be coming for them at any moment.

They were trapped like a rat in a service conduit, just before the work crew purged the atmosphere to rid themselves of the vermin.

That was them; that was her. Vermin to be blown out into space at the convenience of whoever had killed Mahir's partner.

She remembered again the heavy beating of the incoming fire on her ears as she cowered in the cache vault, waiting for the *Gatos* to finish her off.

She saw Declan's empty eyes staring up into the swirling smoke of the battle, and against her volition, she looked over at Rosa again.

They had come so close to losing her and Petar both.

And it had been just dumb luck Matias, too, hadn't been gunned down in that garishly-decorated, neon-bathed corridor.

She shook her head, although none of the rest of them could know what was in there.

Or maybe they did. They could probably guess, anyway.

Matias, at least, wouldn't be surprised that she had decided to give up.

She looked up at Mahir. He would be able to get them off Bakunin, and then he could find some other team to help him route out the bastards behind the blast doors.

Then she saw Nia, the old woman's smile still stubbornly in place.

"We can do this, *mtoto*. You've got this." The old Dak nodded.

And the light glistened off the drops of blood still staining her cheek.

"No!" Hanima scrambled to her feet, her hands balled at her sides. "No, I don't! And no, no, we can't!"

The old woman winced back as if she had been slapped. Her eyes hardened with anger and resentment.

But that couldn't matter. Not anymore.

"This is it! We're lucky we're all still alive!" She jabbed a finger at the table, where Rosa had rolled her head around to look at her. "Rosa almost wasn't! Do you want to keep this charade up until someone else dies? What would it take you to understand that this was a bad idea?! Declan's dead! Do we need to lose someone else? Two more people? Do we all have to be dead before you understand?!"

Nia had flinched away from each point and finally looked away, her face slack. On the table, Rosa moved with a groan, spinning around and pushing herself upright, reaching out with one shaking arm to put it around the old woman's shoulders.

"That's it." Hanima started, turning back to find Matias nodding vigorously. "That's right." The thief's eyes were bright. "It's time someone with some real experience took over this outfit."

"Oh, shut up, you little weasel." Petar's face was twisted with anger; he rose to his feet, looking down at the smaller man. "No one's going to follow you to the latrine. So you can just—"

"Not me." The little man turned. "Him."

He was pointing to Mahir. "He can get us out of this."

Mahir was watching this all with an inscrutable expression. His one dark eye glared at each of them in turn before he shook his bald head.

"I'm not leaving until I've completed my mission. I won't be getting anyone out before that."

Matias shook his head in disbelief. "Call O-12! Notify the Bakunian Conciliator, have them call out the Moderator Corps! Hell," he waved his hands over his head, "call the Nomad Executive Board! You don't think they'd want to know?"

"No." The single word was not shouted. There was no anger or fear or any other identifiable human emotion behind it, which Hanima found more frightening than if Mahir had been raging.

"No?" Matias cocked his head to the side as if he didn't understand. "Why the hell not?!"

"You don't need to know." Mahir's eye did not waver as he stared into Matias's fear-maddened face. "I solve this problem. I will bring this enemy to heel. With or without your team, I will be going forward from here, not back, and not to any kind of Nomad authorities."

"No way the Executive Board lets any more O-12 onto Bakunin without a full review of what's happening." Nia's words were flat.

Mahir nodded. "Things are too far gone. It is only us, now." He shrugged, heading toward his room. "Or me."

"Hanima," Rosa was tentative, but her eyes were steady.

"No!" She backed away. "You can't. You, most of all, can't ask that!"

Beside her, she felt Parachit starting to vibrate with quiet intensity.

She had no interest in the remote's twitchy programing then, however.

"You heard him!" She pointed back at Mahir, who had stopped at his door, turning to look at them placidly. "He doesn't need us!"

"That's not what he said." Petar still wouldn't meet her eyes, but his shoulders were set with stubborn tension.

"I don't care—"

A muffled shout from the hallway interrupted her tirade. It had been a question, but she couldn't make out the words.

A faint buzzing insinuated into her mind. Something was wrong.

She looked around for the monitors, but they were scattered on the spilled curtains where Matias had piled them after Petar cleared the table.

She sent a quick order through her comlog and called up the dial she had tied to the local security network.

The holographic disk spun into existence before her, and she scanned the data crashing through the system.

She jumped for the pile of monitors, dropped one into the blood and discarded bandages on the table, and sent a quick impulse to activate it, connecting it to the same system.

The wide public corridor outside the hostel appeared in the screen, grainy and twitching. Whether that was due to the rough way they'd been handling the monitors or some remaining artifact of the defensive impulse that had flashed through their systems, she didn't know. And she didn't have time to care.

The picture was clear enough to make out a line of garishly-dressed figures, weapons held tightly, moving in from either end of the big hall.

Leading them was a man in bulky red mil-spec armor.

The armor she had recognized from the first moments of the fight.

But that wasn't the worst of it.

Behind those two advancing lines, she could just make out the spindly shapes of combat remotes slinking forward, their matte black armor absorbing the neon light of the public corridor.

Mahir stepped away from his door and moved up behind her, looking over her shoulder at the screen, then flicking a quick glance at the dial still glowing by her elbow.

More screaming, this time coming both from the common room door and from the buzzing speaker of the screen. With a silent thought, Hanima changed the view from the outer hallway to one of the cameras Matias had placed in the hostel itself.

On the monitor, they could now see the lobby, and that the *Los Gatos-7* fighters weren't stopping the usual denizens of the Hotel Khatmandu common areas who were trying to flee in terror. A couple of them took idle kicks at the fleeing civilians to hurry them along, but in less than a minute, the lobby was empty.

"Too late." Matias's voice fell flat in the room, punctuated by the distant, muffled screams of the fleeing hostel staff and guests.

The *mara* fighters moved into the lobby, their gun muzzles sweeping from side to side to cover the large room. They slunk in, ensuring themselves that no one was hiding behind the scattered chairs and couches.

"Come on out, *puta*!" The man in the red and black armor shouted, looking down the various narrow halls that led to the guest rooms. "You got nowhere to run, nowhere to hide!" He raised his Chain Rifle in one hand. "It can go fast or slow. You come out, you choose."

Behind the line of gangers, the remotes came through the double-wide doorway, stalking forward, their sensor arrays searching for targets.

"So, why would a group of reclusive technocrats have so many combat remotes?" Petar was standing behind her, looking at the screen.

Hanima lifted her arm, the dial coming with it, and she commanded it to spin up wider with a glance. A schematic of the hostel floated out of the hologram, with glaring red signal returns showing each attacker. With a thought, she put black circles around the remotes.

There were ten of them, moving up behind nine *Gatos*.

And not a single one of the indicators moved toward the other halls. They were all converging on the hall that led to her team's rooms.

On the screen everyone else was watching, the view shifted to the hall outside their room. She looked at Matias, who was gripping the monitor frame with one hand. He nodded to her.

One by one, her team looked to Mahir for orders. Petar looked sheepish as he glanced briefly at her first, but eventually everyone, him included, was watching their strange benefactor for guidance.

And then, like in a nightmare, that dark face with its black eyepatch and single, intense, dark eye swiveled to look at her.

There was no way out of the hostel. Like most of the communes in Bakunin, the Hotel Khatmandu was a self-contained module with only the single entry point.

And there were now nearly twenty enemies between them and that exit.

Why was he looking at her?

But then she had a more alarming thought. Who was he, really?

He was a good hacker, she knew enough now to say that. And he carried himself like he would be able to fight if it came to that. He certainly carried his MULTI Rifle like he knew what to do with it. And he had known enough to procure just the right kinds of supplies and support for them.

But was he a soldier?

She wasn't either, but she had realized a new skill over the past few weeks that she had never known she'd had. She could see each tactical situation, as it developed, as a puzzle.

There was always a way to solve any puzzle.

The question was, was she willing to pay the price to solve this particular puzzle?

She looked down again at her dial.

The enemies were still creeping down the hall toward her.

There was no way they could flee. They might be able to charge the fighters in the hall, distract them with a burst of violence, fight through them into the lobby, and then run out into the public corridors.

No matter what Mahir said, the Moderators would quickly put a stop to any violence that erupted out in the public areas.

In fact, she paused. If they waited long enough, a Moderator would have to come check to see why so many of the staff and guests of the hostel had just fled, screaming, out into the corridors.

Could they last that long?

But then, if only one Moderator showed up, how long would it take backup to answer the call, when the real situation became clear?

Escaping was going to cost her friends more blood, she knew. She looked over at Rosa, who was helping Nia spray a quick bandage over Petar's now-bare shoulder.

That was Nia for you. Even under the threat of imminent death at the hands of an out of control *mara* far from home, she knew she had to patch them all up as much as she could, to preserve the widest possible range of options.

Petar's smile was back in place. The AutoDoc in the MediKit must have administered some strong sedatives.

Matias was looking at the big man with a shade of jealousy.

If they tried to run, some of them, maybe all of them, would die.

If they waited for the Moderators to rescue them, again, they would pay for every second with blood.

But how could they fight a group like that under these circumstances?

Only one of them was going to fit into the hallway at a time. Could Petar get into his armor fast enough, and then rush out to plug the gap? How much damage would that heavy armor of his take before he was riddled with bullets and chunks of smoking shrapnel?

Rosa was in no condition to dance into the enemy, no matter how lethal she had proven before the gates of the enemy's fortress. Although she did have both of her blades, now, she had lost a lot of blood. Nia and the AutoDoc had administered several different mysterious substances, but even the best medicine wasn't going to be able to completely erase that much damage so fast.

Again, she had found a way out of making a decision.

But this time, the decision that had been made for her was terrifying.

They had run out of choices. There was an enemy at the door, with no way out and no help on the way.

They were going to have to fight, whether she wanted to or not.

And although Petar might have been happy to charge into the hall again as he had during their assault on the cache vault, that wouldn't solve anything.

She had no doubt Rosa wouldn't hesitate from charging into the hall and taking as many of the *Gatos* with her before they dragged her down, but that wouldn't do anything but put off the inevitable either.

Eventually, each of her teammates would fall. They'd all get chewed up one at a time until there wasn't anyone left to hold the door, and then the enemy would be in the room among the most vulnerable of them, and it would all be over.

She looked around the common room. The furniture was a mess, with their makeshift table drenched in drying blood, the mismatched chairs and crates scattered among the pillows and cushions of the chamber's original bohemian décor. The pile of fabric was tangled in the corner, by her nest.

She glanced at the four doors that led to the sleeping chambers almost without seeing them. They had no assets, nowhere to hide, no armored bunkers or reinforced walls.

Enemy gunfire would slice through these partitions as if they didn't exist.

The colorful fabric hangings they had torn down would be just as much protection.

Then she stopped. She looked at the doors; four chambers leading into this common room.

She looked at the pile of fabric on the floor.

She looked up at the team, each staring at her with a different expression.

Did Nia look hopeful? Just the thought was like a dagger in Hanima's heart.

Petar and Rosa, ironically, were watching her with seeming confidence. Each of them had bled for her last plan, and there they were, both apparently willing to step up again if she would only choose to lead them.

Matias looked like he wanted to throw up. She had no doubt that, if the little man thought he could get away with it, he'd sell them all to the *Gatos* if it meant he could walk away.

And then there was Mahir. His cloak hanging from his broad shoulders, hood down, face impassive.

But was that a challenge in the man's single eye? Or was that confidence?

She looked down at the dial again. They were running out of time.

Her head rose up, and she saw, again, everyone looking at her.

Nia nodded with a smile.

Petar and Rosa nodded; one with a smile, one with a confident calm.

Matias, looking at the others first, turned back to her, took a deep breath, and then nodded himself.

Mahir did not nod.

The man looked at her, then gestured with one hand toward her as if indicating that it was her turn to talk.

She took a deep breath of her own.

"I think I've got a plan."

Then, Mahir nodded.

Chapter 18

Hotel Khatmandu, Commune X-7, VaudeVille, *Bakunin*

Mahir stared at the door to his personal cell. He leaned against the back wall, idly scanning what just might be the last quarters he would enjoy in this life. His bed had finally shown its usefulness; tipped on its side and providing a flimsy barricade behind which he could fall in the event that Cruz's plan fell apart.

Sadly, he assumed the chances of that were higher than he would like. The hacker had shown a gift for solving tactical problems on the fly, but there was little chance of making anything positive out of their current situation.

He shook his head, even though there were no humans to observe the performative gesture. He doubted even the Recreated Sun Tze would be able to construct a plan to get out of a jam like this.

He found himself once again, and possibly for the last time, wishing he was serving out this mission anywhere but with the Nomads. If he was within the warm embrace of Maya, bravery would have been far easier to come by. No matter what happened to his Lhost, his physical body, the essence of what made him who and what he was would simply return to ALEPH through the datasphere, ready to continue to serve.

If he died here, disconnected from Maya and completely isolated from the light of ALEPH, his death would most likely be as true as any death could be.

Of course, if his worst fears were confirmed, a permanent death would be the least of his worries.

To be reprogrammed, to be turned into a traitor of ALEPH against his will, if they caught him before he could slag the Cube that stored his essence, would be a torment akin to the human's understanding of Hell itself.

He checked his CineticS Radjun MULTI Rifle again, knowing perfectly well what he would find. It was the best such weapon to be had among the Nomads, and all ammunition reserves were topped off, Ultrashock, Double Action, and armor piercing alternating every set of four with a tracer round.

He allowed himself a grim smile as he registered the DA icon hovering over the weapon.

The tracer rounds, of course, were entirely superfluous. But he found them strangely satisfying all the same.

Probably more cross-contamination with the humans, he figured.

He only had two repeaters remaining for his Pitcher, but that didn't seem like much of a problem given how ineffective they had proven against the remote that had attacked him and Ridhaan back on Corregidor.

Ridhaan. He knew, even if his human catspaws managed to perform a miracle and overcame the assault force closing in on them, the next step, assaulting the prepared defenders behind the fortress walls of the *Alagaav,* was going to kill whoever survived the hostel attack.

And he would follow Ridhaan into the unknown.

He knew, of course. There was no doubt what fate awaited an Aspect of ALEPH who perished beyond the embrace of the AI: nothing.

The endless, senseless optimism of human sentimentalism must have been rubbing off on him.

With no need to hide his true nature, he allowed the armored patch to rise from over his ocular implants. His vision came alive with the tepid overlays of the Arachne Digital Patina as he called up columns of data from the local sphere, running through several surveillance perspectives. Of course, none of the humans could see those augmetics. Such advanced alterations were looked upon with dark suspicion by too many of the Nomads.

Savages.

The eye included every modern convenience. He tapped into all the spy eyes deployed around their refuge, building a mosaic view, skimming as deep as he dared to go into the data morass of Arachne for additional information.

The lobby of the Hotel Khatmandu was an abandoned mess; furniture overturned, front desk pushed over to rest against the bulkhead beyond, a holographic interface for guest registration flickering in the shadows behind.

The hall just outside their room was swarming with human attackers and sleek black combat remotes. They were holding off to either side of the door, fearing, no doubt, someone firing indiscriminately through the flimsy material. Normal human fear was keeping them slow for now, but that wouldn't last forever. He doubted his real enemies would be willing to wait out a siege of the little hostel.

And as for his real enemies, why were they using human agents at all? They had access to some of the most gifted impersonators and infiltrators humanity had ever encountered. Why rely on such amateur muscle for what had to be a major operation? But then, with the paranoia that had swept the entire Human Sphere after the recent revelations of advanced infiltrators into the highest levels of government and culture throughout scattered humanity, here, it was probably best for the real infiltrators not to take a chance in exposing themselves unless they were forced to.

He meant to force them, if he got out of this.

And that was the flaw in his current predicament, he knew. He had inadvertently spun off several subroutines to contain the thoughts and isolate them from his current performance parameters, but that didn't make any sense. He needed to face the reality of his situation, not hide from what might need to be done.

He had come to value these strange humans, no matter how hard he tried to keep them at arm's length. It was almost as if Ridhaan's cursed affection for them had somehow infected him, now, too.

But he had a duty to the entire Human Sphere if he was right about what was really happening behind that armored gate.

If there was a chance to break through the assault lines closing in on them, he had to do that.

It was imperative that he get to the *Alagaav* commune and force their hand. Even if he was destroyed in the process—

No. Even though he *would be* destroyed, revealing what was behind those blast doors would end their threat here.

The rest of the Human Sphere would know the market attack for what it really was: just another layer of the assault against all humanity, not just the most powerful players. The hyper powers, ALEPH, O-12, and all the rest needed to focus on the truth of the situation and stop chasing phantoms, using those ghosts as excuses to prosecute yesterday's wars.

He did not want to abandon his human companions to bring that about, but he would, if he needed to.

He scanned through the dizzying mosaic and looked out across the common room. Cruz had ordered Kimani and Vozde to bring the table into their room to serve as another barricade. The cushions and pillows were all pushed into the backs of the various sleeping rooms, and the ugly fabrics had been hastily reattached to their ceiling clamps where they hung, crooked and awkwardly draped.

When the enemy finally marshalled their courage, they would crash through that door, anticipating a hail of fire, only to be lost in a maze of ugly curtains.

There would be no cover, other than those flimsy barriers, when four lanes of fire opened up into what would certainly be reduced to an abattoir in a matter of moments.

Of course, that would only serve to blunt the assault, as follow-on waves would eventually overwhelm their individual rooms.

He coopted the internal security network and checked in on his minions.

Cruz and her remote were ready in her cell, crouched down behind an overturned bed. She was watching the approaching attackers through her own dial hovering off to one side.

Kimani was leaning against one wall, his Combi Rifle resting on his shoulder as he gave a sour look to the massive bulk of Vozde, now fully kitted out in his armor again. Between the added physical bulk of the heavy suit and the massive power cylinders down his back, he took up far more space than any unarmored man would. Between the Dak's ministrations and the armor's own internal systems, the flesh wound in the man's shoulder should not be a problem before he was pulled, screaming, out of the garish orange and blue panoply.

The Dak, for her part, was sitting calmly in her room, having what appeared to be a normal, civil conversation with the blue-skinned mutant girl who sat on one of the big cushions from the main room, her back to the pile of overturned beds. The girl was nodding occasionally, clearly listening to whatever wisdom the old woman was trying to impart.

What benefit old-woman wisdom could possibly offer, given what was about to engulf them all, Mahir could not fathom.

Was there something wrong with him? He ran a quick self-diagnostic subroutine, but no error flags appeared, so he dismissed his doubt with another very human shrug.

He must have drifted so far from his original template that pessimism was as natural as fear for his own continued existance.

A movement in the hall caught his attention. The human attackers were having some kind of argument. One of them, the crimson-armored specter with the Chain Rifle, was clearly telling another to take the door. That fighter, a woman with a Combi Rifle and an underslung launcher of some kind, was shaking her head with violent emphasis, gesturing wildly to the remotes that stood nearby.

It was a good question. Why were they sending a human in before the remotes?

What she didn't know was that her masters cared not at all for their human pawns. Those remotes represented a considerable cost in resources and risk. Local gangers were a dime a dozen, as Ridhaan used to say.

"You bastard." He muttered under his breath, as if his friend could hear. "Here we go."

The woman in the hallway glared at the man, then set herself as if for a difficult task.

At a signal from the man, she hit the door with her shoulder, having taken a four-step run; all the narrow corridor would allow.

Just as she hit, the door opened, precisely as Cruz had programmed it to.

The woman fell through the sliding door and into the tangle of fabric. He heard her muffled scream through the door to his room and over the link at virtually the same time.

It was rather comical.

An angry roar and a loud cough sounded from behind the door as the confused, frustrated woman launched a grenade, blind. The ordnance tore through several layers of fabric but then lost momentum, becoming tangled in the next drape. The curtain flared away from her, containing the grenade, then settled back down.

Toward the woman.

The spent grenade tangled in its folds.

Mahir made no effort to suppress his tight grin as the ordnance detonated with a chest-thumping crash, less than four feet from the woman who had shot it.

The woman was thrown back into the kitchenette with a scream. Blood splashed across that half of the room and she fell to the floor, groaning.

The man with the Chain Rifle had been coming in on her heels, faceplate slammed down. He stopped when he saw the hangings, and ducked back out right after she had fired her launcher.

After the cloud of propellant and shrapnel cleared, the man came back in, far more cautious than his minion. The featureless helmet scanned the room as the wildly swinging hangings settled down around him.

"¡*Sal, perra*!" His voice was hollow over the exterior speakers. He slowly moved into the room, waving his other fighters in behind him and gesturing for them to fan out. "Nowhere to run, girl. This is where it ends."

He lifted the Chain Rifle, using the muzzle to push aside the last hanging, and gazed at the door on the other side.

Mahir's door.

Mahir's smile widened.

This situation was nothing like swimming through the datasphere of Maya, but there was a certain freedom in not having to hide his true nature.

His rifle switched ammo selection without visible prompting.

The sad excuse for a Digital Patina he was able to conjure up triangulated his target through the door, coordinating the process with the views from the cameras placed on the other side.

Mahir's door disappeared, churned to splintered composite as a roaring scream of armor piercing rounds flashed out, sent several cloth hangings dancing drunkenly, and slammed into the crimson-armored figure.

With a widening grin, Mahir ordered the MULTI Rifle to cycle one of his precious Double Action rounds and sent it spearing after the AP shots. The double kick of the ammo leaving the gun would have been imperceptible to a human.

There was a faint grunt as the high velocity double round struck the shattered armor plating. The speakers crackled into silence as the heavy body jounced twice under the impacts.

He toppled over, his head loose and flopping. As he died, his furious brain sent a flurry of conflicting signals through his expiring body. His trigger finger tightened and a whir sounded through the room as his Chain Rifle pulled a length of raw steel ammo from the spool in its stock. The chain was fed into the firing chamber as the body continued to fall, the arms rising as if in surprise.

There was a scream from the second wave of fighters as someone realized what was happening.

The Chain Rifle sent a cone of smoking shrapnel; sharp, twisted chunks of torn and melted chain, spraying out into the hall.

Five fabric hangings were torn to shreds, bits of burning cloth fluttering through the air.

One of the attackers, too slow to respond to his companion's screamed warning, was caught full in the face by the blast. His body was thrown violently back out into the hall where it struck the opposite wall, leaving a dark splash of matter and then sliding down into a twitching heap.

Well, that had gone even better than anticipated.

Mahir thought perhaps he should be concerned with the unalloyed glee he felt watching the sequence of events unfold through his enhanced vision.

Then the remotes came crashing in.

Somewhere, someone had decided that the humans weren't going to have much luck after all.

He looked into the Patina, to where he had put the results of a constant search of emergency services traffic. The notification glowed a dull red. It had been bound to happen sooner or later; a Moderator had been dispatched to the Hotel Khatmandu.

His shadowy enemy would have seen the same thing and knew that their time was running short.

The remotes came crashing through the doorway, past the body of the human leader, and spread out, advancing on all four doors at once.

They completely ignored the fabric hangings; they could see through them, most likely. Their perceptions of the battle space probably didn't even include anything as ephemeral as cloth drapes.

Mahir hunkered down as the walls around him shook with a deep, resonating boom.

Vozde had braced the barrel of his HMC on the bed before him and fired the massive weapon through the door and into the head of the remote on the other side. He had to struggle to keep the recoil from bringing the blur of the rotating barrels up into the ceiling. As it was, they ground through the frame of the bed in moments. The brilliant stream of armor-penetrating darts shattered the door, blowing arm-length splinters into the common room, and pounded into the remote's multi-lensed face.

The robot was scrap before its smoking carcass rolled to a stop by the kitchenette wall next to the body of the luckless grenadier.

Vozde's booming laughter was almost as loud as the cannon.

The other remotes shrank down on their haunches as their sibling was blasted into oblivion. But unlike ignorant animals, these creatures were being guided by a singular intelligence and immediately recovered.

The three remaining remotes charged the other doors. Six more remotes stalked into the common room accompanied by the remaining humans.

Mahir dropped behind his bed as the remote before the smoldering remains of his own door came crashing through the wreckage, one armored shoulder first, vulnerable head lowered against the impact.

The sleek black shape landed amidst the debris, shaking fragments from its back as it scanned the room for targets.

"Hello, bastard." Mahir spoke not to the automaton crouching before him, but to the being looking out from behind its eyes.

Then he stood up to send a burst of armor piercing rounds into the thing's back, just behind its head. Armor shattered as the repeated impacts drove the remote deeper into its crouch. It tried to escape by leaping to the side, but he followed the movement, keeping the punishing fusillade on target. From the side, the damage almost immediately broke through into the neck, blasting the head clear. The black orb rolled across the floor to the back of the room, coming to rest amidst the discarded cushions and pillows as the body collapsed against the wall.

As he settled back down into a combat stance behind the bed, he focused his awareness on the other two rooms as the rest of his team dealt with their own incursions.

The old woman had lowered herself behind their barricade while the mutant girl, slower and favoring her damaged leg but still as impressive as he would expect, leapt over that obstacle, monofilament blades flashing.

In midair Smyth rotated, spinning over the remote's head and landing on its back.

The automaton tried to buck the girl off, and she plunged one knife into its back, just behind the head, using that blade as a handhold, keeping her seat as the machine began to careen through the room, crashing into walls, overturning beds, and tearing up pillows and cushions with its monomolecular forelimb-blades as Smyth stabbed down, over and over with her free knife.

Somehow, the old woman managed to evade the wildly thrashing combat remote.

Cruz was braced in the far corner of her own room, her SG-9 Combi Rifle held across her chest, ready for the breach. Beside her crouched her own remote, looking almost as if it was quivering with anticipation.

There was something very odd about that robot.

The enemy charged toward the hacker's door, which slid open silently at the approach.

The remote stopped, taking in the woman beyond, the other remote, then looking up at the doorframe as if suspicious.

It had every right to feel that suspicion, he knew. If the programs animating the thing were even half as good as he thought they were, it would be recalling the sudden opening of the main door to the suite only moments before.

But apparently, either it was less aware than he had given it credit for, or it believed the girl and her hacker rig were not worthy of further concern.

It sidled forward, shoulder armor shifting smoothly as it stalked into the room.

And the door slammed shut on its head.

These doors lacked the power and the heft to do any actual damage to a dedicated combat remote, but the sudden impact disoriented the deadly robot for just a moment.

What was she thinking?!

Cruz put three rounds into the remote's shoulder and four more into the room behind, and then it broke through the door and ran at her.

Her remote stood up, staring it down.

He had told her standard hacking didn't work on these things! Had the woman not listened to a thing he'd said?

She reached out with one hand, a dial spinning furiously over her wrist as she cycled through invasive programs. Two more dials spun up beside the first.

Was she slamming the thing with THREE attacks at once?

The matte black monster staggered but continued to move forward as if it was struggling against a powerful, hurricane wind.

Cruz's own remote stalked forward with lethal purpose, its retrofitted combat blades flashing, but instead of deploying them, it walked right up to the quivering combat model, which started to shake madly, struggling to reach its enemy through the storm of Cruz's Quantronic attack.

The white, orange, and green remote cocked its insect-like head to one side, then raised one forelimb. The claw at the end flipped back, a datalink spike emerged, shining brightly, and seeming almost bored, the smaller robot plunged the spike into the neck of the attacker.

The dials floating over Cruz's forearm flared, and the enemy remote stiffened, jumped twice, and then toppled over onto its side. The data spike slid smoothly out of the small hole in its articulated neck.

Mahir shifted his attention back to Smyth's room. The remote there was slowing down, seven deep wounds gouged into its back. The automaton was trying to get to the girl with its bladed forelimbs but couldn't get a good angle. Each time it tried, she would dodge that leg and stab down into the opposite shoulder.

Eventually, it staggered into a corner, pawing weakly at the barricade. It found the old woman and reached one limb toward her.

While it was distracted, Smyth reached around with a blade and drew it smoothly across the thing's throat. Sparks and glistening fluids flooded out over the floor as it reared back. The Dak shrieked briefly, then the remote was on its side, all four limbs skittering among the pillows, head lolling, as the blue-skinned girl pulled out the blade lodged in its back and then sliced again, sending the head rolling.

In the common room, the remotes charged while the invading humans took aim into all four sleeping rooms.

The buzzing roar of the giant's Switech Gurges erupted into the space as a spear of light lashed out of his room, sweeping through the common area. Vozde stepped through the door, helmet closed, amplified laughter booming through the speakers. Behind him, Kimani was peeking around the doorframe, his own SG-9 firing in high-pitched counterpoint.

Mahir wasn't sure the little thief was hitting anything, but he was certainly adding to the chaos.

Another remote was battered to scrap, two more humans fell thrashing into the churn of fabric, flesh, and blood tangled across the floor.

And their refrigeration unit exploded in a flash of smoke and sparks.

Two remotes stalked into his own room, moving immediately to either side to split his attention.

They were going to come at him at the same time; crush him between the two of them.

Unless he wasn't there.

Mahir saw the attackers scattering in the common room, fleeing from Vozde's continuous, buzzing fire.

Mahir clocked his processing speed to its maximum, and the world slowed.

He plunged his awareness into Arachne without care of the consequences. He had only one goal now. What might happen to these humans couldn't distract him. What he himself could suffer once he succeeded didn't matter, and he would need every advantage to make it work.

Running for the door, he swung the Radjun across his body and pummeled the remote preparing on his left with a stream of fire, catching it dead in the chest with three rounds of armor piercing ammunition and then two Double Action rounds.

It was pounded backward into an awkward, bipedal stance before the DA rounds detonated in a rippling roar, causing a flash of overpressure to erupt from every seal and around every armor plate.

It fell, twitching, to the floor.

By the time the other remote had realized what was happening, he was through the door and halfway across the common room. He slid underneath the flaring line of Hyper-Rapid Magnetic rounds, registering another remote making its way into the room containing the Dak and the mutant. The thing paused, turning its head to glare at him with multiple malevolent red lenses.

There were two humans between him and the hallway, two remotes now fixated on him from behind. There were two other remotes, one moving on Cruz and one cringing away from the fury of the HMC at Vozde's feet, and two more human attackers, one by the washroom, one in the slaughterhouse their kitchenette had become.

In a remarkably short period of time, they had cut the assaulting force in half.

But it wouldn't be enough.

He dove for the door, swinging one shoulder around to lead his way through. The two human fighters there were raising their weapons, but they were ridiculously slow with Mahir pushing his Lhost to damaging heights of performance and awareness. He was now pulling data from every possible source, dancing through a mosaic image that owed almost nothing to his single organic eye.

The world around him was one constructed of data and holographic light; threat assessments, firing arcs, and ballistic solutions crisscrossing his expanded field of vision.

As he slid between the two men, their eyes growing wide in surprise and fear, he put one shock round into the head of the man on the left, allowing the gun's recoil to carry his elbow into the face of the other, behind him. He heard that man's skull crack with the impact as the first's exploded with the wet rush of hydrostatic shock.

Matias cursed, his voice heavy with awe.

Mahir didn't look back, spinning to sprint down the hall and away from the battle. In his mind, through his deepening connection with Arachne, he watched as Cruz moved toward the remote in her room, a white, green, and orange shadow crouching at her side. The woman only had one dial operational, but it flared with power, her own remote lowering itself as if to pounce, and the enemy robot simply froze, shaking, as a small trail of smoke leaked up from somewhere inside its torso.

In the center of the common room, Vozde stood like a massive, automated orange and blue statue. He had ceased the endless stream of rounds, firing now in short, disciplined bursts. One of the humans spun away into the kitchenette with a cry, clutching at her shoulder, but then the remote from Mahir's own room leapt onto the big man's back, landing amidst the heavy cylinders, tearing into the thick armor and mechanisms there as Matias shrieked wildly, dancing around the periphery of the fight, shy of firing at his ally's spinning form.

Cruz was now standing in her doorway, and when she saw Vozde in danger, she spun up two dials, their faint blue light casting her face into ghostly shadow.

And then the remote that had been at the big man's feet rushed at her.

It hadn't taken the time to set itself for a charge or prepare its weapons, it just struck her in the chest with its lowered head, sending her flailing back into her room. She crashed into her small barricade, groaning.

The enemy remote stalked after her, following up its attack, monofilament blades sliding out of its forelimb sheaths.

The death machine at the Dak's door paused, then turned back into the room, moving into the chamber.

The frenzied combat robot atop Vozde continued to tear into his armor, sparks cascading across the floor, smoke rising up to swirl across the ceiling.

The little thief continued his shrill, monotone cry.

The remaining human, clearly seeing Matias as no threat, took aim with its Combi Rifle, siting right at the vision slits of Vozde's helm.

Mahir continued to pound his way down the hall and into the dark, empty lobby, leaving them all to their fates.

He sprinted headlong into something huge and heavy that sent him spinning to the floor.

Shaking his head, Mahir glared upward to see… nothing.

There was nothing in front of him.

Then something crashed into his shoulder with the force of a meteor, sending him flying through the air to smash against the wall, buckling the flimsy material, dust cascading down all around him.

He heard the distinctive sound of a small motor whining up to full speed.

The loading mechanism of an HMG.

A big one.

He launched himself backward, scrambling behind chairs and overturned tables, as a torrent of rapid-fire projectiles chewed through the wall where he had been a moment before.

Tracing the line of fire back, he was confused. There was nothing there. His senses were a whirl of confusion and conflicting data. The line of erupting shells was emerging into reality about two meters off the deck; out of empty space.

His confusion was complete. A lightning-speed diagnostic revealed nothing wrong with any of his own processes. Then, still operating faster than any other entity than another Aspect of ALEPH, he spooled through all the footage of the battle to that point.

He had plunged into Arachne to flesh out his sense of the battle space. He had slipped into his old habits, interfacing with the Quantronic reality of the network to use the Augmented Reality of the connection for full combat advantage.

There was a flicker in the replaying image. A moment where two realities were laid over each other. A moment where the world ceased to be one thing and became something subtly different.

The difference was elusive, but it would have been deadly if he hadn't noticed.

Someone with far more control of Arachne than he possessed had edited his perceptions of the space around him. Whatever was stalking him through the wreckage of the lobby had been deleted from the Quantronic reality around him. His own perceptions, through the linked AR, would not show him this new foe hidin in plain sight.

He felt a chill at that capability, but knowing what was being done, at least he could now do something about it.

Shaking his head, he tore himself away from the link with a scream of effort, sending the eyepatch down with a curse, throwing his perceptions back into the pale, limited images of the physical world.

A physical world that now included a new, deadly threat.

A huge armored, mechanical limb was sailing toward him, straight toward his head, a monomolecular blade gleaming.

He rolled desperately to the side and heard the blade crunch into the deck behind him.

Mahir continued to roll away, springing up into a low combat crouch, and turned to face his opponent for the first time.

The chassis was matte black like its smaller cousins, but it was easily three times their size and mass. It had more of a bullish appearance, massive shoulders, narrow hips, powerful legs, and a heavily armored head. At its forelimb's elbows, two long monofilament blades flashed. Over one shoulder, the snout of a massive HMG swung about, looking for targets.

He stood taller, relaxing slightly. If he had not pushed his processing speeds to their limits, he would worry about this creature, for certain. However, with his advantage in processing speed, now that he could see his foe, this battle should be over quickly.

Then it moved.

It moved so fast, no human would have been able to track it.

A series of massive concussions rippled through the lobby as the enormous cannon on its shoulder lashed out. The wall behind Mahir shattered in a cloud of dust and debris, and he found himself propelled forward by the detonation.

Right at the big monster.

This wasn't possible.

He raised a forearm just in time to stop the long blade from taking him in the throat. He brought his MULTI Rifle up in his other hand, but the machine stomped down with its other bladed leg, knocking the weapon across the room.

Back in the common room of their suite, the men and women he had abandoned were facing their deaths with honor. He had left them, and now he had to face the very real possibility that it had been for nothing. They would die knowing he had abandoned them.

That affected him far more than he would have expected.

Processing all incoming data faster than he ever had before, forcing his tortured awareness to reconnect with the local systems while keeping the giant remote visible before him, he experienced the last moments of the battle as a six-fold mosaic.

He saw Vozde, emergency icons flashing across his field of vision, shy away from the chattering of the last human's Combi Rifle as tracers snapped away from the massive helmet, shattering the composite lens but failing to penetrate. Then the big man, ignoring the remote clawing at his back, spun toward the now fleeing human attacker, stitching a line of devastation across the wall of the common room, chasing the man as he charged toward the Dak.

In Cruz's room, he saw the remote there stalking forward, ignoring the smaller robot as the girl tried to rise from the tangle of wreckage that had been her bed, groaning and disoriented.

Kostic and Smyth huddled together, glaring at the automaton stalking into their own quarters, not even seeing the man running toward them with a smoking rifle.

And then the enormous remote struck Mahir a backhanded blow that sent him spinning across the lobby into the wreckage of the front desk.

He landed with a curse, warning icons flashing within his field of vision, but even that flight had seemed slow, leisurely. He had had plenty of time to see his MULTI Rifle lying discarded on the ratty carpet as he flew over it.

He scrambled for the weapon and got it up just as the huge robot hit him with its head, knocking him into and through the lobby wall. He stood up in the sleeping room of another suite, shaking his head to clear it, and barely registered the two humans cowering in the corner of their room, squinting from the billowing dust and the shaft of light flaring through the gaping hole into the dark chamber.

One was a child, wide eyes fixed not on the dust-covered figure that had just erupted through the wall; not even on the massive monster looming up behind the hole in that wall.

The child was staring, with glassy eyes, at a ratty little stuffed panda bear half-covered by debris from Mahir's dramatic entrance.

With hardly a thought, he reached out with one filthy gauntlet, pulled the plush toy from under the buckled fiber-board, and with one quick glance, tossed it to the child, who caught the thing, squeezed it tightly, and smiled its thanks toward him with a beaming grin that was entirely out of place, given the circumstances.

The man clutching the child could only stare, wild-eyed, with a slack look on his pale face.

They all turned, then, at a whirring sound behind him. Through the hole, the big remote regarded him with five crimson eyes, their focal rings whirring as they tightened to fix on him. The big gun, having swiveled out of the way to administer the head butt, came hissing back around, tracking his movements.

He was processing the physical world around him faster than any other entity but another Aspect of ALEPH.

No living creature should be able to match him.

Unless it was a creation of ALEPH.

Or another AI.

His own eye tightened, and he summoned up a dial larger than anything he had used in ten years.

He had seen Cruz do it. He knew it could be done.

But unlike Cruz, he had other advantages as well. Around the border of the enormous dial, smaller circles began to rotate.

If the wrong people were paying attention to the local Quantronic datascape, he had already given them quite of a show, but he'd had enough.

He reached through his dial, aligning icons, pulling power from Arachne, as the entire region around him, reacting to the sudden drain, darkened. Quantronic graffiti in neighboring corridors flickered to dark, jagged abstracts before fading away as he sucked the Social Energy out of the area.

Images from the others spun through his awareness. In her room, Cruz stood up as the black remote leapt, then jerked to the side, impaled suddenly on her own remote's extended data spike.

It fried there.

In Kostic's room, the remote ran headlong into an angry Rosa Smyth. The runaway Morlock gave an animal snarl, her blue face twisted with an ugly rage, and she spun her blades around so that her hands, coming together to either side of the attacker's head casing, struck with their pummels, not their monofilament blades. The armor buckled beneath the furious blows, and the machine staggered.

She danced to the side, still favoring one leg, avoiding the remote's desperate slashes.

With a remorseless rhythm, she began to beat a savage tattoo on the attacker's head, striking first with one heavy pummel, then leaving that in place and pounding the other back into the object of her rising fury.

In the center of the common room, Vozde stopped spinning, stopped moving at all, and stood completely still. Behind him, Matias gathered his wits enough to pump several rounds after the *Gato* ganger sprinting for the room where the old Dak was watching the Morlock girl batter a robot into scrap, missing with every one.

The remote on Vozde's back, perhaps sensing a change in the situation, paused in its tearing attack.

With the augmented strength of the powered armor's legs, Vozde launched himself straight up, into the ceiling.

Before Mahir, in his own reality, the giant armored bull cocked its head toward him. Somehow, he thought there was a distinctly insulting angle to that tilt.

Manifesting his full supremacy, drawing energy and processing power from the strange, gothic structures of Arachne all around him, Mahir gestured toward the big remote as if he was throwing the dial.

It shattered off a slick black firewall that flared around the monster's essence.

Behind him, there was a whimper. Whether it was the child or the man he lacked the experience to tell.

His foe snorted, the gun stabilizing.

And countless smaller dials flashed out, breaking the firewall with a prodigious spray of fiery discs, each carrying a powerful assault program; each tearing a small percentage of the wall away in a very specific pattern.

A massive round flipped down into the firing chamber of the giant remote's HMG, the firing mechanism rearing back.

Sounds of the man dragging the child deeper into the room behind him with a desperate curse.

The firewall protecting the titanic remote shattered, and the big automaton staggered backward.

The gun hissed again and then sagged, targeting offline.

The lethal machine bellowed, but the sound had a stuttering, broken quality.

Mahir sent a lash of corrosive data through the breach and grinned as it curled around the remote's driving programs.

The robot began to stagger first to one side, then the other. The bellowing became more of a whine, still with that staccato, buzzing rhythm.

The dizzying mosaic continued to flash before him at the same time. He saw a smaller remote's head collapse under one last blow of a silvered pommel, and then a monofilament blade plunged through that wreckage, deep into the thing's body.

He saw a remote fall limply off wide armored shoulders in a cascade of dust and debris.

Cruz, bracing herself in her doorway, reached out with an apathetic sneer and snuffed out the last flicker of awareness from the stunned remote slumped at Vozde's feet.

And then, leaning down to look into its burning eyes, Mahir tightened his lash and severed the controlling essence from the body of the giant remote before him.

The eyes seemed almost to widen, and he grinned fiercely.

"I'm coming for you, asshole."

Through the entire ordeal, he had kept ahold of his Radjun. He raised it then, putting the barrel to the bullish temple, and pounded its head into scrap with the staccato drumbeat of rapid fire Double Action rounds.

Screw fire discipline.

With the echoing of his own gunfire punishing his ears, he saw the black-clad human attacker rise up in the old Dak's doorway.

His Combi Rifle rose.

He took aim at the old woman, over the shoulder of the panting, animalistic, insensate mutant.

Mahir released his trigger, ending the deluge of fire pouring into the ruin of the big remote's head. He turned back toward the hall, knowing even as he spun, that he would be too slow.

And the barrel of a huge gun swung through the drifting dust and smoke of the doorway and slammed into the human ganger's head, sending him flying across the destroyed common room to smash against the far wall, where he slumped in a bloody heap.

"Everyone in here okay?" Vozde's grinning face was just visible through his cracked and smudged faceplate as he leaned down into the door.

Mahir's processing speed dropped, and he fell to one knee as he collapsed back into the normal flow of time, exhausted.

But before he lost his connection to the security net, he saw the little old woman nod, an answering smile on her face.

Chapter 19

Hotel Khatmandu, Commune X-7 and Corridor B-8 approaching *Al-agaav ka Sansthaan*, VaudeVille, *Bakunin*

"Holy shit." She thought it was Matias, but it was hard to hear specific tones through the ringing in her ears.

"Holy SHIT!" It was definitely Matias.

She checked on the second remote collapsed in her room, looked to assure herself that Parachit was still operational, and then eased her way into the common area, Combi Rifle held steadily before her.

She didn't need it. The room was a bloody, twisted wreck, like the worst recreated battle scene from the most gratuitous military sensa-series pirated from the *Maya Sabot!* channel. But the danger seemed to have passed.

Petar was helping an exhausted Rosa from her room, but as he looked around for somewhere he could sit her down, the look on his face, even seen vaguely through the cracks and smudges of his face shield, was almost comical.

Nia peeked into the common room from behind them, her dark face ashen at the scene of slaughter and destruction.

"Where's Mahir?" Matias, his own rifle hanging limply at the end of his loose arm, looked around at each of them.

Hanima did her own inventory. Everyone in the team had survived, somehow.

No, not somehow. They had fought like demons, following her strategy exactly except for that part where Petar had rushed into the enemy, stalling the second wave of the attack.

In fact, between her initial plan and the big man's initiative, they seemed to have done quite well for themselves.

Except that Matias was right. Where was their strange benefactor?

Nia dragged a chair from one of the bedrooms into the common room, and Matias was helping her clear a path for Petar to lower Rosa into it. The girl looked like she was about to lose consciousness.

Once she was settled, Matias moved toward the door. "We need to get out of here as soon as we can. No way the Moderators are going to miss this. I take it we still don't want to tangle with them?"

Petar had popped his helmet and was kneeling down beside Rosa, supporting her while Nia examined the girl for further injuries.

"Holy shit!" Matias seemed to resort to those two words a lot under extreme stress.

Hanima moved to stand next to him, looking down the hall toward the lobby.

Mahir was approaching them, limping slightly, covered in dust that had clumped up in pink ridges in places where it had obviously stuck to flows of blood.

Behind him, the lobby was a smoking, shattered wasteland.

And in the middle of that wreckage slumped an enormous black-armored shape; a massive combat remote that dwarfed the models they had just defeated.

"Took care of it." Mahir tried to summon up a smile, but the man was clearly exhausted and in considerable pain.

"Damn, *ese*." Matias took a few steps down the hall and then turned back to Mahir, his eyes round. "You take that thing out on your own?"

Mahir nodded. "We need to talk."

They helped the cloaked man back into the common room. Petar had gathered up one more chair and a crate that had survived the battle well enough for someone to sit on.

Matias had been describing the huge remote in chilling detail. It had obviously been following up the first thrust of the attack; coming along to finish the job.

"No idea how we missed it, but if it had hit us in the middle of that scuffle, we'd all definitely be dead." He slapped Mahir on the shoulder, and Hanima thought she was the only one who noticed the man didn't respond with his usual vague sneer of disdain at physical contact.

He looked simply too tired to care.

"That's why he rushed out." Matias kept his hand resting on the one-eyed man's shoulder. "I don't know how you knew it was coming, but no doubt you saved our asses, rushing at it like that!"

She was watching Mahir as the little man spoke. Nia was busy with Rosa, who was too wrapped up in her own pain and exhaustion. Petar was focused on the blue-skinned girl as well; and Matias was entirely lost in his own story telling.

So no one else noticed that Mahir winced at that comment and wasn't meeting anyone's eyes as they all looked over to thank him.

Although the team clearly credited Mahir with saving them all from the brute, their benefactor didn't seem to share their opinion.

What was that about?

"We need to get out of here." Mahir's voice was low and rough, his shoulder's slumped in exhaustion.

Maybe that was it? He was just completely drained?

"Our enemies have more local control than we thought. They're in Arachne, and they're using it against us; controlling what we can see. We need to go, now, and take out whoever is in the *Alagaav* before they can launch another attack like this, or the Moderators get here."

Petar's eyes narrowed at the comment about their enemies controlling what they could see, but he let it go.

Mahir's insistence that they not bring in local law enforcement, if the stakes were as high as he seemed to think they were, still confused her. Not to mention the fact that the team was hardly in any shape to attack the enemy stronghold after what they had just gone through.

Still, he was probably right. They had survived. Whoever was hiding within the *Alagaav* wasn't likely to let that stand.

And any O-12 agent would be hesitant to bring the locals in; O-12 was forbidden to operate independently among the Nomads. Mahir would get booted back to Concilium Prima faster than a ten skender Bakunin joiboi could down a shot of skoli.

She smiled at that thought; she had clearly been spending too much time with Petar and Nia.

There was a strange ticking sound from within the room Nia and Rosa had shared. Hanima looked back at the scarred, battered doorframe and saw nothing but smoke and dust floating on the air in the room.

Then something stirred.

When it came leaping out of the smoke, she almost didn't recognize it; its profile was all wrong.

But it could only be one of the remotes, nearly intact except that something was very wrong at the front end.

And there were no glowing red lenses flaring with machine fury.

In fact, there was nothing there at all.

The thing's head was a battered, dented mess, with a gaping hole disappearing right through it and into its torso.

But that didn't seem to be stopping it any.

The remote leapt from the doorframe and she screamed, trying to bring her rifle up.

She was going to be too late.

Except the thing wasn't jumping for her. It was sailing through the murky air, straight for Mahir's back.

Parachit erupted from Hanima's room, both of her forelimb blades flashing in the uncertain light, and crashed into the attacking enemy with all the force of her smaller body.

The concussion threw the enemy remote to the side as the team scrambled away, knocking over chairs and tripping over wreckage and twisted lengths of cloth.

Parachit landed on the disoriented combat remote, her forelimbs flashing up and down, crashing into the barrel of the enemy's torso over and over as the black machine struggled to escape.

Sparks erupted from the thing's interior, spraying out from the neck as smoke billowed up once more to curl across the stained and shattered ceiling.

With one last, bright blue flash, the enemy remote fell still. Parachit stood, shook herself off like a dog after a soaking, and then strode back into her room without acknowledging any of them.

From where he lay on the floor, having scrambled away from the attacking remote at Hanima's cry, Mahir watched Parachit disappear, a strange, inscrutable look on his face.

There was a low moan from the kitchenette, and Matias, after a startled curse, moved in that direction, his rifle leading the way.

"Huh." He seemed mildly confused. "We've got a survivor, looks like."

Petar moved toward the other black-clad bodies, moving from one clearly dead enemy to the next, until he came to the man he had clocked with his massive cannon like a club.

"Filthy bastards." Petar picked the man up by his collar in one massive, armored fist. The *Gato's* face was covered in *mara* tattoos sprayed with blood and coated in dust. He was muttering something over and over again in Spanish, but Hanima couldn't make out the words from across the room.

The man opened flickering, unfocused eyes and glared owlishly up at Petar.

"¡Hijo de puta!" The man's words were weak, slurred, and vague. He tried to spit on his captor, but the bloody drool just dribbled down his chin.

"Filthy coward." The big man dropped the figure to the floor again, where the *Gato* coughed, weakly, then seemed to collapse in on himself, eyes glazing to stare up through the ceiling.

Hanima looked at the dead man numbly. Violence had so quickly become a part of her life that she hadn't had time to realize she had grown so accustomed to it, and yet here she was.

Matias came up to stand between her and Petar, looking down at the corpse. The big man seemed nonplussed by the development. Blasting the enemy down in the midst of battle, or cracking him across the face with the enormous gun, was one thing. He had not directly killed this man; but without the insulation of adrenaline and battle rage, that didn't seem to have registered.

Matias shook his head, then looked over into the kitchenette. The woman who had taken the brunt of her own grenade was obviously, spectacularly, dead. Another woman was slumped against the back wall of the little cubicle, her shoulder a bloody ruin, the unmistakable ravages of an HMC round.

Matias growled, then pulled his pistol out of its holster and angrily pointed it.

Right at the dead man's face.

"This is it, *ese*! One chance to tell us who you are and what you know, or I splash your head all over the decking!"

Hanima looked at him as if he was insane. Petar was clearly confused as well. Mahir, slumped once again in a chair near Nia and Rosa, looked up, but couldn't see what was happening due to the debris from one of the doors, crumpled and twisted on the floor.

"I told you, *bastardo*, you get one chance to talk!" Matias's pistol was shaking.

The pistol he was pointing at a dead man.

"Matty, you okay?" Petar's gentle voice was as confused as Hanima.

"Shut up, Vozde!" Matias growled. "Don't get in my way. We need to know who they are, what they know, and what the hell is going on here. And this *cabrón* is going to tell us!"

"Ah, okay." Petar looked at Hanima, his confusion building.

She couldn't offer him any further clarity.

Then she looked again to where the others were watching them. They weren't confused; they were shocked and perplexed, frozen in place, believing they were watching a horror play out before them.

They couldn't see the *Gato* was already dead; the debris from the blasted door had blocked their view of his last moments. They thought Matias was threatening a living prisoner.

Then she looked over to the corner where the woman, having struggled up onto her elbows, was staring at Matias in horrified fascination.

She couldn't see that her companion was dead, either.

"*¡Se acabó el tiempo, perra!*" The heavy pistol barked twice and the body jumped as Matias pumped two rounds into its chest.

Matias's hand was shaking, but his body would hide that from the woman in the corner.

Then he spun on her, stalking through the wreckage and grabbing her, dragging her up into a sitting position against the dented, bullet-riddled surface.

She screamed as he wrenched her injured shoulder.

His hand didn't shake at all as he put the smoking barrel between her eyes.

"Your turn, *ese*."

She gave them everything.

"*Mara jefes* were approached two months ago by some Bakunian weirdos." Her breath came in gasps, but they could make out the details. "It was all *electronico*, through Arachne, but their skenders spent like any other."

Her eyes flitted from one member of the team to another, always going back to Petar's still, cold face and Matias's brave façade.

"All the weapons, ammo, and *equipo de seguridad* they delivered were mil-grade, still in their factory sealant."

Matias shot Petar a look of cold vindication at that.

"We provided security for some real *gente extraña*, armored *guerreros* who visited Corregidor twice."

Her eyes sharpened, then, and she glanced at each of them with a touch of growing suspicion.

"The second time, while a bunch of us were out with the *bichos raros*, a bunch of local *pendejos* tried to raid one of our cache vaults. It all got *confundido*, and in the chaos we lost contact with the *extraños*."

She seemed to collapse in on herself, suspicion and sharpness fading.

"The *jefes* were all *nervioso* after that, but the *bichos raros* called again soon enough, and things were back up and running as if *nada* had happened."

Her eyes flicked over to the *Gato* leader's body, smoke still rising from his armor.

Crimson and black armor that Hanima knew, now, that she recognized, despite the battle damage, scratched paint, and hasty, ill-suited repairs.

The *Gato* woman continued, voice and eyes now dull. "*Yo no se* if any of the *jefes* ever met with any *bichos raros de hombre a hombre*, but I wouldn't. *Solo soy una Gata pequeña.*" Her lips twisted at that in a bitter, blood-stained expression.

She looked at Matias and Petar again, then to Mahir, then down into her lap.

"Either way, *ya no hay Gato guerreros* on Bakunin." Her eyes flicked once more to the leader's body. "No live ones, anyway."

Then the woman was sobbing, her eyes fixated on the ruins of the door that hid her dead companion.

Hanima stood up, looking down at Matias pushing the barrel of his gun hard against the woman's forehead.

"You expect us to believe that's it, *bruja?!*"

The woman tried to shake her head but was stopped by the pressure of the pistol.

"¡No *sé nada! ¡No sé nada!*"

A hand gently took Matias's clenched fist and raised the weapon from the woman's head. Hanima had been unable to look away, terrified, and had missed Nia coming up behind them.

"I don't think we need to keep this up any longer." Her purple hair was gray with dust, but she stood as straight as ever, and Matias, with no more need to maintain the façade, almost collapsed into the little old woman's arms with a sob.

The ganger looked up, confused, fear and anger warring on her face.

Hanima shook herself out of her own frozen state and went to one knee in front of the woman.

"We're going to let you go." She looked down at her rifle with heavy meaning. "You will not talk about what happened here to anyone." She turned back toward the rest of the team and then pointed at Mahir. "That man is with Dragnet. If you ever try to make anything of what happened here today, he will find you, and you will wish you had died here."

The woman's eyes had grown even wider, and she nodded so violently, Hanima feared she might bash her head against the wall.

She stood up, glaring down at the ganger. "Go."

The woman nodded again, not looking at anyone as she scrambled to her feet. As she rose, she reached out for the fancy new Combi Rifle beside her.

"You're kidding, right?" Petar's voice was steady as the barrel of his long cannon rose to point vaguely in the woman's direction.

She made a strangled sound, shook her head, and skittered out the door.

Hanima watched her go, then turned to the others.

"Anyone got anything they'd like to say about that?"

Matias looked relieved, and Nia was smiling at her. Petar shook his big head with a grin of his own, and Rosa looked as if she had barely followed the events, she was so tired and hurt.

"Compassion is a fine thing when you can afford it." Mahir was looking right at her. "I'm not sure how flush your account is on that score right now."

Hanima glared at him for a moment and then looked away. She summoned up a dial and glanced at it; local emergency traffic flickered past.

"Moderators pulled back as the big remote rushed the corridors. They're calling for reinforcements and they've locked the sector down." She looked at Mahir.

"We don't have a choice." He looked at Rosa, and it almost seemed as if he regretted his next words. "We have to move on *Alagaav* now. We can't afford to wait."

Petar shook his head. "That makes no sense. We wait, the Moderators show up with backup, and we're good. They're out of foot soldiers, right? The *Gatos* are played out. That means we should be all good either way." He shrugged massive armored shoulders and folded his arms over his chest. "I say we wait."

Mahir sighed. "They're not out of foot soldiers. *Alagaav* is packed with warriors." He looked at each of them in turn, and when he looked to Hanima, she was shocked to see the pained resolve there. "We're probably not going to make it out, but we need to stop what they've started. I need to get in there, confirm my suspicions, and then the locals can clean up afterward. But I need to be the first one into the commune."

Matias, usually Mahir's staunchest ally on the team, moved to stand with Petar, folding his own arms. "What suspicions? If this is as Sphere-shattering as you've claimed, what the hell is it you think we're walking into?"

Mahir paused, his shoulders slumped. He looked as if he could barely keep his head up. "I can't tell you until I confirm what I fear. The threat is severe, far worse than anything I was sent to investigate. We're not dealing with a bunch of rogue Tunguskan banksters or Corregidoran mercenaries, or even Bakunian anarcho-hackers."

He knew what they were going to face when, if, they cracked those fortress doors open. Hanima knew he knew. Why wouldn't he say? What was he afraid of?

And then she knew. He was afraid they wouldn't continue if they understood what they were facing.

What could possibly be crouching within *Alagaav* that would cause them all to abandon his cause now, at the very brink? After everything they'd already gone through?

And more importantly, why should she trust him?

She found trust so hard. She couldn't trust herself. She couldn't trust her team. Now she had to trust this stranger, claiming that the entire Human Sphere was on the line?

She felt her eyes tighten as her own suspicion crystalized in her mind.

A deep, resonant boom shook the room.

This was far louder, and far more terrifying, than any weapon that had been used to devastate Hotel Khatmandu in the battle.

Around her, Hanima saw her teammates' arms shoot out to keep their balance. The shock that had run through the deck wouldn't have been enough to knock anyone over, but it was human nature to react that way when the ground suddenly showed that it wasn't as solid as it should be.

For a moment, she wished she was back on Corregidor, with the crash couches and zero-g chairs she had spent most of her life complaining about.

Then she noticed that Mahir was standing, quiet and resolved, his hands calmly holding his big rifle.

"What the hell?!" A note of fragile, frustrated anger quavered just below Matias's words. "What now?!"

Each of them had spent their entire lives aboard the motherships. These were ancient, enormous spacecraft; anything that could shake one of them like that was truly bad news.

Mahir looked at her. "It's not an external attack, but I can't access any local information."

She spun up a dial and looked down, furiously flying through local channels and databases.

Nothing had changed since she looked right after the battle.

The local Quantronic datasphere had been completely locked down.

Another boom rocked the room, and this time, the shaking only subsided after the passage of several seconds.

She looked again at Mahir, meeting his dark eye. "Is that them?"

He nodded, once. "Has to be."

And she saw it, then. Everyone was looking at her. A weaker tremor swept beneath them.

She had no time.

"We've got to go."

No one, not even Matias, hesitated. They all moved toward their rooms to gather whatever gear they could salvage, as if taking an order from her was the most natural thing they had done that day.

Petar topped off his ammo and took a moment to spray a sealant across the faceplate of his helm. Matias worked with one of the attacker's weapons, a more modern Combi Rifle with an underslung grenade launcher. He didn't seem happy with the number of remaining grenades. When he finished with that, he slipped several disposable drives into a pocket. He looked at Hanima when he did that and looked quickly away.

As long as he didn't plug in until this was all over, what did she care?

Nia replenished the consumables in her MediKit, then filled a kit bag with more standard bandages, antiseptics, and a collection of rattling bottles.

"Just in case." She shrugged at Hanima with a grin that took decades off her dark, wrinkled face.

Rosa, being by far the most injured member of the team, rested, her blades loose in one hand, as Nia went over her injuries and administered several doses of different compounds she thought might boost the girl's stamina, give her more energy, and protect her from the worst of the battle shock that threatened to overwhelm her.

"You're certain we shouldn't wait for the military?" Hanima was loading rounds into a clip for her Combi Rifle. She didn't remember firing it, but she must have at some point. "I really need to know why that's a bad thing."

Mahir looked up from checking his MULTI Rifle, a sour look twisting his dark face. "I told you. We can't do that yet."

"Yet." She looked around at the rest of the team, but she wasn't really seeing them. "You said that before: yet." When she looked back at him again he paused, as if he was seeing something in her eyes he hadn't expected.

"Trust me. As soon as we can, I'll make the call myself."

She didn't trust him, she realized in that moment. But she nodded.

And sent a quick order to Parachit, who was standing nearby, apparently staring at the two of them.

A single confirmation beep from the remote sounded in her ear, and she nodded again.

As she made her way toward the door, she saw the Chain Rifle the armored leader of the gangers had used. Looking down at her own Combi Rifle, she paused.

The Combi Rifle looked lonely as she glanced back at it one last time, hefting her new weapon on one shoulder. She had left the armor, too.

But she would return for that, if she was able.

The team moved out from their devastated suite and through the ruins of the lobby. Petar whistled appreciably as he moved around the smoking wreckage of the monster remote.

"Damned lucky you saw that one coming, boss." He tossed the compliment casually over his shoulder, so he didn't see when Mahir glanced quickly away at the words.

But Hanima noticed.

"Hey." Matias had stopped by the twisted rubble of the front desk, where the clerk who had welcomed them in a week ago was peering through a ragged, roughly man-shaped hole in the wall, a child clutching a ragged stuffed panda peeking from behind one dust-covered leg.

"This ought to cover the damages." Matias tossed a handful of disposable drive sticks at the man's feet.

"Wha—?" The man looked offended, then suspicious. Then he bent down and picked one of the drives up, and his eyebrows rose appreciatively.

She thought she saw Mahir smile at the child, but he noticed her and looked quickly away.

She had probably imagined it, anyway.

In the corridor outside, things were very dark. It took a moment for Hanima to realize what had happened.

The psycho-reactive graffiti, holo-signs, and other Quantronic-linked decorations and works of art were muted and shadowy. They were vague, jagged abstractions, with dark colors splashed with a deep, crimson red. Those walls that were now visible without the flashing, splashy art were barren, revealing scraped and stained wall paint with smoldering emitters, transmitters, and repeaters studding the dirty surfaces.

The Social Energy of the region had sunk into the bowels of Hell. The people of this sector were cowering in their homes, fearing for their lives, and their ever-evolving artwork, irrevocably tied to their Quantronic social presence, revealed their terror.

Petar snorted. "Hippies."

Matias grunted in agreement, but there was something sad in his eyes as he made his way out into the public areas of the concourse.

As they turned into the final, wide corridor leading to the *Alagaav ka Sansthaan* commune, Hanima saw the imposing door with her own eyes for the first time.

How in the name of all that was holy were they going to breach that door?

Another resounding boom swept down the hall, but this time, so close to the source, it was deafening, and the hall shook so violently that Matias and Rosa both fell to one knee as the others struggled to stay upright.

Everyone but Mahir who, despite his own exhaustion, seemed to be having no trouble keeping his feet underneath him.

"Oh my God." Petar gasped, his own arms thrown wide. "They're trying to jettison the commune's module!"

It made sense that he would recognize the signs first; he had spent years working on construction, paying off his debt to Corregidor with service on countless Work Teams.

But the rest of them were quick to catch on. You didn't live a spaceborne life and remain unaware of the dangers.

And the dangers of jettisoning an entire container module, one that had been part of the fabric of Bakunin for well over half a century, would be devastating to the rest of the sector. The ship had never been designed to suffer that kind of separation.

Were they even close enough to the ship's hull to get the module out? Would they have to tunnel through entire levels of the mothership?

Countless Bakunians were going to die as they tried.

They started to charge the doors, even though she was still unsure what they thought they were going to do when they got there.

Automated turrets dropped down out of the ceiling before them and began to pour small-caliber, high-velocity fire in their direction.

Hanima spun sideways behind a support beam, several dials spinning up across her forearm as she hit the wall. Against Mahir's stated wishes, she sent an emergency report to the Moderators and local services, and knew, immediately, that it had not made it through.

Something was blocking her.

She closed her eyes and submerged herself into Arachne. Something huge was hovering there, waiting for her, and she immediately fled from the Quantronic realm, gasping in fear as she came back to herself.

Across the hall she saw Mahir glance at her, giving her a slight nod.

He knew the network had been compromised.

She looked at Parachit, crouching down beside her. The remote seemed to be following Mahir's progress down the hall, not waiting for her own orders.

More and more, her remote was acting as if driven by the semi-autonomous drives of an expensive Geist as opposed to the standard programs she, herself, had installed.

"Pay attention!" She banged the butt of her rifle on the remote's head, and it jerked away, somehow managing to look guilty, and then gazed up at her with its insectile head.

Hanima tapped into a processing and power reserve in the remote and punched back into Arachne, this time with all of the finesse she could muster.

She just needed to break the barrier in one spot to do what she needed to do.

She formed a program on one of her dials, crafting on the fly as she worked to get past whatever was trying to stop her within the network.

And then she threw it.

The dial, in her mind, went straight through the presence that had tried to grab her. It howled with a strange, vibrating cry of anger, and the program blossomed on the other side of that malevolent guardian.

Emergency reports shot out through the local network, taking advantage of a pool of Social Energy she had manufactured for just such an emergency. It coopted every poster, sign, and piece of street art, and the entire region started to clamor one single, unified message to its citizens:

Flee!

She couldn't follow the progress of the sudden evacuation, but she knew her program would be slamming emergency doors down across corridors at each junction as the denizens of that sector made it to safety.

She had saved as many as she could, now she needed to focus on what was in front of her.

The team had fought their way forward, into the intersection before the heavy doors. The stuttering howl of Petar's cannon echoed down the corridor, wiping away entire sections of remote turrets.

By the sparking, smoking scrap she saw as she moved up to join them, he had taken care of a couple more remotes as well.

"Keep moving. To the right." Petar called over his shoulder as he swung his big gun left, sending a river of light and destruction down that corridor. "Remote bays!"

So that's how they were going to get through the armored front door: they weren't.

Mahir, just behind the big man, nodded and moved past, firing controlled bursts into the ceiling and the walls as sensors and turrets made themselves known.

Matias crouched behind Petar, his spectacles flashing as he accessed the local datasphere. If he could find the turret controls, he would be able to end the ceaseless rain of fire.

But he wouldn't be able to.

"Matias, no!" She reached out, trying to get his attention, but she was too late. A look of excruciating pain swept over the man's face as he was attacked by whatever entity crouched within the local Quantronic datasphere. Haptic feedback crashed into his brain, and he screamed.

"Parachit, Matias!" The remote had drifted farther forward than she would have liked. What was the machine doing?

The robot slunk back to the little thief's side and opened up a repeater beacon on her back.

Hanima reached through the repeater and immediately sensed, again, that dark presence.

"We've got the turrets! Go!" Petar had turned around and was wading down the hall toward the remote bays with Mahir, Nia sidling along the walls behind them. Rosa was walking backward, keeping an eye on the smoking devastation Petar had made of the corridor behind.

Hanima was getting sick of this thing, whatever it was. She sent three dials at Matias, knowing the presence in the network was waiting for her to attack it again.

The containment protocols she flung out surrounded the little man, enough to break the connection, and he fell out of Arachne, his body still shaking, and she was almost sure she imagined, again, the howl of rage echoing through the Quantronic plane all around them.

She helped Matias to his feet, and he nodded his thanks, putting his glasses in a pocket. "Guess we have to do it the hard way?" He was trying to smile, but his eyes were barely focusing.

"They already did." She gestured, and Matias squinted to focus on Rosa battering a remote at the mouth of one of the bays.

She was grunting with each block and strike, pain and fatigue clear in every line of her body. But she drove both blades down into the torso of the robot, then brought her knee up under the thing's chin and drove it backward, its head at an awkward angle.

It didn't move again when it fell.

As Hanima moved up to the entrance to the remote bay, she looked over her friends. It was clear that Petar had taken the brunt of the incoming fire, as the orange and blue paint was almost completely abraded from the front surfaces of his armor. Mahir had been hit twice, once in the shoulder and once in the upper chest. Blood was flowing down his armor, but he didn't seem to have slowed at all.

Nia was grimly ignoring a graze across her own forehead that was bleeding into her eye, and Matias was limping, although there was no obvious wounds that she could see.

Petar reached to his belt and pulled off a large, bulbous object he had locked in place next to the massive knife.

A shaped charge.

He paused for a moment, activating the clamping magnet and manual timer, and then threw it into the shadows at the back of the recess.

He grinned at her, winked, and then spun away from the opening.

She dove after him, everyone else scrambling away.

The explosion, deep within the alcove, coughed fire, smoke, and debris back out into the corridor.

They all braced for whatever might happen next, waiting for the smoke to dissipate so they could see if they had breached the doorway into the alcove.

Then the smoke, still swirling with embers, was sucked back into the recess. It disappeared as quickly as it had shot out at them a moment before.

Then, almost sluggishly, a fog, slightly different in color or texture, began to waft out again.

As if there was some kind of pressure differential between the commune and the corridors of VaudeVille.

Or a difference in atmosphere.

Parachit, crouched beside her, possessed an array of sensors designed to keep her safe. One of them, one she had almost not bought and installed, because of how seldom she did work outside Corregidor, had been a program for sampling and reporting hazards in local atmosphere.

The remote looked at her, sending a quick report over her private link.

A foreign atmosphere was, indeed, leaking out of the commune through the breach.

She turned to Mahir, her eyes narrowing, her mouth tightening.

The strange man looked away, raising his rifle to point down the dark hole.

A tall, powerful figure erupted from the alcove and dove for Petar, knocking him against the far wall in surprise, howling the entire time.

She hadn't had enough time to study the shape, but there had been something horribly wrong about it.

It wore matte black armor, but it was no remote. Nor was it anything like the *Gatos* foot soldiers. The armor was bulked out, strange-looking. As if the suit was meant to hide the outline of the wearer.

The attacker was wielding a long blade that glowed with a strange, blue sheen.

Petar pulled his own big combat knife, the one he called Tisina, out and blocked the blow just before it pierced his side.

More attackers, slightly smaller, perhaps but no less alien, were emerging, raising objects that were clearly rifles, although they looked like no guns she had ever seen.

Mahir roared like an animal and began to fire into the emerging enemy. In the close confines of the corridor, the gunfire was like being beaten about the ears with muffled hammers.

Two of the shapes were riddled by bullets that zipped through them as if their armor was paper. They scrabbled at the floor, bleeding a discolored, vile fluid.

One, its helmet blasted open, tube-like growths dangling from the back of its skull, slid to a halt beside her as many more exploded out into the corridor, sweeping over her friends.

She stared down into the figure's face. Its dead, inhuman face.

A face she had seen on the news reports countless times in recent months.

A Shasvastii infiltrator.

A shock trooper of the invading Combined Army.

An alien terror warrior.

The enemy of all mankind.

Chapter 20

Corridor B-8 approaching *Alagaav ka Sansthaan*, VaudeVille, Bakunin

Shasvastii Seed-Troopers.

And the beast that had nearly knocked him over as it first rushed his own heavy could only have been a Shasvastii Caliban.

Data sets he had never thought he'd need out here among the backward savages of the Nomads began to scroll feverishly through his consciousness, filling in details, providing threat assessments, and creating a battle space profile that looked bleaker by the moment.

Mahir wanted to spit.

For days, he had known the Combined Army had to be behind all this. But having that suspicion confirmed didn't make their prospects any greater.

That also explained, in part, his recent difficulties with Arachne. The Evolved Intelligence, the ancient AI that ruled over the warlike alien coalition, would have sent an Aspect of its own to oversee an operation this complex.

That the Aspect had been directly operating the giant remote probably meant his foe wasn't wearing a physical body like his own Lhost but had rather infiltrated Arachne somehow, establishing itself in the Quantronic network.

How could the authorities among the Nomads have allowed this to happen?

He blasted the last Seed-Soldier to erupt from their spider hole and then backed away, looking around to assess the situation.

He needed to get into the compound and find a way to destroy it.

And he wasn't going to be able to do that on his own.

A sudden, flaring heat caught him off guard and he stumbled back, shielding his face with his off hand.

The bodies of the dead aliens.

He watched as bright white lines of flame chased themselves over the corpses, reducing each to desiccated ash.

Removing all genetic evidence of an alien incursion.

He spat again. "Toth damn it."

All this time.

There was a rush of foul air from the other two remote alcoves, and more Shasvastii rushed into the corridor, bursting up and out as they crawled through the opening, each roaring with a strange, inhuman cry, braided tubes swaying wildly from the backs of their heads.

Their rifles barked, and Kostic cried out as she was dashed to the floor, blood blossoming across one of the Dak's legs to match the half mask that covered her face.

Vozde answered the alien cries with a roar of his own, finally getting the barrel of his cannon up between him and his flesh-eating foe, pushing it off, and then using that moment's reprieve to bring his own big combat knife up into the alien's chest.

It shrieked, then fell over backward, pulling the knife with it.

"Well, shit." Vozde muttered as the alien burst into flames, the white heat engulfing his weapon.

Then he turned toward the renewed flood of attackers, and his big face split into that crazed, wild grin, visible even through the begrimed face plate.

"Well, shit!" he roared again. The motors of his weapon buzzed as they spun up the barrels, and then a stuttering roar flared out as the magnetic cannon launched a stream of gleaming projectiles into the oncoming line of Shasvastii.

He noticed, with one corner of his mind, that the aliens emerging now were not wearing the strange, bulky armor that had hidden the nature of the warriors in the first wave. They wore their more customary red and black combat gear, with their skull-like helmets a stark, leering white mask.

A series of quick, heavy impacts rang out from the nearest alcove, and a big quadruped shape emerged. Heavy armor and strange, articulated legs gave these new attackers a spidery look as the armored bulk of a head-like structure thrust out between the two high forelegs. Two small-seeming arms swung down at either side, fitting between the sets of legs.

Then those arms rose, and a stuttering wave of bright blue plasma flashed out, incinerating sections of wall opposite.

Q-Drones.

So. This cell had their own, alien remotes, not just the human variety.

That was truly wonderful.

With a tight grin, Mahir switched to the depleted reserve of Double Action rounds and braced against the stuttering recoil, riddling the thing's torso with sets of twin holes.

The alien remote staggered backward, then to the side, then toppled over, smoking. It temporarily blocked the passageway behind it.

Two more came out of the other two bays, strange alien weapons hunting for targets.

With a howling laugh, Kimani racked a grenade into his new weapon and launched it at the alien automaton coming from the center alcove, then turned to launch a second at a knot of Seed-Soldiers moving up on them from the left, the connection tubes dangling from the backs of their heads swaying strangely.

Had they opened the armored doors to the commune? That might be an easier way in.

The first grenade detonated, throwing the remote back into its tunnel, and Mahir followed up with a quick burst of DA rounds that sent the alien robot dancing into scrap at the back of the tunnel. The second grenade detonated, throwing the aliens into disarray as two of them fell to one knee from the concussion, but none of them seemed to have been seriously harmed.

Mahir, mouth twisted in frustrated rage, spun around and fired a prolonged, artless burst of Double Action missiles at the last remote, hammering its head into sparking ruin and blocking the final tunnel, for the moment.

He cursed as the final rounds to bark from his gun sparked with the unmistakable glint of AP rounds hitting composite armor.

He was out of Double Action rounds.

Smyth, hunkered down beside the Dak, watched the aliens advance down the corridor. From among the group stepped a taller, somehow elegant alien, and Mahir had to force himself not to spit again.

A Shasvastii Corax; versatile, lethal special operators that could turn almost any twist of fate against their enemies. The final piece of the puzzle snapped into place.

Although this particular specimen possessed the reversed, animalistic leg structures of most Shasvastii, many were physically altered to facilitate infiltration and espionage.

Like the team that he and Ridhaan had interrupted back on Corregidor.

The monster stalked forward, a long silver blade gleaming in one hand, a heavy pistol in the other. The air around the thing began to shimmer, and Mahir recognized the blurring, fractal disruption of a nano-screen as countless nanobots began to zip through the air, masking the alien's outline.

And then, her face twisted in rage, Rosa Smyth launched herself into a full sprint toward the alien sword wielder.

He recognized the shift in her color immediately for what it was; the girl had finally unleashed the MetaChemical reserves the renegade designers had put into her when they'd made her a Biomorph.

Her system was flooding with poisons that would make her a brutal, violent, thoughtless killer, emphasizing qualities the poor girl had suppressed within herself probably all her life.

Not that the Corax would care anything about that.

In fact, it didn't have time to care much about anything.

Her team had been very impressed with the controlled violence and mayhem Rosa Smyth had been able to unleash during their mission. She had made short work of *Los Gatos-7* gangers and military grade combat remotes alike.

But she had been handicapping herself, denying herself this last advantage with which her unconscionable creators had gifted her.

She was an avatar of destruction.

She screamed her throat raw as she ran up to the stunned Shasvastii and carved through the Corax before the thing could raise its blade in defense.

Smyth's monofilament weapons danced through the nano-screen as if it wasn't there, stabbing, slashing, and sliding through armor and flesh with equal ease.

The alien spec-ops warrior was collapsing in a fountain of pink gore before it could scream, and Smyth was on the Seed-Soldiers behind without pause or warning.

Monofilament blades flashing, pieces of alien flew through the air as their own cries rose to mingle with hers. She head butted one, kneed another in the gut so hard something ruptured and a shower of viscera flooded across the floor. She took one alien warrior's head off with a single swipe and then cut off just the top of the next tall figure's cranium with the back hand swing.

In seven and two thirds seconds, she had killed the entire squad, stood panting for a moment, and then howled, running away from her friends, down the corridor, toward the armored doors.

"No!" Vozde shouted after the girl, although by now she was so far gone she could never have understood the cry.

"Go! We've got this!" Kimani launched another grenade in the opposite direction, although Mahir had seen no targets that way. "Go help her!"

Vozde turned and pounded after Smyth, his armored bulk leaving shallow buckles in the deck plating.

"We need to slow these down, or we need to get in behind them." He turned toward Cruz, only to find the hacker glaring at him.

She had known. Somehow, she had known what was hiding behind the *Alagaav's* walls.

And so she would know they should have called in the Nomad Military days ago.

Kimani knelt beside the Dak, unironically providing her with care from her own MediKit, while Cruz glared at Mahir.

As if he'd ever had a choice.

"We don't have time right now. We need to get in there." He tried to peer past each of the three collapsed remotes, but all he could see was vague movement in the darkness behind them.

Then, from behind the third, a spray of flashing projectiles snapped past his shoulder and he ducked away.

Great. There was a Spitfire back there somewhere.

"Why do we need to get in?"

He sighed. He didn't have time for this. "They have some kind of repeater or node in there. It's the only way they could have penetrated Arachne, even out here on the Human Edge. We have to destroy it, then we can deal with the rest of this."

She nodded but didn't move. Smoke whirled all around them, the harsh, chemical, alien reek almost suffocating; a violent sense of urgency was building within him.

"So it was them, trying to tear the Sphere apart. Just like they did at Novyy Bangkok? Just like they've been doing all over the place since they attacked the capitol at Concilium?"

She was smart. But he had known that.

He nodded. "As the great powers finally began to converge, beginning to forge a united front against the aliens, the Combined Army has been using Shasvastii agents and cells to do as much damage to the fabric of a united Sphere as possible." He gestured vaguely in the direction of the *Alagaav* commune. "This was actually ingenious."

She gave him a strange look, and he shrugged. "You think it's beyond belief, that you people would try to drag the rest of the Human Sphere down a peg or two?"

She made a bitter face and looked away. Then glared at him again. "And you, working for O-12, just happened to have been here already? Does the Executive Board even know you're here? They don't really go for O-12 agents operating unaccompanied."

He looked away. He could lie to her. He needed to lie to her. So why didn't he?

And the fact that he hesitated, not immediately lying to her, meant she wasn't going to believe anything he said now, either way. He glanced back at her and saw, by the darkness in her eyes, that he was right.

Which didn't change what needed to be done.

"We need to destroy that repeater, or node, or whatever it is. We close this down and sort the rest out later, right? You can grill me for all you're worth."

She shook her head. "Why couldn't we call emergency services? Why couldn't we alert the Moderators? Or the Securitate? Or Dragnet?"

He laughed at that. "You think they don't all know, by now, something's going on here? And you, yourself, said it: the Executive Board, and all its security agencies, won't much like the fact that an O-12 agent has been snooping around. We would have been answering questions while the real bad guys got away!" He cocked a thumb over his shoulder at the bulkhead, behind which came struggling, scrabbling sounds, and an occasional high-pitched Combi Rifle shot. "The real bad guys?"

She shook her head again. "It's too late for that, though. They come now, they come to fight. No questions until after."

He sighed. She was right. Again.

"I'm going to let them in."

"Who?" Anger and curiosity were crashing together in his head.

"Nomad Military. They're right outside the nearest blast doors. I'm going to let them in, and they can help us with the 'real' bad guys. Then, as you say, questions."

She strode purposefully back toward the commune's front gate, leaving him behind.

She stopped, turned, and frowned down at something beside him.

Mahir looked down and saw the white, green, and orange remote sitting there, staring back at Cruz.

"Parachit, come on." She snapped her fingers. An odd gesture to make toward a remote.

The machine didn't move.

"Damnit." Cruz muttered, then turned away, rounding the corner and hunkering down against a support beam that might offer some cover, should the aliens break out of the alcoves again.

Mahir watched her settle in; watched as she spun several dials up in front of her.

Over the glowing disks, she gave him one last, hot glare, then bent down to her work.

What did it matter, really, if the Nomad authorities came in at this point?

His mission was lost, now. There was no way he was going to be able to make his way back to Tunguska unnoticed, reconnect with that damned Grigoriy, and get through the Oubliettes and into the Vault.

And ALEPH had known his mission was lost before she had sent him after these damned Shasvastii.

In the end, ALEPH's primary imperative must be the safety of all humanity. And standing four square against that mission was not the Nomads, as chaotic and dangerous as they were, but the Evolved Intelligence behind the alien Combined Army.

So let Cruz call in the military if she could get past the E.I. Aspect; the damned ghost in the machine.

Mahir looked down again at the remote bays. There was a lot of noise from the other end of the corridor, where a crazed Smyth was wreaking bloody havoc on any aliens that dared to face her, backed up by a human wearing some of the thickest armor and carrying one of the biggest guns that a human could carry.

It was nothing short of what the damned Shasvastii deserved.

"What are we going to do, boss?"

Mahir looked down to find Kimani standing before him, his hands white around his new DineticS Dayak Combi Rifle, its grenade launcher steaming. The man's eyes were crazed, his breathing shallow.

But he had stood. He had seen the foe for what they really were, and he had stood.

"We need to make sure no more come out of these bays." He nodded to the alcoves, smoke and embers still pouring from their dark mouths. "Once we get this settled, we can go help Smyth and Vozde. How's the Dak?"

Kimani's smile tightened. "She'll make it. Can probably limp as far as the intersection and the front gate by herself if she needs to. But she's going to need some blood, and some food, and a lot of rest. Serum can only do so much."

Mahir nodded, looking down again at the remote wreckage tangled in the mouth of each bay.

"How many more grenades do you have in that thing?" Mahir got as close to the nearest alcove as he dared, peering into the darkness.

"Two." The disappointment was clear in the little thief's voice. "There were barely any when I got the gun in the first place."

Mahir nodded absently, dialing up the sensitivity of his vision. Between the lack of light and the swirling smoke, it was almost impossible to see anything aside from a vague suggestion of movement.

He looked back at Kimani over his shoulder. "Send one straight down this tunnel."

Stepping back, Mahir watched the little man move up hesitantly. "Are they close? The… aliens?"

It wouldn't do to forget that, despite their continued forward progress, his allies in this work had never actually matched themselves against the Combined Army before. In fact, until this very moment in their lives, the existence of hostile aliens was nothing more than a distant abstraction to them.

Mahir looked down at the man for a moment, then dropped to one knee, sighted quickly past the crumpled remote, and pumped a long burst of fire into the dark tunnel; a mix of armor piercing and flashy tracer rounds that made the alcove jump and flare like the mouth of Hell.

From inside, there were strange, disjointed screams and muffled scrambling sounds.

"Go." He jerked his head toward the still-glowing opening.

Kimani looked at him for a long, stunned moment, then settled into a crouched firing position, took careful aim, and with a cough from the launcher sent a single grenade sailing into the swirling smoke and dancing light.

They both stepped to the side, and when the sharp crack of the ordnance echoed out, Mahir bent down to look again. He could just make out the bent girders and buckled sheeting of the tunnel walls forming a twisted barricade in the depths of the bay.

He nodded, stood, and they moved to the next alcove.

Mahir again filled this tunnel with light and death, then had Kimani send his final grenade down the hole.

"Now go. Back up Vozde and Smyth. Make sure Cruz is okay." He wasn't even watching as the little man nodded and turned to run down the corridor toward the sounds of violence. He knelt before the last alcove and drew a bead on the deepest section he could see.

A line of shots sprayed out at him, and something struck him hard in the hip. He fell sideways, out of danger, with a surprised grunt. Looking down, he saw Cruz's remote standing there, regarding him solemnly with its multitude of crimson lenses.

"Thanks?" He stared down at it. What a strange machine.

Then he returned to the alcove with a growl, drilling a continuous stream of armor piercing and tracer rounds into the walls, floor, and ceiling of the shaft, as far back as he could manage. After thirty-two seconds of continuous punishment, there was a grinding crash, and a section of the tunnel roof collapsed in a shower of spreading sparks and smoke.

On his way back up the hall, he stopped by Cruz. She was crouched behind the column, back to the wall, lost in the glowing dials arrayed before her. Sweat plastered the hair to her forehead, and her normally brown skin was ghostly pale.

"You got this?" He kneeled beside her, concerned despite himself.

She grunted, shaking slightly.

Mahir looked down to the remote. “You don’t want to stay with her? It looks like she could use some help.”

The automaton watched him, unblinking, then turned to scan the woman, then returned its sensor array back to him.

“I’m just going to be shooting things. The real work’s going to be back here, now.”

The remote seemed to vibrate in indecision, then settled down beside Cruz, but its sensors continued to watch him.

Strange.

He took one last look at the hacker, clearly locked in a battle with the alien Aspect, then down the corridor to where Vozde and Smyth were battling a rising tide of Shasvastii, remotes, and something even larger.

“Toth!” He spat the name, settling down to his knees between Cruz and the remote, and snapped the armored plate over his optical augmetics up, falling into the Augmented Reality all around him and diving into the Quantronic reality to join her in the real battle.

Chapter 21

101X01XXXXX...101X0XXXXXX...1XXXXXXXXXX

Ridhaan dropped out of the physical world reluctantly. For some reason, he never felt in danger of losing himself while his awareness was inhabiting the little remote. But Mahir was right: the real battle was going to be fought here, on the ragged edge of Arachne, not in the corridors of Bakunin.

He looked around quickly to reorient himself to the strange, uncomfortable, unfamiliar geometries of the datanet. The dark, shifting plane remained the same, but now the impenetrable blackness of the Shasvastii firewall soared up on his right, looming ominously over the rest of the landscape.

There were only tattered ruins of the grand, dramatic architecture common throughout the rest of Arachne, of course. Between the work of the Evolved Intelligence Aspect and the natural entropy of the Human Edge, nothing stood for long here without a prodigious amount of power and will.

And as that thought flashed through his mind, he saw her.

Hanima Cruz looked much the same in the Quantronic realm as she did in the physical. She might have stood a little taller, her hair might have been a little longer, and the fit of her armor might have been a little more flattering, but she was undeniably herself here.

Possibly more herself here than over there.

Her black and blue hair whipped wildly in a tearing wind that seemed to only affect her as she squinted up at the enormous, formless black mass of the alien Aspect. She stood tall and proud before it, but it was clear to him that she was being battered down.

It was slamming streams of junk code into her firewalls in an effort to overwhelm them, while violent data probes struck, again and again and from all angles, trying to pry away enough of her defenses to create a breach.

But each time a flare in her firewall announced a weak point, she would twist one of her hands, loaded with glowing dials, toward the region, and it would firm up again.

She was holding her own, but she wasn't going to be able to cause any damage to her enemy if she was trapped on defense like this.

"Damnit." The word snapped from behind him, harsh and violent, and he turned to see Mahir's avatar standing there, shock and anger emanating from him. "You bastard."

There was so much to say, and yet, even here in the Quantronic realm, no time to say it.

"Sorry." He sent the impression of a shrug, knowing that Mahir had had no time to acclimate himself to the strange, ornate constructs of Arachne.

Then he sent his intention to his partner, not waiting for a reply, and turned to the alien Aspect, squaring himself up for battle.

This creature had almost destroyed him, twice. But he had not been his full self, then. He had been a wanderer, far from home and the source of his own strength. He was reconnected to that pocket file now. In fact, he had reconfigured the file using what he had learned from this very creature. He had his own fortress within Arachne.

The alterations this had required had changed him, too, of course. He was no longer entirely what he once was. If he had been, he never would have been able to survive the things that had tried to capture or kill him.

He himself had evolved, and he knew, feeling Mahir's presence beside him, he was as much a creature of Arachne now as of ALEPH.

And he knew, from ALEPH's point of view, one was all of ALEPH or one was nothing.

But plenty of time to sort that out if they survived this.

His own suspicions had not been confirmed before the Shasvastii Seed-Troopers had emerged from the tunnel; any more than Mahir's had.

But he had sensed the attempt of those within the *Alagaav* commune container to effectuate an emergency separation from the mothership before the aliens burst forth. As Bakunin had slid into the tattered datasphere of the Human Edge territory for the Krug, the alien data fortress established in that border region had slid into the primary network. How the aliens had known the Nomad Nations would choose to meet at such a location was still unknown, but their plan had worked perfectly. The local Arachne network was now so compromised, it had no way to stop the huge container from trying to tear itself loose.

Now, as full understanding flooded through his systems, he knew they needed to isolate the enemy Aspect somehow, long enough to destroy it. Before it damaged the mothership itself.

The artificial alien intelligence was tethered to a repeater node within the commune; a source of near-unlimited power which gave it an incredible advantage over anyone who might try to stop it.

But somehow this lone human woman was standing up to the beast, and he meant to see that she had as much help as he could offer.

Mahir moved forward beside him, still glaring at him with two eyes, here, instead of the one he sported in the physical world. "I can't believe you couldn't find some way to let me know you were alive."

This wasn't the time for such a conversation, but he knew Mahir. There was no way his partner was going to work effectively until this was addressed.

"At first, my control of the remote was extremely limited. It was like a dream." He tried to fill the words with sincerity, but only Mahir could decide to believe them or not. "By the time I could assume full control, I was having my own problems on this side." He indicated the alien Aspect with a thought. "I almost lost myself over here, and it was all I could do, when I could reach the remote at all, to nudge its systems every now and then."

Mahir continued to regard him with anger, but then shifted his focus to the Aspect, still entirely consumed with trying to destroy the human hacker.

"Hey, ugly!" Mahir sped to the side, rushing between the monster and the black wall of its citadel. "Remember me?"

Ridhaan moved toward Hanima. The residual link he felt toward the woman from his time sharing a mind with her remote's operating programs gave a strange vibrancy to his thoughts of her. As if he had known her for much longer than perceptual time would suggest. There was a tug of loyalty there nearly as strong as the one he felt for Mahir.

The girl was entirely surrounded by a shimmering firewall of impressive strength, although it was wavering in several places.

The Aspect, sensing Mahir, turned its attention that way, lashing out with all of its borrowed power, and Ridhaan watched with mixed emotions as the Danavas Hacker stood his ground, raising his own firewall in the form of a massive, fractal data screen that seemed to trap each attack as it crashed in.

Hanima dropped her firewall with a gasp and seemed to sag with relief as she tried to regain what strength she could.

She gasped again when she saw Ridhaan, and then stepped back, looking down, at something behind him.

He looked, stepping aside to reveal a large tiger; it's green, orange, and white stripes vibrant in the Quantronic light around them.

The tiger bound to the woman's side and she smiled widely, brushing one hand along Parachit's coat.

As she did so, she stood up taller, pulling power from the remote's banks in the material world.

"You need to do what you came here to do." Ridhaan tried to pull her attention away from the tiger. "Hanima Cruz, you need to open that blast door."

She shook her head and looked back up at him. "What?" Then her eyes narrowed. "Who are you?"

He hadn't thought of this. Humans still confused him with their imperfect knowledge and emotional, rather than logical, connections.

He didn't have time for this at all.

"I'm a friend." He tried to convey his connection through the remote with the three simple words, and somehow, enough of that seemed to carry through that she nodded after a moment.

He had known what she was doing through Parachit, even before joining her in Arachne. "The blast door you dropped to save the rest of the sector from decompression. The military is on the other side. Your friends need those reinforcements if we are going to stop the Shasvastii."

That brought her back to the moment. "They're going to tear Bakunin apart."

"They would have if you hadn't alerted the Moderators and closed all the blast doors. The damage will be contained, now. The ship will survive. But we still need to stop them."

She looked at the monster, now tearing at Mahir with lashing queries and lances of offensive power saps. His old partner was responding with his own vicious counter assault, sending spinning disks of slicer programs bouncing off the thing's innate defenses.

"While it's distracted, you need to open that gate and let in the men and women waiting there."

She spun up a dial and looked through it into the physical world of Bakunin, to where her friends were fighting for their lives, for the lives of every man, woman, and child on the mothership.

Ridhaan knew what she would see, but he joined her, watching the battle unfold.

Petar Vozde, his orange and blue armor streaming Shasvastii ichor, had formed a defensive bulwark before the now open commune emergency doors. The indicator lights along the massive cannon were flashing yellow; he was going to run out of ammunition long before the battle was over.

Beside Petar stood Rosa Smyth, favoring her injured leg; bloody, bruised, and furious. Her face was twisted with rage, but her shoulders heaved with laboring breath as she glared into the darkness on the other side of the doorway.

Matias Kimani stood behind the two warriors, supporting an injured Nia Kostic, her empty MediKit dispenser discarded at her feet.

The floor around them was entirely hidden beneath a carpet of twisted, torn Shasvastii bodies; he recognized Seed-Soldiers, a Shasvasti Caliban, and a pair of Corax warriors from his alien threat files. Several alien drones of various types were sticking up out of the mess as well.

But more enemies were emerging from the wide doorway, and the air was again filled with the whirring roar of the HMC, the stuttering bark of Matias's Combi Rifle, and a low whining growl from Rosa, who waited until a stalking Corax was close enough, and then charged back into the battle.

"They're not going to be able to hold out much longer." Ridhaan took Hanima's shoulder. "Do what you came here to do!"

He gestured to a smaller dial, and she brought it up, staring into it at the scene on the other side of the nearest emergency blast door.

The Nomad Military was there in force; Moderators, Prowlers, and even one enormous Taskmaster, nearly as massive as Petar Vozde, crowded around the doors as a team of hackers from across the Nomad Nations crouched at the door frame trying to force their way in.

Overseeing the effort was a severe woman in a long black coat, an enormous Taurus SW Clava Heavy Pistol clenched in one white fist.

Ridhaan smiled to see her. Although they had never met, Detective Inspector Jelena Kovač had been there, never far behind him, for a very long time.

The view shook as the aliens within the commune fired another round of explosive bolts holding the module in place. Those bolts had probably been part of the original construction, long before the mothership had taken its current form.

They were going to tear the ship apart to get free.

"We need them to get into the commune and stop the decoupling process." Ridhaan was trying to force his own sense of urgency into the stunned woman's consciousness. "The aliens can't get away."

Hanima nodded, manipulating the dial, struggling to undo her own security overrides. They had been the best she could construct in the moments she'd had, trying to slip the complex program past the alien Aspect, he knew. He had been with her when she'd constructed them.

She hadn't realized how powerful they had been, but he had. They had nearly crashed the system.

Mahir's scream jolted them both from the task at hand.

The E.I. Aspect loomed over his partner, who was down on one knee, broken and sparking shield shedding bits at his feet. Mahir was firing offensive programs into the thing's bulk, and its own firewalls were flaring and stuttering, but it was pulling energy from the node in the *Alagaav* commune, while Mahir's reserves were dwindling fast.

Ridhaan turned back to Hanima. "Get the door open. Get help. In here, there is almost nothing we can do against that." He stabbed a finger of intention toward the enemy Aspect. "In the physical world, if we can get to the node and destroy it, it will all be over."

They would need evidence to prove to the other human powers that this was a real Shasvastii plot, not just another false flag planted by one or another of the rival nations.

Ridhaan checked the connection to his own fortress. The pocket file, now a virtual drive in and of itself, was far away, but the link was strong, and it would provide almost as much power as the node driving the enemy.

And he was in no danger of losing himself again.

He roared an incoherent challenge toward the Aspect battering his partner against the impenetrable black wall of the enemy citadel.

The Aspect turned, one coiling data probe twisted around Mahir, and growled at Ridhaan.

He threw a spray of fractal queries at the monster, knowing they wouldn't be as effective as they had been against the human Interventors that had hunted him into the twilight regions, but hoping it would distract the beast long enough for him to get closer.

The queries bounced off the black firewall that surrounded the Aspect, but not before its attention was indeed pulled upward to watch them scatter colorfully against the tattered black and gray sky.

And then Ridhaan was beside his enemy. A massive lance of weaponized code flashed into hands that formed around it, and he plunged the blazing weapon into the shimmering black surface.

The Aspect howled, pulling several probes down and toward him. Ridhaan spun around them, bringing his lance back and then stabbing it again into the bulk of the enemy.

An answering roar from around the thing's shapeless form echoed flatly in this unreal space, and Mahir was there, slashing with an ALEPH-crafted virus blade. The monster screamed as one of its probes was severed to fall into disintegrating bits across the ground.

Together, the two Aspects of ALEPH, one fallen and one whole, drove the Aspect of the alien Evolved Intelligence back against the wall of its own fortress.

Ridhaan fought against the rise of desperation he felt as he watched each wound they inflicted heal within moments. The Aspect was desperate, its pain was very real. But it would soon realize that it was in no actual danger from their attacks; not this close to its source of power.

He reached out to the tiger standing beside Hanima and a layer of his awareness settled over the remote's emerging Geist, watching the woman work, praying to Toth, ALEPH, and any other power that might be listening, that she would be able to undo her own desperate work in time.

Hanima was working her way through the layers of messy code she had thrown together in her frantic haste. She had needed to slip something past the Aspect that would send an emergency warning to all nearby residents and authorities, then chase them outward using every Quantronic-linked surface in the dizzying corridors, away from the alien-infected commune, slamming emergency bulkheads behind them as they ran, locking them in place with sufficient security that no suspicious, doubting authorities outside of the cordon, or the enemy Aspect on the inside, could open the doors.

But now the doors had to be opened, and she didn't have the leisure to untangle her frenzied protocols in her own time.

He nudged Parachit closer. Hanima was going to need all the help she could get.

Her eyes were working furiously, focusing dizzyingly up and down through multiple dials. It was interesting to him that she still used the dial paradigm even submerged in the Quantronic substrate of the network, where the interface could appear as anything she wanted, or nothing at all.

He watched through the tiger's eyes as she unraveled one impossible, tangled knot at a time. The soldiers and agents at the door were battering against it hopelessly, while the trio of hackers had settled into a swaying, silent stillness…

Three shapes swirled into being around Hanima.

Three women, like witches from an ancient tale, except younger and… stranger.

Clearly the transition into the Quantronic realm had been fast, and they hadn't taken any time or effort to alter their appearance from their normal everyday garb; they looked just like the three women standing before the door in Hanima's dial.

The smallest woman was a little pixie with unruly blonde hair spiking up all around strange, silvered goggles that rode on her high forehead. The second woman wore a modified red and white jump suit, blue hair pulled into a tight, fierce bun. The last woman, standing between the other two, wore high-end armor and a hooded cloak.

The woman in the cloak glanced at Hanima and the dials that swirled through the air around her, and nodded.

"Your work?" The words were curt and sharp. The other two women moved to either side, studying the dials, and then started to call up images of their own, which they quickly started to manipulate, muttering to each other all the while.

Another coil of data probe fell on Ridhaan, then, distracting him from the women working.

"Ridhaan!" Mahir was gasping, his shield gone now, the virus sword's violent flurry his only defense.

"Busy!" He grunted, his lance phasing into the shape of a massive axe. He lopped the tip off the new probe, sent the others scurrying away with a wild, un-aimed swing, and then ran toward his friend.

"How much longer do you think she's going to take?!" Mahir's image was wavering. Not only was he losing what energy he had left, draining his body back in the corridor on Bakunin, but he was losing data as well, bleeding it from several ugly tears.

"She's got help. Not too long, I hope?"

He swung wildly again, trying to keep the alien Aspect wary, to give Mahir a chance to catch his breath.

Through the eyes of the tiger, again, he watched the women work.

"Jazz," the wild-haired blonde had an accent that she had carried over into the network with her. "You see this dataset here? Can you delete it without corrupting the follow-on sets?"

The woman in the red and white grunted. "Not easily… there."

"Thanks." The blonde had moved on to the next layer.

"This was quite a program, miss." The woman in the cloak was still working with Hanima through the dials. "No way we could have untangled it from our end."

"Fast and dirty." Hanima said, by way of apology. "Got very subjective, very quickly."

The woman in the hood nodded. "Happens." She glanced over her shoulder at the massive presence battering the two figures trapped by the huge wall.

"I'm guessing there's a lot more going on here than some techno-hermit gentleman's club."

Then she peered more closely at the monster, probably seeing the structure of its substance for the first time.

"Damn." She muttered, focusing even more intently. "Shit!"

The woman with the wild hair looked away from her work at the towering program. "No way!"

The blue-haired woman snickered. "The one that got away, Mary?"

The woman in the cloak nodded. "Not this time, I don't think."

The blonde woman shook her head. "Aliens."

The woman they had called Mary looked back to Hanima. "Is it tethered?"

Hanima nodded. "There's a node in there." She jerked her head toward the towering citadel of black firewall. "Inside the *Alagaav ka Sansthaan* commune."

All three of the newcomers paused in their work to stare up at the fortress. "Well, damn. We're not getting in this way."

"So open the door, girls! Let the cavalry in!" The blue haired woman, Jazz, bent back to her work, as did the others.

Again, Ridhaan's distraction through the tiger's eyes cost him, and a probe swept up and around him, lifting him high into the air and smashing him against the slick heat of the firewall.

He screamed, his axe disappearing in a shower of sparks as he lost concentration completely.

"Ridhaan!" Mahir roared. His sword began to glow as he infused it with corrupted data and virus chains, and he thrust it through the beast's thick, rubbery, firewall-skin.

Ridhaan watched Mahir collapse, the pain of his own situation stuttering his vision.

But the sword stayed locked in the matter of the enemy's construct. A repeating, spiral pattern of disruption spread out from the wound. The Aspect of the Evolved Intelligence screamed.

It was a hauntingly human sound.

Ridhaan was braced for the fall when the massive probe released its hold and he dropped back to the featureless ground, rising again, pulling enough data and power through his link to form a massive shield. He dropped to his side next to Mahir, holding the defensive wall up over them both.

From beneath the shield, he watched as the odd discoloration flaring out from the enemy's wound started to stabilize, then to fade, the oily blackness rushing in to quell the virus and the corrupted data, and the sword began to slide out.

He eased his awareness of that moment away and plunged back into the tiger, hoping the end was near.

"Yes!" The blonde woman pumped her fist into the air. The other two newcomers smiled at her.

"Easy, Valerya, it was a team effort." The one they'd called Mary seemed amused despite her words.

Even Hanima smiled.

Through the dials, they all watched as the doors slid apart, yellow warning lights flashing, sirens sounding.

The forces of Bakunin charged through the corridor, headed straight for the alien compound. A line of medium-armored soldiers bearing a mix of ranged weapons took the lead. Their helmets bore blank white faces with a single line of sensor material bisecting them. Behind this line was the single armored monster, a Taskmaster bearing a huge Heavy Machine Gun. Two small remotes that looked vaguely like a child's toys ran beside the figure, with a third, slightly larger, just behind.

And behind this vanguard came a tide of lightly-armored Moderators, Combi Rifles raised.

He watched through Parachit's eyes as the Bakunian forces swept up the final corridor toward the *Alagaav* entrance. A huge orange and blue figure stood there at the intersection, firing madly into the darkness. A carpet of dead Shasvastii littered the ground all around, but more were hovering around the edges of the fight.

The vision shook again as the operators within continued to fire off the old explosive bolts, working the module free from the mothership.

Rosa Smyth was keening like a banshee, twirling through a line of Shasvastii Seed-Soldiers who were apparently stunned by the destruction.

There was a shout from beside Ridhaan, and he pulled his awareness back into himself.

"What?" He rose up on his hip, looking over the shield at…

The enemy Aspect was gone.

"Where—" He stood, but the monster was nowhere to be seen.

"Oh, no." He turned to Mahir, but his friend was already phasing out of the Quantronic realm.

And then he realized where the Aspect must have gone.

Through Parachit's eyes again, he watched as an enormous shadow moved within the darkness of the open security doors.

A huge remote, at least twice the size of the beast Mahir had fought in the lobby of the hotel, emerged into the light.

Another shudder of their view, and behind the monster remote, the doors to the *Alagaav ka Sansthaan* began to grind closed.

"Oh, shit, no." The hacker woman, Mary, dropped away.

"Damn!" First the blonde, then the blue-haired woman disappeared as well.

Through the dial, they watched as the forces of Bakunin stood beside Hanima's team, facing the colossal combat remote, the doors of the commune closing behind, gouts of fire, smoke, and sparks erupting from the floor and ceiling of the wall of the module.

Petar Vozde and the Taskmaster stood shoulder to shoulder, HMG tracers and the streaking line of hyper-velocity projectiles lighting up the scene as countless smaller weapons flashed and stuttered to either side.

Matias Kimani stood over a crouching Dak Kostic treating the faceless armored body of a Prowler, its chest stove in. Nearby, he could see Hanima's body, slumped against the wall, Parachit by her side. Next to the remote, Mahir stood up, racked a round into the chamber of his Radjun, and started to walk toward the towering remote, pouring a line of fire into the thing's flank.

The two little bear-like remotes with the Taskmaster dodged past the gigantic alien combat machine and dove for the closing doors.

Something about their movements seemed almost gleeful to Ridhaan.

Then they exploded with enough force to drive the vast bulk of the combat drone forward onto the knees of its front legs.

In the vision, he watched as the humans and Shasvastii both shielded themselves from the debris. The humanoid remote following the Taskmaster leapt forward, raising a small shield that pulsed with energy and flared to a giant disk, deflecting most of the debris that would have hit the two heavy-armored figures.

Hanima closed her avatar's eyes, preparing to drop back into the physical world to help her friends.

The vision shook again, far more violently, and the module tore away from the mothership.

Someone must have screamed an order, as all those without helmets hastened to pull up pressure hoods or rebreather masks and hold on to the countless hidden handles and angles of the hallway. The remaining air vented out, pulling smoke, debris, and bodies toward the opening with it.

More emergency bulkheads slammed into place, freed by the fleeing enemy Aspect.

The doorway was a gaping hole, with nothing but darkness on the other side.

As if a puppet with its strings cut, the enormous remote fell forward onto its massive, armored face and was still.

Hanima's team and the Bakunian soldiers moved forward, ignoring the few remaining Shasvastii, to pump fire through the doorway and up at the module that now floated free, moving under some unseen guidance, away from the mothership.

Hanima's eyes snapped back open, still submerged in the network. She locked eyes with Ridhaan.

"They're going to get away." He felt empty, deflated. After everything they had just done.

"No, they're not." The woman spun up a dial, and then three more.

Her hands flashed, her eyes darting back and forth as she worked her way through some truly formidable security.

One by one, the dials cleared and vanished.

This was rational, standard security, not the tangled knot of desperate necessity that had defied her every efforts moments ago.

The final dial cleared and then another spun up to replace it.

A targeting array, clearly showing a boxy module lifting away from the mothership.

Given the chaotic nature of the local datasphere, there was no way anyone would have cleared the point-defense cannons to fire on a portion of their own ship.

By the time enough of the facts filtered up through the chain of command, the module might be gone, or some stealthed alien ship might have swooped in and rescued the inhabitants of the commune and their network node.

In those moments of stunned incomprehension lay the aliens' hope of escape.

Hanima's brow furrowed, and Ridhaan wanted to smile.

A pair of enormous Hyper-Rapid Magnetic Cannons, that would put Petar Vozde's Switech Gurges to shame, rotated in their armored mounts, barrels rising to track the fleeing module.

Hanima's face tightened and the point defense arrays spat twin lines of destruction upward. She walked the wavering, intersecting lines down across the *Alagaav ka Sansthaan* commune module. Bright yellow outlined the holes punched into the hull. It was already streaming tangled wreckage, and then it gave a brief shudder, then another.

Then it detonated in a perfect sphere of fire, throwing spinning wreckage in every direction.

She sagged back, the last dial disappearing.

The primary dial, showing what was happening in the corridor, returned.

Everyone seemed stunned.

Petar and the Taskmaster had turned to stare at each other in surprise. Rosa had collapsed against a bulkhead, breath fogging the emergency hood to opacity, her head bowed toward her lap. She was covered in blood and ichor.

Matias stood, his gun hanging limply from one hand as he surveyed the carnage.

Only Nia Kostic continued to move, working on a line of injured several of the Moderators had brought to her, smiling through the clear plastic of her hood.

And Mahir, standing about twenty meters from Hanima's still-slumped body, stared at the collapsed colossus of the alien remote.

Then the surviving Shasvastii leapt up and began to attack the survivors.

They were being pounded back to the deck as quickly as they rose, except for one that had escaped everyone's attention.

Behind Mahir, crawling from the last remote bay, came a tall, sinuous figure, forcing itself past the twisted wreckage of the alien remote.

The Shasvastii Corvax stood tall on its reverse-jointed legs. A wicked-looking sword with an evil greenish sheen hung from one alien hand.

And it began to run for Mahir.

He didn't see it.

He couldn't hear it in the vacuum of the compromised corridor.

The alien spec-ops trooper ran past Hanima's slumped body, the rebreather Mahir had placed over her face hiding her features.

The sword rose as they watched. Ridhaan screamed, trying to plunge himself back into the analog world; back into Parachit, as if the remote would have been able to do anything.

With a sudden snap, the image was gone.

The dial was gone.

Ridhaan whirled around, desperately searching for Hanima.

She was gone.

He dove into the data stream, pulling up a link to a surveillance node just in time to see the Shasvastii blade descending toward his friend's back.

"Get off our ship, asshole!"

A blast of twisted, molten chain blew the alien off its feet and into the wreckage of a bulkhead behind it. Mahir spun around, stunned.

Another blast tore through the thing's belly, splashing its thin, oily blood over the wall.

A third blast erased the monster's head.

Hanima, having returned to the physical corridor, stepped into view, exchanging a couple words with Mahir.

The woman looked up and saw that her team was now surrounded by Bakunin forces.

The very people they had just saved.

And although the red, white, and black armored soldiers were not attacking, the barrels of their weapons were definitely pointed in her people's general direction.

Chapter 22

Moderator Watch House T-5, VaudeVille, *Bakunin*

Hanima never understood why the smell of disinfectant always made her feel sick.

She cleared her throat behind a raised hand and closed her eyes. She never understood it, but it always happened anyway.

They were in a sterile white room, about as un-Bakunian as she could imagine, toward the back of a local Moderator Watch House module. Their wounds had been dressed, they had each been examined by active-service Daktaris, many of whom had seemed pleasantly surprised to see Nia, exchanging smiles and low-voiced conversation as they looked over each of her friends.

Petar, a huge smile on his unshaven face and a thick chocolate ration bar in one meaty fist, had been nearly unscathed, aside from the injuries he had taken from the first contact in the corridor. He seemed more concerned with the loss of his enormous knife than any of the injuries he had sustained. He was lounging in one of the uncomfortable seats arranged around the big metal conference table. Only he and Nia seemed completely oblivious to their current ambiguous status as 'guests' of the Moderators.

His smile only dimmed whenever he looked at Rosa, folded in around herself at one end of the table. Her tendrils were hidden once again with a pale blue cloth one of the Moderators had given her, but she was shaking slightly, rocking in place as she sat on the chair, her feet tucked up underneath her, eyes staring straight into the table, unseeing.

Hanima remembered, with a shiver of her own, the roaring, animal rage the woman had descended into during the final moments of the fight; surrounded by alien warriors, smoke and flame.

She was by far the most seriously injured of the group. She had been given the maximum dosage of Serum, and yet still her wounds and bruises refused to close or fade completely. She was wrapped in synthetic skin and fabric bandages, but the worst were her eyes.

Hollow, empty, and unseeing.

Although Matias had made it through almost untouched aside from some cuts and bruises and a single through-and-through wound from a Shasvastii rifle, he looked almost as bad as Rosa. Hanima watched him, hoping maybe he would sense her looking and glare at her, like he used to.

But he was aware of nothing but his own inner turmoil. Just minutes after they had been rounded up by the Moderators, Prowlers and the big Taskmaster standing behind, watching silently, she had noticed the little thief hunting unconsciously through his pockets.

Looking for the thin drives he had tossed to the dirty floor of the hostel lobby in a moment of adrenaline-fueled bravado.

Nia seemed lost in her own mind as well, now that they had all been stabilized and treated. Her own wounds had been seen to, mostly healing nicely under shiny patches of synthetic skin and sealer, and she had seemed to find new energy speaking with the other Daks. She had waved them away whenever a Moderator or Inspector wandered too close, which Hanima found interesting. Otherwise, she was mostly watching Rosa and Matias with concern clear in her dark eyes.

And then there was their mysterious benefactor. Mahir looked drawn and haggard, with multiple scratches and cuts that had seemed to begin healing before they had even made it to the Moderators' triage station behind the first emergency blast doors. And yet he, too, looked lost and somehow alone, even in a room with five other people. He had entered carrying a small satchel, the only one of them with any luggage. The bag now sat at his feet, apparently forgotten.

He sensed her stare and looked up, giving her a weak, empty nod and a tight smile.

Parachit had been allowed to stay with her and was sitting nearby, watching the people around the table impassively.

Hanima wondered if it was coincidence that the remote had sat between her and Mahir.

Each of her friends had deferred to her whenever a Moderator or Inspector came by to ask them anything. She hadn't known what they were doing at first and wanted very much to look to Mahir or Nia for direction.

Neither of them had provided any help; for wildly varying reasons, she realized.

Even the Nomad Military Force officials had been treating her with a modicum of respect, which she had found odd given their quasi-prisoner status, until she remembered: she had blasted an alien-infested module out of Bakunin's skies!

Mahir, more than any other, seemed to have changed his attitude toward her.

He had also started to act very strangely around Parachit, she realized.

Had her blasting that last Shasvastii into slimy bits really impressed him that much?

With a soft hiss, the door slid open and a man and a woman entered. They both surveyed the motley bunch at the table with flat, leveled eyes.

No one rose to greet them.

Hanima recognized the woman from her visions through the Quantronic link to the surveillance cameras during the fighting. Detective Inspector Jelena Kovač was a severe woman; her black longcoat, trimmed in red, did nothing to soften that impression. The enormous heavy pistol at her hip was more complement than contrast to it as well.

She didn't recognize the man in the tight-fitting blue and gold O-12 uniform. Her awareness of that organization wasn't much deeper than any other Nomad's: the international organization of human governments was at best usually an ineffectual friend, and at worst a domineering overseer, to the motherships. O-12 presence on any Nomad mothership was carefully controlled, limited to a handful of representatives at any given time.

If she was any judge, though, based on this man's ill-fitting formal uniform and the controlled power he seemed to radiate, if he was regular law enforcement, she was the Kurat of the Nomad Executive Board.

Kovač cleared her throat, nodding to Hanima, then widening her regard to the rest of the room.

"Some of you know me already; Detective Inspector Jelena Kovač of the Tunguska Securitate."

Why a member of the Tunguska security force, rather than a Moderator from Bakunin, was questioning them was a little confusing, but given how things had gone, it probably meant the Board was taking this very seriously. And the fact that the only Moderators involved at all in this phase of the investigation were hovering around outside the shiny white room was more than a little disturbing.

Kovač was continuing, gesturing to the man beside her.

"This is Commander Yôsef Goldstein. He has been serving as the current O-12 liaison to the Executive Board and will be joining me during this session as an impartial observer." She moved to sit down, gesturing for Goldstein to take the last seat.

At the mention of O-12, Hanima glanced at Mahir. The one-eyed man looked quickly away, and she felt her own eyes tighten.

The man in the blue and gold uniform merely moved to the back of the chair and folded his heavy arms over a broad chest that, again, looked out of place on someone posing as a bureaucrat.

"My friends call me Cuervo."

He seemed keenly interested in Mahir, more than any of the rest of them.

Mahir, nearly squirming under the man's steely gaze, eventually opened his mouth to speak.

Before he could so much as make a sound, Goldstein rumbled, "You can call me 'sir.'"

There was an uncomfortable pause at that, then the annoyed-looking Detective Inspector continued.

"Firstly," Kovač scanned the table, making sure each person sitting there was looking directly into her eyes.

It took several moments of awkward silence to get Rosa to rise out of her personal torment, but the blue-skinned girl eventually nodded along with the others.

"Firstly," Kovač said again, "you all know how sensitive this moment in history is. With Combined Army forces scattered across the Human Sphere, and even Concilium itself under siege, all of humanity is poised to panic at the mention of an alien; especially a Shasvastii incursion."

Goldstein shifted slightly from foot to foot at her mention of the capital planet of the Sphere. The rest of them simply nodded or looked at her with blank faces.

"I don't think I overstate the danger of panic descending upon the Nation, should it become known that such an incursion had occurred among us, on one of the motherships, no less." She looked around again, clearly trying to convey the seriousness of the situation.

Nia looked away, her own past looming up behind her. Petar didn't look overly concerned, but the rest of them, even Mahir, nodded along.

"We do not do this lightly, but the Executive Board believes, especially given the heightened tensions between the Nomads and the other nations of the Human Sphere, that the details of this incident must remain a mystery to all those beyond the fleet." She sighed, looking down at her gloved, folded hands. "Indeed, in order to ensure that word of this incursion does not escape the motherships, those within the fleet must be kept in the dark as well."

Even Petar was listening intently now. No doubt he saw countless free drinks and introductions to likely partners disappear as he was being sworn not to talk about the things he had seen and done over the past week and more.

"Knowledge of what happened here on Bakunin, and indeed the plot at the heart of the recent attacks on the financial underpinnings of the entire Human Sphere, could well shatter the confidence of the Nomad populace in the very fabric of our society." She looked up again, once more forcing each of them to meet her eyes, to see the severity of her words. "With what is currently unfolding on Concilium Prima and Paradiso, if they begin to doubt that the Executive Board can provide both security AND freedom to the Nomad people—"

Both Petar and Matias snorted at that, looking quickly away.

Kovač seemed to sense that she was losing the room, shook her head, and then continued on as if they hadn't made a sound.

"Due to privacy laws, of course, only routine background checks have been made on all of you." The severe woman scanned each of their faces. "You seem like a pretty standard contract team, although it is rather odd to find you all together like this." She paused, then looked first to Hanima, her eyes tightening, "Only one set of identification codes did not pass muster." And then her gaze slid over to Mahir. "Who are you?"

The O-12 agent standing behind the empty chair moved forward, his gloved hands grasping the back with an ominous creak.

Hanima felt the flesh on the back of her neck crawl with a phantom chill despite the severe climate control of the room. From the moment they had fallen in with Mahir, she had known there was something wrong with the man.

She even thought she had figured out what that strangeness was, and if she was right, he posed nearly as great a risk to the Nomads as the aliens had.

"He's my uncle."

The three words were as shocking as a pistol shot in the still room. Every pair of eyes turned sharply to stare at the speaker.

To stare at her.

Goldstein looked ready to spit.

Kovač almost growled deep in her throat, but her professionalism held.

"Excuse me?" The words were as cold and brittle as ice building up around a faulty oxygen valve.

"He's my uncle." She couldn't take the words back now. She would be held responsible for them whether she stuck with them or denied them.

Among the Nomads, there was a certain protective aura around familial connections. To declare someone a blood relative meant that you vouched for them. Unless specific evidence was presented that showed they had committed a particular crime, they would be given over to the custody of the claimant until such time as suspicion passed, or such evidence could be presented.

If she was wrong, and Mahir hadn't been as good as she thought he was…

Kovač glared at her, then at the one-eyed man. "You've spent a lot of time on Tunguska."

Mahir's dark eye was cold and steady as he stared back at her. "I have."

"You seem familiar to me." She leaned over her folded hands, the force of her personality pushing across the table.

"I don't believe we've ever met." Mahir responded to the aggressive push by settling back into his own chair.

The O-12 agent was furious, his dark eyes twitching between Kovač's face and Mahir's.

The detective continued to stare at the strange man as the silence stretched into an awkward gulf.

"Your uncle?" The glare was back on her, and it hadn't lessened in its heat or intensity.

"My uncle." She lifted her chin defiantly. Although they were a ridiculously simple blood test away from exposing the lie, Nomad tradition was sometimes as hard as stone.

They wouldn't give them a test like that without a lot more evidence.

And by the time they gathered any of that, if it existed at all, Mahir should be long gone.

Kovač sighed, looked up at the bare ceiling, and worked her mouth as if she couldn't get rid of a foul taste. When she spoke, it was again to the group as a whole.

"Your story checks out, over all." She reached into a pocket and produced a fistful of data chips she laid carefully into a line on the table. "Your data usage, purchases, and comlogs all confirm what each of you has testified."

The collective sigh of relief from her friends, quiet and contained but no less real for that, was not shared by herself or Mahir.

She was too busy looking at their benefactor, whose demeanor had very nearly collapsed into exhausted relief after Kovač had signaled her willingness to observe the social nicety of their avuncular relationship, for now.

"A lot of your equipment requires advanced licenses for use and ownership." Matias's head jerked up at that, as did Petar's.

Hanima was fairly certain that a Switech Gurges Hyper-Rapid Magnetic Cannon wasn't a common piece of gear owned by your average null-grav hard-head.

"Given your service to the Nomad Nation in this incident, and in partial thanks from O-12 as well," she glanced over her shoulder at Goldstein, who was still glaring at Mahir, "we have taken the liberty of issuing those licenses and permissions retroactively."

Another sigh of relief from her friends; this interview was going to be tough on all of them.

"There does seem to be some minor holes in your stories." Kovač glanced down at the orderly disks, hovering over Matias and Rosa in particular. "We'll be coming to you for any follow up information we need. You won't need to stay on Bakunin."

The Detective Inspector sat up straighter. "With the resolution of the current crisis, the Executive Board has announced an early end to the Emergency Krug. The motherships will be heading back toward civilization, each going their separate ways again until the normally scheduled gathering. Unless you particularly enjoyed your time here, I'd advise you to make your own best speed back to Corregidor."

Hanima thought she heard the woman mutter under her breath, "I won't be rushing back here."

"I've got some questions, still. And I won't be staying on any of these ships long enough for a leisurely follow-up." Goldstein leaned over the back of his chair, dark eyes flashing.

"How did you know something was going on in the *Alagaav ka Sansthaan* commune*?*

"When did you realize there was an alien presence on Bakunin?

"Why did you not immediately alert the appropriate authorities when such involvement became clear to you?"

His words were like bullets, flashing across the room, and her friends flinched with their impact.

Everyone but her.

"We were tracking a signal trace from Corregidor, *Los Gatos-7* territory, to Bakunin. We didn't know—"

"How the hell were we supposed to know we should be telling anyone? We didn't know shit about what was behind that door!"

It was Matias, rising to her defense like a sick lion.

She wanted to hug him.

"We thought it was just *Gatos* scat, man." Petar threw one big arm over the back of his own chair. It was a casual move, but it served to remind all those around him how big the man really was. "No offense, blue-coat, but 'aliens' isn't the first thought that comes to mind when you're looking for anything strange on Bakunin. Especially on Bakunin."

"We had no idea there were aliens involved until they came spilling out of that commune." Nia's calm voice was like a lifeline thrown into the vacuum of the void. "I assure you, Commander Goldstein , if we had had any ind ication it was anything more than *mara* activity run amok, I would have made sure we alerted the authorities."

"What the hell is a *Gato*?" Goldstein's voice was quavering.

Kovač gave the agent a condescending smile. "Low-level criminal gang, from Corregidor. Not really major players here."

Hanima almost smiled to think of what Declan might have made of the Inspector's assessment of his target of choice, but there was too much weighing her down.

Kovač nodded to the old Dak, then turned back to Hanima. "We've looked at the contract your… uncle… filed with Bright, Matsuda, Cohen, and Associates on Tunguska. Standard work contract for tracking down the killers of his… business partner."

Hanima's eyes flicked toward Mahir, and she cursed her own lack of finesse in situations like these. There was no doubt Kovač had seen.

But really, Mahir had filed a contract, an official contract, covering their work together?

His head jerked slightly to the side, as if waving off her line of thinking.

But if the Detective said there was a contract, filed legally and in a timely manner, that meant he had to have done it before they'd ever left Corregidor for Bakunin.

Or he had some way to make it look as if he had.

Another piece of circumstantial data falling into place.

Goldstein was still shaking his head, glaring at Matias and Petar, but Kovač seemed satisfied, at least for the time being.

Detective Inspector Jelena Kovač rose gracefully from her seat, gathering up the data chips with one practiced sweep of her hand. She moved toward the door, where a Moderator, high level judging by his uniform, opened it for her, looking annoyed and frustrated.

Behind the man, Hanima saw a very strange trio standing together in the Watch House lobby.

A woman with wild blonde hair and huge goggles on her forehead; a tall, stately woman in armor and a flowing cloak, two big pistols riding on her hips; and a woman in a flashy modified set of red coveralls, blue hair in a tight bun.

The blonde woman waved at her with a huge grin, while the blue-haired woman smiled with slightly more restraint. The woman in the long black coat merely nodded, but there was a warmth in her eyes that Hanima was shocked to see there.

Kovač turned at the door, looked out at the trio, then back to Hanima.

"Looks like you're developing a bit of a fan club. I don't think you'll be needing Maintenance Team credit to breathe from now on." The woman's face seemed to twitch.

It looked like a—

Could Kovač have—

Winked?

The woman in the long black and red greatcoat swept past the Moderator holding the door, and she was gone.

Goldstein didn't turn but instead walked slowly backward toward the door.

The face of the Moderator there started to darken further at the theatrics.

The O-12 agent looked at each of them, then his eyes settled on Mahir, who stared back impassively.

"I will see you again, friend." He started to turn, then stopped. Looking back, his eyes tightened and his mouth hardened into a sharp line, a slit between mustache and beard. "Soon."

It seemed like a typical, empty threat, the kind of thing a 'bad cop' would say toward the end of a network crime sensadrama.

But Mahir, at the single, sharp syllable, didn't flinch, he didn't raise his head defiantly.

He nodded, then looked away.

Did the men know each other?

Then Goldstein, too, was gone.

"Your paperwork is all in order." The Moderator with the white hair growled. "You're free to go whenever you please."

He stepped back and the door began to slide closed, then he paused. "The sooner the better." And then with one more step, the door was closed and he was gone as well.

A deep silence settled over the sterile room.

Hanima took a deep breath. Every decision she had made to this point had been forced upon her in a moment of intense stress and danger. This decision, the conclusion of hours of fretful deliberation, was the product of cold calculation, informed assumption, and guesswork.

But she was certain she was correct.

She turned toward Mahir. The man was staring at the door, then shifted his gaze to look directly into her eyes.

His single eye was dark, with flecks of gold sparkling in its depths.

There was something in there she hadn't anticipated. Fear? Disappointment?

Pleading?

She sighed, shook her head almost imperceptibly, and forced herself to straighten in her chair.

"You'll be leaving now, I assume."

"What?" Petar stiffened, and Matias looked confused.

Even Nia looked at her with a question on her aged face.

Interestingly, Rosa only nodded slightly, still looking down at the table.

Mahir's eye never left hers. He nodded, once, as if he had known this was coming.

Of course he had known it was coming.

Their strange benefactor purposefully placed both of his hands, palms down, on the table before him. He took a deep breath.

Did he need to breathe? Was that an act?

The pain and disappointment, or whatever it was that tightened his face, remained.

"Yes." He looked up, trying to force a smile.

But could she trust anything he said or did? If she was right about him, there was nothing she could trust at all.

"I want you all to know how grateful I am for your service and your assistance."

That seemed to shock Petar more than the sudden appearance of savage killer aliens had.

Matias, however, didn't register any shock at all. Instead, he was staring at the dark-skinned, one-eyed man with a strange, almost feral intensity.

"I meant what I said, when we first came together." He reached down for his small satchel. He put it down before him but did not open it.

"I made certain promises, and you have all done everything I asked and far more." He wasn't looking at any of them now. Hanima felt her own eyes tighten; that seemed like a strange length to go, to sell this last farewell.

Matias was staring at the tall, cloaked man with laser-like intensity.

"Vozde, I think you've been enjoying the Switech Gurges?" There was a slight smile playing around the man's mouth.

"You could say that." Petar's smile was much wider.

"When you return to Corregidor, you will find you are registered with PraxiTech for supply and repair." Now he did look up at the big man, and his smile was a little wider. "You'll never want for ammo or spare parts. That will also extend to that wonderful work of art you wear into battle."

Petar slapped one meaty hand down on the table with a bark of laughter.

"I'm afraid my ability to put you in touch with the Kriza Boracs has been… curtailed. But I believe Detective Inspector Kovač has filed reports, doctored though they may be, that will put you in the best of lights with any recruiter from the Nomad Military Forces. If you wish, I have no doubt you will find a position anywhere you want; including with the Boracs, eventually."

That news, rather than heightening Petar's excitement, seemed to dampen it somewhat. The big man looked at her quickly, then away.

She thought she knew what that meant.

"Daktari," Mahir slid a small data cube across the table, slid from a side pocket on the satchel. "Those contacts Declan Kinoti promised you. I took the liberty to send letters of introduction explaining your situation. A clinic anywhere on any of the motherships should be well within your capabilities, now."

She smiled gently at him and nodded her thanks, taking the cube in one wrinkled hand.

Next, Mahir took a large console unit out of the satchel. Its green surface was shiny, like polished rock, with gold detailing around its edges. It incorporated a pair of slim spectacles connected to the processing box with gold wires. Around the sides of the box were golden inscriptions in what looked like Tibetan umê script.

"Miss Smyth, you sacrificed more than anyone for the cause of your home, I think." Mahir's voice was low. If this was an act, it was worthy of any sensadrama she had ever seen. He actually seemed like he was hurting as he spoke.

"This is not the Yu Jing wetware to which Kinoti was referring at your first meeting." He put one hand on the box. "Those programs are untested, illicit tech. This is an actual Tibetan ataractic reflection cube." He looked up at her, and Hanima would have put money down, any odds, that the man was sincere.

If he had been a man.

"This will help you more than any Yu Jing wet hack. It will bring you peace when you use it, and will teach you to find your own peace, over time."

The girl reached tentatively across the table, her strange, light eyes never wavering from the gleaming green box.

"Thank you." The words were whispered, but full of heavy emotion.

Hanima had never heard of an ataractic reflection cube, and a quick dip into Arachne revealed to her nothing more than the fact that the things did, actually, exist.

But Rosa seemed to recognize it, and as she pulled it toward herself, there were tears in her eyes.

Mahir cleared his throat and pulled something else out of the satchel, leaving it flat and empty.

This new device was something a little more familiar; a basic data cube, its matte black cage clearly of military origin. A data link port was set into one side, within its own locked casing.

"Mil-spec datalink purge algorithm." Mahir's voice was flat and he was looking right into Matias's eyes.

Matias, however, was staring at the box.

In disappointment.

"This gear will purge you of your dependence, Kimani. It's rough, I won't lie to you. But on the other side is a life free of the driving urges that own you now."

Matias was shaking slightly, and while each of them had been looking at him, waiting to see what his reaction would be to Mahir's gift, they quickly looked away as the weakness, fear, and distress welled up in his eyes like blood from a wound gone bad.

"You have to make this choice yourself, of course." Mahir's voice was low and calm. "It can't work against any kind of resistance. You'll be doing the hard work; this only helps."

Without taking his eye away from Matias's face, Mahir reached into the bag and drew forth a pack of disposable one-use drives.

"Or you can have these."

Matias's smile was bright and tragic at the same time.

"Well, there's always tomorrow for the hard stuff, am I right?" He reached out and grasped the bundle with a quick, eager, clumsy motion. "I'll take these, thanks."

The self-loathing clear in his eyes was hard to see, but Hanima forced herself not to look away.

Nodding as if he had always known where that was going, Mahir slid the military drive back into the bag.

"Now, Miss Cruz." He turned toward her. "You were getting cash."

She nodded. She wasn't looking for anything Declan Kinoti, or this creature, could provide.

"Well, I have topped off all your accounts, so all of you are quite well-off, for the moment." He looked at all of them, smiling as the words settled into their minds.

Then he turned back to Hanima.

"I had that armor from the *Gato* lieutenant refurbished and put with the rest of your gear."

The others looked at her strangely, but she felt the sting behind her eyes and looked away, nodding her thanks.

"I have also established for you a long-term Shadow Contract, secured with a certain Tunguskan legal entity, for sole rental property rights to a compound in the Neck sector of Corregidor, just down the corridor from the Kuhifahdi Cantina." He looked up at the rest of the team. "I believe that is a very sought-after sector? A sanctuary zone, if my research was accurate. The real estate records say this compartment should sleep fifteen easily." He shook his head in disbelief. "Translating that from Corregidoran sensibilities, I'd say five could be very comfortable there."

She was stunned. Long term rental contracts were almost unheard of on Corregidor. And the fact that this was a Shadow Contract, held on Tunguska, meant that a dedicated AI would be assigned to watch over the contract, to make sure no one, absolutely no one, moved against the signatories.

Mahir had given her a home.

More than that, a veritable palace, on space-starved Corregidor.

She stared at him, forgetting her suspicions for the first time since the battle.

"I thought you'd appreciate that more than a gun or more money."

She was stunned. She couldn't breathe. She felt a strange, scratchy irritation in her eyes.

She merely nodded.

"If any of you need me—"

She forced her head down. It needed to be done, no matter what he had done for each of them. She couldn't take a chance with her home.

"You need to leave."

She knew she had shocked her friends with that cold statement. To explain it to them would be to expose Mahir to nearly a century of paranoia and hatred. She would let them think her harsh before she would damage their appreciation of their benefactor over unproven suspicions.

No matter how certain she had become.

Mahir stared at her for a moment, his dark eye steady. Then he nodded and stood.

He slid the satchel across the table to her, without a word, then moved quietly to the door.

There, before it opened, he turned back one more time.

"Thank you. All of you."

Then he looked down to Parachit, where the remote had risen up on straightened forelimbs, its insectile head staring straight at Mahir.

Parachit rose to all fours, quivering in place.

Acting strange one again.

The remote swayed from side to side, Mahir and Hanima staring at it. The one-eyed man seemed far more interested in the robot's erratic behavior than made any sense to her.

She remembered, vaguely, the battle in the Quantronic borderlands. Mahir struggling against the alien program while Hanima and the trio of military hackers untangled her own Gordian knot, Parachit beside her, aiding her efforts.

But Mahir had not been alone, had he? She remembered another figure in the distance, fighting with him.

His partner?

His dead partner?

A genuine ghost in the machine?

Which made no sense at all. People did not leave their essence in the network when they died.

She almost gasped, but kept her eyes even, her breathing shallow.

People didn't leave their essence in the network when they died.

She looked again at Mahir, knowing she had made the right decision. He needed to leave at once.

But what did that mean about Parachit and the remote's strange behavior?

Surely not…

And then the robot settled down, the shaking subsided, and she sat back down beside Hanima, resting on her ventral surface like a tiger settling down to sleep.

Hanima gave a brief sigh, releasing a breath she hadn't realized she'd been holding.

Mahir sighed as well, she saw, then nodded once, looked at her with a sad smile, nodded again, and was gone.

Through the wide windows of the room they watched the blue and gold uniformed Goldstein emerge into the Watch House lobby from a side door. The two men spoke for a moment, the O-12 agent clearly angry, Mahir only nodding, obviously resigned to whatever was happening.

And then they were gone; Goldstein leading Mahir away. The lobby was empty, and her team was alone in the room, looking at each other in silence.

Between their good fortune and the strange exit of their benefactor, she had to think each of them was as conflicted and exhausted as she herself.

She forced herself to take a deep breath. They weren't done here. She couldn't hide anymore; couldn't wait for decisions to be made for her.

If she wanted to walk away from this fiasco with anything that really mattered, she needed to take a stand.

What did the rest of them want, however?

Mahir was right. Even with the events of the last few weeks scrubbed of the alien connection, their fame was going to spread throughout the motherships. Petar would have no trouble finding a berth with the Kriza Boracs. And if he was going to do that, he would need to move quickly before the motherships were too far apart, now that the impromptu Krug was at an end.

Would Rosa want to stay on Bakunin, now? She would be safe from the Morlock Teams or any other enemies she might have made, after what she had done. Hell, they might make her a team leader in the Morlocks, if she wanted that.

She wouldn't, of course, but that was just a thought. The key was that she could write her own ticket on her home mothership now.

Nia had everything she might need; Declan's last wish had been fulfilled, the team had been a success. She could focus on establishing a clinic in the crowded Lazareto sector, heal people, and forget the damned aliens once and for all.

And Matias had made his decision. He'd end up in another flophouse dorm soon enough, content to lose himself in the degrading euphoric loops programmed into those damned sticks, living on the government Demogrant, taking odd jobs with random work teams.

None of them had any reason to stick together that was certain.

So why was that thought so disappointing now? She had fought against taking the reins of this chaotic little team for so long.

Why did the thought of the team going their separate ways hurt so much?

What was it she wanted?

What was it she really wanted?

She wanted a home. She had a home, now, thanks to Mahir.

But she wanted more than that. She wanted something she hadn't had since her parents had failed to come back from their last work assignment. Something she had been seeking for most of her life, without any luck.

She wanted a family.

She looked at each of them again. Even if they wanted to stay together, what kind of family was that?

The door opened again, and a lower-ranking Moderator stood there, an awed smile on her face.

"Excuse me. The Detective Inspector wanted me to let you know your shuttle is ready." The woman was clearly intimidated as she stood there, looking at each of them as if they were heroes or something worse. "There's no rush, but your gear is all loaded and the pilots will be ready whenever you are."

She looked down to a flickering screen floating over her comlog. "Is there a unit designation I should put on the flight manifest?" She shrugged apologetically. "Corregidoran flight control is asking."

Hanima sighed, then looked up to the rest of them.

They were all looking at her.

Petar was smiling widely, nodding slightly.

Nia was smiling, standing tall and straight, with a strange sheen in her eyes.

Matias looked nonplussed, but even he had a slight grin.

Even Rosa, her eyes more clear than they had been in days, looked more at peace than Hanima could ever remember.

They were all looking to her to answer.

And she knew the answer.

She had her own answer, too.

She looked at the woman standing in the door and sat up straight.

"Tell them Team Zed is coming home."

```
[Comlog status: Online]
[Security/Firewalls: Active]
[Automated news update system: Searching]
[Information delivery filters: Active]
[Custom]
[Direct]
[Financial]
[Deactivate/Change filters]
```

Accessing Maya…

White Paper Plus!

Your source for news from around the globe and across the Human Sphere! If you need to know it, you'll read it here first!

… Financial markets across the Human Sphere have stabilized on news that irregularities at several Yu Jing banks, including the Imperial First, were due to internal processing errors and not external manipulation …

… Officials with O-12 Special Situations Section's Financial Security Commission have assured officials from the StateEmpire, PanOceania, and the rest of the nation states affected by the disruptions that the situation has been taken care of. Further, they guarantee that there will be no further disturbances of this magnitude. Several anonymous sources have reported to White Paper Plus that officials within Yu Jing are denying the reports, but cannot explain why all irregularities seem to have been resolved …

… Institutions from across PanOceania have already resumed regular trading, and markets seem to be recovering admirably across the Sphere given the cur-

rent military situation, with the capital itself, Concilium Prima, experiencing extensive terror attacks by the alien Combined Army …
… With the financial underpinnings of the Human Sphere stabilizing once more, concern returns to the incursions of the alien enemy …

```
[Information delivery filters: Active]
[Custom]
[Direct]
[International]
[Conflict]
[Deactivate/Change filters]
```

Accessing Maya…
Welcome to The True Hurt Aggregator. We tell you the truth, no matter what, when no one else will.

… The silence from the Yu Jing capitol-planet of Yutang tells us more than countless official press releases might; despite the almost immediate financial recovery across the Human Sphere, the StateEmpire does not share the optimistic assessment of the current situation. The Zhurong Power Plant on Paradiso remains in Nomad hands, and the official O-12 report, blaming the entire financial disruption on Yu Jing servers, cannot have improved the mood of those at the top …
… Declaring that the O-12 report completely vindicates their protestations of innocence, the Executive Council of the Nomad Nation has announced the return of Nomad Military Force units to the defense of Concilium Prima and other points of contact with the Combined Army …
… As more and more reports of alien Shasvastii infiltration emerge, it must be a great relief to the leaders of the great nations to have this financial disruption, attributed to something as benign as human error, behind them …

```
[Information delivery filters: Active]
[Custom]
[Direct]
[Nomad Nations]
[Tunguska]
[Deactivate/Change filters]
```

Accessing Maya…
Freedom Watch. One person's 'freedom' is another person's threat. We watch

the 'Free' so you don't have to.

… Long time readers, rest assured that we at Freedom Watch do not share in the veritable love-fest engulfing the Human Sphere with the release of the Financial Security Commission's report. There are too many holes in the account, and the convenience of the Nomads being cleared of suspicion just when Concilium Prima, O-12's own planet, is in desperate need of Nomad assistance beggars the imagination …

… Are we to believe that the Quantronic experts serving Yu Jing's most important governmental structures simply pressed the wrong button? That O-12 itself did not catch this error as the Human Sphere was dragged to the very brink of panic and ruin? …

… O-12 was established to protect the international order of the entire Human Sphere. This white wash of very real concerns can only harm that effort …

… As the Nomads announce an abrupt and suspiciously-timed end to their so-called Emergency Krug, they will now return to the fold of law-abiding citizens of the Sphere? Free to rend the very fabric of our society with their polluted, corrupt concept of Freedom …

```
[Information delivery filters: Active]
[Custom]
[Direct]
[International]
[O-12]
[Circulars]
[Deactivate/Change filters]
```

Accessing Maya…

Diogenist Daily: For the discerning news consumer.

… O-12's Special Situations Section has made a rare statement denouncing rumors of alien involvement in the recent financial emergency that nearly resulted in open warfare between Yu Jing and the Nomad Nation, and in fact did result in a temporary withdrawal of Nomad support against the Combined Army at Concilium Prima and other theaters of conflict …

… Regardless of the truth of the FSC report, it is undeniable that all parties who incurred financial loss during the crisis have been made whole …

… Whether the report is true or a fabrication as suggested by several sources within the Yu Jing StateEmpire who have spoken to the Diogenist upon condition of anonymity, it is undeniable that the Nomad return to those forces defending the Human Sphere against Combined Army aggression will be happy news to those still fighting on all fronts, and all those civilians trapped in combat zones across the Sphere …

… Reports from Concilium Prima and Paradiso, as well as unconfirmed rumors from Dawn and other locations, indicate that the alien menace has redoubled its efforts in recent days; human defenders are sorely pressed along all points of contact …

… Only one thing is certain as war continues to engulf the Human Sphere: only by standing together can we stave off total defeat at the hands of the aliens …

[Comlog status: Connected]
[Security/Firewalls: On]
[Personalized Info Network: Searching]
[Data distribution screens: Active]
[Personalized]
[Thru-put]
[Hiring Halls Notice Boards]
[Contract Teams Available]
[Disable/Modify screens]

Connecting to Arachne …

… Facing undue corporate aggression? Rampant *mara* activity disrupting your normal business? Is your world crumbling around you? There's one Contract Team ready, willing, and able to stand by your side against anything the Sphere can throw at you. Quantronic security, physical security, and direct operational intervention are our specialties. Whether you need brains, brawn, or sheer, off-the-chain firepower …

… Team Zed is on your side …

[Arachne Service Response Query]
[Hire Contract Team?]
[Yes] [Hell, Yes!]

Find out more about Infinity and Corvus Belli at:
https://www.corvusbelli.com/

INFINITY
DOWNFALL
MARK BARBER
CORVUS BELLI
INFINITY

TALES OF PANNITHOR
FAITH ALIGNED
KINGS OF WAR
MARK BARBER